Tom Wade
and
The Battle of Sheol

Barbara Mayo-Neville

DEDICATION

To my five children, who have had a magical connection to Adamah all of their lives. I hold the memory of my own Changeling Children in my heart forever. And to Richard, with whom I share all adventures. Also for TW of Lode, Cambridgeshire, from whom I borrowed something important.

Chapter One

The rain was pelting down when Tom opened the door to find Mayteria standing under the eaves holding an open umbrella.

"Thank you, Tom." She closed her umbrella and stepped through the door.

"That's all right," he said, "but I wasn't opening it for you. I'm just about to leave for school."

"You can't go without breakfast."

"We're out of everything," he said, watching as she put her umbrella in the corner.

"I'll find you something."

He started to follow her to the kitchen but she turned around, her face stern and that look in her eyes that he knew only too well. "You stay right here, Tom Wade, I'll get it. Now get your parka on, it's pouring out there."

He grabbed his parka, muttering. "I'm not some little boy to be bossed around" he said, and walked defiantly into the kitchen only to find it empty. Where was she? Tom ran back to the front door, but she was nowhere to be seen. He abruptly turned around to find her standing in front of him, with hot buttered toast and a steaming cup of milky tea. Tom ate the toast, mumbling his thanks. The tea was the perfect temperature, so he downed it in a few swallows.

"Where'd you get this?"

"Get on with you now. You're going be late," she said, picking his backpack up from the floor and holding it out to him.

He stood still, biting the inside of his lip. How many times had she appeared at the house when he needed her? His mum could say what she wanted, but he knew Mayteria was no ordinary housekeeper. These events were never to be questioned, so he shouldered his backpack and opened the door.

He turned back and pointed at her umbrella. "It isn't even wet," he said, and walked out into the rain.

A few minutes later he was shivering beside two other people in the bus shelter. As the bus veered towards the curb, Tom stepped back. He'd been splattered by muddy water last week, and the school bully, Ronald Pecklay, had made his life miserable.

Sure enough, the bus drove straight through the puddle. The murky water sloshed up and splattered dirty marks all over the trousers of the man in front of him. Tom smiled.

As the man stepped back to wipe his legs, a very pleased Tom jumped forward to board the bus. His foot missed the first step and splashed down into a puddle below. Tom groaned as dirty water poured over the top of his shoe saturating all the way through to his grey school sock.

Tom paid his bus fare and walked down the aisle towards an empty seat. The short balding man was in his usual place. So was the thin woman who dressed in brightly coloured suits, red today. She didn't bother Tom. The bald man did. It was impossible not to notice him. He looked up and gave Tom a real once-over with his yellowy-green eyes. Those weird eyes, and what was left of his strange hair, made him stand out from other people. The old chap stared at Tom's wet shoe and snickered.

"Weirdo," Tom muttered as he dropped into a seat beside a plump lady. He turned to look out of the window trying to ignore the thick smell of human humidity that filled the bus. He couldn't see much because the windows were steamy and beaded with droplets of water.

As the bus neared the stop for Colton College, Tom felt that familiar heaviness in the pit of his stomach. He didn't want to attend Colton. He wanted to go to his local college, but his mum made him come all the way across town to attend this private school for its supposed 'Academic Excellence'.

Today, he felt worse than ever. After lunch came PE. He did alright at sports. He actually enjoyed PE if they were playing football. But sometimes PE was brutal. Anything outside the usual games and he became clumsy and awkward, fumbling around, making stupid mistakes. Ronald Pecklay was in his class and loved to let everyone know when Tom blew it.

All that was bad enough, but yesterday Mrs. Mendor said that they were starting fencing today. He was going to die, if not by the sword, then by abject humiliation.

He dragged himself off the bus, his wet sock squelching as he walked. As he came through the gate, he heard a squeal. He knew who it was and nearly walked on, but Porker squealed even louder. Then he heard Ronald's voice and a roar of laughter from the gang.

Tom crept round the corner. Porker, Adam Poker actually, was held up against the wall. It took three of Ronald's cronies to hold Porker there. He was an enormous boy, round-faced, big-bellied and thick-limbed, but he was babyish. He cried easily and squealed loudly (hence his nickname), but he was also a nice chap.

Porker was crying. Ronald had Porker's backpack and was pulling bits and pieces out of it, holding things up for all the others to see. The bullies were howling over every single item that Ronald pulled out, the colourful tissue box, the cute pencil case and even poor Porker's rather large gym shorts.

Tom ran at them, knocking Nathan Shadow to the ground, surprising himself as much as it did the other boys. Tom fell with Shadow and rolled off him. Three boys then ran at Tom while he was trying to get up, one shoved him back down on the ground, another kicked him in the side, while yet another kneed him in the head. At the sound of voices coming around the building, the bullies pulled themselves up, and ran for it. Ronald turned back to sneer as he left, "Are you babies going to rat on us?"

A grateful Porker squeaked 'thank you' over and over. But Tom was humiliated. He picked himself up off the ground, wiping smears of blood from his skinned hands. He headed to class, hating Ronald even more and wondering if his mum would notice the bruise on his face.

James Mason arrived in English Class and sat down beside him. Tom looked over at his best friend and nodded his head. James smacked him on the back in that comforting sort of way.

James whispered, "Hey, I just talked to Porker, you okay?"

Tom nodded. He was saved from revealing his shaky voice by Mrs. Whitman calling the class to order.

Could the day get any worse? Yes, it seemed it could. The first thing Mrs. Whitman did was announce a class debate. She talked on and on about the value of debating before handing out the topics. She gave a card to Tom and one to James.

"You boys have an interesting topic to debate," she said.

Tom looked down at his card. "Time travel is achievable. We only need a new scientific discovery to enable us to take advantage of this exciting possibility." He looked up at Mrs. Whitman. She was smiling maliciously.

"Tom, you will take the positive side of this debate. That is, you will agree with the statement on the card. James, you will disagree." Tom groaned as James punched the air, grinning.

"You nerd," James said, thumping Tom's back again.

But Mrs. Whitman hadn't finished with him yet. "James, Amy Smith will be your partner." She looked up at Amy, "Okay, Amy?" The black-haired, hawk-nosed (but very smart) Amy Smith nodded.

"Yeah, I got a brainy one." James laughed.

Then Mrs. Whitman said, "And Tom, Abigail Meers will join you." The teacher walked on and Tom turned to see if Abigail had heard.

She rolled her eyes and groaned loudly, saying, "Oh crap."

Tom's face felt hot.

Mrs. Whitman gave them a few minutes at the end of class to chat with their partners.

James was scribbling down notes as fast as he could while Amy Smith talked.

Abigail was doodling on a notebook.

Tom coughed and said, "So I reckon we copped the more difficult side of the debate."

Abigail looked up at Tom, her cold, blue eyes glaring, "Duh."

She looked back down, doodling on her notebook again. She was drawing a tiny little dragon. It was one of many little pictures on the pages. They were all drawn in minute detail and were exquisite.

The bell rang. He sighed. They had achieved nothing towards the debate.

Mrs. Whitman's shrill voice rang out, "Now be sure to exchange telephone numbers with your debate partners."

Abigail's book slammed closed and she stood up.

"So, do you want my telephone number?" Tom asked hesitantly.

"Nah, what would I want that for?" Abigail snorted.

"Hummm, we're supposed to…." He faltered.

"You call me if you want. I ain't calling you. Okay, here's me number."

Tom grabbed a pen to write down the number, but dropped it. He tried to remember the number, but couldn't. It hadn't been that easy to follow her, she wasn't like other Colton students, and it certainly showed up when she spoke.

"Here," she said, snatching the pen out of his hand, "I'll write it."

She handed back his paper with her name and phone number. Her writing was beautiful, long slanting letters and numbers, all perfectly formed.

"Wow, you write…"

Abigail rolled her eyes in disgust and walked away.

Tom ate lunch with James Mason, Porker and John Sims. He spent most of the time lamenting his partnership with Abigail. "I mean she's not like other girls, is she?"

His friends snickered and Porker squeaked, "Nah man, I mean, she's real hot."

"No, I mean she's so different."

James held cupped hands up to his chest and wiggled them up and down.

Tom grinned. Abigail was a looker and the boys weren't going to get past it. They knew what he meant anyway. It was well known that Abigail shed her school uniform after school in favour of black leather and wore a pit-bull collar around her neck. Rumours abounded about her boyfriend being a gang member.

Tom felt keyed up. Being paired with Abigail was part of it, but the thought of facing Ronald's gang again caused the worst nervousness. PE was his next subject.

The beginning of PE was as awful as he expected it to be. Ronald came in with a slew of his friends and they were in foul moods. Ronald saw Tom's soggy sock lying on the bench. He grabbed the sock and held it up. "Look at this. Here's why Tom stinks so bad. I mean I've heard of stinking, sweaty feet, but never like this." Ronald laughed loudly and threw the sock at Nathan Shadow.

Tom made the mistake of trying to get it as it flew past. Nathan of course threw it back to Ronald, who bunched it up and threw it up over Tom's head to Matt Benson. Matt happily joined in the game. Tom, on the other hand, was not so happy. He was monkey in the middle, jumping around unable to get his sock, but too embarrassed to stop trying.

The teacher's aide came in and told the boys to get a move on. Ronald threw the sock in a corner, and the boys all got their gear on before heading out to the hall. Some of them were excited by the extra gear and a brand new experience, but Tom walked dispiritedly out to the hall to the waiting Mrs. Mendor. He'd only just gotten into place beside Porker before Mrs. Mendor placed a foil in his hand.

"Are you all right?" she asked, looking closely at him.

Suddenly, Tom remembered how to fence. Sort of like they say about riding a bicycle. He knew he could do it because he had done it before. But how was that possible? He never had never fenced before. His right hand, holding the long, graceful foil, rose with slow elegance. With a soft twist of his wrist, the foil turned lightly to the right.

"Very nicely done," Mrs. Mendor said.

Tom's foil made a smooth slice to the left. He placed one foot back and curved his left arm behind him gracefully.

"Ah, you've had fencing instruction before have you?" Mrs. Mendor asked, starting to walk away.

"N-n-n-n o." Crap, he felt weird. Why did these things happen to him?

"I have, Mrs. Mendor. And my father won the championship cup at his fencing club for the last two years," said Ronald.

Mrs. Mendor turned to look at the strutting figure of Ronald.

"Oh well, that's very good to hear…" Mrs. Mendor said.

"En-Garde," Tom said, his eyes widening with surprise. He hadn't planned to say that. Tom donned his mask and lifted his foil. Ronald's eyes narrowed and a sneer spread across his face. He stepped forward and donned his mask.

The first ting of the foils touching brought all the boys running, forming a wide circle around the two who were locked in combat. Afterwards Mrs. Mendor couldn't understand why she hadn't stopped the boys. They weren't fitted out properly or set up for a bout, yet she let them go. There could have been big trouble if someone had been hurt. But she stood, transfixed, until the clear winner emerged.

All the boys were shouting as they followed the two antagonists across the hall. This was no ordinary sport of fencing, this was mortal combat, and someone's pride was going to be slaughtered today.

At first it seemed Tom would be humiliated. Ronald's confidence of success was evident in the gleam in his eyes and the smirk on his face as they began. There was no doubt that Ronald could fence and he could do it well.

A strange magic was at work, as Tom took the upper hand over Ronald with every touch, every ting, making every point. Ronald's triumphant look changed with each confident stroke from his opponent. Tom's feet took him where he needed to go and his hands commanded the foil with a deft touch. Ronald's eyes became troubled as Tom danced around him. Not that the foil could physically hurt him, but its blunted point was just about to mortify the wrong person.

The clash of the foils was muffled by the sound of the boys round them shouting. Once, twice and three times Ronald stumbled as Tom brought the buttoned tip up to his opponent's stomach, chest and heart. Finally, "Halt. Tom's the winner," Mrs. Mendor declared.

Tom lowered his foil. His hands were tingling and sending that sensation up to his face. Boys were hooting for joy, even Ronald's friends enjoyed seeing him lowered a notch or two.

Next thing Tom knew he was swung around and lifted onto the shoulders of two cheering boys. His best friend, James Mason, was shouting and waving his arms. Boys were hooting, "Way to go, Tom," and, "An awesome defeat of a rat!"

Ronald was standing by, his mouth trembling and his face and ears bright red.

James noticed Ronald and laughed at his heaving chest and watery eyes. "About to cry are you, mate?"

The boys all turned to look. It was clear that Ronald's loyal followers were watching for his reaction, and their allegiance was shaky.

"He's crying cause he lost," squeaked Porker.

"Shut up, Porker," growled Ronald.

Porker stepped back, "Look, he's wiping tears from his eyes."

"You'll squeal loudly now, you…" with that Ronald took a swipe and landed the blunt edge of the foil right across Porker's fat cheek.

Just as Ronald went to strike at Porker again, Tom jumped from his friends shoulders and with a loud ring of foil on foil, he stopped the second attack. "Oh no, you don't, Pecklay."

Porker was already yelling from the first hit, and his reputable high-pitched shriek did sound like a stuck pig. This noise brought Mrs. Mendor around. She soon had the other boys busy practicing while Porker and Ronald were sent to sit at the side, "To be dealt with later."

She turned to Tom with confidence and said, "Please take charge here. Continue giving the boys instructions about holding foil, if you don't mind." She smiled at him before turning to 'deal' with the two boys. She'd never taken much notice of Tom before.

He squeaked, "Yes Miss,'" as though he, too, was a Porker.

As he stood waiting in the bus shelter at the end of school, he couldn't believe this day had turned out to be so marvellous. Even the day itself seemed to acknowledge that life was different. The miserable grey of the morning had given way to a bright yellow. The sun shone, forcing off coats and replacing sullen looks with smiles and cheer. He looked at his watch as the bus came into view. He'd hung around school enjoying his new found respect for too long and now he was late leaving for home.

Tom climbed aboard the bus, paid his fare and turned to walk down the aisle. He froze for a moment. He couldn't believe it. Old yellow-eyed Weirdo was on the bus and looking at him with such intensity.

He tried to read the latest Sci-Fi book by his favourite author, but he couldn't concentrate. He couldn't even revel in today's success. All he could think about were those yellow eyes looking at him like they could see inside his brain.

Chapter Two

Tom stepped off the bus and headed home. He kept thinking about the fencing, so he stopped and held out his hand as if he was clutching a foil again. Dancing about, waving his arms, defeating the imaginary Ronald with greater ease than he had the real one. He dropped his hand and walked on, picking up speed as he went.

His mum probably wasn't home from the university yet. Most days she worked late, preparing lectures, but she often called home to check on him. Maybe he would tell her how good he was at fencing. He stopped and struck a fencing pose again. Then looked around to make sure no one was watching him.

He started walking again. No, he probably wouldn't tell her. He could hardly ever tell her about these strange, inexplicable events that happened to him. She always clammed up when he tried.

He walked up to his front door and unlocked it. As he stepped in, he heard his mum's voice.

"Is that you, Tom?"

Tom looked backwards into the driveway. No, the green Rover wasn't there. Why was she home early today of all days?

"Hey Mum. Why are you home? Where's the car?"

Miriam Wade came down the stairs tying a loose knot around the robe she was wearing.

"It's so stupid. I left work early to get it from the garage, and they haven't fixed it yet. I couldn't believe it. Honestly, I think Ahikar was right when he said, 'The use of modern transportation produces people who move faster to accomplish less.'"

"Who?"

"What?"

"Ahca who?"

His mother blinked her eyes, looking confused.

"What's wrong?" he asked.

"Nothing's wrong. Ahikar was an ancient Babylonian sage. Sometimes I wonder what they teach you at school. Do you learn anything of value?" Miriam turned quickly and went into the kitchen. "Now, what do we want for dinner?"

Tom followed his mum, "Well, mum dear, we certainly don't study ancient Babylonian sages in school."

His mum wrenched the freezer door open. Inside were boxes and bags of frozen pre-made foods. She pulled out a half-open box. "It's early enough we could curl up and watch some silly programme on telly while we eat," she said, dropping a frozen box on the table.

"Fish fingers?"

He curled up his lip. "Yesterday."

She pushed the box back into the over-stuffed freezer and pulled out another. "Chicken fingers?"

He raised eyebrows and laughed.

"Okay, okay, don't say anything."

Another shove. Another pull. "Steak pie. Hey, we haven't had that in a while."

"Okay." he shrugged.

Miriam took the box to the sink and vigorously scraped ice from it. She took scissors and half-cut, half-tore the top off the box.

"Been there a while, hey? I think it's still there from when we went through that pie-a-night binge," Tom said.

"Are you making fun of my cooking, boy?" she asked.

He watched as she pinged the pie onto a tray. She turned to the oven, then back again, pulled the box out of the rubbish, read it and set the temperature. "Probably should preheat it, but oh well."

"Is what you do called cooking, mum? Wouldn't you have to actually have to cook…"

Miriam side-swiped him, laughing.

"Guess we should have some vegetables with it," she said. She went to the freezer to rummage through the bags again.

It wasn't long before he and his mum were sitting holding their dinner plates, flicking through the television channels.

"Don't spill on your robe, mum."

Miriam laughed. "You've always loved this robe, haven't you?" she said warmly. "Since you were a toddler and I cuddled you in it. Calmed you down when nothing else could." Her eyes grew vacant, as though she was seeing those far away years. "When you were a wee lad and we moved to this house. You were so upset by the change. Only wrapping you in this robe would settle you." Miriam smiled, and then looked down, her memories turning from pleasant to sad.

This was a game they often played. He would say something about the exotic robe she would only wear when they were at home and alone, and his mum would tell him about when he was a little boy.

She shook her head. "Come on, boy, eat up."

He picked up his plate and started to eat. His mum continued searching for a programme to watch on the television.

"Mum?"

"Mmm," she answered absent-mindedly.

He was just about to mention his success at fencing, knowing it would please her, but a sudden train of thought caused him to ask, "How could Acqua say that?"

"Who say what?" asked his mother with a grimace.

"That old sage. You know, you quoted him. How could he say that about modern transportation? I mean, if he felt that way about carts and chariots? Think what he would say now…"

Miriam made an odd noise and Tom looked over at her. "Mum, Mum," Tom said, almost laughing at the funny look on his mother's face. "Why are you looking at me like that?"

His mother turned off the television, grabbed her plate and stood up. Walking towards the kitchen she said in a trembling voice, "Can't you leave anything alone?"

Tom sat there, feeling numb. His mother was usually gentle, and so kind, but just occasionally she would get so upset over some small question or comment he made.

He hardly tasted anything as he finished eating. He dreaded taking his plate into the kitchen because he knew what he would find. His mother would be red-eyed from crying, or at least from fighting tears.

"Sorry, Mum," he mumbled, not looking at her.

"No, I'm sorry. That was a silly reaction to your question. I'm just tired, that's all."

They let it drop. He wouldn't ask again and Miriam wouldn't bring it up.

Tom went upstairs, sat on his bed and opened his backpack. He pulled out his homework and his science fiction novel. He sighed. He might as well call Abigail Meers.

He picked up the phone with dread. He believed all the rumours about her, especially the one about the spiky collar around her neck, because she was a bit like a pit-bull.

"Ello," answered a gruff male voice at the other end of the line.

He cleared his throat. "Is Abigail there, please?"

"Abigail." Her father's loud voice echoed over the phone.

It was as difficult setting up a meeting with Abigail, as Tom had expected it to be.

"Where are *we* going to meet up?" Abigail asked.

"I don't know," he replied.

"Honestly, you can't come here," she said.

He didn't particularly want to go there after hearing her father yelling for her, but he hated the way she said it. Finally, they agreed to meet at King's College wall. The first one there could sit and wait for the other. His mum lectured late on Tuesdays and came home well after dinnertime, so he wouldn't even bother telling her.

The next day after school, Tom was the first one at the wall of King's College. He thought he probably would be. He wondered if Abigail would show up at all. He didn't mind being there first. If she was trying to be difficult or embarrass him by asking him to meet in the city, it hadn't worked. He came here often. His mum was over-protective, but this was where she would often meet him when she needed to work really late. They'd meet here, have dinner, then Tom would head home and she could walk back to her college on Grange Road.

Tom unwrapped a slab of flapjack he'd bought at the bakery across the street and hopped on the wall. He sat his coke bottle beside him and munched while waiting, not at all worried by Abigail's tardiness. He opened his book to read, glancing up occasionally.

A tall man with a rather long nose sat down on the wall beside him. Tom recognised the man as someone his mother sometimes spoke to in passing. What was it his mum called him? Was it some connection to the university? A lecturer? No, that didn't seem right.

"What are you reading?" the man asked.

Tom felt embarrassed. The book, *Take Us to Warp Speed,* was about space travel. Though it used a lot of technical sounding jargon, Tom knew it was really just a kid's book. The old gentleman looked at it carefully.

He said, "Mmm, interesting," then handed it back to Tom.

"Warp speed, speed of light, FTL speed. That's not the issue really, is it, boy?"

Tom continued to look at the man, his eyes a little wider, but said nothing.

"Stupid really," said the man. "All those intelligent people trying to answer the wrong questions. They invent things or want some discovery, when really all they need is to find the words, and then it just happens."

"Here boy, this is what you should be reading." He handed Tom a small, tattered old book. "Good bit of scribbled notes on the sides of the pages. Pay attention to them."

Tom opened the book as the man walked away, muttering under his breath, "Fine lad. That should help him."

As the old man disappeared, Abigail came walking up. Tom slipped the book into his jacket pocket.

"Oi, you made it all right then, did you?" She flung herself on the wall and leaned close to him, her white-blonde hair touching his cheek. Tom inhaled. She grabbed his coke, took a swig, and winked at him. Then she put his coke bottle down beside her and looked at him. He watched as her tongue licked her gleaming black lips.

He swallowed as he said, "You're late. We'd better get busy or we'll lose the debate."

Abigail laughed sarcastically. "Time travel really can happen? You think we can win that? It don't matter what we do, we're losers." Abigail laughed, then looked at her watch. "Oi, I gotta be going. My dad'll be furious if I'm late."

"But you just got here. I thought we were going to work."

The girl shrugged carelessly. "Nothing we can do to win. No point." She pulled black lipstick out of her bag and started spreading more of it on her lips. She then took a black leather strip with sliver studs and strapped it around her neck. Tom rolled his eyes. Abigail must be part pit-bull.

"Can you come to my house, since you obviously don't want to be seen with me?" Tom asked.

She raised one eyebrow at him.

"Well, that must be why you don't want to meet at school or your place, right?"

Abigail sat back down on the wall, "You'd fit in me place like a crystal vase in junk shop? Do you know why I'm at Colton College? A scholarship."

Abigail pointed to her head. "Got a good one up there, so I get a scholarship to the high fashion Colton College. Me mum, it was her that did it. Me mum wants something better for me than she had. Right? Now, look at me then, mate."

Tom looked at Abigail with unblinking eyes.

"Do I look like a Colton College girl? No, I don't. Now, I don't fit with me mates from me old school at home, and I only fit the Colton bunch that are just about to get themselves booted out of the place."

She shook her head. "I really have to go. Me dad's not so soft-spoken as some."

"So, my house tomorrow afternoon then," Tom persisted. He felt a bit bad about what she'd confessed to him, but they still had to sort out the debate.

"Right," she said. "I'll come with you straight from school."

Abigail jumped off the wall. She picked up Tom's coke and took another gulp. She leaned close to him to put it back beside him. Her lips nearly touched his cheek. Her soft hair brushed across his face. For a girl dressed in black, she smelled awfully sweet. She walked away without saying anything.

Tom sat on the wall thinking how people are never how they appeared to be. He took a drink of his coke and remembered his flapjack. He poked in his pocket looking for the leftovers. His fingers touched the little tattered book. Tom pulled it out and looked carefully at its frayed pages. It was written in a strange language, with weird curved markings. The side margins were covered in a sloppy scrawl.

He flicked through the book. One page caught his eye. How odd. There was one line printed in gold. Beside the line were normal letters handwritten in red ink. Tom read it out loud, pronouncing each letter carefully.

Lo bamakom hazeh

He continued leafing through the book. Towards the back, he came across more gold print with these letters scrawled beside it in red.

Ba'arets hahi'

He wondered if the two lines were related to each other.

Tom spoke the first string of sounds softly "Lo bamakom hazeh.", and then turned back to the second set and uttered, "Ba'arets hahi'."

He flipped backwards.

There was no reason to lose his balance, yet he was falling off the wall. He kept falling, turning round and round as he plummeted. He fell, and fell and fell. Tom swung his hands out to protect himself. But instead of hitting the ground, his hands flung out beyond him. His arms and fingers were stretched meters beyond the rest of his body.

"What's going on?" he groaned. The words echoed eerily. "What was in that flapjack?" Again, the words quivered around.

Tom jerked his hands to try to rein them in. But that resulted in his elbows extending out behind him. He turned to see his rubbery elbows, and that made his body twist wildly, round and round. It was completely dark and he felt sick, out of control and frightened. He slowly pulled his hands and elbows towards his body. Good. Those parts of him came back into proportion. Now, he gently moved his head in the opposite direction. Yes. The spinning stopped, but suddenly he began to tumble forwards. He did two or three rolls and when he felt he was moving forward again, he pulled up. Right, he got it. He stretched out. This was better, more like flying than falling. Feeling pleased, he nodded his head.

Tom's nose started stretching forward, the way his hands and arms had done. He could see the tip of it out there, as if he were some great human Pinocchio. He started laughing. At first laughing felt good, but then it echoed, and in the blackness it sounded ghoulish. He knew not to try to pull his nose back too quickly, so he made a gentle tug of his head and saw his nose start shrinking back towards him. Then he saw light at the end of the tunnel. As that description came into his head, he shivered. He must be dying, isn't that how all the books talked about dying.

He inhaled as he felt his face rush out of the dark. He landed face-first in a soft turf that looked like a cross between grass and feathers. He must have been stretched long from the waist, because half of him was lying in the grassy-feather stuff and half of him seemed to still be coming in for a landing. He was still trying to come to terms with that weird feeling when he realised that someone was speaking in a strange language. Stranger still, Tom understood them.

"Ai, Suki, they've come. Run. Tell everyone to run," screamed a voice.

"Calm down. I don't think it is a vile creature. I think it is something else."

"What do you suppose then? Do you suppose it's a Peregrine Sol?"

"Well now, I don't know. If it's a Peregrine Sol, it is not very good at landing, is it?"

"No, indeed," answered the first voice. And then the voice spoke with a tremble. "But a Peregrine Sol who can't land is much better than what I was thinking. I thought the doom was upon us."

Tom lifted what he could of his shoulders and neck to look around. This was not easy since from the waist down to his toes, he still wasn't even there.

What occurred next happened very fast. He looked up and saw what looked like two men, but they were no taller than his hand. Just as his eyes met theirs, his backside landed with an enormously loud and painful jolt. The two little men jumped back in terror.

As Tom's rear-end hit his front-side, he let out a horrific scream. The landing was so hard that it created a ricochet that took him back up into the blackness again this time at super-speed. His body was completely stretched. He was flying back, upside down and though he couldn't see it, he could feel that his bum was far beyond the rest of him. His scream was echoing around and he was terrified. Then, with a wallop, he hit hard earth. Bottom first this time. When he opened his eyes the yellowy grey stone of King's College was towering above him. He was lying flat on his back with his feet against the wall.

An older man and his grey-haired wife were staring at him with alarmed eyes. "I'm going to have to have me eyes checked, Mildred." The man said to his wife. "I could have sworn that boy disappeared for a minute."

The wife gave Tom a smile, and said in a watery voice, "You alright, boy?"

He struggled to his feet saying 'Yes', but actually feeling unsure.

He picked his things up and walked away from their curious eyes.

"I must have blacked out. What a weird dream."

He walked to the bus stop. He'd better move if he was going to beat Mum home. He kept brushing himself off as he stood waiting for the bus. He swept his hand over his head. There was something stuck in his hair. He looked at what was in his hand, dropped it and stepped away. The bus pulled up and he climbed on board, paid his fare and then glanced back at the pavement. The door shut, blocking his view of that piece of unearthly, deep-green, feathery grass.

Chapter Three

Tom's heart sank as he neared his house. The car was in the drive. That stupid car. He forgot she'd arranged for someone else to take her class so she could collect the car from the garage.

"Where have you been?" she demanded. "I was just about to call your headmaster."

"Sorry, Mum. I had to meet with a girl from…"

"Meet a girl! You're late because you had to…."

"Come on, Mum. I had to meet her to study."

She relaxed.   "You were studying?"

"Yes."

"At school?"

"Well, er, no. We met at Kings."

 "You know very well, Tom, that you're not supposed to be going off without permission," his mum shouted. "I have to work. I can't help it. So I sure as heck better know where you are all the time. I can't be worrying about you running around the city, anything could happen."

He said quietly "Nothing happened, Mum, we met at Kings and made plans for our debate." He knew the less he said, the quicker this would be over. She was acting as if he made a habit of taking off on his own.

His mother sighed. "If Mandola knew you were in town…" She seemed to relax a little, turning towards the kitchen.

"Is that the name of that tall, thin man? What is he? Oh yeah, I remember, a director or something."

Miriam swung back around, "Did you see the Director? Did he say anything to you?"

Her intensity made him cautious. "No, I just saw him in the distance and remembered you knew him."

Miriam glared at him. "What time were you at King's College wall?"

"I dunno, around half past four till half past six or so."

Miriam's eyes widened, "Nobody spoke to you? Nobody tried to give you anything?"

"No," he lied again. "What is it, Mum? Are you afraid someone's going to give me drugs?" he asked in a bantering tone.

"I don't know. Don't do it again. I want to know where you are. So you either do what you do every day, school and then home; or you make sure I know otherwise."

With that, she walked out of the room and into the kitchen. She continued to be uptight all evening, barking out orders left and right. Tom was pleased with himself for biting his tongue while she pounced around the kitchen like a furious tabby kitten. He found it almost amusing. But he finally lost it over the rubbish.

He didn't mind taking out the rubbish. It was his job, but he didn't like the way she was ordering him about.

Miriam glared at him. "This is the second time I've told you to take the rubbish out. Do it!"

He heaved the black rubbish bag out of the bin and lugged it through the kitchen. Then he swung the bag so hard it thumped on the ground and a sharp edge from a tin cut through the bag spilling a smelly mess onto the ground. Disgusted, Tom cleaned up the mess, and huffed and puffed till he got a second bag up and around the first one. There was no way he was asking his mum for help.

He stepped outside to put the bag in the outside bin. He'd just slammed on the bin lid when a noise made him look up. He saw the rose bush. There was one bud on it.

He stared at the bud. His face felt hot and his eyes got that sore watery feeling. Tom walked over to the rose bush, rubbing his hands on his trouser legs as he walked. They had gone numb. He reached up and touched the rosebud with one cold finger. He plucked off the bud.

He shoved the rosebud into his pocket as a shadow fell across the kitchen window. His mum must be looking out to see why he was taking so long. He went inside the house to find his mother's mood had changed. She was humming softly to herself, looking through one of her many cookbooks. Books she liked to own, but never used to cook.

"Doesn't this look delicious? I bet I could make this if I tried."

Now he felt out of sorts. His mum could change her tune if she wanted, but that didn't mean he would get all cosy with her.

"Oh yeah, sure, as if you would bother," he said and left the room, feeling guilty.

Upstairs in his own room, he pulled his books out of his backpack. He made a stack of the books he had from the library and then sat down.

"Time travel. What a stupid debate." Tom opened a book and lay down on in his bed, but he couldn't read at all. That stupid rosebud. He pulled it out of his pocket and twirled it between his thumb and finger. He started peeling it, wondering what colour it would be. It was too small and green to have a colour yet. He threw the bud across the room and sat up, wiping his eyes.

A rose bush in the back garden, shouldn't that be the most normal thing in the world. Not for him, everything in his life was complex, even the rosebush.

In the spring, little pear-shaped leaves were followed by buds. Those tiny little promises of flowers formed at the tips of the stems. Then, in early summer, something very strange happened. The flowers that came were multi-coloured, blooming beauties. Neon-yellow, black-red, lavender, bright pink, orange, every shade and every colour flower imaginable bloomed on that one bush. As the flowers bloomed, the thorns on the bush disappeared like magic. Tom's mum disappeared too.

Two years ago, he realised there was a connection between his mum's long absences and the blooming roses. It was a day he remembered well.

His best mate, James, and his dad had come to pick up Tom to go biking on a fine spring Saturday morning. James' dad, Mr. Mason, a plump, happy person was always helpful. When they arrived, Mr. Mason immediately said,

"I'll get Tom's bike." And as fast as the words came out of his mouth, he headed out of the back door. Miriam dashed after Mr. Mason, to try to stop him. She never invited anyone into her back garden, and she had forbidden Tom to take his friends there.

By the time Miriam and Tom were out, Mr. Mason was standing stock-still, staring at the rosebush, mouth gaping open. It was that beautiful. Three or four roses lit up each stem. Each rose was a different colour, and each competed to be the most beautiful. The pinks and oranges were so bright that you blinked. The purples made your mouth water as if they were a bunch of grapes instead of flowers. The reds like blood. And one, just starting to open, gleamed black.

Tom knew his mum was leaving soon. It was all organized, his mum would be gone and Mayteria, the housekeeper, would be there when he returned from biking. But when Mayteira rushed through the house just as Miriam was trying to stop Mr. Mason, the whole thing fell into place for Tom.

"You must go, Miriam. Tis late you know," Mayteira said.

Miriam's face was pale as she turned to look at Mayteria. "Mr. Mason, came out here to get Tom's bike."

Mayteria stood still, her hand covering her mouth.

Mr. Mason was raving about the rosebush, using words like unique, phenomenal, and impossible. He seemed to know an awful lot about roses. This made matters worse for Miriam. Tom watched his mum. He knew instinctively she would lie, that for some reason the truth was not an option. But what would she say?

"Okay Bob," she said, "I can see no lie is going to fob you off. I mean, I could tell you a lot of things but…"

Tom lifted his eyebrows. So she was going to tell the truth after all. He'd been wishing to know the truth for years.

"Miriam, you need to go," Mayteira muttered.

Miriam seemed compelled to explain the rosebush. "Bob, the fact of the matter is a friend of mine at the university, a scientist, is doing an experiment."

Tom rolled his eyes and his mum saw him doing it. She scowled at her son and then carried on. "A botanist, that's what he is, Bob. Doing experimental work…" She was stumbling now so Tom stepped in and helped her.

"Asked my mum to bring it home and grow it in the garden here. See if it worked outside the laboratory, you know. It's nice, isn't it? But we've had some problems with it *I can tell you*," he added with emphasis. "Don't expect to see it in the garden shops any too soon," he added with relish.

 Miriam grimaced.

He grinned at her. He knew she wouldn't want him lying, but what was she going to do about it. He was, after all, only following her lead.

"What kind of problems?" Bob Mason started to ask, but Mayteira cut in.

"Miriam."

"Bob," said Miriam, cocking an eyebrow at Tom. "I'm sure Tom, with all his excellent knowledge on the subject, will give you the low-down sometime. I, on the other hand, am very late for my trip."

Miriam started ushering Bob, the bike and the boys out to the Mason's car, saying, "Now I hope you all have a really good time. Remember to wear your helmet, son, and I will see you when I get back."

Tom laid his hand on her arm. "Do you have to go, Mum? Can't you just stay here this time?"

"You know I have these trips to make, Tom. You know I often travel as part of my work."

"Do you really have to go this time? Is it work?"

Miriam paused for a moment, as if she were uncertain. Then she spoke. "Tom Wade, I'm surprised at you. I expected this sort of thing when you were a wee tot, but certainly not now. You're old enough to know better."

Seeing the expression on his face, Miriam softened her tone. "Oh Tom, it won't be that long." She grabbed him in a huge, embarrassing hug. She was holding him so tightly he couldn't even look around to see James' reaction.

She whispered, "I won't be gone long. Think about it, when the last rose blooms, I'll be home."

Mayteira stepped in. She rushed them all away, stopping only to stare directly into Mr Mason's eyes for a moment.

After that, Tom understood the rosebush played some part in their lives. It bloomed and she left; when it stopped blooming, she returned.

He was nervous about the questions James and his father were bound to ask. Mayteira was a very unusual little woman, with her strange lavender eyes and curly hair. But they didn't ask anything about her at all. Maybe they were too sensitive to ask questions about her, or maybe they were afraid Tom would be upset again. He also found he didn't have to make up any more stories for James' dad about the rosebush. Incredibly, Mr. Mason seemed to forget all about it.

Tom didn't forget. Now the rose was blooming. His mother would go away again.

Last year, just one year after Bob Mason had seen the rose bush, Tom saw the first few blooms and he understood what was coming. So he tried to stop her. It didn't work, but he tried.

He plucked the buds from the rosebush. Not just one, like he had tonight. All of them. Every time a bud appeared, he pulled it off. Violently pulled it off. Two the first night, ten more the second night, and dozens the following night. They kept coming and coming, every night more and more and more of those horrid buds appeared, and he would pull them off. Then one morning he came downstairs. His mum was nowhere to be seen, but the back door leading to the garden was open. Tom ran out. Miriam was sitting on the garden bench, legs pulled up, chin down. She lifted her head as he came out; her eyes were teary.

He looked from his mum over to the rosebush. He couldn't say what he expected to see. Maybe he thought the bush would be dead because he'd hacked it so brutally the night before. But it wasn't dead. It was alive. And it was aflame with colour. Every branch and every stem was fuller than usual with blooms. Brilliantly coloured roses had filled the bush overnight. He turned back to his mum. She knew. Miriam knew what he had tried to do, that was why she was crying. And he could see it wasn't going to stop her leaving. Nothing would stop her.

Tom shifted his thoughts from that awful time back to the present. He picked up the now-crumpled rosebud from off the floor and held it in the palm of his hand. He wouldn't pluck another. He would just let them come. There was nothing he could do.

Chapter Four

Tom's key stuck halfway in the lock. He pulled hard to get it loose. Then he stumbled backwards and stepped on Abigail's toes. He tried again but accidently put the key in upside down. On the third try, he managed to unlock his front door.

Abigail stood beside him wearing a smug look. She hardly resembled the girl who left school with him. She'd spent the bus trip to his house redoing herself. Gone was the green school blazer. She was now wearing a black leather jacket. A sliver studded dog-collar was fastened around her neck. Her lips were glossy black. Even her platinum hair was different, now done into six braids, and sticking out in various directions. As the bus pulled into the stop, she was banging a fingernail polish vial against the palm of one hand.

"Guess I'll have to do me nails at your place," she said when she saw Tom stand up.

"Do you do this every day after school?"

"What do you think?" she said, snarling.

He sighed.

The door swung open. Abigail stepped into the house.

"How very posh," she said, dumping her back pack on the floor and wandering off.

Tom cringed. Imagine what his mum would make of this girl's cheek. Abigail went into Miriam's office, fingering the papers, pens and books on the desk.

"Just as I expected. Right neighbourhood and all, perfect little house, everything just cosy like," she said.

Tom sighed and said, "Come upstairs, we can work in my room. We need to get this debate sorted out."

He spread library books on his bed. That was the only place to put them because Abigail had perched on his desk.

"We could be in a bit of trouble with this you know. I don't know why we copped this side of the debate." Tom was talking rapidly, filling the silence, while she seemed completely occupied with painting her fingernails black. He sat down on his bed, hopelessness over-coming him. He was never going to be able to work with Abigail. He might just as well prepare the whole stupid debate himself.

"What's that then?" asked Abigail, picking up the little book that was lying amongst the others.

"Gaw," she continued, "Some odd stuff in here."

He snatched the book out of her hand. He felt oddly protective of it. "It's nothing. It's just a book an old man gave me."

"What's it say there?" she asked, pointing to the gold lettering.

"I don't know," he answered, "and there is another bit on this page." He put his finger on the first page, flipped to the back of the book and showed Abigail. "There's this writing in red that I can sound out," he added.

He used his finger to follow the English letters as he sounded out the words on the first page. Who knows why he did it? Who knows why anyone does anything? As soon as he read the first line, he flipped to the back of the book and sounded out the next phrase. He heard Abigail screaming, but there was nothing he could do about it. He was tumbling in darkness again.

Abigail's screams faded. Tom held his breath to keep himself from yelling. He remembered too well the eerie echoing sound from his last trip.

So it's real, he thought. Or maybe it isn't. Maybe I'm having a fit, lying on the ground shaking or even worse. What if my eyes are rolling around and I'm throwing up. Abigail will tell everyone at school about me.

Whatever was happening, he knew from last time the pain was going to be real and he needed to control his fall. He looked around but could feel his neck stretch out of proportion as he did. He carefully pulled his neck back in. So far, so good. He was falling backwards. He didn't want to hit face down again. Maybe landing on his rear-end would be better. He saw the light shining from behind him. He felt a wave of cool fresh air. He did his best to prepare himself for his landing by curling himself up tightly. As the light grew brighter, he closed his eyes.

He hit, shaped like a ball. He opened his eyes. He was moving upwards. He went back up into the blackness. He came down again. Up again. He was bouncing. Every time he went up, it was into blackness. Every time he came down, he did his best to see where he was falling.

This was a different place than last time. Instead of feathery grass there was something soft and rubbery. That must be why he was bouncing. The next time Tom dropped out of the darkness he saw eyes staring up at him. Some of them were frightened eyes, others furious.

To his dismay, he was bouncing higher into the black tunnel with each rebound and falling deeper into the rubbery surface as he descended. He listened to the voices and strained hard to see the faces that went with the eyes.

"Bekloppt, if it ain't coming a-gin."

Tom turned round quickly, searching for the face belonging to the angry voice.

"I'm going a get mine gun and shoot that Naar."

He went up again terrified about what would greet him as he returned. These strange creatures were downright ugly with squatty fat bodies, stumpy legs and up-turned hairy toes. A few of the creatures wore odd-looking shoes which turned up at the front. Their noses were hideously long and gnarly, their ears like soggy overcooked cauliflower. But their most disgusting feature was the long wiry hairs that protruded out of their noses and ears. Some of the creatures appeared to be females with tight waist belts dividing flubbery upper parts from rounded bottom. The little ones, babies and children, with large rounded eyes and chubby cheeks were almost cute if you could get past the large knotted noses. But they clearly would be as gnarly and ugly as their parents when full-grown. He came down out of the darkness again, his eyes wide open. Would that horrid little beast really shoot him?

Tom yelped as a stinging pain hit his legs. Then he yelled as something hit his back and shouted again as another shot hit his ear. He bounced and shot up again yelping over and over as shot after shot hit him. They were firing tiny green balls at him. He squinted, trying to protect his eyes as the green balls whizzed past his face. What were they shooting at him?

Peering out through his half-closed eyes, he could see the creatures, young and old alike, blowing through long tubes aimed straight at him. It looked like they were using peashooters and, though the pellets were like peas, they felt much worse. Unfortunately for Tom, it seemed they all had rather good aim. Welts were forming all over him.

"That'll teach the nasty creature to be bouncing on mine bed," one yelled, the anger in his voice giving way to glee.

While twisting around to avoid the bullets, he could see that he was bouncing on a bed in a room with yellow walls. He yelped as a shot hit him on the cheek. Fortunately, he was heading upwards again, his arms, legs and backside stinging with pain. He looked up. To his horror, the ceiling was looming. Tom grimaced with fear, but didn't hit anything. He kept going up into the darkness above. He looked down as a little baby lifted its little head from its mother's shoulder. It spoke in a gentle squeaky voice. "Don't hurt it Vater, maybe it's a nice one."

As he hurled upwards he tried to figure out how to get out of this mess. Maybe if he pushed as hard as he could as he landed, it would propel him upwards faster and harder and that might send him back. He got ready to kick as he came down.

He hit the bed and pushed his legs down with all his might. He shot up at a terrific speed. He yelled, "Sorry" as he went up.

The gnome-creatures stared at him, blow guns pulled back from their lips. Just as he was reaching the blackness he heard the little one say, "See I told you Vater, it was a nice one."

He was now ricocheting through the blackness at an incredible speed. He landed with a bounce on his own bed. Abigail jumped, dropping the little book she held in her hand, yelling with fright. Tom sat silent and dazed.

Abigail stared at him, "What happened? What do you think you're playing at?" She grabbed her backpack and thrust a few of her items into it, heading for the door. "I'm going home. You're playing at magic tricks, trying to scare me. Well, I've had enough."

"Wait, Abigail," he tried to stand up. "It wasn't a magic trick. Please come back."

The sound of her feet on the stairs was followed by the slam of the front door.

He sat on the bed feeling rather dazed. It couldn't have happened again. What was wrong with him?

By the time his mum's car pulled into the driveway, he half believed he was having horrible, recurring nightmares. As Miriam came in the front door, he came down the stairs but remained quiet all evening. She kept asking him if he was feeling okay. He just said over and over, "I'm okay".

But he wasn't okay. Was he going crazy? And what about school? How would Abigail react towards him? What would she say to him? Worse... what would she say about him?

His mum was so concerned about him, he easily could have bunked school the next day. But he was going to have to face up to Abigail, so he might just as well get on with it. Maybe Abigail would act as if nothing happened.

He saw Abigail first thing at school. He knew immediately that she also noticed him. Her eyes narrowed, and she turned away.

He wandered through his school day, barely lifting his head. He ate lunch by himself, avoiding his friends and enemies alike. The last class of the day was both ecstasy and agony these days. It was P.E. and they were still fencing. It was soon to end and, when it did, Tom was quite sure it would be back to a ball-based game of some sort. For now it was fencing. That was the excellent bit. Most of the students were improving, but he excelled. The agony was that Ronald never recovered from the sound beating he'd received. Ronald's way of coping with the defeat was to make Tom's life as miserable as possible. He was able to avoid Ronald in most classes, but not P.E.

He wasn't thinking about Ronald as he walked into the changing rooms though. He was too busy thinking about Abigail. As he came through the doors of the changing room his head was down, or he might have seen the dangers that awaited him.

Ronald was waiting, and he had plans for Tom. Nathan Shadow stepped behind Tom and closed the door. It was such a strange act and so noticeable that it caused Tom to lift his head and look around. The feeling in the room was intense. The eyes of every boy in the room were on him. Most of the boys were Ronald's close friends. A few were just those lads who were always happy to see a good fight.

Tom glanced around, assessing the situation. Not one of his friends was in the room. He had been too intent upon his own thoughts to notice that a network had been at play, ensuring that his friends were late. They were only reaching the changing rooms now and finding the doors locked.

Ronald turned and struck a fencing pose, but he wasn't holding a foil. Ronald held up an old, but pristine sword. "Now, let's see who the better man really is?" Ronald said. "Don't worry, I'll let you have the tool you are so good with, you big baby."

Ronald threw Tom a foil.

"What's this? You mean for me to use a foil against your sword?' Tom said, he shook his head with disgust, but deep down he felt raw fear.

Ronald struck quickly, coming at him with no warning and with great speed. The sharp sword lashed Tom's hand and drops of blood fell to the ground. Tom moved away. He would have to outwit Ronald. There was no way a foil could win against a sword.

Ronald came at him with mocking laughter. Tom moved quickly. Two or three of the boys gasped as Tom landed perfectly, with a backward leap, on the bench.

"He's a ruddy musketeer," one chap yelled.

"Way ta go, Tom," shouted another.

Tom light-footed it across the room, on the top of the benches. Two or three of the lads booed him.

"Running away, coward?" Ronald yelled.

"I'm not the one who fights a foil with a sword, mate."

He was tiring and Ronald was on him again with every advantage. He knew only one thing to do. He jumped at Ronald from the high vantage point of the bench and slapped the foil as hard as he could on Ronald's face. Ronald screamed, dropped the sword and stumbled against the side of a bench as he fell.

"Hey, that will not get ya any point," Nathan shouted.

As if Tom cared about point keeping at the moment. He took the chance to escape scrambling around the corner, ducking behind a set of shelves. He could hide here for only a moment.

A sudden silence came over the jeering crowd of boys. Tom heard the door of the changing room banging open. Someone with a key must have arrived to open the door. Before he could tell who it was, he heard the voices of his friends coming through the door calling his name. So that was it, they figured out something was going down and brought back a teacher to help.

"What's going on here, boys?" said Mr. Wells, the art teacher. A breathless Mrs. Mendors called out from the doorway, "Is everything okay?" She hesitated only a moment before continuing in a severe voice, "I'm coming in there."

He didn't know what kind of trouble he was going to be in. All he wanted was out of there. A way out came to his mind and he took it.

"Lo bamaqom hazeh. Ba'arets hahi'." He instantly regretted it as he felt himself falling through the darkness. Where was he going to wind up this time?

When Tom finally walked out of the changing room everyone had gone. He walked out into the school grounds and found the place buzzing with activity. A search for him was on. Then he saw Abigail, James, Porker and even the headmaster running towards him. He felt his heart thumping against his chest, painfully, for the third time that day.

"What happened?" he yelled to the approaching group.

The headmaster, surrounded by Tom's friends drew to a stop in front of him.

"Where's your shirt then, boy?" Abigail blurted out before the headmaster could get his sentence formed.

"Where have you been young man?" the head finally said in stern voice.

"You've been hiding, haven't you, Tom?" asked Porker with a squeak. "I knew you were in there. I told him I heard you shouting. Did they hurt you?" He finished with a high-pitched screech, pointing at Tom's wrist.

The story was taken over by the others, leaving Tom with very little explaining to do. He pulled his gym shirt out of his kit and put it on, listening to them in fascination, as they made up a story for him. All of them, including the headmaster, managed to go on and on, figuring out where he had been during the time the teachers and students were searching for him. They created the whole scenario. He only had to nod in agreement.

He let them go on, making it seem as though he'd slumped away into a corner of the changing rooms terrified of Ronald. How he'd crawled out past the teachers, too embarrassed to talk to anybody. He let them go on describing him as a bullied coward, because he could never tell them the truth. It was easier to bear the story when it was being punctuated by the headmaster's description of what was going to happen to Ronald. Knowing Ronald was out of school, possibly for good, made it a little (only a little) easier to be mistaken for a cowering fool.

He sat just outside the headmaster's office while his mum was phoned. He heard the muffled explanation and could tell his mum was upset. Then he spoke to his mum.

"I'm fine Mum. Really. You don't need to leave work. I'll take the bus home and see you there later."

Tom walked slowly out of the main reception building and was surprised to find Abigail waiting for him.

"What do you want?" he asked. He took in the smug look on her face and said, "I'm going home."

"Guess I'll come with you then."

He couldn't believe Old Yellow-Eyes was on the bus. Tom had never run this late, and what happens the first time he does? Tom swallowed hard, trying to ignore those yellow eyes staring at him.

Abigail immediately asked difficult, pointed questions. "All that bunk about you hiding away whilst they were all searching high and low for you.

What a load of grimy, reeking, fly-drawing ..." She noticed an older lady staring at her. Abigail lifted one eyebrow in a most infuriating way and finished, "crap." The old lady looked away. "Where were you?" she demanded.

Tom remained silent. What was he to say?

"I know something weird is going on with you. I know you disappeared last night at your house. Now come on, tell me what's going on. Does this have something to do with our debate? Are you doing some sort a time travel?" She leaned close to him, "It isn't possible is it, Tom?"

Tom said nothing. He didn't even know where to begin. Abigail didn't like his silence. Suddenly she was the girl Tom had seen so often, and she didn't need her pit-bull collar, black lips or black fingernails to be that girl.

"Let me tell you something, boy. I saw you disappear and I could make trouble for you, I could." Softening a little she continued, "Not that I want to, but..."

"You might as well let me in on it. I already know too much anyway."

Tom let her into it. She did see him disappear and he really needed to talk to someone.

"Do you want to know what happened yesterday in my bedroom?" he began.

"That'll do as a starting place, mate." She replied.

He told her about his horrendous bouncing trip. She laughed at him, but then her face twisted with disbelief.

"Come on, do you really expect me to believe that? Little people shooting you with pea shooters?"

He told her about getting the book while waiting for her at King's. He told her about falling off the wall and about the tiny men seeing him.

"You're not trying to have one over on me, are you? Telling me you're off at Gulliver's land of little people. I ain't stupid."

"Well if you're not going to believe me, I don't know why you even bothered to ask." Tom replied loudly, grabbing his backpack and standing up. He saw the intense yellow eyes staring at him. He headed for the door of the bus. It swung open, allowing him to step off at his stop. He walked quickly towards home. He didn't look back.

"Tom, Tom," Abigail yelled. "Wait up. I didn't mean anything."

Tom turned and waited as the girl ran up to him. "Sorry, but you have to admit, mate, it's a bit of a wild story."

Tom and Abigail sat down on his front doorstep. "So, you said them words again when Ronald attacked you in the changing rooms, didn't you?"

He nodded his head, "I'd been thinking about them all day."

He took a sideways glance at her. "I kept thinking about yesterday, wondering what you were going to say today. And when I dashed around the corner away from Ronald, I was just glad to have a minute's rest. I didn't know how to get away from….well…the situation. Then those words came to my head again. It seemed the only way." He was silent for a few moments.

Then he went on with the story he knew Abigail wanted to hear. "So yes, I did say the words in the changing room, and just like before, as soon as I said the words, I was falling in blackness again. But I'm improving. I had pretty good control of myself. I hardly stretched out at all. I lay down and just flew. But this journey was different from the other two. It was so cold, and the darkness never ended. I figured out how I could land and stay put. I decided to try to land on my feet with my knees bent. And that's what I did. It worked too, except that I jiggled up and down a bit. But at least I wasn't bouncing like I had before. I couldn't stop that up and down movement, but in the end I was glad about that, because once I'd landed, I suddenly realised I didn't know how to get home again. Every other time I was pulled back up by the force of my bouncing."

"So what happened? How did you get out again then?"

"Wait a minute. Don't you want to know what sort of *little* creatures I saw?"

"Course I do, go on then," Abigail spat back.

"I mean I figured it would be some place new. After all, the last two journeys I had landed at different destinations. I reckoned I would be at yet another and, like you, I figured I would again see some sort of little creature. But that wasn't what I found there." Tom stopped, shuddering at the memory.

"Go on, what happened?" Abigail asked in a breathless voice, wanting to know the cause of that shudder.

"I heard voices coming up the tunnel."

"Bit of a nutter aren't you, always hearing voices." Abigail laughed and touched Tom's arm.

He ignored her, lost to all but his thoughts. And those thoughts were seemingly not pleasant. His eyes were narrow, staring into memories that produced a frown and dark lines between his eyes.

"And," Abigail again prompted softly. She was afraid he was getting lost in his dark thoughts.

"There was no light." He turned to Abigail. "No light at the end of the tunnel. Freezing blasts came up, sucking air out of my lungs."

Tom wrapped his arms around his chest. "Then I hit, hard. That's how I knew I was out of the tunnel. It was too dark and cold to tell where I was, and I was still wavering up and down. The cold made me feel sick."

He went quiet again. Abigail waited, biting her lip till he began speaking again.

"Then I heard the voices. They weren't like any voices I'd ever heard before. One voice, a raspy one sounded like the speaker's tongue was thick. Whatever it was made nasty choking sounds. The other voice was really beautiful, almost like music. I know this sounds mad, Abigail," He turned pleading eyes to look at the girl. "But the beautiful voice was cold, really, really cold. And it made me feel even colder than I already felt."

As he continued his story, Abigail shivered. Tom was gone from this place. He was reliving the terrible memory of that journey.

The two voices continued to grow louder. Whoever owned those voices was coming nearer to him. A stench filled the frigid black air around him. Then the words being spoken became clearer and clearer. The words were chilling, even more chilling than the freezing air. Tom had never been more frightened in his life.

"Can't wait, bozz. guuwf. Yaw really can't wait to get that rat. guuwf guuwf."

"Ahh, my time of waiting is almost at the end," said the beautiful voice.

"What ya going to do to him, bozz? guuwf. Ya going to do it slow, hey bozz. Ya going to hurt him real slow. guuwf. Ya going to let me watch ya? Can I watch ya hurt him?"

"I'm going to hurt him ever so slowly, Gug. Ever so slowly. It'll be fun. I will let you watch if you bring him to me in one piece." A laugh rang out across the blackness.

"Can I's help, bozz? guuwf. Please can I help ya do him in? guuwf guuwf"

The rich cold laugh lashed the darkness again. "Maybe you can help. Tell me what you want to do."

A great flapping and fluttering stirred the air around Tom. A stench whirled upwards until the smell became unbearable. "Peck his eyes out. guuwf. Can I? Can I please peck his eyes out? guuwf."

Abigail's gasp brought Tom out of his dark story. "Then all I wanted was out of there, Abigail. I suddenly thought that maybe I could go up, because of the wavering. And I was right. I jumped as hard as I could and started moving up."

Tom paused and faced her, "But I felt a claw touch me. It wasn't quite close enough to actually stop me, but it was close enough to rip my shirt off. That was it. I fell back onto the changing room floor. You know the rest."

He shivered at his memories. The cold, the grey door in the blackness, and the memory of an oddly shaped door handle glinting richly with harshly cut diamonds almost made him tremble. The fear of where that door might lead was horrifying. But these thoughts, Tom kept to himself.

The two friends now sat in silence, tensions high between them. Suddenly, Abigail leaned over and placed her soft lips on Tom's mouth. He kissed her back, putting his hands on her cheeks and pulling her even closer.

Abigail pulled away, wiped her mouth and said, "My boyfriend would kill you if he saw you doing that to me."

"What. You're the one…"

"Shut up, Tom. I'm thinking about this problem and I think we need ta see what's going on. We need to do an experiment…"

But Tom stopped her with the words, "That's my mum's car coming up the road."

Miriam Ward stepped out of her car with a surprised face. Her son was sitting on the front doorstep with a girl at his side.

As the car door opened, Abigail said to him. "I'll meet you at King's College wall, eleven sharp on Saturday morning then."

He was just about to say he'd ask his mum if he was allowed, but it felt too babyish considering this was Abigail. "All right," he agreed. "Quarter past eleven." He would sort things out with his mum later.

There was one good thing though, when he introduced Abigail to his mum, she looked like an ordinary Colton college school girl. She was simply an ash-blonde girl, wearing a green school uniform. Tom's story so engaged her that she'd totally forgotten to don her studded pit-bull collar and black lipstick. This would surely make it easier to talk his mum into letting him meet up with her on Saturday.

Chapter Five

At twenty minutes past eleven, Tom was sitting on the wall in front of King's College, waiting. He was also drinking a coke, which helped soothe the anger he felt towards the late Abigail. She'd better show up. It had been tough getting here. It was the worst fight he ever had with his mum. He'd argued, shouted and finally resorted to being plain mean to get this bit of freedom

"It's this girl, isn't it? Her parents let her run all over the kingdom and you think you should be able to do the same thing. Well, just because her parents don't have the good sense to keep track of her, doesn't mean that I'm going to do the same by you." His mum shouted at him, though she refused to admit it.

"Stop shouting at me, Mum," he shouted at her.

"I'm not shouting at you," she yelled back.

The shouting match continued for a while. Miriam even cried a bit. That usually got to him and he'd give in, but not this time. He braced himself, let her cry and then said exactly what he'd been feeling for a long time.

"What did you say Tom Wade?" asked Miriam, her teary eyes widening.

"I said, I should bloody well be the one crying."

"Watch your language." Miriam wiped her eyes with the flat of her hands.

In the end, he won. Well, it seemed like winning today, sitting in the sunshine. Last night the victory was small compared to the price he paid for it. His mum was hurt and he didn't like hurting her. The moment he said the words and saw her face change, his heart sank.

"You're the one who does a runner every time those wretched flowers bloom. Yet, you think I should be tied to your apron string whenever you decide to be home."

Miriam stopped dead, her mouth gaped open, tears rolled downwards, and her face turned pale. She turned around and walked out of the room. That moment ended the argument. Once he was the winner, he became very reasonable. Later that evening he did his best to make the arrangements as she would want them to be, if she were being reasonable. His mother was mostly silent.

"Are you working Saturday?" he asked. Miriam nodded her head. She worked most Saturday mornings.

"I'll call you as I leave the house," he stated. Miriam nodded her head.

"I'll come to your office when Abigail and I are finished."

"Okay."

"We can have lunch together?" he asked in a hopeful tone.

"All right," his mum said, a small smile forming.

And now here he was waiting at King's College wall. He reached in his pocket and pulled out the tattered little book. He felt a fluttery nervousness in the pit of his stomach, but who could blame him? Abigail wanted to do some sort of experiment. He wasn't sure he wanted anything more to do with this book. He now felt certain the writing in the book was some sort of incantation. But as to where it transported him, he was clueless.

Tom flipped through the printed pages, observing the scribbled writing at the side margins. It was extremely odd. Just a series of squiggles and tiny dots. As he thought about it, this writing was like something that sat on his mother's desk at home. It wasn't the normal writing of the era she studied. Miriam was a medieval scholar. Anglo-Saxon, Middle English, Old French with its many dialects, and of course good old Latin, were the languages she studied and taught (which somewhat explained her desire for him to be at Colton College and taking Latin). Those languages were different from the writing on the crinkly yellow paper that lay protected under a glass-encased frame on her desk. Like the writing in Tom's little book, the sprawling twists and curves hardly seemed like letters.

He asked Miriam about that ancient paper once. All she did was rub her fingers around the ornate wooden frame and across the etched glass which covered it, before finally answering, in a dreamy school girl sort of voice, "Ah such a language, Tom. A language so ancient, yet remains with us forever, to tell us most wonderful things."

"Older than Anglo-Saxon, Mum?" He asked.

She smiled at him and then laughed, "Makes Anglo-Saxon and even Latin seem new."

Tom reached for his coke and pulled his thoughts back to the present. Why? Why did that man give me this book? Did he know what would happen when I said those words?

He looked up, half expecting to see the tall thin man appearing before him, instead in the distance he saw Abigail, at last. "Are you always late?" he yelled at her as she came nearer.

She just grinned, flung her bag to the ground, leaned close to him and grabbed his coke. "Bit early to be drinking this sorta stuff, ain't it? Does your mummy know you're here?"

Tom grimaced. She was in that sort of mood again. He thought yesterday had changed everything. They shared a secret not even James Mason knew, but now this scoffing creature was back. And the kiss, what about that?

"What is it you want to do?" He held out the little book and continued, "I'm not too sure that I want to mess with this thing again."

Abigail glanced at him, tilting her head sideways. "Scared are you?"

"I guess I have reason to be."

"I was thinking about it. I'll hold you down. You say them words, I'll hang on to you, and then, like, we'll see what happens. Right, then?"

"What's the point of doing that?"

"Well it's just a beginning. We can try all sorts of things."

"What sort of things?"

Abigail glared at him. He wondered if she really had any other plans.

"Well then, have you got any better idea?" she asked.

He shook his head.

Abigail stood up and looked around. "I need to find something to hang on to." Abigail walked away from the wall towards the ancient building behind.

She sat down beside a huge rock and anchored her feet under it. He followed her, peering around to see if anyone was watching them. His heart was beating hard in his chest. He stood there, staring down at Abigail. Was she really going to make him do this? Abigail put out her hand. Tom sat down and took it.

"I'll probably just get ripped away from you," he said, but a worse fear entered his head. What if he wasn't ripped away? What if he was just pulled up and out with his arm going all rubbery, leaving only his hand in Abigail's hand? It was too revolting to contemplate.

"Say it," Abigail ordered.

He closed his eyes and slowly said the words, "Lo bamaqom hazeh. Ba'arets hahi'."

The now familiar feeling of falling came, but this time there was the sound of screaming all around him. Then he remembered Abigail and opened his eyes. She was there, still holding his hands. They were pulled miles apart by elongated limbs. Abigail looked hilarious, screaming loudly, her open mouth stretching till it was a cavern. She was flinging and flaying about, causing this leg then the next to stretch out beyond her body. He laughed loudly, watching her. His laughter began to mix with the echoing of her screams. Those sounds in the darkness became ghoulish, reminding him that he was just about to land in an unearthly place. He turned pale and closed his lips tightly on his laughter.

He pulled on Abigail. Abigail floated towards him and he yelled, "Abigail stop that noise." She turned her face towards him. She stopped screaming but her eyes pleaded for help as her screams echoed around them.

"Listen to me," he said, "just move slowly." Abigail pulled her limbs slowly towards her.

"Good one." His words ricocheted around her reassuringly. Once Abigail had literally pulled herself back together, he told her what to do as they landed. She listened quietly but her eyes were fearful.

The light was upon them only seconds after he finished explaining his plan, which worked like a charm. Tom hit first, feet down, bending his knees so the force made him stumble only a little. He and Abigail were still holding hands. She landed on her feet just after him but without his previous experience, she boomeranged upwards. He reckoned on that happening. He felt quite the pro now. He pulled her back down to the ground, yelling, "Buckle your knees." This time Abigail did it. She bent her knees as she came down and fell into him with the force of her landing. The two stood there momentarily, laughing nervously.

"Where are we?" whispered Abigail.

At his feet, he saw the feathery green grass of his first visit. He whispered back, "I think we're near the place I first came."

They searched around to see if they could find a sheltered area. He didn't even think about the fact that he was standing solidly for the first time.

Tom and Abigail ran towards a big boulder sitting in the midst of some smaller ones. They stooped down behind it, discussing in agitated whispers the view that presented itself before them. It was an odd sight. Below them were hundreds of tiny flower-sized trees, green-leaves, brown boughs, twisted and aged, and all blowing gently in the breeze. Daisies, little more than the size of pinheads, grew all around the trees. The boulders and the occasional tuft of normal size grass seemed ridiculously large in the landscape. Little streams, flowing through, were like rushing rivers compared to the little trees and miniscule flowers.

"Can you believe this?" Abigail whispered. "It's like we've entered Lilliputian."

"This is where I first came. I saw those two tiny men, and found the grass in my hair."

"Well now, greetings and welcome, young Peregrine Sol?"

They both jumped and turned around quickly. Standing on one of the smaller boulders behind them was a tiny man.

Tom stammered an answer back to the man. "I-I-I'm sorry. We d-didn't mean to intrude on you or anything."

"Well now that's all right," the little man replied. He took off his pointed hat and bowed to them.

Tom mimicked him. Bowing formally.

"What are you doing?" whispered Abigail. "I mean he seems to understand you, and all. But you go making fun of him and he might get real mad."

Tom said, "Didn't you hear him? He said it was all right."

Abigail gasped. "You mean to say you could understand him?"

"Yeah, couldn't you?"

"No."

They turned back to the tiny man.

The man turned to Abigail, removed his hat for the second time and bowed low. "Halo, perempuan berkalung kucing."

Abigail stared at the little man.

Tom nudged her softly. "Say something to him."

"What?"

"What's wrong with you?"

Abigail rounded on him, "I can't understand him, you fool."

"You can't hear him?" Tom whispered.

"I can hear him. He's speaking in some weird foreign language, surely you can hear that."

"I understand everything he says."

By this time the tiny man had put his hat back on his head. He stared at them suspiciously.

"Peregrine Sol, why have you brought her here?"

Tom just shook his head.

"Come," said the little man.

Tom followed the little man. Abigail huffed, and then followed Tom. The little fellow moved across the feathery grass at an amazing speed. They went around two or three more sets of boulders and then they came upon a group of the little people.

One of the little men called out, "Behold, we have found a Peregrine Sol."

It didn't take the two travellers long to figure out they were interrupting some sort of celebration. For a crowd of such tiny people, the party food was more than plentiful. Plates, normal size for Tom's use but huge for these people, were lying on long tables. Food of various kinds, colours, and shapes filled those plates to over flowing. It soon became clear this was a wedding feast. The bride and groom, dressed in matching silver costumes with golden decorations in their hair, stood in the middle of the group, side by side, their special moment stolen by these over-large people.

Tom bowed and tried to speak eloquently to fit the occasion, "Please excuse my companion and myself for interrupting your celebration."

The bride and groom came forward. The bride looked at Tom and said, "Welcome, strange, uninvited, but not unwanted guest. It has been a long time since we had Peregrine Sols in our midst."

The groom then spoke, turning to address Abigail. "Halo dan salmat datang, perempuan yang aneh."

Tom wondered if Abigail understood the mixed insult and welcome. He was just about to remind her that she was wearing a dog's collar when the man who brought them spoke.

"She doesn't understand," He turned, and pointing at Tom, said, "He has brought an illegal with him."

The gasp from the little group belied their tiny size. One little old man stepped forward. His long beard was speckled grey. The old man spoke, his voice deep, rich and very strong for his size.

"Why have you broken the ancient law code, Peregrine Sol? Why have you defiled our land by bringing this with you?" he waved his hand with disgust at Abigail.

Tom didn't know what to say. But no one seemed in any hurry. They waited patiently. When Tom spoke it was slowly and deliberately. He knew it was important he answered in a way these angry little people would understand. He wasn't sure what they would do, nor what they could do. But the seriousness of their eyes made him think that their anger could be much greater than their size.

"I didn't know there was any law. You call me a Peregrine Sol." (He hoped he said it correctly). Tom paused searching for the right words. "I don't know what that is, or if I'm one. I'm not sure I'm supposed to be here anymore than Abigail. I just know that somehow I have found my way here and that, without knowing how to bring her, not trying to bring her, Abigail has come too." He took a deep breath.

The little people remained silent. Even the children seemed to understand that this was too important for noise. They were so serious and solemn.

He couldn't take the silence any longer, he straightened his shoulders and said, "I believe I'm supposed to be here, and so is Abigail. "

"I'm Karmono, leader of these people. I also believe you should be here, though I do not know why. Maybe it's also true that this other is to be with you. I will not judge." Karmono turned to face his people. "Come, you must all now make merry."

The little people obeyed, turned away, and began to chat and laugh among themselves. Karmono beckoned and Tom and Abigail followed him.

Karmono lead them to another area of scattered boulders. Karmono climbed on a boulder and indicated that Tom and Abigail should sit on the ground beside him. They all sat quietly, watching a young wee man build a fire.

Once the fire was roaring, the young man climbed on the boulder and sat down beside Karmono. The warmth coming from the blaze was comforting.

"Well now, I should introduce my son, Eddi." Karmono said when they were settled. "You must tell your friend our names," he said to Tom.

Tom repeated it all to Abigail.

The old man sighed and said, "I'm sorry you can't understand us. I'm sorry that your welcome seems less than it should." He then looked at Tom to translate for him.

When Tom finished, the little man nodded.

"Do you understand everything I say to her as well as what I say to you?"

He nodded again.

"Why? How?" Tom asked.

"Well now. There is an intense magic in this land you have entered my boy. A very deep and powerful magic it is." The old man took a tiny pipe out of his breast coat pocket. He lit the pipe and drew two long puffs from it. The faint smell of cloves filled the air.

"This magic, boy, it's at work now. You say you don't know if you are a Peregrine Sol, but we know." stated the old man, pointing with his pipe from himself to his son. "We know."

"How?"

"You understand us. You belong. You will understand everyone in every part of Adamah, as we all do, though we speak in different tongues. But this strange collared female, she does not, and she never will without a special magic performed."

"What kind of special magic?"

"Enchantment." Tom shivered at the word.

The two little men laughed. "Spells. Incantations. Charms. Maybe these are the words you prefer young Peregrine Sol. Something said to her, nothing done to her, you see, that makes her understand."

"Who does this magic? Can you do it?"

"Well now, lad. Not me. Not any of us here can do such things." He stated still using his pipe as an indicator.

"No, this is only done by the wisest and oldest of our world. Such wise ones, you will only find by going to certain places in Adamah. I'm no such wizard," he said, laughing again.

Two more little men climbed up on the boulder. They whispered something to the father and son. The old man tipped back his head, roaring with laughter.

He waved his pipe as though he *were* a wizard with a wand said, "So you have been here before Peregrine Sol."

Tom felt a hot red flush cover his face. So that was why those two were so familiar. They were the ones who witnessed his horrific first landing.

"Well now. You have improved my young friend." And again the old man bellowed out laughter, joined this time by his three small companions.

As Tom told Abigail what they were talking about, two more little people climbed up the boulder. This time it was the bride and groom.

"Ah now," said Karmono, "this is my reminder that I have a wedding celebration to attend. This is my daughter getting married." Again the pipe was a pointer.

"She's beautiful," Abigail blurted out.

"Abigail says your daughter's beautiful." repeated Tom.

"Well now," said Karmono, turning towards Abigail. "All our women are beautiful."

Tom translated.

Karmono continued, "and all our men are handsome."

Abigail joined the laughter with the little people as Tom translated. It was true, the little people were perfectly lovely. Smooth brown skin, dark eyes and shinny black hair.

It was time to go. Peace had settled between them. Tom wanted to go before something broke it. Then suddenly he remembered.

"I don't know how to go home," he whispered in a panicky voice to Abigail.

"Well now, I must return to my celebration and you must return to your home and your destiny." Karmono's eyes narrowed. He looked closely at Tom. "This is not such a good time, my young Peregrine Sol, to travel. Though the time of peace is nearly upon us, until it is here there are dangers, you know."

"Time of peace? What's happening here?"

"Ah, terrible things can happen," replied the old man, slowly shaking his head, his face overcome with sadness. "An open battle we can handle Peregrine Sol. But they steal in upon us without warning…." The little man's face wrinkled with worry.

Karmono stood. "I must go now, Peregrine Sol. Remember to be careful."

They began to descend from the boulder. With a wave, Karmono led his people away.

Tom and Abigail watched until they were gone. Tom repeated Karmono's final words to Abigail. She didn't seem to hear him. "Blast you, Tom Wade, you've got no idea how to get us out of here, have you?"

"No. Not really," he said honestly, lifting his hands.

Abigail wore such vulnerable expression that for the first time she seemed exactly what she was, a girl his same age.

"Peregrine Sol."

Tom turned. It was Eddi. "Yes, and my name is Tom."

"My father says that it's always the converse. Travelling, that is. It's always the converse."

"Thank you… I think," Tom stated.

"And Peregrine Sol Tom, I give you this." The little man handed him a small tubular shaped parchment. "Sometimes," he continued, "only a little will do. This will call me to you, where ever you are in this land."

"Thank you Eddi." Tom said. The little man turned and walked away again. Tom again repeated it all to Abigail.

"So what's that supposed to mean?" Abigail put her hands on her hips.

"Converse," Tom muttered, "What's it mean?"

"Talking with each other." Abigail then said, "Hey, it can also mean backwards."

Tom pulled out his tattered book. He tried saying the first line backwards. Nothing happened. Then he turned to the back of the book and read those words first. "Ba'arets hahi'." Then he said, "Lo bamaqom hazeh." He grabbed Abigail's hand quickly to keep from leaving her behind.

When they landed at King's College they were on the other side of the building.

"Wow," said Abigail.

Tom shook his head. "It's certainly real. Now we have both been there."

"Dead to rights, and I think you should follow that little chap's advice and stay out."

"You mean you wouldn't want to go back?" he asked with surprise.

"Not on your life. Would you after the warning he gave you? You'd have to be a fool."

Tom said nothing. But he did want to go back. It was true what he said to Eddi, he felt he was travelling there for a purpose. He felt he needed to go back.

Chapter Six

Tom and Abigail walked and talked. The more they talked about what happened, the more unreal it became. They stopped on the street outside Seldon College. Abigail was going on to meet with some friends. She was late, but said she didn't care. Her friends would probably be late anyway.

They were standing close, face to face on the street. He didn't want her to leave. A strand of hair was hanging across her face and he was overcome by a desire to push it back behind her ear. He did it and found her hair was soft.

"Something makes me feel we're just playing a kid's game of pretend. The more we talk, the more I think maybe we just made the whole thing up."

That feeling was growing in Tom too, and he wanted it to be real. Then he thought of a way to keep Abigail with him. He grabbed her hand and said, "Lo bamaqom hazeh. Ba'arets hahi'."

"You fool, what the hell are you doing?" Abigail's echoing scream travelled across the darkness. The expression on her face was not fear this time, it was pure fury.

"There's nothing you can do about it now. If you don't want to smash on your face like I did my first time, you'd better listen to me."

Coming out of the darkness, he felt nerves in the pit of his stomach again. But it all worked perfectly, even better than the last time. They landed on their feet and neither fell over or even stumbled. But as they settled, Abigail's anger returned.

"What do you think you're up to, you idiot?" She grew angrier as she spoke. She shouted, "I told you I didn't want to come back to this horrible place."

"I realised that it did seem unreal and I wanted to check it out again."

A noise made him turn. He hadn't even noticed his surroundings yet. A large yellow-stone building towered above them. His heart skipped a beat as he saw three people coming around the corner of the building, each carrying long-pole spears and wearing brass breastplates beneath unsmiling faces.

One of the warriors stepped between him and Abigail. Another guard walked behind Abigail and one stood in front of Tom, gesturing before turning to lead the way around the corner of the stone building. It was clear what they wanted and Tom compliantly followed. Abigail resisted, set her face and would not move. Without a word or even a look of malice, a brown-faced warrior lifted a spear and pointed it at her. She jogged along quickly to catch up.

"I don't know why you bother being so stubborn. We're obviously going to have to go where people with spears say we have to go."

"Well, I wouldn't be having to go nowhere, if you'd have left me alone like I said," she replied, her upper lip in a snarl.

"If the sharp end of that spear leaves a mark on your backside, I won't ever have to prove we have been here again."

Abigail huffed at him and kept marching along.

They had landed behind a large square building. As they rounded the corner, they came upon a glorious scene. An avenue of trees led to a large green, gently rolling park. Wooden benches were scattered here and there against flower gardens and copses of trees. Umbrella-covered tables with comfortable chairs dotted the entry way of a magnificent manor house. Most striking was the gaiety in the park. As far as the eye could see, and filling the air with sound, was play.

Tom felt a poke on his back, the sombre faces and sharp pointed spears where a contrast from the scene that they were now walking through. Their captors were rather intimidating despite being only average adult height and rather slim. Round faces, large almond shaped eyes, and full lips were framed by straight, ear-length hair. The guards were distinguishable only by their different coloured hair. The most prominent feature of the guards was their countenance. The longer he was around them, the sadder Tom felt. They seemed to radiate sadness.

The friends were led through a dark hallway, into a large manor and through to a luxurious formal room. One guard indicated they should sit on a small sofa. The guards then turned to leave, all except one, who remained at the door. Abigail sat down. She was silent, which was so rare a state in Abigail that it made Tom watch her face closely as he sat down beside her.

Abigail turned to him, her eyes wide, "Ain't they sad? Did you see what was out there in the garden? Say them words and let's get out of here."

Before he had a chance to respond to any of Abigail's rushed comments, a group of children entered the room. They were so obviously the offspring of the beings that held him and Abigail captive. A light creamy material jumpsuit covered each child's soft skin. The little ones had rounded bodies and limbs, and the same rounded faces, almond shaped eyes and straight, short hair of their older counterparts. They ran round and round the room, jumping on the sofas and chairs. They jabbered and chattered to one another the entire time. He couldn't understand them, though Abigail kept asking him what they were saying. It wasn't that he didn't understand the language. It was that they spoke so rapidly and nonsensically that he could not follow them.

The little ones became braver, finally coming right up and poking him and Abigail with short stubby fingers. Then all but two of them scampered away, out of the door. The other two sat down quietly by Tom's knees, staring up at him with unblinking brown eyes, twirling their black hair between their little fingers. He glanced down at them, up to Abigail, and then swiftly back down again. They now were watching him with unblinking blue eyes and red hair. Their skin was a light shade of green. Abigail gasped.

He laughed and said, "Did what I thought happen, really happen?"

She just pointed down at the little ones.

He looked down again, shaking with laughter. Now they were blue, with bright purple eyes. Their hair was still red. Then before his eyes, the children changed again. They were back to their brown skin, but one had orange hair and the other brilliant blue. Their red eyes glimmered spookily.

The two little ones seemed fascinated by Abigail and Tom's reaction to their changes. They tilted their heads, opened their eyes wide and began to rapidly change colours all over their bodies, like little living Christmas

decorations.

The sound of clicking heels and clapping made them all start. A woman

standing in the doorway said, "Now children, off you go. You're wasting your

lovely play-day."

The little ones jumped up and grinned at each other. They spoke and Tom

finally understood them. "Let's play that I'm a rabbit and you're a wolf who's

after me." one said to the other.

"Okay," squeaked the other.

Tom jumped up. At his knee was a rabbit and a wolf. The rabbit jumped

away calling and laughing in that same childish voice. The wolf stopped, licked

his hand then bounded out of the room after his prey. Tom sat back down in

amazement.

The tall, elegant woman swept over to them and gracefully sat down in a

chair. She was glorious. She had the same heart-shaped face and almond eyes as

the guards, but her dress and manner transformed her. She wore a long flowing

dress of shimmering silky green, a graceful cape of deeper green and a head-

dress full of long, soft pastel feathers and brightly coloured silk. The head-dress

framed her face, giving her the appearance of soft, multi-coloured hair. The

woman was regal.

"I am Mother."

"Mother?" asked Tom.

"Mother," Abigail repeated.

"My name is Mim. My children call me Mimmi rather like children of your world say Mummy, Mommy, or Mama. All others call me simply Mim."

Abigail curled her lip. "So why call yourself Mother, then?"

"Well, Mim is 'Mother' in my language."

"You speak English," Tom said, suddenly realising he was hearing his own language.

"I have been to your world." She searched his face with her eyes.

"You've been to Earth?"

The woman laughed, throwing back her head. "Earth, they call it. As if it is the only one. Yes, I have been to Earth."

"How?" He asked.

Her eyes narrowed. Now he saw that she, too, had that sadness that filled all but the little ones in this place.

"I, too, am a Peregrine Sol."

"So why did you set those guards on us, then?" asked Abigail.

Beautiful Mim leaned forward, "I did not set guards on you, girl. The guards came upon unknown creatures within our borders and they did what they must." Her eyes became terrible and her voice worse than her eyes, "If you offered resistance, they would have killed you."

Mim leaned back in her chair. "But you were peaceful so they brought you to me. It is the way it is. A necessary evil which is the result of a most terrible tragedy in our history." Her voice was now matter of fact.

"These guards or whatever, are they men or women?" Abigail asked, her curiosity overcoming her dislike.

"Both male and female," answered Mim.

"And the ones out there taking care of those, mmmm, children, are they men or women?" Abigail ventured again.

"Both male and female," Mim said. She laughed, "Even in your world they are finally learning that both can care for the little ones."

Mim looked again at Tom. "Why are you here?"

"Well," he said. "I don't really have a lot of control as to where I go. I just seem to land places." He looked back at Mim, feeling rather foolish.

Mim laughed, "Ahh, I know that feeling well." For a moment her sea-blue eyes took on a glistening faraway look. Then she straightened herself in her chair and spoke rapidly. "But why come at all, there must be a reason? You've been given a key?"

"Key?"

"Yes, a key to come here."

"Tom ain't got no key. See. He only has a book written in some squiggly language."

Mim looked at Abigail, arching the eyebrows above those knowing eyes again.

Abigail whispered, "The key?"

Mim smiled haughtily at her and nodded her head.

Looking back at Tom, Mim said sternly, "The key would not have come to you without cause. You are a Peregrine Sol. That much is clear. You must have a calling or a quest. I ask again, why are you here?"

He looked down at his hands.

"Come, surely you can see that I can be trusted. I am Mother of Erets and a Peregrine Sol like you."

"I don't know. I really don't…. The man who gave me the book didn't say anything about a quest. He didn't even tell me what would happen to me. I had no idea I would come here. Maybe it's all just a mistake." He gave Mim a worried look.

"The dark times come to Adamah quite suddenly. You must have a purpose for coming. Especially in light of the evil I have heard of this day." Mim shivered slightly and wrapped her cape around her arms.

"Come." she commanded.

Abigail stood first, following quickly after Mim. Here again was this warning about something happening in this place. She wasn't going to let Mim out of her sight.

Tom hurried behind Abigail. They went out of the door, past the guard and into the garden park. Children and creatures were at play, the sound of their laughter, giggling, and joy, riotously filled the space. Mim stopped, a slight smile playing about her lips as she took in the scene around her. Tom saw two little children near him pop suddenly out of the forms of two puppies. One of the little ones yelled to the other, "Pretend I'm the princess and you are the Vile One coming to get me." The child disappeared and a small princess dressed in bright colours stood in her place. The other former puppy began to cry, "I don't want to be the Vile One. I don't want..."

Before the second cry could come all the way out of the little one's lips, another grown-up came running. This adult looked much like a guard, but was dressed in a thin, light-coloured robe and was holding a book instead of a spear. "Come, come Eli. Come Rochelle. Let's look at a picture book. We can find a new pretend," she called. The little ones, once again child-like in appearance, joined hands and trotted off to a bench.

Tom was just turning to speak to Mim about the children's transformation, when two large snakes slithered between Abigail's feet. She let out a piercing scream. The next instance, they were laughing children, rolling away. Abigail's eyes darted with fury, she moved abruptly towards the little ones. The sound of galloping hoofs thundered towards her. Only the raised hand of Mim kept the huge, snorting horse from bearing down on Abigail. The horse stopped, sliding through the grass leaving a torn trail, then turned to gallop away. A few trots and it was a guard, walking at a steady pace.

Mim's face showed no emotion and her voice was quiet, "Be very careful girl, we protect our young in Erets. Sus could have trampled you. He's never been in your world, where angry threats are often empty. We know uncontrolled passions lead to terrible actions."

Mim picked up the children, whose little faces would no longer frighten anyone. She petted and cuddled them, saying. "What a silly game, now off you go, to play nicely." She set the two little ones down.

"Your people, I've never seen anything like it." Tom stammered.

Mim looked around her, with love painted on her otherwise dispassionate face. "Changelings. They are Changeling children."

"You mean all of you can just pop into anything you want to be?"

"No, not all of us can change into anything." Sorrow filled the air as she spoke. "Do you think the children of Erets are special? In your world have you seen children at play and you could almost believe they were what they were pretending? The monkey's tails, feathers on the bird, the authority in the King's voice, have these things ever been visible to you in the play of a child? Almost visible. That is what we have with our little ones. Pretend that is reality. Joy unabashed." Mim closed her sea-blue eyes as she continued, "Childhood so deliciously sweet that lasts as long as life…"

Tom, who had been watching Mim's passionate face, spoke, "As long as life?"

Mim's eyes flew open. "We've wasted enough time. Come."

Mim moved at a quick pace across the lovely gardens towards a clump of trees. Tom and Abigail had to jog to keep up with her. But they couldn't help looking around as they went.

The gardens were full of little creatures transforming from one thing to another. Their protectors stayed close at hand. A little monkey jumped from a branch, reaching out towards the limb of another tree. He missed. Falling, the panic of his yell stopped Tom, Abigail and Mim in their tracks. Mim turned pale. But before the child, now back in his Changeling shape, could hit the ground, a swan was under him and he landed in a gentle thud on feathers.

Mim called out, "Well done Barbur."

The former swan allowed a momentary smile of pleasure to cross its face.

Mim hurried on.

"She was pleased by your praise," Tom said.

"Yes. But she was just doing her duty," Mim answered abruptly, as she led them into a wooded area.

"And what about the guards and the ones who care for the little ones, can they change too? What are you, a grown up Changeling? Why so few grown-ups compared to so very many young ones?" As Tom asked the questions, he could see her expression change. He was pushing his luck.

As they came out the other side of the trees, Mim stopped. "Here we are. This is what I wanted to show you," she stated.

He could still hear the sound of the play, but he could not see through the thick trees. The view opposite the woods was only a long, rolling landscape, with one distant hill.

"Up there."

He looked where Mim was pointing and then back at her again, unsure of what he should be finding.

"The hill. The All Seeing Hill. That's where you need to go. From there you can see all of Adamah clearly. If you have a destiny here, you may find it up there. Many go to the All Seeing Hill for clarity."

Mim turned to walk back to the Erets.

"Wait," he called urgently, "I don't understand. How do I get there? What do I do?"

"You are a Peregrine Sol. You must travel there. Do whatever it takes, that's what we all must do. Walk, if you have to." Her voice was now stern and uncompromising.

Tom stood still, looking at her, confused.

"Go back. Go back to your earth, little boy, take the little girl with you. You reminded me of someone and I thought you were up to the task. You are not. When you're stronger, come back, not before."

"Ah, you think you can call us little boy and girl to hurt our feelings. You're the one acting childish. What is it *Mother dearest*, did no one ever help you?" Abigail asked, her voice dripping with sarcasm.

"I've been helped many a time. But you two... I cannot understand how you can have no knowledge. You have the book."

"I told you," Abigail yelled, "that book has some sort of strange language. Tom and me, we can't read that stuff."

Mim's face hardened, she arched her eyebrows, about to speak, but Tom piped up first.

"Mim, I can't read it. If there really is something I'm supposed to do here, I don't have time to learn, even if I knew someone who could teach me. I need your help. I promise I'll do my best. I'll try to learn all that I can. Please, Mim, will you please help me get started?"

Mim's face softened. "Right then. We are Changelings, but we older ones are different. We're Changelings still, but no longer can we change like the children. We can only transfigure."

"Transfigure?" they asked at the same time.

"Transform into only one other form."

"So you change into something you wanna be?" Abigail asked.

"We do not so much choose as discover what we want to be. We find that as we grow, we make a difficult, but irresistible choice. The form we select is in fact ourselves." Mim's voice had become quiet and sad.

"So, you know what you should be, and that's what you can transfigure into?"

"Yes Tom, well said. But you'll never understand the pain, for you will never have to go through it."

"Well," said Abigail slowly. "That doesn't explain why there are so many little ones compared to the adults."

"There are not as many adults, but there are more than you saw, they serve across Adamah. Many a fortunate Changeling Child remains a child forever. But this is of no value to your cause. I only answered your question to say that we all have painful experiences in our journeys. Ours is different than yours, but it's all a part of taking on the quest at hand. That's what you must do, boy. You must reach out and make each decision you know is the right one. I think the moment of truth is just at hand for you, seize it, boy. Seize it."

Tom nodded his head. He felt as if Mim was handing him a burden. He wanted to know more. "Mim, is Adamah the name of this world?" He asked.

Mim nodded.

"Please Mim, tell me more about it. I have seen the little people and I have seen some ugly gnomes. And I have heard some truly frightening things. What else is there, Mim? You keep talking about dark times. So did the little people. What's happening? Maybe that will help me more than anything else?"

"So what do you turn into?" Abigail asked.

Mim kept her eyes on Tom as she answered Abigail, "A Rara Avis. I transfigure as a Rara Avis."

Leaving Abigail to wonder, Mim spoke to Tom, "You've been far. Further than I thought. Our world, Adamah, is special. It is full of special people. I guess you feel that way about your world too. But our people, unlike yours, are innocent. Oh, you have seen only a small portion of the people here. Good people. In the border lands of the Etz live the Dryad peoples who look like trees, Yam is inhabited by Naiad water folk. Nymphs blow like wind through the lands to the east."

Mim's face was tender as she spoke. "To the west and to the north, you will find the lands full of creatures so extraordinary that your imagination could never conceive them. Have you ever seen a Gambit, a Gropher or a Droll? You might laugh or cry or shiver if you did. But all these delightful beings are under a most terrible threat. And something horrible has happened."

Mim's voice lowered to a husky whisper, "You must understand that the far south is a different place than most of Adamah. We call it Sheol. There, all you see and hear, can chill you to your heart. The Vile One sits on the throne and all disgusting things cling to his feet. It is he…"

They leaned forward to hear Mim as her voice had lowered to a hoarse whisper. "He and his gruesome, flesh-eating, foul followers are the reason that Adamah is now in such terrible pain. It's not yet been an hour since the reports reached us. And knowing they have made this victory will cause those despicable creatures to become bolder. Already they are crossing the borders, driving through the Enchanted Hedge, and menacing the people of our land. We are all called upon to be in Readiness. We are all watchful."

Movement in the trees caught Tom's eyes. Suddenly a large rank of the Eret's guards burst through the woods. These guards no longer looked sad, their faces were stern, angry and worried. He knew his time with Mim was soon to be over. He asked quickly, "What is it? What horrible thing has happened that has made everyone so afraid?"

The guards drew closer, their loud voices calling to Mim. "We have marauders on the west boundaries Mim."

Mim's eyes and face filled with fear. "I must away to protect my children." She spoke with urgency. "You must go find your calling. I must go fulfil what I already know is mine." With those words, Mim turned and ran with such speed that her cape and head-dress flew out behind her.

"Oh Abigail, we still don't know what has happened that has them all so frightened."

"I don't think I even want to know. Please just take us home. Anything that can frighten that strange woman is bound to be really scary."

He took Abigail's hand and slowly uttered the first word. She closed her eyes tight in anticipation of the journey with no plans of opening them till she was safely in front of Seldon College. Tom spoke the incantation backwards. As he did, he looked around one last time. Out of the trees to the west, he saw a strange sight, a magnificent, enormous, and wildly colourful bird rose in swift and purposeful flight.

Chapter Seven

Tom and Abigail walked back to the entrance of Seldon College. Abigail wasn't angry anymore because their experience had been so interesting. But she wanted nothing more to do with any of it, and she made that quite clear. "That's it, okay. No more stunts like that or you've had it."

Tom smiled at her and reluctantly said goodbye. Abigail turned to leave, then turned back and gave him a quick kiss on the cheek. Tom watched her for a few moments before heading into the college grounds to find his mum.

He didn't feel the way Abigail did. Right now he wanted nothing more than to go back to Adamah. Before he went back, he needed some time to think things through. It would be great to get away, but he'd have to do lunch with his mum first. He walked into the courtyard to find his mum was already there, standing in a crowd of people. They were an odd assortment, all dressed differently, four Asian men wore suits, a black woman was in traditional African dress. There were a few men, one fat chap had a tucked in shirt that gaped open to show his belly-button. A few of the women were older with varying shades of grey hair, and a young woman, her hair pulled severely back from her face, was wearing an academic gown. But after being in Adamah, this strange group was nothing.

Miriam saw him coming and rushed over, "Tom, I'm so sorry. I didn't know these visitors were here today. I know we had our little problems last night and I seemed stubborn...."

He raised his eyebrow at his mum.

"Could you grab a sandwich for lunch?" His mum smiled, wrinkling her nose in the rather cute way she did when she wanted something. "We could have afternoon tea together instead. Okay? I'll be a couple of hours."

"Perfect," He thought to himself but said, "I'll come back here in two hours, Mum. I'll wait in the back garden for you. I guess I'll be in town all on my own." He smirked as his mother grimaced.

He went back to the city and bought a sandwich, a flapjack, and a small coke. He wandered around looking at shops, but it was boring, so he headed back to Seldon College.

He went around groups of people who were holding wine glasses and nibbling delicacies from passing trays. He walked past the chapel and into the garden. Time alone, just what he wanted. He sat down on a bench and munched his sandwich thinking about Erets. What were they doing there now? Were the little ones playing outside or did they have to stay indoors? Tom's stomach turned at the thought of some despicable creature hurting one of those little Changelings.

Was it true that he had a quest? Karmono thought Tom had a calling and Mim seemed sure of it. He stared into space for a minute. Then he stood up. He had to get to the All Seeing Hill. But how? He needed to think logically.

He went to a new place in Adamah every time he said the incantation in a new place. When he came back from his journey, he came back to the same starting place, *unless* he changed places in Adamah, then he returned to a different place. When he and Abigail followed Karmono and Eddi, they came back on the other side of King's College. Today, when they followed Mim to the other side of Eret's Manor, he and Abigail landed on the corner, a block away from Seldon. Maybe from here in the garden of Seldon, he would land somewhere close to Erets and could make his way to All Seeing Hill.

He took a quick look to make sure no one was around. Then he said, "Lo bamaqom hazeh. Ba'arets hahi'." Away he fell.

He only felt the falling sensation for a moment before he gained control. Then he flew. For the first time, he felt relaxed. He laughed and twirled himself round, holding out his hands. It was glorious, like rolling in laughter.

He saw the light. He repositioned himself to land feet first. Only then did he feel that queasy flutter in the pit of his stomach.

He landed, hit a little harder than he anticipated, and stumbled. He looked around to make sure no one was going to attack him. Even peashooters seemed lethal at times. No one was there, it was deadly quiet. There was also no manor, no copse of trees, no distant view of the hill and no sound of play. He hadn't managed it. He didn't get back to Erets.

His disappointment lasted only for a moment. He realised he was standing on a hill. He ran to the edge and let out a shout of joy when he saw Erets Manor. He was standing on the All Seeing Hill.

He stared at the manor. It was so far away, yet his eyes focused and he could clearly see people moving, and even recognise individuals. He didn't know them well, he had only been there once after all, but that guard at the right, he was sure that was Sus, the horseman.

There was a small group of heavily guarded children playing on the grass. Tom watched as the guards called the children together, counted them carefully, and lead them indoors. As that group of children went in the manor, another small group came out, all obviously full of unspent energy. They ran, jumped, and played, changing into all manner of creatures. That was not all that was happening in Erets. There were groups of guards out everywhere, some were patrolling the borders, but others were searching for someone. His heart gave a jolt. Was Mother missing?

"No," he whispered, "I bet it's a little one." He squinted. The view focused a little more, becoming even shaper. Now he could see sheer agony on the face of every guard.

He stepped back to the middle of the hill and looked beyond Erets. The landscape was immense. Huge forests, hills, and valleys of emerald green tumbled over one another. Rushing rivers gushed through the land down to a great, distant blue ocean. He could see far out north where mighty white-capped mountains blocked his view in that direction. He turned rapidly around, taking in plains, woods, hilly regions and marshes. He could see hundreds of miles of a beautiful ever-changing land. As his gaze turned northwest, the land flattened, becoming a desolate plain, but his view stopped at a massive hedgerow. Beyond the huge hedgerow, both long and high, was nothing but blackness.

Tom stopped for a moment. No wonder this was called the All Seeing Hill, he could see all of Adamah while standing and looking out, but when he stopped and focused on one place, his vision cleared and zoomed into that place as though he were wearing the most powerful of binoculars. He could see all the fine details distinctly. He could even see tiny red berries hanging on a far-off bush. It didn't seem to matter how far, or how near, when he stopped to focus on any one place, that place came into close range.

Now he looked, not widely, but closely, taking in amazing sights from all over. What was that? In the wind? It looked like a woman. She was laughing, her ivy hair blowing wildly. The woman was holding out her hands, rolling and laughing like he did on this last journey. She was lovely, like a carving of a beautiful woman made in wood. Coming out from behind her were not feet and toes, but long roots. Then he saw what she was laughing at, another face, that of a young man, in the river below her.

Tom recognized them, of course. A Naiad and a Nymph, no longer just mythical creatures. Tom gasped as the watery face leapt up, raging in the waves. He could hear nothing, but his sight was so clear he could read the Naiad's lips shouting, "No. No. No. You can't drink anymore," while liquid fists beat against stones lining the riverside.

The woman dived down towards the water and stuck her long root-toes into it, despite the angry protests of its resident. The Naiad slapped his wave arms against her body. The wooden beauty opened her mouth in laughter and a waterspout flowed out over the Naiad back into the river. The Naiad gazed up at the lovely sight and the waves settled and the water lapped gently.

Tom shifted his gaze. He smiled sheepishly at the sight of the gnome-people. "Little creeps," he thought. But they weren't shooting anybody now. They were working in a large vegetable garden.

Tom walked around. The All Seeing Hill gave him a real understanding of this world. He stopped again. A ball game of some sort was taking place. Balls of all sizes were rolling here and there, but there were no players. Tom was confused until he saw eyes, noses, and even ears. The balls were alive.

He moved along again watching mundane activities occurring, but such unusual creatures doing them.

He noticed four weird creatures in the distance. Dressed as warriors, they appeared to be heading towards the massive thorny hedge beyond which was only darkness. Tom's eye travelled along the hedge for a moment. It was not only immense in height but in length as well. It seemed to act as a border.

He looked back at the warriors. These creatures were different. They seemed foul. He laughed at his own pun, "Foul - Fowl." They were huge, half human, half vulture creatures. Under their helmets they had human-like faces with small beady eyes, thick, scarred skin, and pointed beaks. Enormous winged shoulders, a human chest and legs came down to shoeless feet which could have made them seem like winged humans. There again the vulture took over, their feet were claws with sharp talons. Talon-like hands protruded from human arms under the vulture wings. With fascination Tom watched as the group of warrior-vultures moved a black bundle. Flapping and pushing at it while pecking at each other.

"What a nasty flock," Tom muttered, ready to turn his gaze onward. Then the baggage they were moving struggled. He stared at the bundle. It kicked. It was alive. Tom felt his stomach heave. "Oh no, they have some half-dead creature to eat. Yuck."

Again, just as he was ready to move on, the scene transfixed him. One of the vultures dropped his side of the bundle and lunged at his companion, scratching with bared talons. A clawing, pecking and biting fight ensued as the remaining vultures, unable to resist the brawl, joined in. The bundle lay still only for a moment. It began to edge away from the fighting by rolling and shuffling itself. Tom gave a whispered cheer. "Keep going mate. Keep going."

But there was no hope of it getting away. One of the vultures looked over and leapt towards it. The others lowered their claws and came after the prey as well. They were all dripping with a grey sweat and thick brown blood. A vulture kicked at the bundle, his talons puncturing the side. Another beast ripped some of the black casing off the victim. A large bit of the black came loose and was tossed away carelessly. The black binding was certainly not cloth. It must have been some kind of metal. The black piece flew through the air and hit another vulture. That warrior fell to the ground, writhing in agony.

The others reaction to their wounded comrade was grotesque. They jumped on him, tearing at him with their beak, lacerating him with their claws. The prey started to edge away.

"Oh no," Tom moaned. Now with so much of the black pulled away, he could see that the prey was a person, a human.

Now Tom yelled, "No" as once again the monstrous vultures saw the moving bundle. They lunged at it. The captured prey's face guard fell away and Tom saw a very young man.

"I must help. I must get down there," He was yelling into empty space. Frantically, he looked for a way down. Moving from side to side, trying to figure the best way down the steep hill, a rising panic consuming him. A noise from behind froze him.

"It's too far away."

Tom turned. Behind him stood a Changeling child.

The Changeling child's serious, scarlet eyes blinked. His straight black hair and soft brown skin contrasted sharply with his cream jump suit. He smiled at Tom, but his face was sad. Like the faces of the grown-ups in Erets.

"What are you doing here?" Tom asked.

"Watching. Like you," he stated, his eyes shifting away to the scene below.

The Changeling child came and stood by Tom. Having turned to speak to the Changeling child, Tom's focus was taken from the scene. Now as he looked back, having lost his focus, he realised how far away it all was from where he was standing. This terrible scene that he could see closely was actually taking place over a plain and a river and well past a huge forest. There was no way he could have run down to rescue the poor young man.

"They have been dragging him for ages," the child said softly. The little Changeling walked to the other side of the hill. "I have been watching them since there," he stated. Another degree of grief settled on the Changeling's face. "There was nothing I could do."

"You should be in Erets with the other children."

"I ran here when I saw Mother fly away. I heard the Nannies whispering. They said all was lost. I felt so afraid. I've never felt that before." The Changeling looked at Tom, his eyes were now deep-ocean blue. "I was so afraid. I wanted to know all I could know, so when the Guards and the Nannies were gathering everyone together to go inside, I ran away and pretended to be a bird, a beautiful bird, like Mim, and I flew here." Finally the childish joy came back into the little face and voice.

"Is that you they're searching for in Erets."

The Changeling nodded. His face sad once more. "I'm sorry to cause such worry."

"Come, I'll take you back. They need to know you are safe."

"Look," said the Changeling, pointing with his chubby finger.

The hideous creatures below were circling the prey. The young prisoner had broken free while Tom and the Changeling were talking. The young man was weak and very frightened. The vultures were closing in on him. Tom watched helplessly. The eyes of that young man seemed familiar.

"I feel so helpless," Tom groaned. The Changeling hung his head.

The vultures recaptured their prey, wrapping him tightly in a vine from a tree. Pain etched the youth's face. In silence, together, Tom and the little one watched as the vultures prodded, pulled and shoved their victim onwards. The fourth vulture now lay dead on the road, killed by his comrades.

The ghastly party reached the large thorny hedgerow. The poor wretch, held fast between the awful vultures, was now still. They propped him up against a fallen log. He was obviously too spent to try to escape. One of the vultures stayed as guard while the other two moved towards the hedge.

"Don't hurt him. Don't hurt him," Tom commanded uselessly. The two moved about the hedge flapping their wings and chucking their ugly heads up and down like chickens in a farmyard. What they were doing had a strange effect. The hedgerow parted.

The parting of the bush kept Tom's attention from the young man for a few minutes. It wasn't until the vultures stopped their chicken dance in front of the hedgerow and turned their attention back to their prey, that Tom turned to look also.. He yelled, "Don't you dare. Stop, Stop," as if his yells could have any effect.

The guard's perverse appetite for warm flesh had overcome him. He was attacking the young man, mouth wide open, trying to pick bits of red flesh from the prisoner's sores. The other two tried to stop their colleague, flapping, scratching and pecking at him as they three had done earlier to their first fallen comrade. The vulture-guard beat off the other two as best he could, while remaining intent on his purpose. His hunger was driving him. One vulture flew above the errant guard, driving his talons down into his comrade's shoulders. The guard stumbled. The other vulture knocked the guard on the head. The blow sent the guard's helmet sailing across the road. The flying one again zoomed downward. This time the talons drove a death-strike into the guard's head. The guard faltered, then fell.

The young prisoner lay still. Tom held his breath. Was he dead? The warrior landed on the ground beside the prisoner. He kicked at the body. The young victim moved slightly. Tom let out his breath again.

Tom squatted beside the Changeling as the two remaining vultures shuffled their burden between them towards the opening in the hedge. They jerked and fluttered about as they edged closer and closer. Either their burden was heavier with only two left to carry it, or they were nervous.

The hedgerow opened even wider and a grisly army waiting on the other side became visible. The deranged looking army opened their mouths as one, clearly releasing a vulgar shriek of victory, as the two vulture-warriors made a final shove of the body through the hedge.

The army was terrible to behold. It was made up of thick skinned, runny eyed, purple lipped beings, but they were men in some perverted form.

At the front, and leading the army, was a man, as young as the victim. He was completely unlike those in the army. He was beautiful, soft curling hair fell to his shoulders and his body was tight and strong. His mount was a fierce, black-winged animal with the body of a large, muscular horse and the head of a dragon. The young man was wearing a crown. He dismounted from his steed and walked to the battered victim lying on the ground. He stood over the prisoner looking down. A sudden flash of hatred marred the handsome face, his features changed to the cold grey bones of a skull, fire shot from his eye burning the prisoner. Black smoke churned around the now disfigured, mutated prince. The army laughed and the steed roared, spraying fire.

Tom jumped up, backing away. Fright filled his senses. Tom was breathing heavily as the prince walked away from the prisoner. The prince's features changed once again. His face was passive, his countenance beautiful. But Tom knew he was ugly and foul to his very bones. Tom saw the evil prince's red mouth scream, "Take him to the castle." and then he mounted his terrible steed. The hedgerow closed as a small group of those twisted soldiers gathered around the young body of the prisoner.

"So it's finished. I guess they'll kill him now," Tom said.

"No," the Changeling said.

"How do you know? What do you think they'll do?" Tom lifted his head.

"Same as his mother. They will torment him."

Tom looked wide-eyed at the Changeling. "Do you know who he is?"

"He is Amos, son of Sir Gwain, the great Knight and Protector of the Realm."

"Oh." Tom didn't know what else to say.

The Changeling looked at Tom, his eyes now forest green. "That's why everyone is so afraid. I heard them whispering in Erets. Sir Gwain leads the knights against the Vile One. His son has been taken, as his first wife was taken. He knows that if he sees Amos again, it will be only a battered broken person, not really Amos anymore."

As the Changeling spoke his eyes grew wider, his sorrow stronger, and, it seemed to Tom, his body a little bigger.

"Sir Gwain is paralysed with grief." The little Changeling's voice quivered, "and they said… I heard my nanny say, The Vile One has cast a great bewitchment over all the knights. The curse has even taken Sir Gwain, the strongest of them all. The knights do nothing. She sounded so frightened, so I ran away."

"You mean no one is looking for Amos?" Tom demanded.

"The knights are all searching. But they run in circles, greatly confused and their efforts are useless. The knights are searching still, but bewitched as they are, everything is in complete disarray."

"Why didn't the knights come here? Surely they know about the magic of this place?"

A tear rolled down the Changeling's face. "They're truly cursed. They do nothing right. If our knights are destroyed, then all could be lost."

Tom looked out in the direction where the Changeling pointed. Far out to the west, Tom saw hundreds of knights, all dressed in black armour, like Amos had been. The plan of their enemy had been well set, for the knights searched in circles, wandering as though directionless. One young knight pulled his black face guard from his head to wipe sweat from his forehead and neck. He looked weary, frightened and confused.

"They are usually so noble and brave, but now they are lost. The knights of Adamah for generation after generation have kept the land safe, but now… I have watched it all from here ever since I ran from Erets. But like you, I could do nothing.”

“What’s your name?”

“Eli.”

Suddenly all Tom wanted to do was to go home.

“I’m Tom. Come on Eli, I’ll take you home before I leave.”

“I’m not going home.”

“Of course you’re going home.” Tom stated, forcefully.   “Where else would you go?”

“I’m going with you.”

“With me?” Tom spat, “back to my world?”

“No.” said Eli slowly. “If you must go back to your world first, then I will wait here for you.”

“Go where, Eli? What are you talking about? Where do you think I’m going?”

“To get Amos.”

“What?”

“To get Amos. You said you were going to go help Amos.”

“I said that in a moment of panic. I tried to run down the hill.” Tom felt a rush of fear. “You’re the one who stopped me, Eli.”

Eli put his hands on his hips. He once again seemed a little bigger, a little older than he had been previously.

"Honestly Eli, what could we do? Look at all those knights down there. They're the ones who will have to find him."

"You're not going to go help Amos?" Eli asked, shocked.

Tom and Eli stood looking at one another. Finally Eli whispered, "I thought you were the one."

Then Tom knew, without any doubt, that he was the one. This was it. This was his quest. He had to go and help Amos, try to help at least. Eli was right, Tom had no choice but to make an attempt.

"All right Eli. You're right. I do have to go help Amos. I don't know what I'll do. But...I'll try."

Eli jumped up and down and clapped, looking very much like a little child again.

"But," Tom continued. "I'm taking you home again, first. You're much too young to come with me. I hardly know what to do myself. I don't want to have to take care of you as well."

The clapping stopped. Eli looked sternly at Tom. His little face ageing, yet again. "I must go with you. I am your Ach. You can't succeed if I'm not with you."

"You're my what?" Tom demanded.

"I'm your Ach." Eli's eyes changed colours as he searched for words. "I am your brother."

Tom shook his head. "Look Eli, that's nice. But you're not my brother, I don't have a brother."

Eli's face fell. Sadness, on the already sorrowful face of a Changeling, is an unbearable sight.

"I'm your companion." Eli spoke softly, "I know that I'm your Ach. When you came to Erets. When you were walking with Mim. I could not play. Rochel and I were trying to play, but I didn't want to anymore. You will not succeed without me. Amos will die. You will fail." Eli paused for a moment.

"To succeed, you must have your Ach," Eli said simply, as if it were a natural law.

Tom looked closely at the Changeling's face. Eli no longer looked babyish. Was that only Tom's imagination? Was he trying to convince himself that Eli was old enough to go with him?

"Eli, this place is strange to me. Everything here is weird. I'm afraid to go alone, to tell the truth, I'm afraid to go at all. Everyone keeps telling me I have a reason to be here. Maybe you know more than me too. Maybe you *are* supposed to be my companion."

Eli didn't clap, he smiled, yet his face remained sorrowful.

"I think I'd best go back to my world first, Eli. I have some things I need to sort out there before we start. Will you really stay here on the hill waiting for me? Don't you need anything?"

Eli shook his head. He went over and sat down, "I will wait here." Tom said his incantation and was flying away.

Chapter Eight

"Tom, are you here?"

He heard his mum's voice from his uncomfortable position under a bush. He'd been so busy planning his return to Adamah, he'd forgotten about landing on Earth. When he saw light he tried to get ready, but it was too late. He thumped on the ground and rolled, just before his mum started calling him.

Tom crawled out, staying close to the bushes. Then he stood up and sauntered out to greet his mother, hopefully looking unruffled.

He was so distracted during afternoon tea that even the large piece of chocolate gateau his mother bought him couldn't keep his attention. Guilt was setting in, how could he get away without worrying his mum? She was already stressed out, asking him over and again if he was okay. He kissed her cheek as they came back out on the footpath, feeling a little sad at the surprised look in her eyes.

"Are you sure you are okay?" she asked again. "Look, I know we had a nasty row last night, and I was a tad unreasonable. I'm trying to lighten up. I really am. Please don't stay so mad at me, all right?"

"It's okay, Mum. Really it is." Even as Tom said it, he was planning to use her feelings against her. So he kissed her cheek again.

Tom went home and gathered as much snack food as he could cram into his backpack. He threw in a few bottles of water and his little book with the incantations. Then he wrote a note to his mum.

Dear Mum,

I'm going to James's for the night. His family have invited me to go on a picnic on Sunday. I know you have to work all weekend again and, since you are giving me more freedom now, I went ahead and said I would go with them. We're getting up early to leave on the train. Should be fun. I will call you when we get back. Thanks for being more reasonable and giving me some space.
Love, Tom.

He knew the letter would hurt his mum, but hopefully it would also mean she wouldn't try to call. He'd text her later and say he'd arrived at James's. Lie on lie, but if she did try to call, it would be okay, James and his family had gone away for the weekend. He just hoped he would live long enough to apologise to his mum. There was no way he could get back without her knowing he had gone. Would he ever be able to tell her where he had been?

Next, he needed to find Abigail. If he had a quest to fulfil in Adamah, then she had a purpose there too. All he had left to do was talk her into coming with him.

"Nothing with Abigail is easy," he thought, waiting in front of her door after ringing the bell.

He could hear someone yelling, "Ain't nobody going git tha' door?"

The door flew open and there he stood, Abigail's father. Tom expected a big burly man, but instead her dad was short and thin, with sandy hair.

"Which one do you wan' then?" he asked roughly.

"Abigail," Tom squeaked.

"Ab'gail." His loud voice made a mockery of his short stature.

Abigail came down the stairs, took one look at Tom and said, "Ah blimey, what's he doing here?"

"What's a matter, luv? This here boy bothering you?" Mr. Meers laughed, then went on, "Don't look as if'n he could do much harm."

"It's okay Da. I'll talk to him."

They walked upstairs to her room. Her door, and the room itself, were decorated with death signs and rock posters. The curtains were pulled, leaving a hazy red glow. But her bedroom was tidier than Tom's.

Abigail listened intently as he told her about Amos. She kept painting her fingernails, but she turned off her loud music as the story progressed. The description of the events he'd witnessed produced groans of sympathy for the poor, young prisoner.

He ended the story saying, "That's when I knew rescuing Amos was my mission. The calling that Mim and Karmono said I had."

Abigail was silent, staring at him, wide-eyed. Finally, she spoke. "You fool. There ain't nothing you can do to help that poor bloke. You needn't go rushing off on your own."

"I wasn't intending to go on my own," he replied. He smiled at Abigail. "You have to come with me."

Abigail jumped up, smearing a black mark of fingernail polish across her duvet. "Get out," she yelled. "Get out now."

"Why are you acting that way?" he yelled back. He wasn't too worried about her family's reaction to their yelling. There was loud music coming from the room next door and a TV blasting away somewhere downstairs.

"Just get out of here." She opened her bedroom door.

"You know you're supposed to come," he said, standing still. "That's why you're so mad. You're just fighting what you know you should do."

Abigail closed her bedroom door but kept her furious expression.

"Come on Abigail," he said. "It could be a bit of fun. Like you said, it'll be a bit of an adventure."

A funny expression came across Abigail's face. "I'm furious with me mum and da, right now. It would be a bit of a lark, taking off and not telling them."

"I left a note for my mum," he said softly.

"Naw, I'll have a really good barney with me da and walk out." She laughed at the thought.

"But they'll be so worried."

"I've done it before, mate. Usually me mum and da check with all me mates till they find me. But they'll just reckon that I off and run away to one of me Colton mates. Me mum's been trying to get me to tell her who me friends are at school. She don't know I hardly have any. It'll be okay." Abigail tossed her hair and looked at Tom, obviously laughing at him.

He left Abigail's house feeling nervous about her plans. He agreed to meet up with her in two hours, just outside Seldon College.

He returned a couple of library books in town, just in case he didn't make it back before they were due. He bought a flapjack from the bakery across from King's College, hoping it wasn't his last meal. Sometimes it seemed like a game, but there were moments when he couldn't breathe for fear.

Three hours later he felt nothing but anger. He was still standing outside Seldon College, waiting for Abigail. Any time now his mum would finish work and walk through the college. He was going to have to go without Abigail.

Then he saw her, walking up the street, taking her sweet time.

She only protested mildly when he grabbed her hand, dragged her through the College to the gardens, and said the words.

The landing was perfect. Eli was curled up sleeping beside a rock. The Changeling woke up, yawned and stretched like a small cat, then stood. He was taller than Tom remembered.

He looked at Tom. "Why did you bring the dog-girl back with you?"

"What did he say?" Abigail asked.

Tom laughed and translated with glee.

"Hey you little change freak, I ain't no dog-girl."

"What did she say?"

Tom didn't translate this time.

"Can't she change all the way?" Eli asked.

"No Eli, she isn't really a dog-girl." He grinned at Abigail. "It's just a way some people dress in our world."

Eli's eyes grew so sad that even Abigail softened. "Tell her I'm sorry she can't change all the way." Eli was never going to understand that Abigail wasn't trying to pretend to be a dog. So Tom just told her that Eli was sorry.

Abigail reached out her hand to pat the top of Eli's head, but pulled it back again when she looked at his sombre face. There was something untouchably royal about Changelings.

"So what are we going to do?" Tom wondered out loud.

"Find Amos," Eli answered.

"What did he say?"

"This is going to be miserable always having to tell you two everything the other says. He says we should find Amos, but I have no idea how to find Amos." He felt defeated before he even began.

"The Wise Ones can help, they can do anything. They can help us with both problems." Eli stated.

"What did he say?"

Tom sighed. Looking at Eli, he asked, "You mean these Wise Ones could help Abigail understand you?"

Eli nodded. "And they can help with finding Amos too."

"Are you sure Eli? I mean what can they do?"

Eli's eyes grew round. He leaned closer to Tom.

"They have magic," he whispered. "They can change. Not like me, I can only change myself. They can change everything."

Magical powers sounded really good to Tom right now. "Where do we find them?"

"They dwell in Hokmah."

"Do you know the way?"

Eli thought for a moment. "I think I can find the way."

Abigail was starting to tap her foot.

"Eli says there are Wise Ones who can help you understand him. He says they can even help us find Amos." He shook his head. "I don't know. If they are that powerful, Eli, why couldn't they just change things so that those horrible creatures disappear?"

"Or turn good or something?" piped in Abigail. She hoped this adventure would be like a short television show, where bad guys suddenly turned good.

Eli's mouth turned downwards. "I don't know."

Tom looked at Eli closely. The Changeling's face seemed older. He stepped closer to him. The little Changeling's head now came up to his chest. He was sure Eli was a foot taller than he had been. Tom stepped back, looking darkly at the little fellow.

"Let's find these Wise Ones."

Eli led the way down the steep hill. The foliage growing on the hillside was unlike any Tom had ever seen. Young pyramid trees bearing shiny yellow cones cut through the undergrowth, reaching skyward. Trees with silken brown bark split at the tops and shot out curling fern leaves of golden green. Spindly vines, full of heart shaped leaves, snaked along through the tall grass, spitting out bright red flowers here and there. Thorny bushes, dripping in un-ripened green berries, filled in the undergrowth.

At first it was different and interesting, but soon pushing back the branches became more tiring than exciting. Each step was a battle against the underbrush. Abigail was at the rear and Tom, forgetting about her, let the branches he pushed out of his way fly back and hit her in the face.

"Hey you idiot!" she shouted at him. "Would you mind? I'm back here you know."

He turned around, then let go of the large branch in his hand. He yelled out an unapologetic "sorry" as it slapped her in the face again.

He then ran to catch Eli. Abigail started running, ducking under the low hanging branches. She yelled, "You're in right trouble now, Tom Wade!"

Abigail caught up to him and shoved a handful of green leaves down his back. He was about to try to hit her with a branch when Eli disappeared.

A small sound made Abigail look down. She squealed, then yelled, "It's Eli!" There was a lizard at her feet. Its fork tongue flicked out with a lizard-sounding laugh and then it took off through the undergrowth.

Abigail threw Tom a challenging look and ran after the lizard, letting branches fly out of her hand as she went. Tom ran after her, shrieking as loudly as he could every time a branch came his way. The underbrush thinned and then disappeared. Tom and Abigail were now racing in the open. They finished the descent from the hill, and each claimed victory. They fell beside the feet of the lizard, exhausted. It was sitting on a rock blinking at them. Eli transformed back into his Changeling form.

"That was a fun pretend."

Tom told Abigail what Eli said. Her only reply was, "Boy, am I hungry."

Tom pulled off his backpack, unzipped it, and began to unload the many goodies he had stuffed in. He laid them out on the grass.

Abigail sat up, "Brilliant." She smiled, choosing a snack bar.

Eli took one of the offered treats, a small chocolate covered biscuit. He followed Abigail's example, unwrapping it carefully. He took one bite and began coughing. He threw the biscuit down, making a face.

Abigail smirked, "Can't take sweet stuff hey, Eli?"

Tom laughed as he translated the remark. Then he pulled three small bottles of water out, handing one to each of his companions. He unscrewed the lid on his own and took a swig. It wasn't quite cool enough, but it was still very thirst-quenching. Eli followed Tom's actions, a look of wonder on his face as he unscrewed the lid. Then he too took a swig of the drink. With a groan Eli spit the water out, spraying Tom in the face.

"Hey, what's the matter with you?" Tom yelled at the Changeling.

Eli dropped the bottle and the water glugged out. Tom grabbed it and screwed the lid on, saying, "Hey Eli, be careful will you? I have no idea when we'll be able get some good water again."

Eli was nowhere to be seen.

Tom took a couple of bites out of a biscuit, and then said to Abigail. "I'd better find him."

Abigail wiped her hands on the side of her trousers and stood up. "Let's go, then."

They walked down the path Eli had taken, and went into a woody area. Eli was sitting beside a small stream, dipping his cupped hands into the water, drinking. He had shimmering water droplets all over him.

"This is good," he said, with a smile. "I have been a fish."

The cool water was so inviting. Tom stooped, dipped his cupped hands into the river and lifted it to his mouth.

"Wow." Tom dipped his hands again and again, sucking the water up as fast as he could.

Abigail bent down. Hesitantly, she put her hand into the water and took a sip. She too drank up. She wiped her mouth with the back of her hand. "Blimey, that's incredible," she said. "It tastes like…" Abigail laughed. "It tastes like water. You know, like water looks on them adverts for bottled water. I can taste the shimmers and the drops."

Tom laughed. "You sound like an advert, and I'd think you were crazy, but you're right."

Tom bathed his face in the water, licking the drops as they ran down his cheeks.

"Come," Eli yelled, and ran back into the woods.

Abigail and Tom followed him.

Eli led them to a bush. Red and black berries hung like clusters of grapes from its branches. Eli plucked a few off and held them out in his open palm.

"Ask him if he is sure these are safe Tom," Abigail said, shaking her head.

"Very good," Eli stated, popping one red berry from his open palm into his mouth.

Abigail took one of the red berries and slowly placed it in her mouth. She bit down. She straightened her back, her eyes brightened.

"What does it taste like, Abby?"

"Red."

"What did you say?"

"Red. It tastes…red."

Tom said, "It tastes red?" He then took one of the berries. A burst of red flavour filled his mouth.

The two began plucking red berries and popping them into their mouths, emitting purring noises of satisfaction. Eli's fingers appeared in front of Tom's nose holding a black berry. Tom took it, and with a little sigh of happiness, popped it into his mouth.

At first there was nothing, just a little soft ball in his mouth. Then it burst. Tom shook his head.

"What?" Abigail demanded, "What does that one taste like?"

Tom plucked another black berry and put it into his mouth. It happened again. Nothing, then a burst of flavour.

"I'm full," he said.

"Was it good? Should I eat one?" Abigail demanded. Tom held one out for Abigail. She put it into her mouth.

"So can you describe it?"

"No….naw really. It's a feeling more than a taste." Abigail went over and sat down by the stream.

"I feel so full." She settled down, resting her head against a low rock. "No wonder Eli spit out our stuff," she said, closing her eyes.

Tom and Eli settled themselves beside Abigail. The peaceful setting and full stomach made Tom feel drowsy. Abigail made a soft snoring sound. Eli giggled.

"Guess she fell asleep."

"A happy sleep from berries," Eli answered. "Not horrible like food from your world."

"Well, I must tell you that I didn't bring the healthiest snacks, mate."

"Not good food?"

"Well, I mean I brought chocolates and junk. But you didn't like the water either."

"What water?"

"In the bottles, Eli. The water I gave you."

Eli snickered.

"Okay, so our water doesn't much compare to yours."

"I heard before that everything in Ha`ehad is spoilt. Now I know it's true," Eli said.

"You mean my world?"

"Yes. When the parents came to Adamah, the beauty blinded them. They found streams that sparkled like crystal, and fruit that satisfied the soul as well as the body.'"

Tom sat up, turning to look at the Changeling. Eli's round face now belonged to a tall, thin body. "What are you saying, Eli? Are you saying that people came from my world to settle in this world? That can't be, we have no one like the people of Adamah on Earth."

Eli blinked his eyes, as if coming into the light. "I don't know." He stumbled on his words. "I was only repeating things I've heard in stories and poems."

Tom laughed softly. "Stories and myths from your world, I see. Yes we have those and they have no truth in our world either." Tom leaned back again, "You really had me going there for a moment. I thought maybe you were saying your ancestors were from earth."

Eli's voice came from beside Tom again. They were both stretched, out looking up at the blue sky. "I think when the Vile One came he spoilt the land here too. But not all of it. Only where he goes and only what he or his evil people touch. The taste leaves the fruit. And the water blackens. Or so it is said."Tom listened to Abigail's soft sleepy breaths. Eli's voice began again as soft as a lullaby.

> "Adamah. Land so pure.
> Where children can be free.
> Adamah. Land so rich.
> Hungry always feed.
>
> A land for those whose lives are torn,

apart by war and greed.
A land where those hot and thirsty,
are cooled by gentle breeze.

The parents came to find a home
away from pain and sorrow.
The people followed to find a land,
to heal heart, soul and marrow.

Adamah. Land so marvellous.
We'll protect you if we can
from the Vile One among us."

The next thing Tom knew, he was opening his eyes. The sun was low in the sky and he realised he'd been sleeping for a long time. He sat up and said, "What are we doing? We need to get moving."

The others were gone. Tom jumped up, looking around him, running by the stream into the bushes then back again. "Abigail, Eli," he shouted into the empty space. They were nowhere to be seen.

Abigail yelled back, "Stop shouting, for goodness sake, you idiot." Abigail emerged from the trees, followed by Eli.

"Where have you been?" Tom demanded angrily.

"We've been sorting out the direction we should take from here, sleepy head. You were snoring away, so we went off."

Tom huffed, "Did you find out which way to go?"

"Yeah. Well, Eli did. I mean I can't understand a word he says, but we've got hand signals down like a charm." Abigail said, waving her hands around making all sorts of gestures. Eli grinned at Tom.

Eli led the way and Abigail went next. Tom followed. He felt rather put out by the chummy attitude Eli and Abigail seemed to have developed.

Abigail bent down and picked a few acorn-like nuts from the ground. She cracked open the shell and ate them.

Tom scrunched up his face. "Are you sure you should be doing that?" he asked

"Mmm. They're yummy. Here try one. They're sort of like hazelnut creams."

Tom took the de-shelled nut from Abigail's hand and popped it into his mouth. Instead of the crunch of a nut, it melted softly like a cream sweet.

"Oh, like chocolate-covered, hazelnut creams," he sighed.

"Yeah some of them are, others are just a creamy hazelnut flavour. What a place."

Abigail ran back up to Eli and handed him a de-shelled nut to eat. The Changeling smiled at her. Tom gasped. Eli was as tall as Abigail and looked a strange version of a boy just their age. Tom felt a tingly sensation wash over him. What was happening to Eli?

Abigail yelled back with glee. "Quick, Tom. Look here. Look here. This is what we found. We wanted to surprise you."

The trees thinned out and in the distance Tom could see a great grey stone building. It loomed up over the trees and was completely carved with pictures and strange writings.

Eli spoke, his voice soft and respectful. "This is Hokmah."

"Isn't it beautiful." Abigail's voice held the same respect as Eli's.

They walked round and round the huge building admiring it. At various places, turrets bounded to the sky. Along the sides, gargoyles leaped out of the stone with claws exposed. Abigail stood under one of the magnificent stone characters. From a distance, it was hard to see the creature was stone, and Abigail looked in danger of it. The grey, stone face was fierce with strong, staring eyes, and pointed horns. Its front legs extended out a great distance ending in huge sharp-clawed paws

"It's almost as if they're protecting something," Abigail said.

"Hey wait a minute," Tom yelled, taking off at a run around the building again. He came back around where Eli and Abigail stood under the two gargoyles and looked at his two companions angrily.

"There's no way in."

Eli, Tom and Abigail walked round the building, searching carefully. It was true. There was not a door, an entry, or even a window to be seen.

"Great job, Eli," Tom said sarcastically. "Now what are we supposed to do?"

Tom threw himself onto the grass in front of the gargoyles. Eli walked away and sat down, his head hanging low. Tom turned away to avoid seeing Eli's sad face.

Abigail kept walking slowly, round and round the building. Eli said nothing, just dropped his head lower. Tom's anger passed into sadness, with three long sighs.

Abigail walked past, and then disappeared again. The silence between Eli and Tom was heavy. Abigail appeared, walking past her two companions and then away around the corner. Tom turned to Eli, breaking the awful silence separating them.

"Look Eli, I'm sorry. I shouldn't have said that. You did the right thing bringing us here, I was being a pig."

Eli blinked. "A pig?"

Tom half-groaned, half-laughed. "It's just an expression in our world. It means I wasn't very nice."

Eli smiled, but only a Changeling could smile with such intense pain. "But there is no way in."

"That's not your fault, Eli." Tom said.

"There is a way in," Abigail yelled.

"Where?" Tom shouted as he and Eli jumped up.

"It's right here, where we are now." Abigail pointed to a tiny crevice in the wall. "I've checked all around. There's nothing like it anywhere else on the building." Seeing the look of mistrust on Tom's face she continued. "And Tom, all the other gargoyles are tame, like, compared to these ones. I'm telling you this is the way in and these here gargoyles are the ones that protect the entry way."

Tom translated all that Abigail said to Eli. But since Tom didn't actually speak Eli's language, but was simply understood by Eli while speaking English, Abigail could understand everything he said. So in typical Abigail fashion, she felt free to correct him And she did, over and over again until Tom was nearly mad. Finally Tom said,

"Oh have mercy, I wish we could get through that tiny hole so you two could get to understand each other without me. This is driving me crazy."

"Don't you get it idiot?" demanded Abigail.

Tom just shook his head.

"Eli." she laughed. "Eli just has to change into some kind of little creature and get in there and tell them to open the door. Eli said these Wise Ones change, right? That's probably how they get in and out. We have Eli."

Tom gave a shout, punching the air. Eli's face brightened at Tom's happiness.

Tom translated and Eli jumped up and down clapping his hands, acting once again like the little Changeling that Tom had first met.

Eli walked up to the building close to the crevice. He turned back to his two companions, looking Tom in the eye. Eli smiled. Then he turned back to face the wall.

Tom and Abigail waited. Watching Eli's back, they waited. Nothing happened.

Eli started to wail. He ran to Tom and Abigail, dropping in the grass by their feet.

"What is it Eli? What is it?" Tom cried, dropping on his knees beside his Ach. Tom felt overwhelmed by the pain in Eli's cry.

Eli's tear-streaked face lifted up to Tom and said, "I can't change. I'm not a mouse. I can't be a mouse."

"Why Eli? Can't you just pretend to be a mouse? What's the matter?"

Eli sobbed again, "I'm not a mouse. I can't be a mouse."

"What's going on?" Abigail demanded.

Tom looked up at Abigail. "I don't understand it, but he says he can't change into a mouse because he's not a mouse." Tom hunched his shoulders. "I don't know why he can't pretend it. It must have something to do with what Mim said to us about adult Changelings. Did you notice how he was growing? I'm worried Abigail, why is he growing so fast? I'm afraid something's wrong."

Eli dropped his head into his hands. He was almost hysterical. "I'm growing. I can't be what I can't be. Oh, it's going. All of the joy is leaving me."

Abigail stooped down beside Tom and he whispered to her. "Eli said all the joy is going because he cannot be what he isn't. He's growing up."

Abigail threw herself on the grass beside Eli and moved close beside him. Tom felt alone. He looked at the massive building in front of him. Hokmah, the place of answers was closed to him. And his questions and problems were only growing.

Chapter Nine

Tom carefully covered Eli with his own jacket and sat down on the grass. The Changeling let out another shuddering breath, all that was in him after a long terrible cry. Abigail sat up, her eyes red and puffy. She offered her jacket for Eli, but Tom shook his head. Tom's face was pale. Unlike the spent Changeling lying next to him, and the red-faced girl sitting beside him, Tom's tears were invisible.

Tom stared at the massive grey building in front of him, studying it as if it were a fine piece of art. The more he considered the building, the more it did seem like art. It was elegant, but the horrible faces of the gargoyles kept it from being too pretty. Silhouettes were etched into the stone. Tom reached into his backpack and pulled out his little book and let it flip open in his hand. "Look."

Abigail looked up when Tom spoke. She followed his finger to where it was pointing as he said, "It's the same writing as in my book."   Abigail shuffled closer to Tom. The squiggly marks in the book of incantations were the same as those carved into the stone.

"Fat lot of good that does us, we can't read the book or the blooming wall," Abigail said.

Tom looked up at the wall, down at his book, then back up to the building again. He was trying to figure out if any of the words were the same. Abigail stared at the building. "Hey, look at them pictures up there. They remind me of stuff done on mummy tombs."

Tom stared up at the building, his book lying open. A small round tube fell out of his book. He picked it up and untied the tiny golden thread that bound it. Abigail lost interest in the writing on the wall, turning her attention to Tom.

"What's that?" she asked.

Tom unrolled the little parchment and groaned.

"What is it?" demanded Abigail.

"Whatever it is, it's written in another language."

"Let me have a look."

Tom handed the tiny parchment to Abigail. The writing was so small that she held it close to her face. "No look, first it's a strange language but it changes. Look, it's English," she shouted happily.

She was right, tiny but readable English followed the other language. It read:

> Kadang-kadang tugas yang paling besar
> menuntut orang yang kecil.
> Apabila ada perlu,
> panggil saja.
> Sometimes the biggest task,
> requires the smallest soul.
> When in need,
> you only have to call.

"What the heck does that mean?" Abigail said.

Tom thought for a minute before jumping up. "Eddi," he yelled.

"What?"

"Eddi is the one who gave that to me. Remember?"

"That's right."

"Eddi," he yelled again. "What does it mean Abby? How do I call Eddi here?"

Abigail shrugged. "I don't know."

"Eddi, Eddi," Tom kept yelling. "Do you think we need to say what's on the paper?" he asked.

"That'll do, Tom."

Tom swung round. Standing behind him on a rock, was the little man.

"Eddi," Tom yelled, this time in glee rather than panic.

"If you keep yelling so, you will awaken this sleeping one," Eddi stated.

"I'm so glad to see you. I didn't know how to get you to hear me."

"I've been waiting impatiently for your call. I want to fulfil my destiny. It's not been easy waiting."

Tom sat down beside Eddi, and told him what had happened. He ended the rather long story saying, "So Eli can't change into anything, not even a mouse, to see if he can get in that crevice."

Eddi was silent till the end, then he gasped and said, "That's it? That's what I'm to do? I thought I would play a larger part."

"What do you mean?" Tom asked.

"I thought I might do something bigger."

"This is important Eddi. We must get help."

"I will, of course, do as I'm asked. But you must see that having a calling based on my size is sad indeed." Eddi walked through the crevice, and disappeared from their sight.

Suddenly alone again, with only a sleeping Eli at their feet, Abigail and Tom stared at the hole in the grey wall. They were silent for a very long time.

Finally, Abigail whispered. "You realise don't you, Tom, we don't actually know what we've just sent Eddi into?"

"But Eli said…" He looked down at the Changeling and closed his mouth. Tom pulled up his knees and dropped his head, face down, onto them. Waiting.

A loud crack split the air, followed by a ferocious roar. Tom jumped up, realising as he did so that Abigail was clinging to him. The gargoyles on the wall were coming forward, no longer made of stone. They were now large, terrifying beasts, their grey stone turned to vivid coloured fur.

"Who stands at the door of Hokmah?" the beasts bellowed in unison.

Before they could stop quivering and think of an answer, the beasts once again turned to stone, this time, full-bodied, standing erect, facing each other a short distance apart. The grey stone melted between the gargoyles, creating an arched entryway not unlike the miniature one Eddi had disappeared into.

Tom held as closely to Abigail as she did to him. A tall man, dressed in a magnificent robe, appeared just inside the arch. His hand was held up in front of him, balled into a fist. He walked slowly towards them. He was not alone, a misty hoard of creatures followed him. His face was grim. Tom thought of Eli, lying in front of him, unprotected, and stepped over his sleeping friend to protect him. The man kept coming. His long blue robe with bright red swirls, shimmered brightly. The man also wore a high, peaked cap with a red silk scarf which waved behind him as he walked.

"He's a wizard, isn't he, Tom?" Abigail whispered, trembling with fear.

Tom shrugged his shoulders. Tom gasped as the wizard opened up his long bony hand. He was holding Eddi.

"Hey, you let him go," Tom yelled, with all the authority he could muster.

"By what authority do you order me to do so?"

"Because…" he said, trying to think of a good answer. "I'm the leader of this group and he was acting on my orders when he entered your castle. If you must take someone, you should take me. Or, or you'll have my anger to deal with." Tom had heard this kind of thing said on telly and it sounded tough. The words were braver than he really felt. He stood straight and puffed out his chest trying to look the part.

The wizard laughed. Echoing laughter came from behind him. Eddi rose into the air and floated. Tom grabbed at Eddi, but he flew past. Tom looked into the eyes of the wizard, and then held out his hand, extended flat like the wizard's. Eddi landed in Tom's palm.

"You're a mere boy, and your words were foolish, but your heart is good. Therefore, I honour you, Peregrine Sol Tom. Now if you are finished threatening me, you can come into, not my castle, but our temple-city, as we were coming to invite you to do."

The laughter from behind the wizard sounded once again. Eddi gave Tom a wobbly smile. "That was some way to meet Sannyasis, the head wizard, young Peregrine Sol."

Abigail whispered over Tom's shoulders. "I could understand the wizard guy. Wonder why I could understand him? Is it safe?"

Tom looked back at Abigail, making a face. "Eddi says I just made a terrible fool of myself in front of the head guy."

"Oh, so you're just being your normal hopeless self then, eh?"

Two winged creatures flew through the arch and picked Eli up. They nodded formally to one another causing their golden bodies to shimmer in the sunlight. Then slowly and reverently they carried Eli through the entryway. The crowds behind the wizard bowed as they passed by.

Tom called, "Will he be okay?"

"Do you doubt me still, Peregrine Sol?" Sanyassi asked. He walked back through the arch into the temple-city and beckoned Tom and Abigail to follow.

Tom, holding Eddi, led Abigail between the gargoyles. The air went cold. The stone beasts became real again, with striking colour and terrifying faces. The beasts sound angry as they growled, "Who dares to enter Hokmah?" Tom stumbled, desperate to turn back. He felt Abigail tug his arm. He forced himself to take two more steps past the beasts. Once past them, the terrifying beasts returned once again to stone.

Tom stepped through the entryway. to find he was outside again. But this outside was better. The light was brighter and without any glare. Colours were vivid. The smell of flowers filled the air.

"Marvellous, isn't it, Peregrine Sol?" Eddi said.

"Amazing," Tom replied.

"Welcome," Sanyasis said loudly.

A chorus of voices joined in, "Welcome."

When Tom saw the crowd that had welcomed him, he gasped. Abigail said, "Blimey."

He was an avid watcher of science fiction shows, but it didn't prepare Tom for this. These beings were not plastic. In every face and every pair of eyes, was humanity. One creature was a woman in tree-form. Others were half-goat, half-human fauns, winged creatures of gold and silver, and a man whose body was liquid. There were many more beings of all shapes and kinds. They were tall, short, fat, thin, ugly and beautiful beyond description, and all were real and as alive as anyone on earth.

"It's like standing in a blooming fairy tale, it is," Abigail said. Tom could only nod in agreement. It was true, mythical creatures surrounded them. Dwarfs, giants, and pixies were standing there in the flesh, along with creatures no myth or dream had ever conjured.

"Come, we must perform the first ritual of welcoming," a voice called out from the crowd.

Sanyasis beckoned them to follow him. Tom and Abigail clung tightly together as they walked. Tom whispered to Eddi, "What kind of ritual is he talking about?"

"I don't know, Peregrine Sol Tom. But we're in Hokmah and it'll be wondrous."

They passed between great white columns and entered a long corridor. Chalk white walls rose high on either side of a smooth shiny floor. A small man, the tip of his head reaching only to Tom's waist, moved close to Tom's side.

"This is Stoa, a sacred place in Hokmah," he whispered to Tom.

Tom looked down at the man. His long knobbed nose with protruding hairs, floppy hairy ears and round body were all too familiar. Tom looked quickly at the small man's hands, but he was not holding a peashooter.

"Why is it a sacred place? It only looks like a walkway," Tom asked.

"Ah," said the little man, "many walk this colonnade, talking. And those who walk here have discussed mysteries of the deepest kind. These walls will sometimes echo our past, our future or even our inward self. Maybe you will be so fortunate as to hear the Voice of Endless Wisdom in Stoa."

"I'm not sure I want to be hearing any dismembered voice in a hallway, "Tom said, then added, "I think I've been to your part of Adamah."

"You have been to Nibelung? It's been many years since I walked the gardens of Nibelung. Did they feed you a dish prepared for eating only minutes after taking it from the garden dirt?"

Tom shook his head. "It was one of the first times I made my journey and… well, I didn't make a very good job of it. I seemed to bounce on someone's bed."

Instead of the laughter Tom expected to hear, the small man uttered a sigh. "I'm afraid my fellow Nibelungs have little experience with the outside world."

Tom cleared his throat and said, "They are very good shots."

"I don't live among them any longer, but I love them dearly. They don't know that I, along with others in Hokmah, live for their protection. Don't hate them for their ignorance, dear Peregrine Sol. It's their innocence that makes them good, as well as difficult."

The little man was so much like those Tom had encountered, whose silly faces he would never forget, but he was also was very different. His face was kinder and held a look of wisdom.

Tom smiled and hurried to catch up with Sanyassi. They entered a grand hall, lit with candles shining yellow, blue and soft white. The crowd, who had been following, now rushed past Tom and his friends into the hall. They moved quickly to sit at the heavy wooden tables. They knew what to do. Tom and Abigail, who was holding Eddi, could only stand and watch.

Every creature sat down at a place suited to his or her size and shape. There were tall, long-legged seats for the short, low stools for the giants, soft curvy cushions for the blowsy nymph people. At the end of one large table, was a tiny little table with miniature chairs.

Sanyassi hushed the crowd. "We are assembled here to welcome the Peregrine Sol Tom and his travelling companions."

There was a loud cheer.

"We will welcome our guests in the usual way."

At this, Sanyassi clapped his hands three times. A table appeared out of nowhere with seats enough for Tom, Abigail, Sanyassi, and two other odd but dignified looking wizards standing next to him. There was even a miniature table with a tiny chair sitting beside Tom's place at the table. Abigail held out her hand and Eddi walked out onto the large table to sit in his tiny seat. Before

Tom could slide his chair under the table, Sanyassi clapped his hands again, and dishes started flying through swinging doors at the side of the hall. Each dish was laden with food from which steam rose. The plates floated around the room, wafting a delicious smell throughout the hall. The dishes landed various places, eliciting a cheer from the residents at the table.

An old wizard sitting by Sanyassi stood and said loudly,

> "May we always eat with knowledge,
> May our hearts be ever true,
> So that the land of Adamah,
> will be ever blessed by You."

A hum filled the hall as creatures of every kind dished food onto their plates and began eating and chatting. "So I guess we should eat too," Abigail said.

"I guess so," he said, passing her a big plate filled with pasties. He watched as she took one and bit it. Her eyes grew wide and she let out a sound of delight. Tom took a bite of one too and began reaching for more plates of food. He should have known that a place where the wild berries and nuts were so delicious would produce perfectly beautiful food to eat at a banquet. And the way that the wonderful food was eaten made it even better.

Everyone ate with their fingers. There was no cutlery. Tom took bits from a platter in the middle of the table and popped them onto his plate. He then shovelled the food into his mouth with his fingers. He cleaned his fingers for the next bite by licking them. He was only doing what every other person in the room was doing. It was delicious fun.

Eddi actually got up from his little table and wandered along the High Table looking for something to his taste which he then dragged back to his little table. It was the quantity of food he took that was shocking. He filled his plate to overflowing with pasties, vegetables and brightly coloured titbits. Eddi kept eating and getting more, piling his plate much higher than Tom dared fill his. Could one little man really eat that much?

Tom was busy devouring some fluffy drops that tasted like buttery mashed potatoes, orange disks that reminded him of Tandori chicken, and red jelly dots tasting of strawberry cream. Sanyassi and the two other wizards sitting at the table were doing more serious talking in low voices than eating. Tom looked up to catch Sanyassi looking at him. The old wizard then turned back to the other two wizards with whom he was talking. Tom stopped eating. He wondered what they were talking about. At that moment, Abigail leaned over, a strange gleam in her eyes.

"Do you know what I'm thinking."

"No, how could I know what goes on in that brain of yours?"

"Lay off, will you? I was thinking we might have gone into the past, coming here. It might have something to do with our debate."

"Into the past?" Tom raised an eyebrow and smirked at her.

"Yes, do you know all those pictures we saw on this Hokmah building."

Tom nodded.

"Well…" Abigail seemed determined to take her time, "Remember I was telling you that I thought they look a lot like Egyptian Mummy thingys."

"Egyptian Mummy thingys, whatever are you talking about?"

"You know, pictures on Mummies."

"Hieroglyphics?"

"Yeah, hieroglyphics thingys."

At first Tom shook his head, but the pictures on the outer walls of Hokmah came into his mind again and he knew she was right. They did look like hieroglyphics

"So."

"Well, Tom." Abigail narrowed her eyes at him, not liking his tone of voice. "When that ugly little man was talking to you, he sounded like he was speaking German. It was one of my subjects in school last year. He sounded German, but not German too. I wondered if it was old German or Anglo-Saxon like in Beowulf."

"What are you talking about, Abigail?"

"I told you. I saw that writing and started figuring it looked like Egyptian stuff..."

"Then you leapt to Anglo Saxon..."

"I explained that too. I've been hearing all this talk around that sounds the same as when my teacher read Beowulf to us."

"There's no way we have returned to the past, Abby. Look around you, for goodness sake. Do you see anything here that could be our ancestors?"

"Peregrine Sol Tom," Sanyassi said, interrupting their discussion. "May I introduce my two fellow High Counsel members to you? This is Geey and Lingua."

Lingua's long leathery face wrinkled with a smile as he pushed back a strand of his scraggly, black hair. "You're enjoying your Welcoming Feast, I see."

"It's brilliant," Abigail answered. Tom looked at his friend's face and felt his nerves tingle. She had that determined look about her again.

"But what I want to know is why I can understand you and him," she said, pointing at Sanyassi, "when I can't understand anybody else here."

"Have you understood no one else in Adamah?"

"Mim," Abigail answered, confident that they would understand who she meant.

"And why could you understand Mim?" the other wizard, Geey, asked. He was a small, googly-eyed, hairy-faced creature.

Abigail looked at him. He was perhaps the strangest being in the room. Geey's face was nearly hidden by a long grey-green beard. His long hair, which was the same unusual colour, fell down his back and over his shoulders, blending with the hair of his beard so that only his eyes could be seen. But they were eyes that drew you to look into them, large eyes, slightly bulging, and so intense they gleamed. Yet they were mud-brown and earthy, as though this wizard reflected the very land upon which he stood. As Abigail looked into the wizard's odd eyes, she felt the world around her slow down, almost stop being, as though only what she could see in Geey's eyes was real. She felt her eyes asking him, "Why am I here if I'm not a Peregrine Sol? Why should I be here at all?"

Then Abigail saw herself, dressed in white, looking pale and exhausted as though recovering from some terrible sickness. Was this a vision, showing her what this quest would do to her? Abigail shivered against the possibility and shook her head to try to get that vision away. Finally, she answered, "Mim said she was speaking English."

The three wizards merely nodded their heads.

Tom spoke up, "So you are all speaking English. But is there any way that Abigail can speak all these languages like I do?"

Sanyassi laughed and said, "It's not so much a gift of speaking that you have, Peregrine Sol. It's a gift of understanding. You talk as you always do, the gift you're given is that the people of Adamah understand you. They speak the language of their kind, your gift is to understand them. This is a gift that is rarely found in any beings beyond those of Adamah. It's one of the special things about this world, creatures in Adamah understand one another. But it's a gift that's only rarely bestowed on others by the ones who *can* give it."

Sanyassi turned to the black-haired wizard at his right. "It's up to you, Lingua."

Lingua placed his hands on the side of his head and looked down, closing his eyes.

Geey, the odd earthy wizard, stared at Tom. The world slowed, almost stopped and Tom felt confused. He was alone. No, not alone, there was someone lying in a heap at his feet and Tom was crying. Tom heard his own voice echoing in his head, "Mum, Mum." His mother didn't answer. Tom cried, "Dad, Dad. Oh please listen to me…" To his absolute shock, Tom heard a distant answer. Tom never knew his father, knew nothing about him. His mother told him long ago that she would tell him about it someday. Tom didn't really mind, you couldn't miss something you never knew.

As Tom came out of Geey's mesmerising eyes, he heard Lingua say, "I think she has a part to play."

Lingua said, "I think she has a very important part to play."

Lingua stood up, placed his two wrinkled hands over Abigail's ears, and touched her mouth. He bowed to all those at the table, and walked away.

Abigail sat for a moment, looking around happily. "I can understand them." She pointed at a group sitting near her corner of the table. "It's like a necklace see," Abigail said pulling at her dog collar. "Did you hear them?" she asked Tom. "They were talking about me. They like my dog collar."

The group that were talking about Abigail came over. A flowery girl with bright swirling colours, falling like petals round her spoke for the group, "Come with us, dog-girl, we'll show you Hokmah."

Tom looked at Abigail, expecting an angry reply. But to his shock, she stood up quickly, immediately ready to go. "I'm going with them." Her voice defied Tom's disagreement. "They're *my* friends." A watery laugh echoed from the group and a liquid arm reached round Abigail's shoulder. Abigail jumped.

"Are you sure you're okay?" Tom asked.

Abigail leaned close to Tom. She put her hand on his cheek. Tom breathed deeply. He lifted his hand, ready to put it tenderly over her hand. Abigail planted two firm pats on Tom's face, smirked at him and said, "I'm a big girl, remember." She walked away with her new friends.

Chapter Ten

Tom heard the wizards laughing as Abigail walked away. He turned to them, trying to regain his dignity. "Now do I get some answers for myself?"

Sanyassi nodded, but said, "After we hear a little about what has brought you to us."

Tom told them his story, carefully, leaving out how he came by the book, and saying nothing about his mother. When he was finished, he said, "I've told you what you wanted to know, now will you give me some answers?"

Sanyassi raised an eyebrow at Tom, saying, "Have you told us everything?"

"Well," Tom answered, "I've told you everything you need to know."

"Okay, Peregrine Sol, we will tell you things and we will help you. I will also give you something you want."

"What?"

"I will take you to see your Ach."

"Eli," Tom said, immediately standing up.

Tom turned to say good-bye to Eddi and laughed loudly when he found the little man was still shovelling food into his mouth as if he had never eaten. His plate was nearly empty.

Sanyassi clapped. Dirty plates and cups jumped from the tables, revved up like little sport cars and zoomed towards the double doors, looking rather like a car chase in a modern movie as they tipped and turned to avoid one another, zooming and even honking at anything in their way.

"Do all dishes do that here?" Tom asked.

"Oh no, Peregrine Sol, this is a special gift of mine. I rather like it,"
Sanyassi said. He had a rather smug look on his wise face.

Eddi stayed behind, chatting to a group of tiny people. He grinned at Tom
and said, "Tis a great honour for me. I'm here with Patrick the Wise. And
Peregrine Sol, I'm in the presence of Pixie folk and Brownies. Good folk that I
have never had the honour to meet before." Tom patted his little friend on the
back with one finger before walking away with the two wizards.

"What's happening to Eli?" Tom asked as they walked.

Sanyassi spoke quietly, "I think Geey should be the one to explain. He
knows more about Changelings than I."

Sanyassi told Tom to sit on a bench in the walkway. Tom sat down. "This
is Stoa, isn't it?" he asked.

"You have already learned this, Peregrine Sol?"

"A little guy from Nibelung told me."

"Ahh, Westermann."

Geey sat beside Tom. The old wizard's long grey-green hair came down
over his shoulders and his skin was lightly green. He was dressed sombrely in a
monk-brown, cloth robe. He wore no shoes, and had earthy-brown feet. Geey's
face and eyes drew Tom's attention and held it.

Tom whispered, "Eli?"

Geey asked, "What is it you wish to know about the Changeling?"

"Will he be all right? What's wrong with him?"

"Yes, he will be all right, though full health and acceptance will be a slow process." Geey smiled at Tom. "Your other question Tom, 'What is wrong with him?' That takes the ages of Adamah to understand."

Then Geey folded his hands and bowed his head. Sanyassi too bowed his head. Tom sat looking at the two old wizards wondering what was wrong with them. Then he heard a rumbling and a deep, rich voice echoed around him.

Let's fashion a people unlike any other.
Let's give them joy that is yet unknown.
They will play upon the earth forever,
never knowing the pain of having to grow.

The fun they will have as their laughter rings freely.
The carefree and innocent lives they will lead.
But who will care for these lovely creatures.
That must be our careful heed.

To some of these special people will be given,
the duty to give up the life they enjoy.
This duty will be a destiny's burden,
that only the chosen will choose to abide.

And so it has been for ages uncounted,
The Changelings have played on this ground so carefree.
But in every age there are special ones chosen
to give up life's joy and to duty be bound.

The Mother, Protectors, the Nannies and Guards,
in pain they protect the ones they adore.
Knowing they care for a treasure so precious,
they give up their childhood forever and more.

The rumble continued when the voice stopped. Tom waited, then looked in the now raised eyes of the wizards. "Yes, I thought that was what Mim might have meant. She said some things that made me think that all the grown-up

Changelings must have given up being children by some choice and for some reason. But I didn't think how hard that must have been."

Geey sighed, a long, sad sigh. "It's very painful. For they give up childhood pleasure and take on adult responsibility. Of course, many do that, but most of us don't have to choose to do so, it is thrust upon us, therefore it comes naturally and much slower. For the Changeling, once the destiny is accepted, the painful process of growing happens very rapidly."

Sanyassi added, "And a Changeling must also give up the joy of being able to be whatever he or she wants to be. Can you imagine making such a choice? And then it must endure the pain of finding only one being, the being that is themselves. After that, they can only transfigure into that one being."

All three sat in silence, thinking about that painful process without any real knowledge of the experience. But the more Tom thought about it, the more he knew it must be awful.

It was Geey who broke the silence, "And that, Peregrine Sol, is what Eli is suffering."

"But, why Eli? Is he going to go back and be a guard or something?"

The two old wizards considered Tom for a moment before Sanyassi said, "We hoped that you, Tom, would tell us what is happening here. You see, in some rare circumstances, a Changeling takes on a task, his destiny, which is beyond the realm of Erets. A very few become Peregrine Sols like yourself."

Tom piped in, "Mim did."

"Yes, Mim did. But she returned to her people to fulfil her destiny. And a few become companions." Sanyassi looked at Tom, bending close to him to see into the boy's eyes. "And this is what Eli said to you? That he was to be your Ach?"

Tom nodded, feeling rather haunted by the deep way Sanyassi and Geey were looking at him. The wizards turned from Tom and looked at each other. "I can't understand it," Sanyassi said softly, shaking his head.

"Why?" Tom demanded. "What's the matter with that?"

"As far back in history as we can see," Geey answered, "a Changeling has only ever been an Ach to a prince."

Tom sat silent for a few minutes. "There's always a first time," he said, hopefully. When the two wizards didn't answer, Tom said, "Or maybe Eli made a mistake."

The silence was barely broken by Sanyassi's whispered "Maybe."

Tom ventured another question, "Mim said something horrible happened in Erets. Was that to a Changeling child? Can you tell me what that was?"

Sanyassi jumped, as if coming out of a deep thought. "It's time for you to see your Ach. That's a question he can answer for you. He'll make you feel the pain of this history, as only a Changeling can."

Tom was led through a dark corridor into a dimly lit room with many crisply made beds. "Is this a hospital?" he started to ask Sanyassi. But the two wizards were gone.

He only had time to feel a little confused before a woman entered. She was incredibly tall. Her hair was ivy and her skin a soft-green, like Geey's. But unlike that ugly wizard, the woman was beautiful. She was wearing a loose-fitting gown of soft woven leaves. "Come, I will take you to your Ach."

Chapter Eleven

Tom ran to the bed. "Eli, are you all right?"

Eli was smiling. "I'm okay, Tom. I'm sorry for what you have been through because of me."

"I haven't been through anything Eli. I've worried about you."

"That's what I mean. I'm no help."

"It didn't matter you couldn't change into a mouse. I was supposed to call Eddi. It sorted out fine. Eddi was waiting for me."

"I know. But instead of being by your side, I've been a worry for you. That's not what an Ach should be."

"Well," Tom said. "I don't know if an Ach should make a person worry, you are my first after all. But I know friends often make each other worry."

Eli smiled.

"There is just one thing Eli. The wizards were wondering about it too. Are you sure you're supposed to be my Ach."

That fleeting sadness passed over Eli's face and Tom hurried on to explain himself. "Just because they say in the history of Adamah, a Changeling has only ever been an Ach to a princeling."

"Maybe this is the first time in history," Eli said.

"That's just what I said to them."

After a few quiet seconds, Tom went on. "Eli, the wizards told me I should ask you about something."

Eli raised his eyebrows.

"I wonder about something Mim told me. She said there was a great tragedy in the past that made her protective of the little ones. When I saw the guards looking for you they were so upset. I thought maybe a little one was lost…"

Eli groaned.

"Are you okay?"

"I feel bad they were looking for me. I know they must have been afraid I was taken…just like he was taken. I'm sending a message soon. The healing sage, she promised to send a message and tell them I'm here and fulfilling my calling. Soon they won't have to worry."

"Like who? Who was taken?"

Eli didn't answer, he just looked away. Tom waited. Finally, Eli replied in a whisper, "It was so long ago, but my people remember as if it were yesterday." Eli's voice turned harsh as he spoke, "Arovoit was stolen away by the Vile One. That Master of Horror had only been in this world a few years. The devils that serve him came with him, but he wanted more. He wanted an army of strong and able beings. But any who serve that Vile Master must be horrible to the core. So he needed to turn good beings bad. Arovoit was one who was taken."

Eli turned his serious face toward Tom. "Other people in Adamah were taken too. They were made into beings to serve the Vile One, but Arovoit was a

Changeling." Eli's voice dropped into a whisper, "Arovoit could be made into an Ach for Evil, and he could find a self to transfigure into as strong and cruel as anything could be.

Arovoit who once was so good…became the most evil of all. And the descendants of Arovoit are the most gruesome of all the Vile One's servants. They sit by his throne and act at his command. And when they transfigure, Adamah becomes perilous. All Changelings shiver when they remember those dreadful beasts are our brothers."

Eli went silent, and Tom thoughtful. The only noise was the gentle sound of someone tending the herb gardens outside the window.

Eli started to hum. Then he spoke, and Tom felt the pain all Changeling's feel.

Arovoit, oh Arovoit
a change was wrought on thee.
Aroviot, oh Arovoit,
thine ruined destiny.

A gentle child, a changeling child,
at play so gracefully.
A cat, a bear, a snake, a rat,
What do you want to be?

Arovoit, oh Arovoit,
a change was wrought on thee.
Arovoit, oh Arovoit,
thine ruined destiny.

Changeling children all at play,
pretending creatures new.
Transforming, reshaping,

eyes of brown or blue.

Arovoit, oh Arovoit,
a change was wrought on thee.
Arovoit, oh Arovoit,
thine ruined destiny.

A heedless moment, unaware
and from us you were snatched.
His vile command sent evil hands,
profane was their intent.

Arovoit, oh Arovoit,
a change was wrought on thee.
Arovoit, oh Arovoit,
thine ruined destiny.

The pain and torment you endured,
corrupting you within,
A twisted demon lives inside,
The Changeling child died.

Arovoit, oh Arovoit,
a change was wrought on thee.
Arovoit, oh Arovoit,
thine ruined destiny.

Now misshapen, hurt and brazen,
when choosing what to be,
your descendants all transfigure
into cruelty.

Eli lay quietly. A voice came from the doorway. "I think it's time for Eli to rest." Tom looked up to see the green lady beckoning him. Tom touched Eli's shoulder and left.

"I'm Galenic. I care for the sick and wounded who come to Hokmah seeking a cure."

"Do many come here wounded?" Tom asked her.

"It depends on what is happening in Adamah, Peregrine Sol. During times of war, when the Vile One attacks us, we have many. During times of peace, there are almost none. In between, there are a few because of the skirmishes with the Evil Army on the borders."

"And now?" Tom queried.

"Only a few."

Galenic led Tom through a garden rich with the fragrant smell of deep green leaves. "Do you know your herbs, Peregrine Sol?"

Tom touched a leaf, "this looks like lavender. But are the herbs the same here on Adamah as they are in my world?"

"I don't know," Galenic answered, "but that is lavender. Do they use herbs for healing in your world?"

"Well, sometimes, but we also have more powerful drugs than herbs."

"More powerful than herbs, growing fresh in the dirt of the land? Ahh, I think that must be because your world is tainted now." Galenic walked on. "I hope the Vile One is never able to destroy Adamah as was done to Ha`ehad."

Galenic stopped at a doorway. She pointed, "You walk through there, it will lead you back to the great hall. The High Counsel waits to speak to you."

Galenic turned to go. Tom called to her "What do you mean when you say Ha`ehad?"

She turned back to Tom from the middle of her garden. She looked very much a part of her surroundings. "The first place."

"The first place? And was the Vile One there too?"

"Do you not know?" Galenic looked confused. "Ha`ehad was destroyed, made shapeless and empty. Do you not learn this history? Are your people so spoiled they do not remember the past? Or maybe I'm confused and you are not from the world we call Ha`ehad. "

"And the Vile One came here from there?"

"Yes, he came from there. Many years after the Parents, he found the way. First he wrecked the remade Ha`ehad, then he came here. But at least we fight him."

Galenic turned away saying, "The Counsel waits for you, they will know the answers to your questions better than I."

Tom walked through the doorway, to find himself in a long dark hallway. At the end of the hallway, Tom was once again in Stoa. His thoughts were occupied with Galenic's story of the Vile One. Could it be that Adamah was connected to earth? Surely not, Galenic must be confused. Surely Ha`ehad was really a different place altogether.

Tom heard a rumbling and felt the ground shaking under his feet. He stood still and a Voice filled the air.

Run, run. Destruction is upon us.
Pick up your children, gather no other thing,
the land is putrid as the demons enter, nasty voices ringing,
the song of the Destroyer is all they can sing.

The columns of Stoa stayed very still, but the floor rose and fell like a tidal wave and the walls came alive with pictures of frightened faces and crowds rushing away. Then the picture on the wall turned dark and a black cloud came into the ancient walkway. Fear engulfed Tom as though he needed to run from the Vile One too.

It all stopped, just as suddenly as it started. Tom moved to hurry on, but before he could, the rumbling began again. Tom held on to a large white column.

Hide little children in caves and crevices.
Be safe where only the smallest can go.
The followers of the Vile One,
will never find you hiding here.
And fight we will now,
for the land we love so.

Now the pictures on the walls were of mothers crying over their children. Finally it stopped, Tom waited and sure enough the voice spoke again, but this time it was gentle.

Come now ye remnant,
to the land that we have found for you.
Come see a peaceful land,
land of beauty rich.

Come now ye remnant,
to the land we call Adamah,
leaving the Vile One,
to Ha`ehad's unrest.

Tom looked up. Sanyassi was in the walkway looking at him.

"I came to find you Peregrine Sol. You have been blessed to hear our history from the Voice of Endless Wisdom, something many of our own people have never been privileged to hear."

"Sanyassi, I have so many questions."

"Not now Peregrine Sol. You must wait and speak to the High Counsel. Come we must hurry, time is always passing outside."

Tom entered the great hall again, but it looked very different. Torches against the walls lit the room with a low glow. Twelve men and women sat around a huge circular iron table.

Two seats were empty. Tom sat beside Sanyassi, his eagerness dampened by the sight of the Wizards of the High Counsel.

Sanyassi spoke first, "I found our young Peregrine Sol in Stoa. The Voice of Endless Wisdom blessed him with some history of Adamah." The wizards smiled at Tom and nodded their heads.

"Tom has many questions. I have asked him to bring those questions here as time is pressing. Tom, before we tell you why we have brought you to our Counsel, you may ask your questions of us. But remember, time is passing quickly and Amos is in the hands of the enemy."

Tom thought for a minute then asked, "People here refer to a place called Ha`ehad. Is that my earth?"

The Wise Ones exchanged glances and then a Geey answered Tom. "That is not so simple. There are many opinions. It takes time to study ancient history and form a conclusion. Many wizards here in Hokmah spend their lives trying to unravel this mystery. Do you want to spend time now, Peregrine Sol, when Amos is suffering, to talk about this mystery?"

Tom shook his head.

"Do you have another question?"

"I know I have this quest but I wonder why? Aren't you wizards? Can't you just do something to get him back?"

A soft voice answered Tom. Tom looked round the table to see who was speaking. Then he could not move his eyes from her face. Her fair skin and green eyes glowed with beauty. She was simply dressed in a long, white robe. Her thick long hair fell to waist with tiny white flowers adorning it. She was an elf. Tom was sure she was, because of her pointed ears.

"Peregrine Sol Tom, we're not wizards as you think of them from the stories and myths of your world. We are wise from years, hundreds and even thousands of years of learning. We are more Wise Ones than wizards as you think of the word. " At this she smiled at Sanyassi, Geey and Lingua. "We do no tricks of illusion, nor do we have powers of control. We act only by our special abilities and gifts, which do sometimes seem magical to those who do not possess them."

All the wizards at the table nodded their heads in agreement. Sanyassi said, "I wish, indeed, Tom, we all wish that we could stop the evil that has invaded

Adamah, but like our ancestors who were unable to stop the evil in Ha`ehad and fled to Adamah, we are unable to stop the Vile One."

Tom looked back at the woman, "Are you an Elf?"

She raised her eyebrows and then laughed, "An elf? A mischievous and mystical creature of your fables? I am not. I am Iris, of the people Elvene, a strong and noble race. We are not those of your make-believe, a pretty people who sing songs. My people sit on counsels of wisdom. Can you boast the same?"

Iris turned her smirk into a smile saying, "But come Tom, you are not responsible for the fables of your world, I'll not tease you. We have brought you before this counsel to give you what little help we can. We will use what magic, as you call it, that we are able, to help you in this quest. The Voice of Stoa has already been given. Gifts from the Armatura will also be made available. Our Mapkeekers will give you guidance for your journey, our herbs and food will fill your packs, but... "

Lingua spoke, "We're troubled, Peregrine Sol, by the lack of help we're able to give you. We've looked for a word or a prophecy but none has come."

Tom looked around. Their strange faces were all sad. "I didn't really know you might have a prophecy so I can hardly miss it, can I?"

"Sometimes the things we don't know about are the ones we miss the most," Sanyassi said.

"I've tried to find it," a little man with bulging eyes and balding head said. He seemed familiar. Tom knew someone who looked like this man with strange curly hair, a bald spot and bright eyes.

Sanyassi whispered to Tom. "This is Libiri, Keeper of the Books of Prophecy."

"But I can't even find a written prophecy that fits this occasion," Libiri continued.

The little man jumped up, ran through the room and stopped dead still. Three enormous bookcases slammed down in front of him, startling everyone in the room. He pulled books from the shelf, tossing them onto the iron table. The books sailed across the room, pages flapping open, and looked ready to hit the floor. Then up they zoomed, landing in a perfect pile. Tom laughed, but stopped because of the grim faces around him.

The little wizard ran back to his place at the iron table with the same speed, and passed books out to his fellow wizards.

"Just look, look at these books. Open them, open them. Nothing in any of them talks of such happenings as we have here today. No prince snatched by the Vile One is told of, no Changeling adopting a common boy. This Peregrine Sol is never predicted in the Books of Prophecy."

Tom looked around him, wondering what this meant.

"Did you search for a word about an odd fellowship of four?" asked a chilly voice. The being was leaning forward, his hair stood stiffly backwards as if a freezing wind kept it there. He was rubbing blue-tipped fingers over his chaffed red cheeks.

"Of course I did," replied Libiri. "There is nothing written about this group with its common boy leader. Nothing about a dog-girl, or a company of four including a Changeling and a Luchorpan."

"A Changeling and a what?" Tom asked.

"A little man," Sanyassi answered.

"A common boy?" Tom asked.

"You do not understand, Peregrine Sol," Libiri said in his quick way. "When Miriam the Huge pushed back the assault on Largus, thereby saving her kind, we saw it coming. When Helena planted the hedge of protection we knew and agreed, for it was prophesied that such a thing would happen. When Theodora the High turned her back on her people and became the handmaiden of the Vile One, we mourned but were not shocked for the Books of Prophecy had already foretold the sad story. Even when, as a young man, Gwain defeated the fire of the drakon, that we also saw."

"Gwain defeated what? What is the fire of drakon? It sounds like a myth of Sir Gwain and the Green Dragon."

"We Elvene people have also been treated so by your kind, making a child's story from pain they have never endured."

Sanyassi patted Tom's arm. "This is Iris, the Wise Elvene."

Iris the Elvene continued, "The Drakon was an invention of the Vile One and his army. A great mechanical beast that spit out fiery bombs."

"And Sir Gwain," Tom said quietly. "Is this Sir Gwain, Amos's father?" Several of the wizards nodded.

"He has known many bitter days, Tom," Sanyassi said.

Libiri continued rapidly, flipping pages as he spoke. "We are waiting still for some prophecies to come to pass. We know for instance that a great warrior will ride the clouds to rescue a young woman, and that a storm will beat down the hedge of protection, letting a foul army run amuck on Adamah which can only be defeated by a woman of great knowledge. We also know that a brother will save a brother unaware, bringing peace to Adamah for a year, and we know that the Vile One will someday be driven from Adamah."

"So you know you will win against the Vile One?" Tom asked, cheering a little.

Sanyassi laid his hand on Tom's shoulder. "Prophecies are fragile things, dear Tom, easily broken by events before them. We can't know for certain, but we hope."

Libiri interrupted with an abrupt voice. "There are many more prophecies, but none for you."

And all were silent.

"Does that mean I should not be here," Tom asked.

"No, Peregrine Sol Tom, it means that we didn't know about you. Also, that we have little help to give."

"So what good was coming here?" Tom asked bitterly.

"Your Ach's health is restored," stated Iris.

"Your friend Abigail can understand and be understood," Lingua reminded him.

"And we will give you the gifts of Hokmah that we are able, dear Tom," Sanyassi finished softly. "In fact, come now, young Peregrine Sol, let us see what Armatura gives you."

Everyone stood and pushed back their heavy chairs. It seemed everyone wished to see what gifts Tom would receive.

Tom felt a little nervous as Sanyassi led the way through the Stoa, he didn't want to hear that rumbling voice again.

They went to another large room. The grey walls were bare and the stone floor empty. Tom heard the door open and turned to see Abigail and her friends entering. Abigail came and stood beside Tom.

"Oh Tom, I'm so excited. Aren't you?"

He looked at her, "Why?"

"We're getting presents from this here thing. It's supposed to be a great honour."

He sighed deeply. "I wonder what kind of gift it gives."

"I could do with a bit o' lipstick. I've done gone and lost mine." Tom grimaced. "I was just kidding. What you done then, lost your sense of humour?" Everyone went quiet. Tom turned to look at Sanyassi. The wizard's head was bowed low.

"Fire, ice, heat and cold.
Gifts of might, yours to bestow.
These gifts are used in the fight for the just.
The Vile One's end and the innocent's best."
A tall thin woman, whose outfit was much like Sanyassi's, came and took Abigail's arm. She led the girl to the far wall and stood her against it. Abigail looked frightened for a moment and suddenly held up her hands. In one she held a long knife and the other, a cut-crystal phial of orange liquid. Everyone in the room clapped.

"The gifts you hold in your hand are a knife that will always hit its mark and a phial of sustenance. If you are hungry and without food, a drop or two will fill you as though you have feasted at a banquet," the woman said.

Sanyassi held up his hands high over his head and called out loudly, "These are great gifts for a quest of courage." A cheer rose from the others in the room. Then they all fell silent again.

The woman came and led Tom to the wall. Tom stood with his back against the cold wall. Sanyassi smiled at him reassuringly. Tom felt so afraid.

The wall seemed to close in around him as the wizards and Abigail disappeared into blackness. Did Abigail feel this too? Tom heard humming and felt a soft warm substance encasing him. He felt cold hard metal hit into his hand, and a heavy burden slung upon his shoulder. The cold stone slowly moved back and Tom opened his eyes. He was looking into the solemn face of Sanyassi. No one else was in the room. "Where did everyone go?" Tom asked.

"They have gone to eat and rest. You've been many hours in the Inner Sanctuary of the Armatura, Peregrine Sol."

"Hours?"

"Yes, look at yourself."

Tom looked down. He was dressed in black. In his hand he held a long, thin-edged sword and a heavy black shield was slung over his shoulder. Tom thumped his hand against his thigh. It clanged like metal, yet felt warm to the touch.

Sanyassi's face came close to his own.

"Many of our young come to Hokmah after months of learning how to protect their regions from the forces of the Vile One. After studying the art of warfare against the Vile One and his army they come here to learn the wisdom of peace and to hear prophecies to guide their destiny. These good people prepare to give their lives for their families, friends and neighbours. The very last thing we do is to bring these eager youths here to the Armatura to receive a gift. Eddi received his prophecy and gift many years ago. Most people who come here receive something like Abigail received. They go back and serve their region of Adamah. They join in all normal work but they are prepared, when called upon, to form the Militia that will protect their people if the enemy invades.

Just occasionally, Tom, indeed rarely, a young person is brought to the wall and we step back as the Inner Armatura surrounds that person. We know hours will pass before it opens again, and we know a Knight will emerge."

Tom whispered, "A Knight?"

"We have been in Counsel for many hours with all our wisdom and gifts poured out on the Iron Table. Libiri has searched all the books again, for never, Tom, has any one from outside Adamah been made a Knight by the Armatura. As we wizards stood and saw the sanctuary surround you, we gasped with wonder, for no one could believe that a boy from your world would be made a Knight of Adamah."

Sanyassi stood looking at Tom, his faced pinched with thought, he continued quietly, "The armour of a knight, designed for you alone, has been placed upon you. A sword, wrought from the finest steel and made to fit only your hand, has been given to you. A shield has been placed on your shoulder. This is what happens to every knight of Adamah. And on that shield is placed the symbol of an Order of Knights. That order is where the knight will serve all his life. There are many symbols, for example, some shields show the blue unicorn and serve the Order of St. Gallant. Those with the white horse serve the Order of Sir Christopher the Pure. A red lion puts you under the order of Barnabas the Wild while the golden eagle means you are a knight of St Joachim.

When you were taken into the Inner Armatura, we knew you would come forth a Knight. Now we must see what banner you bear. For your quest will not continue. You will instead be placed in your order of Knights and serve Adamah with them.”

Sanyassi reached out and took the shield from Tom’s shoulder. With a shocked voice he said, “It’s blank. No order. I don’t understand.”

“Has anyone else ever had a pure black shield?” Tom whispered.

Sanyassi shook his head. “No, never. A knight who has all four symbols, one on each corner, is the High Commander of all. Sir Gwain has all on his shield. But never has a shield been black. I don’t know what to do. Where are you to go? Who are you to serve?”

Iris’s voice startled both Tom and Sanyassi. She walked gracefully across the room towards Tom and the wizard. “Maybe Sanyassi, Tom was not placed in an order because it is all he serves in this quest. The quest must go forward.

My scouts are back from their foray. Tom’s story is true. Amos is indeed behind the enemy line. The hedge has been breached and breached again. Already, my men say, the enemy raiders have new courage to harry the people of our land. But the worst news is also confirmed. Sir Gwain is sick with grief, and has fallen under a bewitchment as have all the knights. Sir Gwain is preparing for surrender. Adamah is near the end, if these things continue. Tom is now a knight of Adamah, never has our need been greater than it is now.”

Iris again looked at Tom, a single tear rolled down her cheek. "Our fate in the hands of a mere boy."

Sanyassi's face was grey. "Our hope rests in you, Peregrine Sol. Sir Gwain, the leader of our people, is about to surrender Adamah to the Enemy. The only thing that can stop him is to see his son safe again."

Chapter Twelve

"Sleep is what you need now, Tom."

"I'm not tired," He wondered if he sounded like a toddler. Sanyassi led Tom to a room filled with soft cushions.

"The experience in the Armatura is more exhausting than you realise. Rest now."

Tom sat down on a large cushion. He really didn't want to sleep, he had so many questions in his head. "Why is everyone so frightened if there's a prophecy saying the Vile One will be defeated?"

Sanyassi toyed with the scarf that fell from his cap. "The future is always a dark horse," the old wizard said, "as if a veil lies over its face. Prophecies tell what will happen if all goes a certain way. They can be distorted and changed. This taking of Amos, this wrecking of Sir Gwain, it all could be the undoing of future things. You see, Tom, the Vile One knows of these prophecies too. Everything he does is an attempt to change the future and make it what he wants it to be. And there is always that awful chance he could succeed."

Sanyassi shook his head. "It's a terrible weight for an old wizard like myself. It's a very heavy yoke to put on a boy like you, even if you are clothed as a Knight."

Tom lay down on the cushions. He was keyed up. There was no way he would be able to sleep. Sanyassi, touched his forehead. "May nothing trouble your thoughts, may your dreams be sweet. And when you wake, may your path be true."

Then Tom woke up. He blinked twice and stood up feeling completely refreshed, knowing he had slept well and long. He stretched and laughed. "No wonder Sanyassi was so sure I would sleep, he put a spell on me to make sure I did."

Tom opened the door of the room to find a squatty woman, sitting on a chair. She said nothing, but took his hand and led him back to the great hall which was different yet again. This time a small table, a chair and an enormous breakfast waited for him. He was ravenous and the food was as delicious as anything he had ever eaten.

He ate heartily, until two visitors arrived. His discussion with them put him off eating even the warm, buttery bread he was having with his cup of tea. He was happy the arrival of Abigail and Eddi ended that visit. He didn't even want to think about what those two creatures had told him.

"Come on you. We're supposed to be out there waiting for that wizard bloke. We got to get moving on now," Abigail said. "Eli will be coming and Sanyassi will open the gates for us to go on out and get Amos."

Tom turned to look at her. The ease with which she spoke of the quest surprised him. If only it would be that easy. If only they could just, "go out and get Amos." He followed her out to the courtyard. She was looking around. She saw Tom watching her.

"My friends said they'd be here to say goodbye and all. They reckoned nearly everyone here in Hokmah would send us off. They're all putting their hopes in us. Can you imagine?" Abigail shook her head and looked around for her friends.

Tom looked down at his armour-clad feet wishing it were the game Abigail's words made it sound. Though crowds milled around and various creatures came to speak with them, all he could think about was how afraid he felt.

Eli followed Sanyassi into the courtyard. Tom calmed down. Everything would be okay now, Eli was here.

Sanyassi hushed the crowds, and called out, "Let the doors of Hokmah open wide, to send these companions out to fulfil their quest."

Out of the stone, an entry appeared, and outside the doors, Tom could see the guarding beasts. They were real again, not stone. A fear came over him at the thought of passing beneath their fiery gaze again.

Sanyassi came close to the little company of travellers and smiled. "There's no more I can say to you. Blessings and success, I can only hope, will be yours." And he stepped back to allow them to pass.

Tom picked up a small bag at his feet and hitched his shield up over his shoulder. He saw Abigail fling a bag on her back. Tom looked left then right, and stepped out. The crowd was silent unlike the welcoming, whispering crowd that greeted him and his companions at their coming.

Tom led the way out through the archway. Shivering, he walked between the beasts, their hot breath on his cheeks and savage whispering in his ear.

"Go back. Go back to the safety of Hokmah. Adamah is perilous and your quest, impossible. Go back, go back…."   And then he was out from under them. He looked back for a final wave to those who had come to mean so much to him, but it was impossible. The beasts were once again stone gargoyles on the wall without an entryway. Hokmah was sealed as if impenetrable.

Tom took one look at the sad faces of his companions and started walking forward. Putting on a cheerful voice, he said, "Well come on then, you all, let's get out of here and find Amos. I have a feeling that there will be a big party with all our friends when we bring him back."

Tom's cheerful start gave way as they went along, and soon the companions were walking in a heavy silence. They walked for hours. Tom held fast to the map he was given in Hokmah by the Mapkeepers, following exactly the path they had mapped out. It was easy now, as they went through the forest surrounding Hokmah, up a hill and then down into the valley below. They were already in the forest and the walking was still easy but the undergrowth was beginning to become dense. He knew what was coming and it troubled Tom.

"Oh great leader, how long are we going to have to walk through this blooming forest before you let us have a wee break?"

Tom looked back. Eddi was dozing on Abigail's shoulder. "Sorry, Abby. I thought everyone was okay."

"I'm okay. I just want me afternoon tea, that's all. I could go on if there was some need or something, just as easy as you could. But look, Eddi is snoring in me ear. And Eli is just getting better after all." Abigail arched her eye at Tom. "You should of thought about that since you're the leader."

He looked at his Ach, who smiled back at him. Tom laughed, "All right, all right Abigail, you will get your afternoon tea break."

Abigail flung her bag to the ground and carefully lowered herself to lean against it. She moved slowly so she wouldn't wake Eddi, and dug deep into her bag, pulled out a flask and poured steaming hot tea into a cup. Looking up, catching Tom's eye, she held out the cup, which he gratefully took. She then poured one for Eli and herself. Eli was sitting close to Abigail. His now rather tall body was bent close to her as he listened to her chatting.

Tom watched them, no longer feeling upset about their friendship. He didn't know why. Maybe the burden of leading his friends was enough. Or maybe he simply accepted his relationship with his Ach well enough now to relax.

Tom leaned back against the tree after taking a sip of his tea. It was not too sweet and just hot enough. He relaxed then bolted forward again. The map. It was okay, still clutched in his hand. He released his fingers. His grip was so tight it almost hurt to let up. A long round tube fell out of from his hand and rolled a short distance. Tom smiled and picked it up.

"What's that, Tom?" Abigail called.

Tom held it up.

"Is it a peashooter?"

"Yeah, Westermann handed it to me just as we were about to leave."

Abigail took another bite of the piece of cake she was eating and Tom returned to his thoughts, still rolling the peashooter around between his fingers. A little smiled played about his lips as he recalled that moment in the courtyard of Hokmah when Westermann ran up to him. It happened before Sanyassi had even come out with Eli. Tom had been tense and waiting, worrying about the journey and looking forward to seeing his Ach Eli. He felt a tug on his sleeve and looked down. There stood the little, hairy-nosed Nibelung, with a worried look on his face and the peashooter held out in his hand.

"Only a moment of your time, Peregrine Sol. I feel I must.... I truly feel compelled... You must take this weapon. It's the weapon of my people and it's very effective."

Tom took the tube from the Nibelung and said with equal sincerity, "I completely understand its effectiveness. But, Westermann, surely you can see I've been given great weapons by the Armatura."

The serious, worried look intensified on the face of the short man. "I know the Armatura is wise. I know there are many wizards here whose years of study and knowledge far outweigh my own. That's why I can't understand it, when the fierce weaponry of Nibelung is never among the gifts of the Armatura. The other wizards here, for all their intelligence, seem not to understand the deficiency."

Tom smiled at the Nibelung. Standing in the sun in beautiful Hokmah, Tom took the little tube saying thank you to the little man. Tom never let on that he reckoned the greatest use for this weapon would be to irritate James when he got back home.

The last thing Westermann said was, "Be careful, Peregrine Sol, it's loaded."

Tom held the little weapon up to the sun, closed one eye, and looked into the tube. It was blocked. "Mmm," he thought, "some magic or mechanism keeps the little pea-bullets up there."

Tom put the shooter into his breast pocket under his armour, took a sip of his drink and unrolled the map. This was the reason he could not rest now, and the reason he lost his appetite at breakfast. Tom knew what lay ahead of them.

Pale, big-eyed creatures called The Mapkeepers had scurried noiselessly into the room while Tom was having breakfast. They bowed low, stretched the map out on the table, flattening it with gentle, loving strokes.

"We have come to show you the way to the Enchanted Hedge. That's as far as our maps can help you. We know nothing of the terrible beyond called Sheol. To the hedge, we can help you go, yes we can."

They looked down at the map with tender eyes, caressing it lovingly. And their long fingers pointed the way across the crinkly yellow paper. It was after those fingers made paths through the Simkah Forest, down Chere hill and across Joiee valley, that the big, liquid-brown eyes looked into Tom's face.

Those eyes turned fearful and compassionate when they glanced up at him. The creatures drew a path through dark and dreadful places with mean names. The path they showed him now crossed the Torrent River and went over Biting Ridge. The map revealed jagged rocks and steep cliff edges.

Then The Mapkeeper's fingers moved across the Plain of Desolation. Tom looked closely at the map as the long grey fingers trailed across the plain. He could see the Enchanted Hedge, drawn with thorns and red dots, but the plain had strange markings. Tom looked up and found penetrating eyes staring back at him.

"What strange symbols those are on the Plain of Desolation. Who lives there?"

A gentle creature, maybe female, spoke to Tom. "Nothing lives there any more, yet creatures wander through." Her voice lowered, "Fear what creeps through that land."

That's when Abigail came in with Eddi on her shoulder. Tom greeted them. The Mapkeepers hurriedly folded the map, pressing it into Tom's hand before shuffling out of the room. Tom forgot about the map when he saw his friends. It was all far away while he was warm and laughing with Abigail.

The frightening images he saw on the map returned the moment he passed under the gargoyles. All Tom could think about since he left Hokmah was the scary places The Mapkeeper's had showed him.

Abigail's loud laughter brought Tom back to the forest again and awoke Eddi. Abigail pulled off a hunk of her cake and held it up to the tiny man who consumed it rapidly and held out his hand demanding more.

Tom watched them for a moment before forcing a cheery, "Come on, you lot. We'll never get there, sitting here." Tom picked up the map and flung his bag and shield onto his shoulder.

They walked for a while before Abigail's complaints became unbearable. "He says move, and he' expects us to do whatever he says. Why does he think he can just order us about like that I would like to know."

Eli spoke softly, "It's Tom's duty, Abby. Ours is to follow."

Abigail's voice came back harshly, "Well, maybe it's your duty Eli. You seem to have something going with him, but it's not mine. I didn't really even want to be here. He dragged me into this you know."

Tom had been trying to ignore her, but when she went quiet, it became harder than when she was being noisy. He strained to hear what was being said behind his back. Tom glanced back only to see a look exchanged between Eli and Abigail.

Abigail spoke again, "Well, of course I want to be here now, you lot couldn't get much done without me."

The path soon grew tiring again. The undergrowth thickened and it became a battle to move through the tangle. Tom felt sweat rolling down his face, and he could feel his nerves tingling. As he grew tired, his fear became heavier and The Mapkeepers' warning echoed in his ear.

"So when should we be worried about running into trouble?"

The Mapkeepers straightened up from bending over the map. They stared at Tom with those huge eyes.

A raspy voice answered him, "Peregrine Sol, all of Adamah is in travail." The Mapkeeper moved his fingers lightly across the map touching Erets, Nibelung, the Valley of the Luchorpan, Simpkin Forrest, Hokmah and regions Tom didn't know. "The enemy is invading all of Adamah. Take care, oh Knight of Adamah, every sound you hear in forest or valley, could be the sound of the Vile One's warriors."

Now walking through this forest, Tom heard sounds all around him. Abigail on the other hand was surprisingly quiet, her weariness showing in her silence. Tom stopped often to listen, bending his head this way and that. Abigail didn't comment, just followed silently.

Tom stopped again, looking up as a flock of bird abruptly took to the air out of the tree. "Are you tired? We could stop for a rest," he said. "But I would rather get out of these woods before night-fall."

Abigail was looking up at the birds. Eli answered, "We'll follow you."

Tom led on, walking and walking, pushing away leafy branches that slapped back into his face. The weariness was making s him numb. Dusk fell grey and wet on the travelers. Tom no longer stopped or turned for each sound. He only walked on.

A loud noise rushed through and forest and Tom stumbled and fell on his face. He landed on something soft and heard rumbling all around, but he couldn't see anything. His nostrils filled with a dusty smell and a rough fur rubbed his face. Tom screamed 'Eli!' but as he did his mouth filled with fur. Something had grabbed him and was squeezing him so tightly it was nearly smothering him. Tom heard muffled yells from his companions, and knew they too had been captured. Tom had failed. His companions were taken by the enemy.

Chapter Thirteen

He was flung over the back of a huge fur covered beast. He couldn't see anything, for the night had turned the forest black. He could hear the thump of running feet behind and see shadowy figures. He hoped that his friends were held by those who came behind. He tried to free himself.

A growling voice said, "Settle down. We're almost there. It's my duty to carry you. You must lay still."

Tom kept struggling and the beast tightened its grip. Now he could not struggle or even move, all he could do is whisper, "Please keep them safe. Please help me get free." The brute kept squeezing him tighter and tighter, finally Tom passed out.

Tom was flung to the ground, and landed with a thud on downy grass. He groaned then lay unconscious for some time. When he came to and lifted his head, the sight that met his eye was terrifying. He was in a clearing of the dense forest. A large bonfire was burning in the middle of the clearing and shapes moved all around it. Beasts, strange beasts were gathered in this open space.

Tom swallowed a gasp and pushed himself up on his elbows. Where were his friends and how would he ever get them out of here alive? He could hear the grunts, growls and muted mutters of the beasts. It was an odd assortment of creatures. Having been through Hokmah, Tom now knew that many kinds of beings lived in Adamah, but the beings here were different again. These were beasts. Giant bears were prowling, stopping occasionally to sit on their haunches to join in with the discussion that was taking place around the fire.

There were also large, fierce-eyed horses and small wiry-legged antelope. Some of the antelope were winged. They would become excited by something and run about, whinnying in high-pitched voices. Then they would leap in the air, their tiny wings lifting them magically high.

Some of the beasts were part human. The centaurs, Tom knew from earthly myths. But these angry, horse-faced men with short shaggy manes were not what Tom envisioned when he read stories. Two were female. They were tall and strong looking, much like the male centaurs except with long-hair and manes. Some creatures reminded Tom of the fauns in stories he read as a little boy. But these too were different. They looked less human, more animal. And some of them had horses' tails. All together, the scene was frightening.

Tom lay back further. He didn't want them to know he was awake. He wanted to listen, maybe he would over hear something to help him. He lay very still. The muted voices came to him like whiffs in the smoke. As he listened he realised he could understand the beasts. Even the growls of the bears became words as he strained to hear.

Tom bolted upright. The low, growling sound of a bear's voice was talking now. It was the answering the voice that caused Tom to sit upright.

"I was not too rough. I was just cuddling 'im. And I really laid 'im down quite softly too." The bear was actually whining. It was talking in that sort of wheedling, grovelling way toddlers use to try to convince others of something not quite true.

Then the first person spoke again. Tom stood right up onto his feet when he heard, "You're not telling the truth, mate. He may not be a hero or anything, but Tom wouldn't just pass out cause of a little bear hug."

Someone in front of the fire stood up. "Tom," Eli shouted. "Are you all right?"

Tom was surrounded then by many small, excitable beasts. He was pushed towards the blaze where Abigail, Eddi and Eli all stood. Piles of grapes, apple slices, figs and a few unknown fruits and assorted foods were sitting on plates in front of the fire. Tom looked around at his friends and the others gathered with them. Now it all felt more like a party than a counsel of enemies.

"They were watching for us Tom. Expecting us all along," Abigail said. "Seems one of them is like Eli and Eddi here. He has this calling he thinks he must fulfil, so he needs to go with us to get Amos."

The big bear sitting slightly off from the rest of the crowd began to wail. Two or three of the small bears went into a huddle round him, petting and soothing him. Tom heard a growly voice say, "Its okay, we just don't know 'ow strong we are compared to them, that's all."

Eli came and put his hand on Tom's shoulder. "He's upset because everyone's been angry with him for hurting you. The bear brigade was supposed to bring us here."

A centaur came close to Tom, his strong body and fierce face a tad overwhelming. "I made the mistake of telling the woolly-coated, thick-headed beasts to round you up and bring you in. They took it too literally and went out of here like wild things."

The big bear had obviously been listening, for his wailing cry, which had been tapering off, began with renewed vigour. Eli looked at Tom with a funny sad face. Tom walked over to the bears. The small ones, which were actually quite big when Tom came closer to them, moved aside. Tom walked round to the front of the large bear, swallowing back his fear. This beast was huge. It towered above Tom even while sitting on its haunches. But when Tom stood in front of the bear, its puppy-dog innocent face melted all Tom's fears. Tom reached up and patted it. "It's okay. I'm all right. No harm done."

The bear smiled a silly smile and then grabbed Tom in a great bear hug. Tom spluttered and coughed. The bear released Tom, looking around with wide, tear-filled eyes.

He started blubbering, "Oh no, I did it again…" Everyone was quiet, not sure what to say. Tom finished coughing and started laughing, which brought laughter from everyone.

Tom backed away. "It's all right, really. No more hugs, but it's all right."

"Come," called a large, determined looking female centaur. "We have things to discuss before the night is gone. No more wasting time." The way the animals responded, convinced Tom the centaurs were the leaders of the forest.

Tom followed the others, happy to let someone else be in charge. He sat down between Abigail and Eli. Eddi climbed onto Tom's knee and sat cross-legged there. Tom watched the beasts all gather round, the antelopes leaping over one another trying to get the best position. The little bears all huddled around the big one, trying cheer him up.

The beasts formed a circle around the fire as a stern look from a centaur quietened them. A centaur nodded to Tom who just looked back wide-eyed. Surely this big brute didn't expect him to take charge of the meeting.

The centaur spoke, hesitantly, "With your permission, Peregrine Sol, I, Cimber, shall explain why we wished for your presence enough to send these bears after you." A sniff came from the direction of the big bear.

The centaur's stern look was accompanied by an equally stern command, "Brutus, enough from you." The big bear, with a pouting lower lip, looked the other way.

Cimber began speaking again, "We know of your journey to try to save the life of our prince, the young knight Amos. We thank you for taking on this quest." A cheer went through the crowd.

"We have special information about this, for we have one among us who had visions of this day. I confess..." The centaur halted, clearing his throat. "I confess we never took him seriously. He told us of his vision of this terrible time. He felt he had a part to play. But we…. We only laughed at him."

Cimber looked around at Tom sitting with his companions and then at his own fellow creatures. "We never believed him. We thought he was too foolish to have a true vision." Tom noticed that many of the creatures standing around the fire were hanging their heads down.

Cimber cleared his throat again. "But we never believed the enemy could ride straight into the heart of Adamah, strike against a young but strong knight, and take the son of Sir Gwain." Cimber shook his mane fiercely. "Now we know that can happen, has happened. And we know the vision was true. What we called the dreams of a fool, have become a reality." The creatures were all now staring straight at Cimber.

"I'm kinda lost here. Who are ya talking about? Some visionary person, is it?" demanded Abigail.

"You'll never guess," a beast in the crowd laughed.

"Is it Brutus?" asked Tom slowly.

A voice from the crowd called out, "You would probably refuse to take him, wouldn't you?"

Brutus let out a shivering sniff.

Tom looked over at the big furry mass. "Actually, I was kind of hoping it was him. We could really use a powerful person on this quest."

Brutus stood up and ran, stretching out his arms, he grabbed Tom in yet another bear hug. "I knew you were a good bloke, I jist knew it," Brutus said, over and over again. He released Tom who fell in a big heap on the ground, coughing and gasping for air. Brutus looked down, "Oops."

The crowd laughed as once again Cimber called for order. "Are you alright, Peregrine Sol?

Tom nodded as Brutus slunk back to his spot among the bears. Cimber cleared his throat and said, "This visionary amongst us, as you say, is…." At that, the crowd spurted with laughter, calming only after yet another harsh command from Cimber. The centaur then continued, "The person we are talking about is…Pan."

Out of the crowd stepped a short, incredibly ugly, little faun. His sharp chin, round nose, and bright green eyes could not compensate for his bland caramel complexion and muddy-coloured fur. Pan appeared a dull creature, all brown and dreary.

But Pan was anything but dull. He stepped out into view, waving his arms about wildly. "It's me, it's me. I'm the chosen one. Me." Some in the crowd tittered as if uncertain. They were accustom to laughing at the faun, but were not sure it was proper to do so now that he was a prophet. Tom and Abigail looked at each other with raised eyebrows, then back at the dramatic but ugly creature.

The faun looked around at those watching him, grinning with delight at the attention. "Yes it's me. I'm the one who saw the future. I'm the one who saw Amos being taken and tried to warn the elders." Saying this he gave the centaurs a disapproving look. "If only they had heeded my words and gone to Sir Gwain, how different things might now be." Pan put his little round nose into the air, raising one eyebrow. "They didn't heed me and look what has happened."

Tom interrupted. "Okay, so you saw Amos would be taken. But what part do you see for yourself in our quest?" They had enough small helpless people going on this journey, why would they need another?

"Oh Peregrine Sol, I saw the praise I was given in a vision. Proclamations were exclaimed from the highest treetops of Simkah Forest. My fellow creatures came from every nook and hole to praise my name. In my vision, creatures cantered from clearings to see me, they flew from eyries to catch a glimpse of me, they tunnelled up from deep in the earth just to hear me speak. Everyone honoured me because I saved the quest, and Amos, and all of Adamah." The faun was smiling, gazing upwards, and lifting his hands in victory.

"So without you the quest will fail? What do you do?" Tom repeated, startling Pan. The faun jumped and said, "I don't know. But I'll know when the time comes. I could feel that during my vision too."

Cimber stepped forward. "I feel I must be honest with you, Peregrine Sol. There are reasons we did not believe this particular faun. He has….well he has a history."

A whinny came from the background. A centaur with a beautiful, white-horse body stepped up and spoke in loud voice. "Pan is a fool. He's talked of glory for himself before this, it's still hard for us to believe he might be correct. I feel, and I think I speak for others too, that even now I worry about sending him with you on a quest so important for our land." A murmur of agreement rippled through the crowd.

Pan ran to stand on a nearby rock, yelling at the top of his voice, "Oh people of Simkah Forest. How you continue to doubt me! Yet my prophecy of Amos came true. You will see, as you bow at my feet in honour, that I was right. My former prophecy will also be fulfilled. I will be honoured as a master of the vine, even more than my great-grandfather Dionysus."

Abigail leaned over and whispered into Tom's ear, "Wasn't that one of them Greek gods?"

A young antelope laughed, "I've heard many of our historic people are worshipped in your world. Would you really worship Pan's great-grandfather just because he *claims* to have invented wine?"

"We don't wor…."

Tom shushed Abigail. This mixing of the two worlds was troubling, but Cimber was speaking again and he needed to hear.

"Your desire to create a new wine to bring you fame, Pan, has nothing to do with the issues at hand tonight. I only want to know if the Peregrine Sol is willing to let you join the quest."

All eyes turned to Tom. He started speaking, not really knowing what he was going to say, "Look at my company, we're not a strong group to march into the territory of such a horrible enemy." Tom shook his head, they did not need one more helpless person. What they needed, Tom felt like saying, was the strength of a Brutus and the stern wisdom of a Cimber. Why couldn't they accompany the rescuers instead of little Pan? Instead Tom said, "I don't know why Eddi, Abigail, Eli and I were the ones chosen for this quest. I don't understand why the brave knights of Adamah are all powerless. I don't know if we will succeed or fail, but I do know we will be faithful to our calling. And if Pan is called to go with us, let him come and be faithful with us, even if it is to his death." Then Tom stepped back as the crowd murmured approval.

"Bit dramatic ain't you, mate?" Abigail whispered. "You sound as if you actually meant it."

Tom looked at his friend. "Don't you?"

Abigail smirked. Then she looked at Tom's face and stopped smiling and turned away.

"The Peregrine Sol has spoken. Pan will join the quest. Let us have a celebration in anticipation of their success." The creatures of Simkah Forest all hurried away in a burst of activity. Tom went and sat down, feeling exhausted, Eli came to sit next to him. "Your words were very wise, Tom. Wiser than you know."

Tom looked over at his Ach. "I didn't mean to say all that, Eli, but as I was talking I realised for some reason we have been chosen for this task. Sometimes I worry, really worry that we have been chosen to fail, that we're the ones to bring about the end of Adamah." Now Tom was whispering, "Maybe that is why such young, inexperienced people were chosen." Tom shuddered at the thought of Adamah's destruction.

Eli put his arm around Tom's shoulder. "No," he said sternly. "Whether we fail or succeed, Adamah will not fall. That will not happen." Eli's voice was so strong, so certain, Tom felt better.

Abigail, with Eddi riding on her shoulder, came up to the two companions. "Come on then, you lot. You're missing out on all the good stuff."

Tom and Eli looked up. The clearing was transformed. There were far more animals than previously and more kinds too. Squirrels were busy roasting nuts over the fire, rabbits were bringing in lovely multi-coloured salads, and the bears were making piles of fruits and nuts in alternating layers. A mighty feast was just about prepared.

Tom joined in the feast, putting aside his worries. Many of the animals came to talk to him. Some were serious and talked in low voices about their fears for the future, but some were light-hearted and fun. The little bears were all jokers. The jokes were similar to those Tom and his friends might have tried on each other a few years back, but seemed to have an earthier theme.

"Knock, Knock, Peregrine Sol," one little bear said.

"Who's there?"

"Acorn."

"Acorn who?" asked Tom, trying not to laugh at the hilarious bear, jumping with excitement.

"A corny joke is all you are going to hear in Simkah Forest," said the bear, doubling over with laughter.

Brutus was the most amusing, and the poor thing was trying to be serious. He sauntered up to Tom while the merry-making was in full swing. Tom could hardly hear him, so they went away from the crowd to the side of the clearing.

"I'm sorry to pull you away from the feast, Peregrine Sol."

"That's all right, Brutus," Tom replied, stepping back a few feet.

"It's just that I thought I should tell you, I won't be able to go with you."

"Thank you for letting me know."

"I know it'll be a great disappointment for you," Brutus said, stepping a bit closer to Tom. "I know you were 'oping a big strong person like me'self would join you." The big brute pulled himself up a little taller and straighter.

Tom stepped away again. "Well, I understand…"

"It's just that Cimber told me I really shouldn't come." Brutus looked down his giant nose at Tom. "Not that Cimber can boss me around or anything. I don't think 'e would even try to boss around a strong courageous bear like me'self."

"No, I guess not," Tom stepped back two steps again.

"But Cimber needs me. That just what 'e said. Cimber used those exact words. 'I need you to 'elp protect the forest. So you see, I 'ave to stay 'ere." Brutus opened his big arms, and Tom jumped back in fright. "I guess you will 'ave to go without me," Brutus repeated, as he reached out but found Tom a bit too far to grasp.

Tom stepped back again with wide eyes. "We'll do our best without you. Hey, I think we should go back now, someone may be missing us."

Tom turned and ran back to the crowd gathered round the huge bonfire. He was hugely relieved to have avoided another bear hug.

Later, as the celebration was calming, it was Cimber himself who came close to Tom. "Just a word if you please, Peregrine Sol. I just have a couple of things I need to discuss with you."

Again Tom walked away from the inner circle, out to the edges of the clearing. This time as Tom walked out, he stepped over three or four little creatures that had grown weary of the party and curled up to sleep.

"We will all soon rest Tom. The small creatures are already growing tired."

Tom smiled at a little squirrel curled up not far from him. "Yes, I can see that."

"We will part company soon, you will depart on your quest, I will go out to patrol my forest and keep my people safe here." Cimber paused. It was a thoughtful pause that did not require Tom to say anything.

"I will be thinking of you as what happens on your quest deeply affects what happens in my land." Tom nodded his head.

"I've held Brutus back from joining you. I know you feel you need his strength, but you do not know that bear. He's as good of heart as any creature could be, but I fear he'd let you down. I'm already sending one with you… I

best not dwell on that." Cimber paused for a moment, staring at the ground as if

it would show him something he needed to see.

Finally, he went on, "I told the bear it was a strange company that you

led, strange indeed so many frail creatures have been called…as you yourself

said, Peregrine Sol. I told him I really felt only the called ones should go on this

quest. It's too important a task to be meddled with by mere creatures. Something

bigger is happening here. Of course, the bear was going to insist, so I talked him

into staying by telling him I needed his strength here in the forest."

Tom laughed, "Well, you must have pleased him, because all he could talk

about was how much you needed him."

Cimber tipped back his head and gave a wild laugh that sounded much

like the neigh of a horse. Tom jumped. Creatures around the fire broke into

laughter at the exciting sound. It was an odd sight and even stranger sound, this

huge solemn creature laughing so heartily. Up until this point, neither Cimber,

nor any other centaur, had even so much as smiled.

Cimber calmed and became serious as quickly as he laughed. "Peregrine

Sol, I wanted also to tell you, we'll not be here when you awake in the morning.

This is the best way we can send you off. We'll sleep here together, but when

the dawn breaks the creatures of Simkah Forest and I will be gone, leaving you

to resume your journey quietly, in case there are eyes watching in the forest."

Cimber looked around at the dark trees outlining the clearing. "I'm sure there are eyes out there, Peregrine Sol."

Cimber's name was called by another other centaur and he galloped away before Tom could speak. Tom shook his head. Well he would say good-bye to the centaur later, at dawn. How could Cimber think Tom wouldn't wake up when hundreds of beasts left in the morning?

Some animals were already curled up sleeping. Others were talking, laughing and singing quietly around the fire. Abigail was with a group of winged antelope. They were trying their best to teach her to fly. She jumped, ran and flapped her arms, and leapt off rocks, but of course she did not fly. Tom sat laughing at her, while she and the antelope tried to talk him into trying too.

Eli was chatting with a group of centaurs. Their conversation seemed deep and meaningful, so much so that though Tom wanted to, he did not feel he could go over and join in. Eddi was talking with the squirrels. Luchorpans and squirrels share one particular habit, they hoard nuts. Tom listened to them talk. The conversation revolved around ideas for keeping nuts fresh in storage. Then Tom watched the fire, and soon he was dozing off, head falling in nodding drops to his chest. Tom leaned over, curled against a rock, warmed from the fire's glow, and fell asleep.

Chapter Fourteen

The sun was full on Tom's face when he awoke. He started moving but something was holding him down. That 'something' turned out to be Abigail lying on top of his legs. Eli was not far away, curled up with a soft horse blanket spread over him. Eddi was nowhere to be seen. Only Tom's new companion was awake.

Pan was sitting beside the fire. The ground around the fire was blackened from having been burnt when the fire was larger. The little faun, his bottom smudged, was sitting on the charred earth. He was cooking something in a pot over the fire. Tom shuffled a grumpy Abigail off his legs and stood to stretch himself. Walking over to Pan, he said, "What are you doing?"

"Cooking up a secret recipe," Pan said, not even bothering to look up at Tom. "It's going to be the finest wine anyone has ever tasted, and yet not be made from grapes."

"What's in it?" Tom asked, raising his eyebrows.

"That's the secret," Pan said. He waved his wooden spoon triumphantly.

"Will you lot please be quiet? Some of us are still sleeping," Abigail grumbled.

Pan pulled the pot away from the fire. He stirred the liquid round and round with a wooden spoon.

Tom watched Pan for a moment wondering how Cimber and the other creatures had done it. The clearing was empty. Not only were the animals gone, but every plate, cup, and platter of food was gone too. The rocks, which were once placed as furnishing around the clearing, were now scattered. Only the fire and the burnt ground showed any sign of last night's celebration. Not even a footprint was left to show their trail.

"Ugh." Pan was spitting, wearing a horrible expression on his ugly, little face.

"What's the matter with you?" Tom asked.

"Those little beasts, they tricked me. Here, you taste it yourself. It's awful." Pan spat again.

"You're wine?" Tom couldn't help but grin.

"Yes." Pan held out his pot. "Taste it, taste it. It's horrible."

"I don't want to taste it. Who tricked you?"

Pan screeched, "Those dirty, little squirrels. They told me it would be delicious. They told me to bottle it, age it and it would be the most wonderful nutty-tasting wine in the world. Oh, I'm going to get them. They said, 'save it for a special occasion.' Little liars said not to taste it, just keep it for a surprise, but I always taste my mixture before I age it. Just as well. Those horrid monkeys will pay for this. They were trying to trick me. It's awful. Taste it, you'll see, it's very bitter." Pan was holding out a spoonful of the hot liquid, sloshing it about as he tried to force Tom to taste the nasty stuff.

Eddi came crawling out of a tree stump. He was laughing. "Of course it's bitter. Even Luchorpans don't eat the nut of the Oak Tree, silly faun. Only squirrels, who love a bitter taste, will eat an acorn."

Abigail, rubbing her eyes sleepily, joined them. "Maybe they weren't tricking you. Maybe they like it, so they thought you would like it too."

Eddi laughed. "Oh, they were fooling him, all right. They laughed about it all night."

The faun poured his mixture on to the small fire. "They'll be sorry when I get back from this quest. I, the hero of Simkah Forest, will not speak to them." He stalked off, leaving his new companions grinning at each other.

Tom and Eli spent part of the morning mapping out the quickest route towards the Enchanted Hedge from this new starting place. They then led a surprisingly refreshed and encouraged group back into the forest to walk on. Pan raced ahead, keeping just a step or two ahead of Tom.

"We know very little about this quest, hey, Peregrine Sol? But we do know I'm important, that I save the quest, so I best stay close to you. Isn't that so?" Pan said.

The company journeyed on in this way for hours without rest. Tom made sure this time to occasionally ask Abigail if she needed her tea break, but the girl seemed to have developed a sense of urgency and was ready to push on. Finally, Tom himself called for a stop. He was tired, and felt the company was slowing its pace. He pulled out his map. The forest was now thin, the trees small and spread out. Eddi was eating hurriedly, gulping down as much as he could, but Tom ate and drank only what his Ach handed to him. The others were silent. The tiredness and fear of danger were growing stronger.

Only Pan was not sitting and resting. He was up, walking about, looking at various plants. Pan found some little plant he thought interesting. He moved closer to the rest of the group and squatted down to start a fire.

"Looks like he's going to try it again," said Eddi.

As the faun mixed his concoction to put over the fire, Tom showed the others where they were going. "You see, we're about here. That's why the walking has been hard. We've been going steadily up hill. Even the scrawny, sparse trees are just as they are on the map. Now we'll go down Chere Hill and into Joee Valley."

Everyone but Pan was watching Tom's finger as it pointed at the map. They were silent, listening to him, leaning closer as his voice sank lower and lower. "At the lowest point of the valley we must cross the river. It looks to be a rather wild one, for it's where Chere River meets Music River and becomes the Torrent River. The Mapkeepers told me that it's very dangerous to cross. After that, we walk up Biting Ridge. It's not long, but it's very steep and the path is narrow. All we have to do after that is cross the Plain of Desolation." Tom looked into the wide eyes of his companions.

"That's all?" Abigail said. "We do all that only to get to a dangerous place." Abigail stood up and walked away from the group.

Pan was the only one not worried. He was busy. Though they were staring at him, they were not really seeing what he was doing, until the sound of a small explosion made them all jump. Pan stood up, a tuff of fur on his chest was slightly burnt. He smiled weakly at the others. "I guess that didn't work."

"Pan, we really don't need that kind of noise. We don't want to be attracting attention."

Pan poured his mixture onto the ground, where it sparked and flared, then slowly sputtered out. He stood dejectedly looking down at it.

A snarly noise emanated from the trees. Tom stood up as a low growl joined the sound.

"Oh," said Pan, "it's good, old Brutus."

Tom relaxed and Pan started running, yelling as he went. "Come on out Brutus, you dumb bear. We can hear you for a mile."

Out of the darkness of the trees came a bear figure, but it was not Brutus. It was twisted. The bear body was massive, as big as Brutus, but its face was that of an evil man, hatred filled its red eyes. The beast's hands were paw-like but able to hold a sword befitting his great size. The others leapt to their feet, as Pan skidded to a stop, turned around and ran to hide behind his companions.

The Beast was moving fast. As he drew close to the company, two more of the same kind emerged from the forest. Their half-human, half-animal state was as grotesque as a Centaurs' was beautiful. Tom, breathing deeply, pulled his long sword out of its sheath. He saw Abigail lift her knife.

The beast lifted a massive sword over its head as it barrelled into their midst. Tom stood still, unsure if it was bravery or fear that kept him in his place. The beast opened its mouth, yelling, its breath stinking as it came upon Tom. The beast's attack was fast and furious. Tom could hear Pan screaming, Eli shouting and Abigail crying, but he could not look around to see what was happening to his friends. He had to fight, fight for his life against this horrible half-beast.

The enemy's sword hit Tom's head with a sickening thud. He stumbled backwards, but the blow glanced off his helmet without doing lasting damage. The beast's sword then hit Tom in the stomach, knocking him back, but once again it bounced off the armour leaving Tom only slightly winded. Tom struck the beast. Up to this point his blows had been useless. This time, however, his sword hit the beast full in the chest. The sword twanged violently, and then stuck. The beast bellowed, stumbling. Tom clung to his sword's handle, determined to pull it out of the creature's flesh. Though he pulled with all his strength, he could not pull it loose. The beast fell backwards while Tom was clinging to the sword, digging his heels into the ground. The sword pulled free with a wet splosh as the enemy's huge body hit the ground. The beast lay dead.

A quick look around revealed that his friends had scattered. Tom ran to try to find them. He heard sounds of fear and battle in the distance. A beast appearedin front of him pursuing Pan. Tom felt a rush of anger and he reacted. He ran as fast as he could and attacked the beast. He leaped on its back and grabbed it by the throat. Pan shrieking loudly ran on, leaving Tom to fight the creature alone. The beast spun around trying to shake Tom. The long sword was awkward to manoeuvre. Tom was wrestling with both the beast and his sword. Finally, Tom won command of his weapon and brought the sword down into the heart of the second beast.

He was panting with tiredness as he stood beside the creature's dead body. Tom listened, his chest heaving. Then, hearing a distant yell, he turned and ran again, hoping to help another of his companions. The shouts seemed to come from behind. He ran back and found the shouts were to his left. He ran left and heard the shouts again, way in the distance. Tom stood still, and yelled out in frustration, "Where are you?"

Then he saw them, some feet away in the forest. Abigail and Eli were fighting with all their might against another beast. Abigail was waving her knife while Eli stood beside her, no weapon in his hand. She looked tired. Tom ran to help them, never taking his eyes off the fight. Suddenly, Eli was a lion. The beast's face turned from angry to fearful. It hesitated just long enough and Abigail flung her knife toward its heart in a wild fashion. The knife plunged in and Tom arrived just as the beast stumbled, and fell to the ground.

Abigail turned her pale face towards Tom. Her lips trembled and a tear ran down her cheek. "We killed it." She turned away from the dead body lying on the ground. "I've never killed anything more than an insect before. And sometimes I even feel guilty about killing them."

Tom put a hand on her shoulder and led her away. "I killed two, but they're worse than insects, Abigail," he said, his voice shaky.

Eli laid his hand on Abigial's other shoulder. "We'd be dead if you hadn't fought for us, Abigail." The Changeling looked sadly at Tom. "I couldn't find anything I could transform into until the very end."

Tom looked around, "Where's Eddi? I saw Pan and went to help him but he ran off while I was fighting. I'm not sure which direction he went. We need to find both of them."

"I don't know where Eddi is. We were fighting so hard. I felt him slip off my shoulder but couldn't leave Abigail to deal with the beast alone to keep an eye on Eddi. The beast kept us moving, wearing us down." Eli's face looked stricken.

"It's okay, Eli. We'll just go and search till we find the two of them. Come on. Let's take a look at these things we were fighting first."

Eli and Tom walked over to the beast. Abigail turned away. "I'm not looking at its ugly face."

When Tom and Eli came to the place where the beast had fallen, there was nothing but fur left. "Its gone, Abigail," Tom shouted.

Abigail ran to them. Clumps of fur lay on the ground. The breeze picked up bits of the fur and blew it across the grass. There would soon be nothing left. Abigail shivered. "That's so weird. Why would they just disappear like that?"

The three friends began their new quest, that of finding their companions. They were sure that finding tiny Eddi would be the most difficult, but the little chap was sitting on a rock waiting for them, looking rather depressed.

Tom sat down on the rock beside him and held out his hand. The very glum little chap walked onto Tom's palm.

"What's the matter, mate?" asked Abigail.

"I'm worse than useless. That's what's the matter. I can't fight the enemy. I only cause you to lose time looking for me."

"Oh, Eddi, that's not true. None of us yet know what part we are going to play. Come on. Cheer up. I'm just glad we found you," Tom replied, standing up. "I hope it will be as easy to find Pan."

"Did he really run away and leave you to fight on your own?" Eli asked.

Tom shrugged his shoulders. "It doesn't matter. He'd only have been in the way."

"Yeah, but I bet he still reckons he's the most important part of the quest," Abigail said. She had her nose all wrinkled up. Tom could have laughed, but sighed instead. "Well we better start looking for him," he said as he turned to lead the way.

Chapter Fifteen

Tom, Eli and Abigail walked through the woods calling Pan's name as they went. Eddi sat in silent depression on Tom's shoulder. There was no sight of, or sound from the little faun.

"I can't imagine where he is," Tom stated wearily, as they came to the place where they were first attacked.

Tom walked to a nearby tree and sat down against it, closing his eyes. The others surrounded him in powwow fashion. Eli voiced the fear rising in them by saying, "Could there have been a fourth beast? Could he have been taken by another we didn't know about?"

Tom lifted his head. "That's the only thing I can think. I didn't see another, but when the first reached me, I really didn't see anything but its horrid face." He shook his head. "I'm afraid it is possible."

The four sat still, each searching for another possibility. Eddi broke the silence. "We must go on, Peregrine Sol. We can't abandon our quest because one of our party's gone. The quest is bigger than any one of us. It's more important than all of us."

"You're right, of course, Eddi. I know we must go on. But what if he is out there alone?"

"If he's out there alone then everything is fine," Eli said. "He's a creature of this forest. He'd be all right here on his own. And if he has been taken…"

"Then," Tom said decisively, standing, "They're probably taking him where we're going any way. Let's go. We've wasted enough time."

And so the quest began again. The journey uphill, through the thinning forest, should have been easier for the group of adventurers, but now their hearts were heavy and their minds weary. It felt long and hard. When they finally made it to the top, they stood and looked at the beautiful Joiee Valley below.

"This is a perfect place to have a break," Abigail said, flopping down on the grass. "It's lovely to look at. Hard to believe there's any trouble at all in the world."

Tom rested this time, not even bothering to look at the now very familiar map. It was just as the symbols on the map made it seem. Perfect and peaceful. It was impossible to believe that nasty creatures could be wandering in that valley. Yet, Tom knew that it would be so. And they might have Pan in their wretched hands. Tom shivered at the thought. Eli, who had started a fire and was busy stirring a pot. He poured a hot liquid into a cup and handed it to Tom. It tasted like a caramel chocolate.

"Mmm, that is delicious, Eli. I thought for a minute you were making a brew like Pan," Tom said without thinking. No one laughed. Tom sipped his drink, trying to keep his fears at bay.

They sat munching on titbits left from Hokmah and Simkah Forest. No one talked about how quickly they were working their way through the food in their bags. They didn't even give it much thought. Tom leaned back on his shield, feeling full and tired. "We'd best not rest here too long," he said, closing his eyes.

It was only minutes later when they heard a sound. Now more cautious than they once were, all the company came to their feet. It was a large bird, circling the air above them. It was so high that no one, not even the keen-eyed little Luchorpan could tell what sort it was.

Abigail sat back down. "Well, I don't know why you even try to tell what it was, Eddi. I can't tell one of them big birds from another even when I sees them close up in the zoo."

The others settled down, watching only for a few moments as the big bird soared around in the air above them. "Well," said Tom, starting to pack up his things into his bag, "let's get on our way."

Eddi, sitting on a rock beside Tom, stood up to go. Suddenly, the huge buzzard zoomed down. It was then Tom recognised the nasty thing. Its human face was marred by hanging pink flesh and a sharp beak. Tom yelled, but the bird picked Eddi up by its beak and flew straight up.

Abigail screamed. Tom waved his sword, but he could do nothing against such an enemy. Then he remembered the peashooter. Running, he followed the way the bird was flying as best he could from the ground below. He put the shooter to his mouth and blew. Tom was breathless from running and the bullet fell way short of the mark.

Tom was panting heavily. A bright flash crossed his vision and he looked sideways. A sliver horse was galloping beside him. No, not galloping, it was flying. Tom turned to look at the animal. It was a winged horse. Its wings shone like crystal. Tom knew instantly it was Eli. The horse neighed and Tom recognized Eli's voice saying, "Hurry or it will get away."

Tom jumped on Eli's back and held on to his mane as he was lifted skyward. Eli soared in the wind, rising farther, moving faster than the creature carrying Eddi. Tom put the peashooter to his mouth and shot without thinking. The tiny bullet sped across the sky, landing in the wide-open eye of the buzzard.

"Oh hell, what have I done?" yelled Tom as the bird, Eddi still firmly gripped in its mouth, went spiralling downward.

Eli pointed his long nose down. Tom had to hang on for life as he watched the ground growing closer. Eli neighed, "Reach for Eddi as I go in close."

Tom could not imagine letting go of Eli's mane, which he now gripped tightly with both hands. He opened his eyes, trying not to look at the earth looming ever closer. Eli made a sidewards dash through the air. Tom let go of the mane with his right hand, swinging out for a terrified, screaming Eddi. He missed. Eli lunged back again, jerking Tom. Tom slipped, falling to Eli's firm flanks, barely holding onto the mane with one hand. As Eli neared the bird again, Tom pulled himself up onto Eli's back. Eli was nearing the nasty creature. Tom was going to have to lunge for Eddi with his left hand this time. He lunged, tugged violently and at last pulled the tiny man out of the beak. Eli dashed skywards. Tom was shouting gloriously at the top of his lungs, holding Eddi in his hand. The buzzard hit the ground with a thud.

"Peregrine Sol, Peregrine Sol," coughed Eddi, "Please let up your grip, you're squeezing me to death."

Tom straightened up on the back of Eli, and let up his grip. "Sorry, mate, I was afraid I would drop you."

Eli flew them back to the waiting Abigail and landed beside her. Her face was pale, and she didn't speak.

Eli was just Eli again as he said, "Abigail, are you okay?"

Abigail, very unlike herself, burst into tears. "I wish I was home. I never thought it would be like this. It was just a little game we was playing at." She wiped her eyes with her sleeve. "Then you all went off, Eddi gone, Tom running off, and then you, Eli. You turned into that, that thing and took off after Tom. I could only stand here, all alone. And all I could think was what if you all never came back. What if I was left here alone? I couldn't go home. Only Tom can take me home. And I don't even know where we are going or how we are going to do what we have set out to do."

Abigail sat down in a heap, crying. The three others stood watching her, afraid to speak. Then, just as suddenly, Abigail stood up, her white, tear-stained face looking determined. "Let's go then. Let's get out there and get this thing done."

The four travellers started downhill. It could have been fun. The hill was beautiful, the grass soft and the sky blue. It would have been the perfect day for a picnic and walk, but they were all too aware that this was no picnic, and no ordinary walk.

As they half-slid the rest of the way down the steep hill, a dusky sky was settling over the valley. Tom was debating within himself whether they should make camp for the night on this side of the Torrent River or cross it before stopping for the night.

One look at the river gave Tom his answer. "I don't think we should attempt that wild looking thing without full light to help us," Tom said, as they stood looking at the white-capped swells rushing past them.

They all worked to gather enough wood to make a large fire. It was very comforting when the blaze rose up high, bringing warmth and light. A look into the bags reminded the travellers they'd been none too careful with their provisions. Eli and Eddi decided to try their hand at catching a few fish, and Abigail wandered off to watch. Tom sat staring at the fire, trying to remember how many nights he'd spent in Adamah. It was the first time he really thought about his mother. What was she doing? She must be worried by now. Had he and Abigail been reported missing?

It seemed unreal. That other world, where he used to live, was so unreal. Tom put his hand up to his chest. Under his armour he was still wearing his old shirt. Tom opened one of the metallic plates of his armour, and put his hand in and felt the useful little Nibelung weapon. Beside the peashooter was his little tattered book. How long ago since he opened that book and said the incantation to come to Adamah? At least he could still say those words and go home. If the quest was unsuccessful, all Adamah might change, but Tom and Abigail could still go home. His mother would never believe where he had been and what he had been doing. But what of all the inhabitants of Adamah, what would happen to them? It was a question he didn't want answered.

Abigail walked up. "Why are you shaking your head? Did you ask yourself for something and tell yourself no?" She laughed at her own joke.

"I was just thinking about home. Do you realise how many nights we have been here? Is it three or four or more?"

"Mmm, not sure. I lost count in Hokmah. Time is weird in that place."

"Do you wonder what your parents must be thinking?"

Abigail looked at Tom and made a funny little smile. "I've already had my little wobbly about that, mate. You about to have yours, then?"

Tom looked away. "No," he answered sullenly. "I just wonder about my mum."

Tom decided to change the subject. "So, were they catching anything over there?" he asked, pointing back to the river.

"Yep, but they cheated. Eli turned into a shark. Poor little fish didn't have half a chance."

Abigail obviously didn't feel like switching subjects. She said, "Do you think there is some kind of connection from here to our world, Tom?"

"Yes. There's definitely something. We seem to have something in common with the history of Adamah."

"But it's like you said, Tom. How could we have history in common, there are no creatures on our Earth like anything we've met here."

"I know, Abby, but we do hear stories, don't we? Myths…"

Abigail opened her mouth, looking astonished. She was about to say that they were just pretend. But how could she say that, sitting by a fire in Adamah? "Good point. I can't help but think I'm just going to wake up soon."

Eli and Eddi interrupted them when they came back with a huge catch of fish. Soon the crackle of the fire and smell of roasting fish filled the air. It was fun, like a camping trip, holding the fish over the fire on long sharp sticks. The smell was delicious and eating them even better. They settled down to sleep after their meal. The feeling of fun ended as the companions grew quiet and the sounds around became threatening. The hope of a good night sleep faded.

When they awoke, not one felt rested and the river crossing faced them. Torrent River seemed even more difficult in the light of dawn. Tom looked and looked for a different route, but there seemed no other way.

Abigail already knew the river was icy cold. She'd gone and washed her face and came back freezing. They packed up a little slowly, dreading the moment. Tom led the way. He stepped into the icy water, holding his breath as the water quickly came up to his knees, then to his waist. It was cold, very cold. The others were all close behind him. He could hear Abigail's teeth chattering.

Tom kept on. The water was close to chest high when he felt it. So unexpected. A strong undercurrent grabbed Tom's body, sucking him down and away. As he went down, he saw Eli's dark hair go down and Abigail's hand fighting the water.

Tom was pulled along and dashed into jagged rocks sticking up from the bottom and out of the side of the bank. The rocks couldn't do him much harm as his armour protected him. But even in the midst of fighting for his own life, he worried about the others.

Suddenly a large dolphin appeared beside him. "Eli," Tom yelled, his mouth filling with water. Eli ducked under Tom, lifting him. He swam up stream and dumped Tom out onto the dry land. Tom spluttered and spat.

"Are you okay, Peregrine Sol?" Eddi asked.

"Oh Eddi, I'm so happy to see you. Did you get washed away by that undercurrent?"

"No. I was very lucky. I was riding on Eli's shoulder and he quickly turned into a fishy thing and swam with me."

The dolphin came leaping out of the water and dumped Abigail on the shore beside Tom. She lay still, gasping for breath. Her face was bleeding from a gash on her left cheek and a large pale bruise was already forming under her eye. Tom scrambled to kneel beside her. "Are you all right, Abby? Are you going to be okay?"

Abigail coughed convulsively and spat out water. She rolled over on her stomach and lay groaning, but Tom could tell by the amount of noise she was producing that she was actually okay. Eli came walking up out of the water and sat down beside Abigail. She turned over on her side, looking at him with an angry expression. Eli's steady gazed fixed on her face, waiting.

"Don't call me Abby again. Do you hear me, Tom Wade? Why did you wait till we're half-drowned before turning into a fish to save us, Eli? Why didn't you just take us across on your back in the first place?"

"I guess you're okay, Abigail," Tom said.

Eli turned his face towards the river. "When I was a little boy, I could pretend to be anything."

"What, two days ago?" Abigail laughed sarcastically.

Ignoring her, Eli continued, "Anything I wanted to be, suddenly that was what I was. But now it's all so different." Eli stopped, his face was thoughtful. "Now, I find myself a lion, a dolphin, a pegasus with wings, not because I wanted to be, but just because I am that thing. I can't will it, it's just me."

Tom stood up and patted Eli on the back. "It's just as well for us that you were a dolphin. Come on, we need to get dry and move on."

The drying process took a while. No one had an extra change of clothing. So they built a large fire and took off what they could to dry in its heat. To get themselves dry, they moved close to the fire. Tom was better off than the others. He was dry inside his armour. He stepped close to the fire for only a few minutes to let the outside of his armour dry. He moved back to give his friends more space. He watched them as they struggled with their wet gear and hoped they didn't notice how much easier it was for him. The disgusted look that Abigail threw him showed she, at least, was aware.

Eli went back to the river, returning with fish for frying again. No one asked him what he became to get this food, they just all ate hungrily and gratefully. When they were full, they were also all dry. They dressed themselves in starchy clothing, reeking of smoke. And the journey began yet again. This time they were walking slowly and carefully up Biting Ridge.

It was a quiet company of travellers. Abigail made a few noises. She let out an occasional huff, or muttered lightly under her breath about stinking of smoke. But everyone, including Abigail, was watchful and alert. This was the sort of place evil could lurk. No grass was growing on the ridge. The only plant life was thorny bushes that gouged and scratched at legs as the travellers walked. The path was narrow, and inclined steeply so that each step became more dangerous than the last. It did not take long for the cliff edge to become high enough that the drop would kill anyone that fell. The other side of the path was lined by sharp grey rocks that jutted out. Passing by the sharp rocks forced them to go precariously close to the steep edge. There were also caverns big and small along the way. They seemed perfect hideaways for evil creatures.

Tom led the way, his sword extended. The others walked closely behind him, jumping at every sound. It was not a long walk up the ridge, but they were tense and frightened the entire journey.

When they reached the top of Biting Ridge, they ran across the flat plateau to get away from the journey they had just made. An exhausted, pale Tom threw himself on the ground to rest.

"I can't believe it. I thought for sure we would be attacked out of one of those caverns, but nothing. Nothing at all," Tom huffed and puffed loudly as he spoke, not from the run, but from the fright. "I was ready for anything that came at us, but nothing came." Tom lay with his face upturned towards the sky, so exhausted.

"Have you lost your gourd, Tom? You sound disappointed. You're daft, that's what you are." Abigail was lying beside him.

Tom couldn't explain the feeling. He'd been so prepared, so ready. His body couldn't have been tenser. If some creature, claws and fangs bared, had thrust itself upon Tom, he could have fought it for hours. At the end of such a battle, he would be no more exhausted than he was now. The fear was enough.

Eli leaned over to Tom. "I think that there's more than one way the Vile Enemy can attack us, Peregrine Sol." Tom sat upright at the word attack.

"I think," continued Eli, "the Vile One can use our own fear against us." Tom leaned back, closing his eyes. There was no way he was going to let himself sleep, even though his body was aching with weariness.

Chapter Sixteen

Eddi ran across Tom's chest and then up on his shoulders. Tom sat up. "Oi, be careful would you?" Eddi bellowed into Tom's ear. Then poor Eddi ducked, as Tom groggily raked his fingers through his hair.

"Sorry, Eddi," Tom muttered. "I can't believe I fell asleep when Amos needs us."

The thought of the young knight in the hands of the Vile One made him ill. He looked out in the distance. The plain was dotted with rock and stones. He wanted to move on and see what was out there.

Distances on the flat terrain were deceptive. It seemed to take forever to reach even the first huge stone. There were more in the distance, even larger. He could also see crumbling formations of brick.

His energy was depleted. The endless walking and worrying were getting to be too much. He stayed in front of the others, watching the sky, and turning frequently to look around in case something moved in the distance.

Eli hurried forward to walk beside Tom. "Are you okay, Peregrine Sol?"

"I feel like the Vile One is watching for us."

"But he doesn't even know of our quest, does he?" Eli asked.

"Surely news of our travels has gone out. Cimber thought there were spies in the forest."

Eli spoke softly, "I don't think the Vile One would expect us. A few weak creatures to rescue Amos, the son Sir Gwain? No. He's watching for the surrender of the knights. If he thought there would be an attack, I'm sure he would expect an army. That's our advantage and your fear is our weakness. Can you let it go?"

Tom didn't answer. Having Eli walk beside him didn't rid him of his fear but it was a comfort. The sun was coming up, filling the plain with warmth and light. He took a swig from his water bottle, reckoning it would soon be hot.

The formations of rock and brick grew larger and larger. They were fascinating and Tom's fears dropped away as he became absorbed in figuring out what they were. He quickened his pace and started chatting with his companions. "Wow, there must have been a village here once."

Crumbly, brown bricks and yellowed stone lay all around. Remains of a rock wall jutted up here and there, rising to various heights. At one particularly high point, there was an arch-shaped hole.

"My mother would love this," he said, turning around and around inside the ruin. "She just loves old stuff and all of this, here, in another world. Wow, she would go mad."

Eli lifted himself up onto a crumbly bit of wall. Abigail held out her hand and Eddi clambered onto the wall too. Abigail then hoisted herself up beside the other two and the three companions watched as Tom wandered around the ruin. Eli smiled as Tom became more and more relaxed.

"Do you know anything about this place?" Tom asked out loud, but to no one in particular.

Eddi answered, "They say, Peregrine Sol, the people who lived here were not of our kind."

"What do you mean 'not of our kind? You mean they weren't little people?" Tom asked.

"I mean not descended from those who came with the Parents from Ha`ehad."

Tom stared at Eddi amazed, "You mean these ruins are…" Tom struggled to find the word, "from prehistoric times."

Eli laughed, "Pre-historic. That's a funny word. I think the people were in history, just not our history."

Tom smiled, and said, "On my earth, we call something prehistoric when it happened before things were written down."

"Oh," Eli said thoughtfully. "Then these are not prehistoric, Tom, for I think it has been written about." He turned to look at Eddi who was humming. "Do you know something written about these walls?"

Eddi smiled. "Only a song and I don't sing well, but it goes something like this." He began to sing. He'd lied. Eddi sang beautifully.

I've been to heaven this very night,
for I've walked the garden path of sheer delight.

Bellus, oh Bellus, a place to be.
Sights of beauty and as fragrant as the sea,
Flowers mingle, their colours so grand,
Paths weave a trail through all this fair land.

I've been to heaven this very night,
for I've walked the garden path of sheer delight,

A people so gentle who planted this land,
Never caring for war or defending their bands.
They tended and mended and gardened and grew,

loving the land where the wild birds flew.

I've been to heaven this very night,
for I've walked the garden path of sheer delight,

They're gone now, these people we never knew,
who tended the land where as children we grew.
Some evil took them far from the place,
where their handiwork lingers, giving voice to their face.

I've been to heaven this very night,
for I've walked the garden path of sheer delight,

The garden they tended is the land that we love,
It is moulded and fashioned to fit like a glove.
Our people live in its plains, hills and trees,
Its valleys and mountains and rivers all please.

I've been to heaven this very night,
for I've walked the garden path of sheer delight,

When day is finished, my work is complete,
And I rest in the place where they used to meet.
I try to remember that others long gone,
Who once called this land, their lovely home.

Eddi looked embarrassed as the others clapped for him.

"So what happened to them?" asked Abigail.

Eli smiled at her. "I don't know. There are fragments left that the Wise Ones study, trying to learn about them. All I know, and I'm sure others know more, is some great evil came upon them and they had to leave the land we now call Adamah. It seems rather sad, especially since our ancestors came here so we could have peace. They must have left many years before our people came to Adamah."

"Mmm," Eddi said. "My dad liked to use the story to remind me to be grateful when I was tiny lad. 'We could lose all we have," he would say, 'like the First Ones'."

"The First Ones, is that what you call them?" Tom asked.

"My people call them the Clayans," said Eli, "because they tended the dirt from which they came."

"What do you mean by that?" demanded Abigail.

"I don't know, really," replied Eli. "I know Wise Ones come from Hokmah to dig deep in the earth to find out more about the people who lived here. It seems the more we know about the Clayans, the more we know about Adamah."

"You mean they do archaeological digs here in Adamah." Tom said, starting to laugh. "That's what my mum does. She goes on all these digs. It would blow her mind if she knew there was a whole other world where they did the same thing." He stood there, looking around and then said, "and if she knew I was standing here in a whole other world, she'd probably go ballistic." He climbed up to the arch, pulling himself up on the jagged bits of rock sticking out.

"Watch out, that may just fall apart under your feet, you idiot," Abigail yelled.

When he reached the arched window, he hung on to the ledge and looked out across the desolate plain. "Well," said he thoughtfully "I can't see this ever being the garden in your song, Eddi." As far as he could see, the land was just flat and dry. Tom reached down and to give a hand up to Abigail who, despite calling him an idiot for doing it, couldn't resist climbing up herself.

"This reminds me a bit of a primary school trip to Bury St Edmond," she said, looking out at the ruins.

"Doesn't look like a garden though, hey?" Tom asked.

Eddi scrambled up to the arch to sit by Tom too. He put his hand up to shield his eyes from the sun and said, "This is the dwelling. Adamah is the garden."

"What do mean?" Tom asked.

"Get out your map, Peregrine Sol," Eli said.

Tom jumped down from the wall and moved aside to let Abigail do the same, Eddi held in her hand. Then, he pulled out his map and spread it out on the flat dirt, smoothing it with his hand. He took out a tiny bit of his remaining food, a small chunk of bread and a thin slice of cheese. The others did the same and they all nibbled their dry bread as they looked at the map.

"This map only shows a small part of Adamah, but look here and here," said Eli pointing at the map. "And there and there, can you see it?"

The longer Tom looked, the more he could see it. There were avenues of trees, woodlands, and flat grasslands bordered by flower gardens. Each place on the map, some of them places Tom knew already, formed a pattern like a plan that a gardener would make when planning a proper garden. Even the streams seemed planned.

"It is strange isn't it, Peregrine Sol. My father told me when the Parents found Adamah, a place they could bring those who had survived the war in their world, every kind of creature found a place perfectly suited to it's kind," Eddi said.

Eli smiled at Eddi, "Like the lawn and trees of Erets fit for the playing of hundreds of little Changelings."

"Yes," replied Eddi, "and Bumi, my land with miniature plants as well as the big, that made my people happy."

A short pause was broken by when both Eli and Eddi said the word, "Rufus." They looked at each other and laughed.

"What is it?" Abigail asked. She and Tom joined in laughing, though they didn't know why.

Eddi smiled as he spoke. "The Rufus people live in the land we call Edom. A land where all the plants, earth and even the rocks are red."

"Red?"

"Red or at tinged with red. Even the sun glows red there," Eddi said.

 "Why would that land fit them?" Abigail asked.

"They are red creatures."

Tom rolled up his map. "That's amazing. So I guess the First People made Adamah for these people?"

Eli answered slowly, "I don't know. No one ever says the Clayans designed the land for us. Just that it was their garden and it fitted us. I do wonder about that though."

Tom leaned back to rest, making sure he was in the shade to protect himself from the hot sun. The companions were all quiet. The weariness from their journey seemed to settle on them as they rested.

Tom heard Abigail's breathing turn deep with sleep. Eddi too, breathed deeply, then a whistle came from his nose and then he started snoring. Tom snickered, and Eli laughed softly. Tom whispered, "I can't believe such a little body can make that much noise."

Tom lay still, but sleep would not come. He was aware that Eli wasn't resting either. Eli said, "You know even the land beyond the Enchanted Hedge was once a homeland of our people."

"Of the Changelings?"

"No, not of *my* people. It was called Roweh Goy, homeland of the Roweh people. It was taken by the Vile One. He tried to advance further, but the Knights stopped him."

"What happened to the people who lived there?" Tom whispered, hardly wanting to know the answer.

"Most of them escaped. They lost only a few because they are shepherds."

"Shepherds? Do they have sheep?"

Eli hummed to himself again, "No, they are carers, always looking after others. Only their royalty were taken or killed by the Vile One. Roweh rule by caring. Upper people look after those below them, who care for those below and so forth."

"Care for them, like being in charge?" Tom asked

"No, more like serving."

"Hah, that's the opposite of where I come from. Where I come from, the higher up a person gets, the less they care for others. So where are they now? Did they get a new land?"

"They are scattered, living here and there. Wherever they live, they are honoured for their caring ways. Some are wizards, living in Hokmah so they can tend to the needs of everyone."

"Have I met one?" queried Tom. "What do they look like?"

"They are our height, with intense eyes and curly hair."

"Oh, like Libiri, the Wizard who keeps the Books of Prophecy in Hokmah."

"Yes, he is a Roweh."

Tom was trying to think who else he knew that met the description when he suddenly remembered another question he'd wanted to ask Eli, if they were ever alone. "Eli, do you know anything about Amos?"

Eli made that little humming noise he now seemed to make when he was thinking. Tom smiled to himself, maybe Eli was part cat.

"I only know little things about him, Peregrine Sol. Now I wish I listened more when I was in Erets, but then I was just little." Eli's voice took on that wistful tone, remembering what he had given up.

Eli sighed and continued, "But we used to like to pretend to be Sir Gwain and his son when we played, so we did ask our Nannies about him. I also asked some questions of my healer in Hokmah." Eli looked sideways and grinned at Tom. "Galenic knew a good bit about our Amos. I think…" Eli's grin broadened. "I think she fancies him a bit."

Tom smiled. "So what did she tell you?"

"She said he is brave, but gentle of heart. She doesn't think he should be a knight at all. Of course she is a healer, and they do not care for things of war. That may be the only reason she feels that way."

Tom and Eli were quite for a while but the slumbering breaths of their two companions still did not lull them to sleep.

"I remember something else, Tom."

"What?"

"I remember that Amos carries a strange shield. He must have dropped it before we saw him from The All Seeing Hill."

"What kind of shield?"

"The shield is like all that are given in the Armatura, made of the same strong magical materials as yours. But Galenic said that when Amos emerged, all the wizards, even Sanyassi and Lingua, were waiting anxiously and hoping that Amos would emerge with a shield marked the same as his father's. For that would show that he was heir to Sir Gwain and the future leader of all the knights."

"And it didn't?" Tom asked. "What does Sir Gwain's shield look like?"

"Sir Gwain's shield is same as that of his father's and grandfather's. The symbols of every order of knights is crested upon it."

"And what about Amos' shield?"

"A white dove, sitting on a vine, with grapes in its mouth. Isn't that an odd symbol for a Knight?"

"A dove sometimes means peace where I come from, does it mean that here?"

"I don't know, but Galenic said that the vine branch and leaves mean healing."

"So what did they do?"

"Nothing. Amos went back to his father and helped him as he had done since he was a little boy. They are very close Sir Gwain and Amos. Amos' mother died after she was brought back from the lands of the Vile One. Father and son became nearly inseparable. Everyone thought the Armatura was starting a new Order of Knights with Amos, but no others received the symbol after him. So, many years have passed, and as the young came through, they were given a symbol on their shield to match an Order already established. None have ever received the symbol of Amos. That is until you, which was different again. No symbol at all. Galenic says that is even odder than what happened to Amos."

Tom touched the shield that lay beside him. It was hard under his hand, but not cold, warm as always, soothing for a weapon. Tom closed his eyes, he could feel sleep at last taking him.

He woke to the whispering voices of his companions and sat up. They all looked rested. The sun was high in the sky and Abigail was digging through her backpack. She smiled at Tom and said, "Good morning to you or afternoon more like. We're all just getting bits and pieces out of our bags to see if we can get enough to eat. I'm starving."

Tom joined the hunt for food, and they all gathered their bits together. There was very little left, so they took only a mouthful each. They still had a little water, which was just as well as they needed it to wash away the stale taste from their mouths after eating.

Abigail curled her upper lip at Tom and said, "Well the food gets just as bad here as it does in our world after a while."

Tom laughed in agreement and then began gathering up his things to lead the group once again. They walked for few hours before slowing. It should have been easy to travel over this flat land, but some inner heaviness made them drag their feet.

They walked till the sun was completely gone before stopping. Then they ate the few remaining bits of food and slept restlessly till the sun broke the sky at dawn. They rose, sipped a little water, no one even tried to find food, and began to walk again. The walking was harder than ever, though the land continued flat. Hunger was now a great enemy.All Tom could think about was eating, but he said nothing, hoping that by keeping his mouth shut, the others would not think of food. Or lack of food really.

The journey continued, the view never changing, and though they walked they hardly seemed to move forward. "Look at something in the distance," Tom said. "Seeing something grow a little bit bigger helps me see I'm moving." He took a swig of water and his eyes met Eli's and Abigail's. "My water is getting low, how about you?" They nodded their heads wearily in answer. Hunger was

soon going to be accompanied by thirst.

Eddi was the first to complain. "Oh, I have to have something to eat." He

rubbed his stomach vigorously as he spoke.

Tom said as cheerfully as he could, "Well, Eddi, you are just going to have

to wait till we come upon a spring or a pond again. Then maybe Eli will turn

into a shark and fetch you some fish to eat."

Tom's eyes met Eli's. Eli had studied the map and he knew as well as Tom

that there was no pond, no spring, not even a tiny stream in this desolate place.

"Come on then, be staunch, Eddi. Tell us a legend of your people to help

everyone keep their minds off their hunger," Eli said.

Eddi settled against Abigail's hair and began to chant.

In the county, where the normal folk live,
A man came a-walking, who was way too big.
His head was a boulder, made of solid rock,
His voice was leaden, and his words very thick.

The ground beneath him made a trembling noise,
The trees were a-quiver and the waters all rose.
The Luporchan mothers with their little babes,
All a started screaming, at the noise he made.

The gentlemen hid behind tall trees,
Watching the big man as long as they pleased.
He lumbered along, with his hands in pockets,
Toying with something, making a racket.

Suddenly they realised, it was tinkling of gold,
Carrying it in his pocket was awfully bold.
This was a chance and they needed a plan
A swig of the gin was taken by each man.

"Can you imagine-the size of that gold?
And how many pieces that big man could hold?

It would be quiet a job, but it could all be ours,
If we put our minds to it and work really hard."

They formed up a plan, that made the normal folk big,
And brought down that giant, who landed on his head.
They tied up the big man, staking him to the ground,
And took from his pocket, all the gold that they found.

When the giant yelled, "Why you little thieves.
The Luporchans chanted "It's a toll if you please.
You've stamped through our land, making babies cry,
Bringing down trees, with your giant stride,

This is the pay for the trouble you caused,
You should be please it's your life that is not lost.
Remember to walk with a gentle stride,
'Cause thumping through here is going to cost.

The giant man roared, his rage was so great,
The stakes started loosening, the ties begun to break.
The Luporchan people, all ran to hide
The giant never found them, though he tried very hard.

That's how it is, as all people know,
Size doesn't matter when it comes to blows,
The Luporchan people though not very big,
Outwit all the rest; it's just the way it is.

They laughed, and clapped for Eddi. He stood on Abigail's shoulder and

took a bow.

"We have a few stories like that in our world too, Eddi," Tom said. "But in

ours the little people don't always come out looking so smart."

Eddi sat up eagerly. "Are my people in your world, Peregrine Sol?"

Tom shook his head no. "It's just stories. But they do talk about big people

looking for gold, trying to catch the little people who have it."

"Ours are all almost always about my people out-foxing big people. And

quite often it is gold we take from the big ones." Eddi laughed.

"It's funny, you know," Abigail piped in, "because we have a really old myth about a normal man wandering into the land of little people and being staked to the ground to by them."

"Normal people?" Eddi roared in her ear, "We're the normal ones, it's you lot who are the odd people, so large and clumsy." Eddi wriggled on Abigial's shoulder, huffing and puffing.

"Yeah right," Abigail said, preparing to argue.

Eli smiled thoughtfully, then said, "Really, neither of you are normal."

Before anyone could say anything else, Eddi ended the argument by saying. "I'm still hungry." At that his stomach rumbled loudly.

Everyone stopped in their tracks, looking at him. Abigail stood rubbing her ear. "Was that really your stomach? Good lord, how could that noise come from such a little person? Man, it hurt my ear."

Tom and Eli howled with laughter and the girl and little man who had been glaring at each other, burst out laughing as well. Then Eddi's stomach let out another roar. Again the four laughed long and loud.

They kept up the journey for a few more hours, continuing to find Eddi's stomach pains amusing. Soon that humour disappeared. The poor man's pain grew more ferocious with every rumble. He was looking weary and ill, lying on Eli's shoulder. It was more worrying when the noises stopped. His body had lost so much strength that it couldn't complain.

Tom," Eli called. Tom looked back. Abigail's face was weary, Eli's worried and Eddi was a barely noticeable lump on a shoulder. Tom halted.

"I'm worried about Eddi. He's so little. I think if he doesn't get food, he might…"

"Look, there in the distance. There are more ruins. The walls look high enough to protect us from this sun. Let's get there and we can dig in our packs again. Surely even crumbs can help Eddi."

Tom hoped he was right. He'd always been amazed at the amount the little chap ate. But surely, any little bit could help him.

The thought served to spur the travelers on. When they finally reached the wall, they threw themselves down on the ground in the shade and searched desperately through their bags, finding what few bits they could. Poor Eddi was too weak to chew, so they wetted the crumbs with a bit of their water and dribbled them into his mouth. Colour came back to his face, but he was still very weak.

"I'm sorry. I've been no help, only a hindrance." Then Eddi closed his eyes and slept.

Eli took a very small sip from his flask.

Tom was looking at the map. "Look," he said with excitement. "We're almost to the edge of this plain. I can tell because the ruins are getting closer and closer together just like it shows on the map. That's great. We'll soon be at the Enchanted Hedge. We just have to hang on until then."

Eli leaned over and looked at the map. "But Tom, what good does it do for us to reach this place if we have no food. If we go into Sheol with no food, we'll be in trouble. In a day or two we will all be like Eddi. I doubt we can get food once we pass the boundaries of that land because all things are foul in Sheol."

"What's it like, this Sheol?" asked Abigail.

"It was once beautiful place, but now, it is said, it's as vile and foul as he. We can't eat food there, nor do I think we should drink the water."

Tom put his head down. "You're right again, of course, Eli. We'll be useless there if we are starving."

Tom's stomach knotted up, hunger hurting it less than worry. He leaned back against the stone wall and closed his eyes. Abigail and Eli were quiet too.

Abigail broke the silence, "You read all those space travel books back on Earth didn't you, Tom? You should have been reading survival books instead.

Chapter Seventeen

A loud moan woke the travellers. Tom, Eli and Abigail scrambled to their feet in fright. It was poor Eddi, in terrible pain. His breathing was shallow. Tom was afraid the little man was dying.

"Oh, oh, oh. Why didn't I remember, why didn't I think about it," Abigail suddenly cried out.

"Abigail, stop yelling," Tom said. "Can't you see that Eddi is dying?"

Abigail dropped to the ground and started pulling things out of her backpack. "It's in here. Oh, it's in here."

"What in the name of Adamah is wrong with you?" Eli asked, exasperation showing in the voice of the normally calm Changeling.

"You weren't the only one given a gift in the Armatura, you know."

Tom remembered and dropped to his knees to help pull stuff out of Abigail's bag.

"I only wished I remembered it sooner." Abgail whispered. Then she yelled, "There," as she held up a cut-crystal bottle full of orange liquid. "Remember Eli, the Armatura gave me this bottle with…I don't know what they called it, but it's supposed to work for food."

"I wonder if it will workfor poor Eddi, as he is now?" Tom said sadly.

"Well it is not my fault I…I just didn't remember." Abagai wiped a tear away.

"I wasn't trying to blame you…"

"It sounded like it, you…."

"Abigail and Tom, while you are arguing our little friend is dying," Eli said. "Why don't you try it first, Abigail, though I'm sure anything that was given in Hokmah will indeed work."

Abigail pulled the stopper out of her pretty, little bottle and let a drop fall on her tongue. She swallowed and said, "Sanyassi said only a drop would fill… Oh wow. That felt weird. It definitely works."

She turned and knelt beside Eddi. His mouth was already open, gasping for air. Abigail carefully tipped the bottle allowing one little drop to fall into the Luporchan's mouth. The orange drop bubbled up over his tiny mouth, lingering there, bobbling slightly like gelatine. Was he too far gone to swallow? The three companions held their breath.

The drop wiggled. It swirled round like water going down the drain-hole of a sink and slid down Eddi's throat. Still the three friends did not move, they watched their little friend closely. The tiny man just lay there. Abigail looked up, tears in her eyes, "If only I'd remembered sooner." Eddi's eyes flew open and he sat up. "Can I have some more?"

Abigail laughed and cried at the same time. "How can you possibly want more, a drop filled me completely up? I couldn't eat anything else right now."

But the little man opened his mouth wide. Abigail poured another little drop into Eddi's mouth. It lay there, shimmering for just a moment, then wiggling and gleaming, it slid down his throat. Eddi let out a huge burp. The three friends laughed hesitantly.

"I feel better," Eddi said.

Abigail lifted the tiny man up in her hand and held him close to her face. It was as close as she could come to giving him a hug. She arched an eyebrow at Tom, daring him to say something about her small act of tenderness. Tom grinned but said nothing. It wasn't worth the risk of bringing out her claws.

Tom sat down with a thump, putting his head between his knees. The others just stared at him, worried he was crying. He lifted his head and grinned again. "I can't believe it." He said, shaking his head. "What a bunch of losers we are."

Eli and Tom each took a drop from Abigail's cut-crystal phial. Tom let the drop linger on his tongue. It didn't taste great, but it also wasn't foul. It shimmered in his mouth and down his throat as if alive, swelling, filling his whole body, not only with the sense of being full, but of being healthy and well. He felt completely refreshed. No wonder Eddi had wanted more.

"Can I have another wee drop?" Eddi asked hopefully.

"Eddi," Abigail said, with a cheerful exasperation in her voice. She held up the bottle. The five missing drops had left their mark.

"Go ahead and give him another," Tom said to Abigail. "But Eddi," Tom turned a serious face to the Luporchan, "this is because you have been so poorly. We can't afford to waste this cordial. We have no idea how long our quest will continue. So please, from now on, only take some when you are really in need."

The little Luporchan looked shame faced, but opened his mouth anyway. It was fascinating the way the liquid lingered on his little mouth, shimmering and glistening then rushing down.

Eddi smiled at them and said, "I think I'll rest a bit more now." Eli covered him with a small bit of cloth Abigail handed him from her pack.

Abigail came and sat by Tom, "Where's your map?" she queried. Tom pulled the map out looking at her. This was the first interest she'd shown.

"Okay, so there's the Enchanted hedge, right?" she asked, pointing at the thorny symbol. "So where do you think we are now?"

Tom showed her on the map. "You see we're at the beginning of this area. From here on the bits of wall become closer and closer together. You look too, Eli. When we reach here, this last bit of wall is just a short way from the hedge. I guess from there we will have to figure a way through the hedge and then we are truly in dangerous country."

Eli shivered. "I never thought I would ever go past the Enchanted Hedge."

"Do you know anything about it, Eli? How are we supposed to get over the blasted thing?"

Eli said, "I think everyone in Adamah knows about the Enchanted Hedge. It's our protection." Eli made that little humming sound, almost like a gentle neigh, then spoke again. "When the Vile One came to Adamah, it was in Roweh Goy that he first appeared. He brought with him an army, what they were, I'm not sure. I think they were humans, like you. You call yourselves human, is that right? As though you are the only ones?"

"Yes," Abigail stated, "We're human."

Tom looked at her and said, "But I know what he is saying Abby. Now that I've come here I realise that I don't really understand what a *human* is at all.

Isn't Eli a human? Or Eddi? Or Sanyassi? Even Cimber, Brutus and poor little

Pan seem human too, don't they?"

Abigail nodded. Everyone was thoughtful for a few moments at the

mention of the little fawn's name. Then Eli began again.

"Those creatures in the Vile One's army are vicious and cruel. Their teeth

drip with blood. If they cannot get the blood and flesh of other creatures, then

they attack one another. There is always war in Sheol, even when they are not

attacking Adamah. When they are not warring with us, then they war against

each other."

Tom looked at Abigail, "They do sound a bit like our kind."

Abigail looked at Tom, wrinkling her nose, "My teeth certainly don't drip

with blood, I don't know about you. You say Sheol was Roweh Goy?"

"When the Vile One came to Roweh Goy, he killed and drove out the

people. I've already told Tom much of this. But it wasn't just the people he

maimed or killed, it was the land too." Eli shivered again. "Why would you

torture the land that nurtures you? I cannot understand it. Now the land there is

sick and twisted, the same as the living beings that he has taken, the same as

Arovoit whom he stole and Theodora who went to him of her own accord."

Abigail listened intently, as did Tom. But she was not getting her question

answered soon enough and interrupted. "But you still haven't said…"

Eli ignored her and said, "The land was no longer the home of the Roweh,

so it could not be Roweh Goy any longer. In fact, the land was so changed, made so horrible that it is really no longer Adamah. It is different. Other. It's

Sheol, the homeland of Evil."

Eli went quiet. In the distance, a bird cried out, as if saddened by Eli's

story.

"And the hedge?" Tom asked softly, reminding the Changeling why he had

begun this sad story.

"The Enchanted Hedge came many years after the Vile One first took the

land of the Roweh. First, the Knights of Adamah arrived. They were our first

defenders, our first protection. They came bearing the standard of the red lion.

That order is the oldest of all the knights in Adamah. Sir Gwain served in that

order until he became the Leader. Those first knights were all like you." Eli

paused and did the soft neigh.

"I do not know where they come from, but I know they were not

descendants of the Parents of Adamah. When they came, they fought many

fierce battles, holding the Vile One's armies back from taking more of our land.

It is said they defended Adamah because they felt responsible for the evil

unleashed on our world. The Vile One is the offspring of the evil of their world.

But the Knights could not be everywhere, and the enemy often attacked

Adamah. The enemy made many forays into Adamah and were able to harm the

people and land."

Eli was quiet yet again. Eddi was snoring, though only gently. A flock of

birds passed by high overhead. Tom and the others shuffled back further under

the protection of the high wall.

Then Eli continued, "Helena, of the land of Roweh Goy, whose hair was the colour of dripping honey and on whose brow the fragrance of flowers rested, planted the hedge. No one knew, then, that it was enchanted. She dropped the seed along the border, where the blood of many young knights had been spilled defending Adamah. Overnight, the hedge took root and began to grow, a thorny ugly thing.

At first, the people cried out with anger against Helena, for the hedge kept our warriors from making inroads into the enemy land and the thorns could not keep out the thick-skinned creatures of Sheol. Then the season changed and the Shoshanna buds came, and blossomed, the sweet fragrance lingered in the air for miles all around. The foul creatures of that deranged land would not come near to the hedge then. The sweet enchantment was too strong for those vile beings. It kept them far back in their lands and so Adamah experienced peace for the first time in many long years. Adamah had not experienced such peace since the Vile One first came to our world.

Then the people realised that even during the season of thorns, the Enchanted Hedge protected the land. The forays into our land were fewer and the knights could patrol the border to keep the enemy at bay. But Helena died before her great deed was fully known. Now in Adamah we sing her praise.

Helena so fair and sweet,
your noble deed lingers on.
The peoples' anger was replaced
with honour, praise and glory.

The seed you planted long ago

has bloomed across the land,
it fragrance lovely fills the air,
with peace, repose and calm.

And when we see the fragrant blossoms bloom,
our honour also grows
And we wish that Helena could know,
Our love to her bestowed.

Eli smiled at his companions. "And so it has been since those days long ago. Every season, the Enchanted Hedge blossoms with the beautiful and fragrant Shoshanna flowers and peace comes to Adamah. All the knights return to their homelands, enjoying their families and resting. It is a wonderful time in our world. A time of celebration. It will soon be the season again, but not quite yet."

"Well that's fine and all," Abigail said. "But it doesn't sound like we are going to be able to cross the hedge."

Eli looked at Abigail thoughtfully. "Helena of the Roweh did right when she planted the hedge that kept them away but also didn't let us go there. We do not wish to foray into the land of Sheol, even though the land belonged to one of our peoples. We are not the kind who would go in and kill to take it back. We only wish to be left in peace. But we will defend our land. So we did not need a hedge that allowed us to attack them."

"Yet," continued Eli slowly. "The hedge has been breached from our side before. Not often. I only know of two times. Once when Theodora went to the Vile One of her own accord, to become the handmaiden of Evil." Eli shuddered.

"Why would any woman in her right mind do's something as daft as that?" Abigail asked, shaking her head.

Eli made that little purring neigh again and said, "Theodora the High, always wishing to be higher than she was born. Made the choice for evil, it's a rare choice in Adamah."

"And the other time?" questioned Tom.

"One other time that I know. It was when the Knights of Adamah found the way in and attacked Sheol to rescue Maree, mother of Amos."

Tom stared at Eli, "So it can be done."

"So it can be done," his Ach echoed.

"How? That's what I want to know," said Abigail.

"That I don't know," replied the Changeling sadly.

"At least, we know it can be done," said Tom in a determined voice. He smoothed out the map that had become crumpled when they'd moved further against the wall. He studied it, his neck and shoulders hunched over. "Look," he finally said. "If we could make it a little further before nightfall then we could rest here and only be few feet away from the Enchanted Hedge." He looked in his friends' worried eyes. "If we get there, then we can face getting through that stinking hedge in the morning after a night's rest."

"Oh you misunderstood me, Peregrine Sol. It does not stink. It smells wonderful, sweet and pure."

Tom grinned at Abigail who rolled her eyes.

They woke Eddi, who stretched his arms and legs and yawned widely, but was looking much like his old self. "Peregrine Sol, do you think…"

"Only if you really need some Eddi," Tom said somewhat sternly. "If you can wait, please do."

The little Luporchan sighed loudly, "Okay, I think I can wait."

As they set out, the sun was going down and the heat was less intense. Tom felt a certain confidence. They had come through many dangers now, and had more than survived them. He began to whistle. They walked well, taking long hard steps, moving at a solid pace.

But once again it did not take long for the journey to feel tiring. It seemed endless. Tom put his mind to figuring out how they would cross the hedge and rescue Amos. That made it all the worse, as he had no idea how to breach the hedge. He didn't even know what they were facing if they could get across to the other side. How could he form any plan?

"Peregrine Sol, are you listening?"

Tom looked up. Eli was speaking to him. "Sorry Eli, I was lost in my thoughts. What did you say?"

"Look up there. Do you see those large birds?"

Tom stood still, and looked up, then back at Eli. They'd seen birds flying over this plain ever since they first put their feet on it. It was one of the few changing scenes.

"I don't like the look of those," Eddi said. He stood up on Eli's shoulder, a look of terror on his face.

Tom looked up again. The birds had flown some distance and were now circling around.

"Run," yelled Tom. "Run for the wall."

The companions ran with all that was in them. Little Eddi clung to Eli's hair, screaming into the Changeling's ear. "Run Eli, run"

The three large friends hit the wall at high speed, flattening themselves against it. Eddi swung out on a lock of Eli's hair. Eli reached out his hand and pushed the tiny man back on his shoulder. All were breathing deep, quick breaths, even Eddi, for the fright was enough to steal breath away, even without the running.

The birds came, flying fast, to where the travellers were hiding. They circled overhead. Eddi gasped, rolling into a frightened ball on the Changeling's shoulder. The birds continued to circle, lowering as they came, till even Tom's eyes, much less sharp than those of the little Luporchan, could see the nasty creatures. They were undoubtedly the same half-human, half-vulture warriors that carried Eddi away and captured Amos. Tom could barely breathe, and from the corner of his eye, he saw Abigail holding a hand over her mouth.

The vultures swept low, squawking at one another. Then they lifted again, flying upwards, out and away towards the Torrent River.

"Do you think they were looking for us?" whispered Eddi.

Tom didn't know what to answer, for that was his fear.

"No, I don't," answered Eli. "But I do think we need to be very, very careful. Secrecy is our only advantage. We have no other."

"I don't know how you can be so sure, Eli," said Tom, looking at his Ach with furrowed eyebrows.

Eli made his thinking noise, before answering, "The Vile One has no courage. I don't think he understands courage and never expects it. He doesn't come out to battle with our Knights on his own. They never see him. Only his armies, his foul warriors, and his son, the Vile Prince, are ever seen. He would never think Adamah would send us, and that is our advantage."

Tom nodded his head. "Maybe you're right. I know you're right about one thing. We need to be very, very careful now. We are so close to the border of his land. What do you think those nasty creatures were doing then?"

Eli's soft brown eyes were deep, "I believe, Peregrine Sol, that while we try to find our way into the land of Sheol, those beasts are coming out of it and attacking the people of Adamah. These are new creatures of the Vile One. He has twisted more creatures for his pleasure and work. These Vultures can fly above the hedge and foray into Adamah. There must be terrible things happening in my land."

The travellers waited a few more minutes to make sure the way was clear, then they moved out slowly, keeping a watchful eye. This time they ran, a tip-toed run, keeping very low as they went. They rested at the crumbled remains of walls as they reached them, breathing deeply and saying little. Then they ran again. It was just as well the remains were now close together, for they ran as fast as they could, to the next hiding place, and rested there. Tension built. They kept going only because their exhaustion was outweighed by fear of detection.

Twice they saw flocks of those horrid vultures flying overhead. Soon the travellers were so weary that when they reached shelter, they fell on the dry, brittle earth, lying as still as possible. When they felt ready, they would get up, look around, and run again.

It was with great relief that they made their final run for the last bit of decaying wall. They could see the hedge in the distance, but it was to the stone and brick they scrambled, lying against it without talking, feeling they were safe for the moment.

Eddi broke the silence with a hesitant question. "Peregrine Sol, do you think that perhaps I might have a little drop from that wonderful bottle of Abigail's."

Tom said, "Oh Eddi, I think that would be fine. In fact, I think we all could use a drop."

The refreshing feeling resulting from a mere drop on the tongue from Abigail's bottle came over them and a sense of well-being and safety took hold. They leaned against the wall, the warmth from the sun still lingering in its stone, warmed them and they were silent.

Tom dozed, then awoke, tense and listening. It wasn't noise so much that woke him, but a trembling, rumbling along the ground. Night had fallen while he slept. The dark was broken only by a soft glow from the pale moon.

He felt Eli move, and Abigail lift her head. Eddi stood up, flattening himself against the wall. The rumbling grew more intense, shaking the ground beneath them. Then from around their boulder, to the left, and to the right, appeared masses of creatures, man-like, but not like any man Tom had ever seen, marching in a disorderly array. They spewed around the ruins behind which the frightened travellers huddled.

The horrific army was intent on their purpose and marched forward in hurrying, hard steps. Tom pushed himself up to a sitting position against the old wall, turning his head left then right, taking in what was happening around him. These were the same creatures Tom and Eli had seen from the top of The All Seeing Hill. It was the Vile One's foul army.

The Riders came next, whips in their hands. They were a different kind of creature than the foot soldiers. They were grey-faced and man-like with white hair shinning under their helmets. Cold grey eyes glistened in their hard faces. They whipped the foot soldiers, yelling at those under them with harsh words. "Move on, you mangy beasts, we have our Master's work to do." The soldiers ran harder as the rider's whips lashed out.

Line upon line of soldiers marched out of Sheol into the once peaceful land of Adamah, and all Tom and his company could do was watch.

More riders with whips followed the first to keep the troops marching. The foot soldiers weren't reluctant to go to war, they laughed and seemed anxious for the battle, but they were unfocused. It took the riders and their whips to keep the soldiers in order. If the riders fell back, even for a moment the soldiers turned their sharp claws and blood stained teeth upon each other. Abigail shivered as the army passed by, scratching and slashing at one another.

The last of the riders came riding through, pushing the troops onward. The rumbling and snarling sounds moved into the distance, until all that was left was the trembling ground which first woke the travellers.

Eddi swallowed back tears as he looked at the others. "War, they're going to war against Adamah, aren't they? It's been many years since they have managed to breach the hedge and be so bold."

"Our job is even more important, Eddi," Tom said. He looked around at his companions and continued, "We must keep our minds on our quest. That is the best we can do for Adamah. Our only hope is to break the curse upon the knights so they can fight for Adamah."

They all nodded, but Tom saw the fear in their faces that he felt himself. He scooted around and peered back at the hedge, hoping it was open. It wasn't. Whatever secret the Enemy had used to open the Enchanted Hedge and allow his army to enter Adamah was no longer working.

"We must take whatever rest we can tonight," Tom said. "Tomorrow we will enter that horrid land. At least we know that if they have crossed the hedge, we should be able to find a way to do so too."

Abigail shuffled her bags about and moved around trying to get comfortable. "At least there will be less of those horrible beasts in there for us to have to deal with," she stated.

"That's true. But that's a small comfort, Abigail," Eli said softly.

Tom curled up in a ball. He lay there, looking up at the stars and soft moon. It was a lovely evening. Cool, but not so much that he was uncomfortable with just his jacket pulled up over him. It was unbelievable to think that this beautiful world was in such terrible trouble. Tom thought of that horrible army marching on Adamah and the pain it would cause. He thought of all the people he had met on his journeys into this world, the innocent Changeling children, the little forest creatures, Galenic in her herb garden, the wise wizards of Hokmah, even the silly Nibelungs. He wanted them safe. They were more real to him and meant more to him than anything else he knew, even more than the people of his world. He would do anything he could do to keep them safe.

Chapter Eighteen

Boom. The sound of an explosion split the silence. Tom, who had been dozing off and on, woke and yelled, "Crack of Dawn," immediately feeling ridiculous. Eddi let out a whoop of fright and Abigail grabbed him and put her finger over his mouth.

The four companions sat stone-still, listening. Was another army about to be unleashed upon Adamah? Nothing happened. Tom cautiously moved to the edge of the stone wall. He peered around. A curl of smoke hurried skywards near the hedge. He leaned back in and looked at the others.

"Something's happened out there, but I'm not sure what." Tom leaned back out. The smoke was a mere wisp making its away quickly upwards. "Smoke," he whispered back to his friends.

Tom looked back around again, moving his body further and further forward. He was suddenly jerked backwards. Eli's brown hand was on his back, Abigail's furious face in front of his.

"What do you think you're doing, idiot?" she hissed at him.

Tom shrugged Eli's hand off and said, "There's nothing out there. Look, we've no choice, we've got to get moving and try to get across that hedge."

Eli peered round the wall this time, looking out for what felt like eternity, then he turned back to them and said, "I only see a bit of smoke. It looks safe."

Tom led the way, edging out slowly, looking both ways and even up to the sky. There was nothing to be seen. The others followed and slowly but surely, they moved towards the hedge. Then they ran to reach it. Once there, they sat down. Tom put his head in his hands saying, "I have no idea what to do now."

Suddenly, the hedge began to move and moan. The travellers leapt back with fright as the hedge shook even more violently.

"Ahhh," Abigail and Eddi were both screaming. They ran round about, finding nowhere to hide. Tom jumped, look around and then without thinking he too ran, straight back towards the wall. All Tom could see of Eli was the backside of a horse with wings, flying upwards.

Tom stopped, what was he doing? He was the leader. He looked back and saw Abigail with Eddi on her shoulder, standing stock-still staring at a small shape that was crawling out from under the hedge. Its colour was much the same as the brown of the earth. Was Abigail going to face whatever it was that was coming from Sheol on her own? Tom turned to run back to her, pulling his sword from its hilt as he ran. He stopped dead in his tracks. Eli flew back down again.

Standing before Abigail, holding a small bottle in his hands, was a dirty, little faun with a dirt-smudged face.

Abigail broke the shocked silence, "Pan?"

Pan ignored her and turned to look at Tom instead. "Well, Peregrine Sol, it's about time you arrived. There's been a lot happening here, you really needed to hurry it up a bit."

Fury hit Tom like a bat. "You, you, you….little goat," he yelled. Moving closer to the faun, he shouted, "Where have you been? We looked and looked for you. If we're the least bit delayed, it's because of you."

Tom never felt such anger, it consumed him and he was screaming by the end. He lifted his hand with every intention of belting Pan in the face. Then he felt a hand on his shoulder, and looked back. The deep blue of Eli's eyes stopped Tom's anger. Tom swallowed deeply. The fury suddenly replaced itself with the desire to cry. Both emotions were despicable to him.

Pan stepped back, his tail nearly in the prickles of the hedge. "I," he stated, with a haughty voice, "have been here waiting for you. I know my duty to this quest."

Tom's anger returned, but he controlled it. Abigail snorted. "What after leaving Tom to fight a beast alone?"

Pan turned his nose upward, "I know my place in this company and it's not to fight warriors. Tom was doing just fine on his own."

"How did you get here before us?" Tom asked, cooling his anger as best he could.

"I went up river to Surety Bridge."

"A bridge, a blooming bridge," Abigail yelled, first at Pan and then turned on Tom. "Why didn't we go up the river to a bridge, O great leader?"

Tom shook his head at her in amazement. "I didn't know about any bridge. And that little monkey, that goat…" Tom pointed at the faun, "he ran off. It's not exactly my fault."

"Peregrine Sol, that's the second time you have insulted me. I'm a faun not a monkey and I'm certainly not a goat. *Some* people, ignorant people to my mind, say that we have certain physical similarities to the species capra, commonly called goats. I, for one, have never seen it. I highly resent the reference to goat when referring to *me*."

"That's it with you, isn't it Pan? It's always about you. Everything is about you," Tom yelled at him.

"Well, I don't believe I ever could be accused of elevating *myself*. But I do know that my place in this quest is most important."

Tom let out a huff of anger.

Eli stepped forward, "This is getting us nowhere. We need to be thinking about how to get across that hedge, not fighting with Pan. Besides that, Peregrine Sol," Eli turned and looked at Tom, "aren't we really pleased that the little faun is safe?"

Tom took two hard breaths and then nodded his head. "I'm happy to see you, Pan, even though I'm angry too. I was afraid that you had been taken by one of those horrible beasts."

The little faun smiled knowingly, "No, I sensibly ran away and made my way here. And don't think it has been so easy for me. Yesterday was so scary. I shivered and hid under the hedge farther down there." Pan pointed down the hedge. "Great numbers of nasty looking creatures have been coming out of Sheol."

"Yes, we saw them too." Eli replied.

Pan walked back to the edge of the Enchanted Hedge and pulled out his small pot and spoon. "Fortunately, I didn't waste too much time while waiting for you. I was able to try a few more recipes for my wine." Pan looked down at his pot, and gave a gentle swish of the liquid in it. The others looked at the faun, too amazed by his cheek to even speak.

"You will be sorry to learn I've not been very successful. Two attempts along the way tasted very bad." Pan looked up at the four faces. He was expecting interest in his efforts. "And this last attempt was most disappointing. You might have heard the little pop it made when I accidentally spilled a bit as I took it from the fire this morning."

"That was you who nearly scared us to death?"

As Pan finished talking, he gave his concoction another little swirl and threw it over his shoulder. It hit the Enchanted Hedge with a watery splat and exploded with the sound of thunder.

"Look at that," Eddi yelled. The explosion had blown a hole in the hedge.

Tom was stuttering and stammering, "I can't believe..."

Pan was silent only for a moment. Then he burst into tears. Eli gasped, yelling out, "Tom, look the hedge is growing back." When Tom looked back, the hedge was, indeed, rapidly repairing itself.

"Quickly everyone, get your things and get through that hedge," Tom commanded. Abigail grabbed Eddi and her backpack before running through the gap. Eli stepped through just before she did. Tom was close behind, but Pan did not move. He still stood there wailing.

"Come on, Pan, move it."

Still the faun stood there, his bellowing continuing to escalate in pitch.

Tom looked at the hedge. "Pan, hurry, the hedge is closing."

"Just leave him, Tom, and come on yourself," Abigail shouted.

Tom could not leave Pan again. What if the faun really did have an important part to play in the quest? He ran back, grabbed the faun by the scruff of his neck and dragged him through the narrow gap. He tripped and fell on Pan. The hedge closed. They were in Sheol.

Tom was lying on top of the faun.

"I don't know why you even bothered with him," Abigail said. Tom sat up. The faun was still crying uncontrollably. Tom wiped oozing blood off his cheek. "He really might have a part to play in this quest, Abby."

At those words Pan's cry once again became a wail. "Ai. Ai. Ai," he yelled and started banging his head against his hands.

"Oh, stow it, you little git. For goodness sake, Tom nearly risked not getting through that hole to bring you in here. So shut up, now you can get on with whatever you think you're supposed to do."

Pan gulped, and with hiccoughing sobs, he spoke. "I've done it. I just did what I came to do." And with that the faun burst into tears again.

Tom felt a hysterical laugh well up in him. "That was it? You mean that blowing a hole in the hedge with your wine concoction was your great act for the quest."

"You could have left him on the other side after all," Abigail said.

Eli asked, "Are you sure, Pan? Maybe there is something else too. You never know."

"But I do know," sobbed Pan, lying on the ground, his voice muffled. "I told you from the beginning that part of my vision included the fact that I would know when my great deed was done. I knew from the moment the hedge burst open that this was my great deed, an accidental explosion of my wine." Pan lifted his head and howled loudly, then dropped it back down to sob on the ground.

Eli knelt down beside the little faun. "But it was a very important thing." The Changeling looked up at his friends, his eyes stern. "We had no idea how we were going to cross the Enchanted Hedge. Pan's part has been invaluable."

Tom did his best to swallow back his laughter. Pan sat up and brushed himself off. He got to his feet. His face was streaked with tear lines. His pointed chin and lips quivered. Then he burst out crying again. "They're going to make such fun of me in Simkah Forest when they find out that my part was with yet another (Pan let out a shuttering cry) bad wine mixture."

Tom bit his lip, hard, and said with a straight face, "No Pan, Eli's right, your part has been invaluable. We may not have been able to proceed any further if you hadn't exploded your wine mixture." Then Tom felt the humour of the situation welling up inside him again and he could see Abigail shaking with laughter too. Eli's stern look quietened him down again.

"Right then, we're in. Now what do we do?" Abigail asked, her voice still edged with laughter.

Tom looked up. "I have no idea. The map I was given by the Mapkeepers of Hokmah was blank past the Enchanted Hedge. Any suggestions?"

Pan was sitting on the ground again, still wiping away tears that ran down his dirty face, but no longer making any noise. Eli's back was turned to his companions. He was looking out over the land they had just entered. Eli made his thoughtful neigh, then chanted softly,

All paths lead down
All roads are rough
Into the darkness,
of pain and death.

In Sheol black,
the evil place,
where all the paths
lead to his vile face.

"Yep, that's said in my country too. All the roads of Sheol end at the dwelling of the Vile One." Eddi shivered.

Well then," said Abigail, taking a swig from her water bottle and wiping the back of her hand across her mouth. She started walking straight away from the hedge.

"Hey wait up, Abigail," Tom shouted.

Abigail stopped and looked behind her. "What's the matter? Am I taking your place, Oh Great Leader?"

"Cut it out, Abby," Tom replied. "I just want to walk beside you."

"Don't call me that."

Tom caught up with her and looked out at the distance. There was a dark line of trees. "I guess the landscape will change up there, hey?" he said.

Abigail nodded her head then turned to his look at him. "After that long flat journey, you'd think we'd be really glad to see some trees." She looked ahead at the black scraggly line on the horizon and finished, "Somehow those don't look so good."

Tom agreed. He glanced back at his Ach. Eli was no longer pulling Pan along but the little faun was still hanging back, his eyes red and his nose redder. Tom felt guilty for making fun of him and wanted to do something to cheer him up. He called out merrily, "Come on, Pan, let's see if Abigail will give us a break, since she seems to be the leader now."

Eli ran up to Tom. "Think where you are. We must stay quiet."

Tom swallowed. He hadn't given much thought about the fact they were now in the enemy territory. Coming in had been so much easier than he had anticipated.

The scraggly line of trees came closer and closer into their view. And soon they could see, as Abigail had anticipated, it was no pretty little wood.

Fear grew as they drew nearer. The trees on the forefront of the little woods were large and bent, thick black bark covered the trunk and branches. The trees stooped so low that in places the branches swept the dry parched land beneath them. Tom didn't feel like going under those menacing trees.

As they walked, a stench filled the air. It stung their noses and throats. And a cold, sharp wind cut through the forest stinging their faces. Every step made the companions want to turn back. But no one dared speak that desire.

The wind stopped as the travellers came into the trees, but the stench grew stronger. It was still cold, but now it was clammy, as though some rancid water seeped through the atmosphere. A tree brushed Tom's cheek. "Ouch, get off," he said, pushing the branch away from his face. There was a burn on his face where it had touched him.

The travellers were immediately even more cautious than before. The sense of hidden evil grew. The trunks of gnarled trees, cold grey boulders, and holes in the earth, seemed made to hide the enemy. Feelings of desperation seeped into Tom, he wanted out of this eerie wood. He strained his eyes, hoping to see a light in the distance to indicate an end to this place. But no light came. It grew darker as they walked deeper into the midst of the trees.

Soon they could barely see and were stumbling over twisted roots and scattered rocks. The noises in the forest were frightening in the dark. The scuffling of feet and sniffing sounds of unknown animals came close to them as they huddled together. The occasional flash of some pale luminous eyes darted away past in the shadows.

"Do you think even the woodland here animals will be evil?" Tom asked no one in particular.

Eddi spoke, "No, many are not. When the Vile One took Roweh Goy, there were many animals living here, in this wood, it was named Fair Forest. Sunlight filtered through the leaves of the trees and it was a magical shimmering place. The Vile One and his slaves destroyed the forest, but it was home to many who would not leave it for safer lands. They live here still."

"How do you know all this, Eddi?" Abigail asked.

"The burrowing animals meet in deep underground tunnels where hedges do not bar the way. These little creatures from one forest speak to those of another. So this news comes to the animals of Simkah Forest. The Wise Ones of Hokmah find out many things from animals. My people learn much from our close friends the squirrels. The moles tell the squirrels and the squirrels talk to us."

"I could have told you too," stated Pan haughtily, speaking for the first time since they left the hedge side.

Tom ignored Pan and said thoughtfully, "I'm glad to know, because there are a lot of things scurrying around out there and I would hate to think they might run and tell the Vile One we're coming."

Eddi spoke again slowly. "There are some of my kind living here."

"Really?"

"Yes, but they bring shame to my people."

"Why is that?" asked Tom, stumbling over another root. "Oh, let's take a break," he said, sitting down on the ground under a tree, being careful not to touch it.

The others also sat down close together, huddled for warmth and comfort. Tom said, "Now tell us, Eddi."

"The people who came to this forest were outcasts," Eddi said. He looked out into the shadows were dead leaves lay, and then he continued slowly, "A baby was born one spring, with golden hair and wings. As you know, my people all have skin and hair of brown, and we certainly have no wings. Pixies have wings, but not Luporchans. She was not normal, this baby. Her parents named her Pipitin. As she grew, she became beautiful, but my people hated her. Markus took her as wife and the next spring their baby was born, fair again and with wings. Within days, another baby was born with wings. Fear consumed the Luporchans. 'We will become a winged kind if we let this go on,' they cried.

Blame was laid on Pipitin, the first. They drove her, Markus and their child away. Pipitin took the other winged baby with her as they went, for the parents did not want their son, a despised offspring. Pipitin and Markus came here to Fair Forest. Pipitin's daughter, Marquee, and the other child made their home here in this Once Fair Forest. Their descendants are the winged Luporchans of Once Fair Forest."

Abigail lifted her eyebrows at Tom and said, "Faeries."

Eddi laughed. "Faeries, that's a nice name for the people of this forest."

The companions stood up, ready to move on. Suddenly, Tom let out a small whoop of joy, there was light in the distance. The travellers picked up their pace, wanting to get out the forest as quickly as possible.

A ray of sunlight glinted through the leaves of the thinning forest. Tom stopped walking so he could catch the warmth on his face. "Oi there, let me have a bit." Abigail laughed, knocking him aside. She and Eddi shared the ray.

Eli watched smiling. He said, "It's definitely lighter now, even without fighting to stand in the sunlight. Too bad it's not warmer. But we must be coming close to the edge of the woods. "

"Beat you out of here," called Tom and he ran, racing for the distant light.

The others followed. Tom came out of the trees, followed closely by his companions. They bumped into him as they emerged. The sight that greeted them immediately froze their fun.

Chapter Nineteen

A cold mist hit Tom's face as he came out of the trees. The freezing air and sight that greeted him stopped him in his tracks. Abigail, then Eli bumped into his back. A foul smell made them gag.

A large grey castle dominated the grounds and seemed to emanate a strange penetrating cold that chilled all the way to the depths of their being. The castle grounds were filled with the most terrifying beings that Tom had ever seen. The reality of the task he'd undertaken struck him with an almighty force, as they slunk back into the veil of the trees.

"I guess we now understand better what is before us," Eddi said softly.

"I might as well just remain here," said Pan, looking the other way.

"You'll do no such thing. You're not running out on us again," Abigail snarled. Pan turned his nose up at her and looked away.

Tom sighed and stood up. "We'd best get on with it."

"And what's it your plan, Oh Great Leader? Have you forgotten what's out there?"

Tom looked through the trees and felt a raw pain in his chest. "No."

The castle itself was square with pointed towers that leapt up at various places giving it an angular, barbed look. One huge tower rose high, dominating the building. The grounds around were yellowed grass with numerous paths all leading straight to the castle entryway. It seemed that all roads did indeed lead to the dwelling place of the Vile One.

The entry doors were shiny black marble with thin streaks of grey. They were the only beautiful thing in the entire place. They rose high and were shadowed by ornately carved over-hangings with mantles that came down to form an entry hall around the doors. There were no gargoyles to protect the entrance, and Tom could understand why. Who would want to go through those beautiful doors and enter that awful place? No one, of course, yet he must.

Though the doors weren't guarded, the grounds were full of creatures that would scare away anyone with sense. It was those creatures, not the more distant thought of what was in the castle, which kept Tom's companions sitting huddled on the forest floor.

Creatures fit for nightmares filled the grounds around the castle. They made Tom (and the others too) just want to curl up in a ball until he had enough courage to run home.

The grey-faced riders were swaggering around, yelling curses both at each other and at other creatures. The foot soldiers were there too, standing in packs, the sound of their voices, harsh laughter, and bellowing filled the icy air. The Vulture Warriors were perched on bars made just for them. They dived from their heights occasionally to knock some unexpected worker on the head, either for fun or for food.

A group of creatures sat around a bubbling pond. They acted like merry-makers on holiday, relaxing on lawn chairs except for their long heads, sharp teeth and red eyes. They spat, in unison, into the bubbling pond. It hissed and steamed, letting off a nasty stench. Tom felt ill. Eli looked at his Ach. "We need a plan, Peregrine Sol."

"Yes, I know, Eli, but I don't know how to make a plan." Tom looked out at the hopeless scene once again. He watched the scene beyond the trees, feeling helpless to act. As time passed, the scene changed little. The same curses, yells, and harsh laughter echoed through the cold. The nastiness continued with hate spilling in every direction. The creatures bit, spit and scratched while Tom sat there, watching them, not able to think of any way forward.

Three foot-soldiers came running into the grounds. They caterwauled back and forth with spurts of rasping laughter. They passed the creatures lounging by the pool just as one of those long creatures spat. The spittle shot passed the pool, and landed with a mucousy splat on the shoulder of a foot solider.

The foot-soldier roared with anger and jumped on the creature who had spat on him. He bit the creature's long neck, killing it instantly. Screaming, the other long-headed creatures attacked the foot soldier. His comrades joined in the fight. Soon all the creatures were slashing and tearing at each other. They kicked, punched and head-butted. When they could get close enough, they bit, their teeth sinking down into the flesh of their victim.

The fighting grew intense as various kinds of creatures from all over the ground ran to the fray. Some yelled encouragements to the foot-soldiers and others for the long creatures, many seemed to swap sides, always cheering for the creatures who were winning. Many others creatures joined in the fight, aimlessly throwing punches.

Tom watched the fight, astounded by the intensity. Then he heard a whisper. Whose voice it was, he couldn't be sure. Maybe it was his own voice. "This is our chance." And whoever it was (Could it have been him?) must have spoken out loud, for with sudden swift movement, all the companions gathered their bags and stood. Eddi scrambled up onto Tom's shoulder as he stooped to grab his pack. They ran, hunched down. Tom's arms hung low, his fingers nearly dragging the ground as he ran. Eddi whispered loudly in his right ear, "I will watch the creatures, you just keep running." And Tom did run, his companions following him as he went, bending as their leader did.

Tom and his companions past swiftly by through the grounds, unnoticed by the feuding creatures. The companions didn't know it, but they could have been posing as a group of Grovlin creatures. The poor Grovlins were the most despised creatures of Sheol. They were slaves, serving the wants of every other kind of creature in that awful land. The years of toil and mistreatment showed on them and they walked always hunching over low, protecting their faces from the hits and blows of any and every one. Tom's company would never know they looked like these poor beasts, and so would never completely understand why it was they passed through the grounds and into the entryway of the castle without being seen.

The fight was waning as the friends reached the protective covering of the entryway. The creatures that were not part of the original fray began to scatter. Dead bodies lay in heaps around the pool. Some dark desire for blood was satisfied and the fighters picked up the dead of their own kind and dumped the bodies into the steaming pool. They jumped back to avoid the splash made by the putrid water, then dusted off their hands. The coldness of their actions was as astonishing as any other part of the affair.

With a hiss at their opponents, they moved on. The pool bubbled and brewed. The lawn chairs were set back up and the long creatures took their places as if nothing had happened to disturb their little holiday mood. Their lost companions were forgotten in a moment.

Tom shook his head and looked at the castle walls, now surrounding him. The magnificent doors towered beside him and cast a shadow over all the company. They were protected from the view of the creatures in the grounds by the surrounding entryway. It was larger than it looked from the woods but the companions bunched tightly together trying to feel secure.

Tom stood up for a moment to see if he could find out what was going on in the grounds now. He didn't want to look at his friends because he knew he would see the fear he felt reflected in their eyes. They were stuck in this tight place without a way to get in those doors. He knew he needed to think fast.

At the sound of heavy thumping Tom looked out again. Foot-soldiers were running towards the castle. There were at least a dozen of them. Tom flattened himself against the wall for fear of being seen, but then the soldiers veered off to the left and out of his view. He breathed out a sigh of relief and heard the others exhale as well. Then, just as suddenly, the foot soldiers were back in view and running towards the castle. Tom stiffened. They veered again, this time running away from the castle. Tom kept still, watching the soldiers until they turned again, as he thought they might. They were chasing something. It was some kind

of a game and they were laughing and yelling as they ran.

Tom leaned out as far as he could, to see what they were chasing.

Whatever it was, it was very small and running like a mad thing to get away

from the horrible beasts.

"What is it?" Eli asked from behind him.

"They're chasing something, trying to stomp it. I think…" said Tom. "I

think it's a mouse or something."

They watched the creatures carousing around the grounds after the little

mouse. Tom once had a pet mouse and what they were doing made him feel

sick. He didn't want to see them stomp the mouse to death, but he had to keep

an eye on them. They steadily came nearer to the castle in that same zigzag

fashion. Then Tom gasped. The little creature they were chasing and stomping

was not a mouse. It was a tiny golden-haired, winged girl. A Luporchan. A

faerie.

Tom squinted, trying to believe his eyes. The little, winged Luporchan was

half-running, half-flying on one wing. The other wing was dragging the ground.

Her face was a picture of anguish.

"Oh no," Tom groaned. "I can't believe it."

"What, what do you see?" Abigail whispered.

Tom turned around as best he could to speak. The others were tight against

him, also trying to see. He looked at Eddi as he spoke. "It wasn't a mouse they were chasing. It, well, it's…" Tom took a deep breath and avoiding Eddi's eyes as he said, "it's a winged Luporchan."

Eddi made a flinging leap onto Tom's shoulder to look out. Just then, a foot hit the winged girl, crushing her already wounded wing. Though they could not hear it, they saw her utter a gasp of pain.

"Oh, what are we going to do? What are we going to do? We have to do something." Eddi was jumping up and down on Tom's shoulder.

They were going to catch her soon. Tom could see that. The little faerie was tiring. Tom could get no thoughts in his head, only fear.

Then more of the nasty creatures entered the chase. They seemed to love pain and death. There were now so many of the creatures after the poor little faerie that they were pushing, and shoving. That is what saved her. The creatures began to fight amongst themselves.

"I'm going out there to help her," Eddi said. He looked over at Tom, then back at his other three companions. "I'll do what I can to lead them away from here and give you a chance to get into the castle."

Just before Eddi jumped off, Tom gave the tiny man his last command. "Eddi, if you do get away. If you make it…. come back here. We shall all try to meet up here in this alcove, if any of us make it."

Tom knelt down and Eddi jumped off Tom's shoulder, running. They watched his tiny body disappear around the mass of twisted booted feet and he was gone. The only sign that he might have reached the girl, was a loud shout that came from the front of the crowd and the view of them veering off right and out of sight.

"At least he will be remembered for having a noble part in our quest." Pan sniffed.

"Shut your gob. That's not why he's doing it, you little git. He's doing it to help that poor girl," Abigial said.

Tom looked at his companions. "We best try this door—to honour Eddi's courage." He looked up at the door towering over his head. There seemed to be no way in. No doorknob marred its smooth surface. There were no levers, and no buttons, only a bar across the door from one side to the other.

Tom reached out and touched the black marble door. Something leapt from a hole in the ornate carvings above the doors. It fell on the floor in front of him, landing lightly on four velvet paws. Its sleek black coat glimmered with black-blue highlights. There was a collar about its neck studded with white diamonds. Green eyes narrowed as it stared at the companions. It was an evil thing with the body of a cat and the face of a woman. She had long black hair and dark red lips. She stood up on two legs, leaning casually against the beautiful marble doors of the castle.

She purred softly, and then said in a silky, deep voice, "So visitors have come to call." The cat dropped down on all fours and rubbed a paw against the whiskers coming from her human face in a cute, kittenish manner. Walking on all fours, she paced in front of them. Tom saw then that she was not just any cat. She was a leopard, and she was beautiful, sleek and elegant.

"Why are they here?" she asked softly, her voice smooth and gentle. "Are they toys sent by my master for my pleasure?" She stopped by Pan. "No," she said. "They are too useless." Pan reeled backwards as if hit by a fist.

The cat-woman stepped two paces forward and was now in front of Eli. "And too strange," she said. Eli's head flung backwards and he blinked his eyes. Two steps more brought the leopard woman directly in front of Abigail. "And much too ugly."

"Ouch," Abigail yelled, and touched her cheek. When she moved her hand away, Tom could see a large red swell beginning to form on her face.

Then the cat stood in front of Tom. He looked into her eyes and saw black slits where the pupil of her eyes should be. "And they can't be food, they're too small, for that." As the cat-woman said the word 'small', Tom felt a stinging under his armour, down his chest, as if claws had dug deeply into his skin ripping downwards.

Abigail stepped forward. "Who are you, I'd like to know?" she asked in a cheeky voice. "Someone's little pussy-cat?"

The leopard hissed as if hurt and in a leap, turned to face Abigail. "Dog girl," she spat back at Abigail.

Abby flinched with pain and shouted back at the cat, "Here kitty-kitty."

The cat leapt forward, standing eye to eye with Abigail. Tom noticed for the first time that blood was oozing down the left side of the cat's back. She went right up to Abigail and lifted her human face up to hiss, "Hairless Wonder."

A gash appeared along Abigail's neck. Abby yelled, "Cat-eyed freak."

The cat-woman reeled then jumped back, pawing her eyes. "Tinted-hair witch," she hissed.

Abigail's head jerked back. She rubbed the back of her head, groaning. Tom had seen enough, he stepped forward and Eli came to stand beside him. Abigail's eyes were dark with pain from the last words the cat had spoken. "You can't help here, you two. This is mine," Abigail said. She laughed softly but without any humour. "Neither of you would be up to this one. This uses my gift, doesn't it? Mean words are my speciality."

Abigail turned back to the cat-woman, who was once again washing her whiskers with her paws, wearing a self-satisfied look on her face. Abigail licked her lips and leaned forward, speaking softly, she snarled, "Stubble-faced Feline."

The cat yowled with pain, rubbing her nose vigorously. She jumped lightly into the air, landing on all fours with an arched back and the fur rising along her spine. "Slick-skin Biped," the cat screamed.

Abigail fell, her legs flying out from under her. Tom could see she was fighting back tears. "Rubbish-Guzzling Thief," Abigail shouted.

The cat clutched her stomach and closed her eyes for a moment. Then she hissed, "Slop-tongue, Gabber Girl."

Blood oozed from Abigail's mouth and her chin trembled. Tom looked at her. "That's enough Abby. I've had enough."

Abigail turned watery eyes to him. "She'll kill you with words if I don' take her down. And she will drag you in and lay you at her master's feet. I have to go on." Abigail reached out and touched Pan's head. "I know what my part is as well." Abigail licked her lips, and blood spread across her mouth from the gaping wound on her tongue.

The cat didn't wait this time. She now knew she was matched against a formidable opponent. She bounded upwards, pawing at the air and shrieked at Abigail, "You Wishy-washy, Others-lover."

Abigail spun, falling back into Eli. He stood her up, putting his hand on her shoulder to steady her. Abigail yelled, "Prancey-footed, Wool-Doormat." And without waiting to see what effect her words would have on her opponent, Abigail yelled again, "Brown-nose, bootlicking, grovelling lap-cat." Her voice ended with a tom-cat screech.

The cat-woman flew backwards, landing in a heap by the outer wall of the alcove. She groaned and meowed loudly, but did not rise. Abigail smiled, but it was a sickly red grin from the blood in her mouth.

The cat rose up. Her face was menacing. She walked slowly and gracefully forward. "Flat-chested, Book-loving, Punctilious, School-Girl."

Abigail humped over, coughing. She turned back towards the inner wall and vomited violently. Then turning back, still holding her stomach, Abigail hissed, "Dry-mouthed, Rat-eating, Snake-Tail."

The leopard wailed with pain and went round and round, reaching for her tail, and after finally reaching it, she licked it over and over.

Seizing her chance Abigail shouted again. "Smooth-moving, Stealth-seeking, Rump-snuggler." The cat wailed and groaned.

Abigail stood upright, looking brighter than she had since starting her war of words with the cat-woman, she whooped, "Sand-wetting, Fly-drawing, Kitty Litter Lover."

The leopard screamed with pain as Abigail sent yet more her way. Moving closer to the writhing half-cat, Abigail whispered viciously, "Sniveling, Surly, Lily-livered Minx."

The cat-woman could no longer get up on her four legs. She lay there moaning, finally she cried out. "Silly girl."

Abigail laughed.

The cat howled, "Fat girl"

Abigail laughed again and spoke in a harsh voice, "You don't hurt me anymore, you Four-footed, Weak-willed, Rough-tongued, Vassal of a Vile Master."

The cat closed her eyes with pain and blood came streaming out of her mouth. She could barely speak and her voice came as a gentle whisper. "My Master would love you."

Abigail's head flew back, her body propelled back violently and she hit the wall behind her, closing her eyes. Tom and Eli ran to her as Pan stood wild-eyed looking around helplessly. "Keep an eye on that cat," Tom ordered him.

Abigail was unconscious for only a moment. She opened her eyes, but did not speak. Tears started streaming down. "I can't move," she whispered, "Such pain."

Tom and Eli settled her down as best they could on the cold hard floor of the entryway. They took off their jackets and laid them over her. Tom put his arm on Eli, telling the Changeling to stay there, and he went over to look at the cat-woman. She too was unconscious, breathing heavily on the floor. Tom went back to his friends. He whispered to Eli, "The cat's still alive. What are we going to do?"

Abigail opened her eyes, tears came again. She whispered up imploringly to Tom and Eli. "She said her master would love me. He would love me," the girl cried bitterly.

Tom leaned over Abigail and said, "He would not love you. He would hate you. You didn't say those things just to hurt somebody else. You said them to save our lives."

Abigail spoke again, the pain making her voice more of a whimper. "It came easy."

Eli patted Abigail's shoulder. "Not that easy, Abigail, I saw your face."

Abigail turned towards the wall and closed her eyes. Her breathing deepened and Tom hoped she would sleep. He rose and looked down at his Ach kneeling beside their friend. "We have to figure out where to put Abigail to keep her safe. We also need to figure out what to do with that cat." He pointed at the bundle of black fur lying against the outer wall.

Tom and Eli carefully moved Abigail as far as possible from the marble doors. Pan scurried along before them, making a pillow out of a backpack. Then they covered her with their jackets again. Tom shivered with the cold. Abigail groaned softly, but seemed to go to sleep. The three stood over her, looking down with worried eyes.

Finally, they turned to deal with her vicious opponent. They gathered up what bits of cloth they could find from their packs and made twisted ropes to bind the cat's legs. They used the straps of their backpacks to finish wrapping the cat up as best they could. Then they pushed and shoved until the cat was far against the outer wall. She didn't wake up though she hissed and snarled in her unconscious state.

Tom stood and surveyed the entry hall. Anyone who came through could see Abigail and the cat, but they could also walk by without noticing. It was the best he could do. He sure didn't want to leave Abigail here alone.

"How are we going to get in?" Tom wondered out loud. Eli pointed up at the hole where the cat had jumped out. Tom smiled oddly and nodded his head. The cat had shown the way.

Tom turned to Pan. "Eli and I are going to have to scramble up and jump through to the other side. I have no idea what we will meet when we get in there." He looked at the little faun. "You're staying here with Abigail."

Pan opened his mouth, but shut it when Tom spoke again with a stern voice. "I'm the leader. You said your part was done. I say no. I say you still have a part to play, but this time the part is in obeying my orders. Abigail cannot be left here alone as she is. You think Eddi and Abby have played noble parts. It's your turn to be noble. You will stand as a protection to one who gave all she had to protect you, and me and Eli."

Pan straightened himself and Tom was pleased to see a light enter his dark little eyes. "Do you understand, Pan?"

"I understand. I'm Abigail's protector."

Tom nodded. He looked another moment at the little faun without saying anything. Would that resolve hold if actual trouble came? Tom wasn't sure.

"Eddi may come back here too." Eli added. "You'll be here for both of them."

Pan puffed up just a little more.

Tom and Eli walked over to the imposing doors. Tom put his hand out and touched the doors again, looking up quickly to make sure nothing leaped out again. He pulled back his hands, already red with the freezing temperature of the doors. Tom looked at Eli with a grimace. "Well, here we go," he said to his Ach. With a sigh, he pulled himself up onto the bar that crossed the doors. Balancing carefully, he stood. Eli put his hand on Tom's thigh to help him remain steady. Tom tiptoed, pulling himself as high as he could, just managing to get the tips of his fingers to the hole. "I can't quiet reach it," he said.

"Here," said Eli. "Stand on my hands."

Tom stepped on to Eli's hands. With trembling arms, Eli pushed Tom up higher.

"Got it," Tom whispered. Tom's grasp on the flap was now firm. He pulled himself up until he could balance on the edge of the hole. "You come now," he whispered down to Eli. Eli climbed on to the bar. They clasped hands and Tom pulled until Eli was balanced beside him. With a wave at Pan, Tom and Eli jumped lightly down.

As Tom landed, the cold pierced him. It was a frigid, evil place and he was in it.

Chapter Twenty

Tom hugged himself against the cold and whispered to his Ach, "Could you turn into something warm and cuddly."

"I can't believe you can joke at a time like this, Peregrine Sol. And in this place," Eli answered.

They had dropped down into a large open foyer and were feeling exposed, so they moved quietly and cautiously towards a distant wall. They had no idea which way to go to find Amos. They naturally moved in the direction they were facing when they landed on their feet. Once at the wall they could relax a little and look around. Going straight would lead them down a narrow corridor, a turn to the right went up a flight of stairs and to the left of them was the castle wall. Abigail was just the other side of it. Tom stood there wondering which way to go. He didn't have any information so how could he decide? A thought struck him. Tom leaned over and whispered into Eli's ear, "I bet the Vile One would want to see everything that happens in his land. I think he just loves all that fighting we saw out there."

Eli nodded, and waited for Tom to go on.

"I think he's up there in the tower," Tom said, pointed up the stairs. "And look, this whole place seems to converge on those stairs. If all paths in Sheol lead to his castle, maybe all corridors in his house lead to him."

"So should we go up?" Eli asked with a quivering voice.

"No," Tom answered decisively. "We shouldn't. Meeting up with him will do Amos no good. First we find Amos, and then maybe we can get away without ever even seeing the Vile One."

Two options were left but neither was very good. Going back into the great hall would leave them very exposed to sight. The passage way was narrow, so if anyone came down it, Tom and Eli were sure to be seen. Tom stood, with Eli at his side, for a long time trying to decide. He listened to see if sounds might tell him where creatures were roaming in the castle. There was nothing but stony silence all around. At least down the corridor, they could try to escape through one of the many doors.

Finally, he said, "Let's go down the passage way. Maybe we'll see or hear something that will tell us where we should look for Amos."

As quietly as they could, the two companions walked down the corridor. Tom felt fear in his throat and was tense and watchful. It was a long corridor with walls as smooth as ice. Along the left wall, doors came at varying intervals. All were closed.

Tom turned his head at the sound of weird voices filtering down the corridor. The creak of a door opening made Tom jump. With a glance at Eli, Tom moved to open the door beside them. The risk of what they might find inside the door seemed a little better than meeting up with the owners' of those harsh voices. They stepped inside the room and to their relief it was empty.

The light in the room was dim, the walls the same dull grey as in every other part of this cold drab castle. But in the room there were wall hangings of various sizes. Tom inhaled. These were not pretty pictures or portraits, but weapons of cruelty. Tom had seen such things before at an exhibit of medieval weapons and objects for torture on a school trip. But those were old rusty tools, never to be used again. The wall hangings here were new and obviously still being used. Blood smeared many of the edges. Eli looked at Tom with horror.

"I wonder were Amos is," Eli whispered.

The heavy footsteps were passing now. Tom envisioned the huge brutes that were out there. He heard speaking. The words being used sounded harsh.

Then a gentle and rather beautiful voice spoke as if answering a question. "Yes, Gug, I did have a good time. But we don't want it to end too soon. We must make our play go slowly. We'll leave the pasty fellow waiting. He will fear our return, won't he?" A bright laugh rang out in the hall joined by a harsh-rasping chortle.

"Now we must go to my father. Oh, you cower, don't you, at the thought of him? So you should. Then I will come back and we can finish off the maggot of Adamah."

The clomping of heavy feet continued down the passage way and into the hall. Tom heard the slam of a distant door, and still he waited. He listened, tense and fearful, for more sounds. It was silent but even that seemed ominous.

Tom whispered, "They must have just left Amos. He's got to be down this corridor. Are you ready to go out there again?" Eli nodded with a tiny shake of his head.

Tom walked through the door as Eli opened it. The corridor was empty. They stepped out and continued walking down the passage, now more hopeful that this was the right way to find Amos

There was only one more room. This must be it. Tom's heart seemed to stop beating for a moment, then it started again, beating faster than ever. The handle of this door shocked him. He had seen this beautiful diamond shape before. He had been here before.

Was Amos alone, or was someone there with him? Eli put his hand on Tom's shoulder. Tom drew his sword and opened the door. The room was darker than the last one. Tom stepped further into the room. His eyes adjusted slowly to the dimness. It was colder here than anywhere else so far.

The same horrible tools were on the walls. A table stood in the middle of the room. Eli grabbed Tom's arm with a vice-like grip. His Ach whispered hoarsely, "There is someone over there."

Tom and Eli stood still waiting for some movement. But the person lying on the table said nothing and made no sound. Tom moved slowly forward. A knot in Tom's throat choked him. These evil creatures would take such delight from springing up to attack him and Eli.

Tom stood over the bed and looked down. He could not believe it. It couldn't be so easy to find Amos. But there he was, lying on this bench, his shattered, broken black armour in bits. He was easy to identify.

"Poor Amos," Eli said. "They have been very cruel to him. Is he dead?"

Tom felt a tingling fear as he put his hand down to touch Amos's neck. He had seen this done on shows, but Tom wasn't really quite sure how to take someone's pulse. The moment he touched Amos's warm skin, the young man groaned.

Eli breathed with a sigh of relief. "He's alive."

"It's been too easy Eli. I'm afraid this is a trap. Are you sure that this is Amos?"

Eli looked at Tom. "You think finding him was easy, after all we have been through?"

"But to walk into a room, and find him straight away. That doesn't seem right."

The Changeling made the gentle whinny that he now seemed to make when he was thinking. "Yes, it could have been much harder. But my only hope is that the quest continues to go so smoothly."

.   Tom sighed, "I guess you're right and we still have to figure out how to get him out of here."

Amos's eyes fluttered open. Terror took over his face as he tried to scramble away, yelling, "No. No. No more please."

Eli ran light-footed to the door and closed it gently.

"Shhh. Please Amos, be quiet. You're okay. We're not going to hurt you. We're here to try and help," Tom whispered urgently to him.

Amos stopped yelling, but he continued to thrash around, his eyes wild. Then he slowed down and stopped, staring all the while at Tom. Eli was still by the door with his ear against its coldness.

"You," Amos said to Tom, his voice low and urgent.

Tom whispered, "We've come to try to help you."

Amos again said passionately, "You are here."

Tom looked quizzically at Amos. Then, feeling that he understood the young man, he said, "Yes, we are here in Sheol. We have come to try and rescue you, though even now that we have found you I don't know how to rescue you." Tom finished helplessly.

Eli walked slowly over to the couch. He looked back and forth between his Ach and the prince, watching them closely.

Amos struggled to sit up. Tom helped as best he could, but it was clear that he was in a lot of pain. With a trembling hand, Amos reached out and touched Tom's face. The pain in Amos' eyes diminished as he touched Tom and was replaced by some emotion Tom didn't recognize. Then Amos said it again, with a stronger voice, "I just can't believe you're here, Tom."

"Eli, help me lift him up by the arms. Let's see if he can walk."

Tom and Eli helped the unsteady Amos to his feet. His legs buckled and then gave way. Tom and Eli bent quickly and pulled him back up. Tom looked round the young knight to Eli's face. "I hope the corridor is still clear. Maybe we should check."

"Wait." Amos' voice was quiet but urgent.

Tom looked at him, "What is it, Amos?"

Amos said, "I can't go yet." He pulled so hard that Tom and Eli had to lower him back on the couch. "I can't leave without my Ach." The young knight looked up imploringly at Eli, "You must understand. I must find my Ach."

"I'm not sure your Ach is here, Prince Amos. We saw you being taken. We were standing on The All Seeing Hill, but you were alone. There was no Changeling with you."

"They took him before they found me. I was out looking for him when…." Amos shook his head, grimaced with pain and hugged his stomach. "He thinks he's at fault. I've seen him here. I told him it not his fault. But still he is so upset and sad, and they have hurt him. They're brutal. They love inflicting pain." Amos' voice became hard, and his body tensed and shivered. "Please, he must be rescued too. I couldn't leave him, he's like a brother. And a brother would never leave a brother." Amos put his hand on Tom's shoulder.

"Do you know where they're holding him, Prince Amos?" Eli asked.

Amos moved and pointed across to the other side of the room. "That door, it leads into a short passage way. At the end of it is another door. That door goes out to a corral. They have Enoch tethered there."

Eli looked over at Tom. "I'll go, Peregrine Sol. I'll try to find Enoch and bring him back here." Eli looked back at the Prince. "Is he badly hurt? Can he still transform?"

"I think so. But I'm not sure."

Eli nodded and made to move across the room. Then, turning back, he looked at Tom then at Amos. "Two knights and so alike," he said and walked out of the door.

Tom looked at the door for a long time, listening. His mind was fully bent on willing safety for Eli. Then he looked at Amos. The young knight's eyes were closed tightly. His face was drawn with pain. It was clear he was normally a strong and fine looking young man. Brown hair fell across his forehead, reaching almost down to his eyebrows. There were small lines that came from his eyes, as though he laughed or smiled a lot. Amos opened his eyes, they were deeply green, but now they held more pain than colour.

"Here, Amos, why don't you lay back down while we are waiting for Eli to bring your Ach," Tom said.

Amos lay back on the table again. He attempted to smile up at Tom. "When I lay here before and opened my eyes, I expected…" Amos closed his eyes in pain then opened them again. "I won't tell you what I thought it was going to be. But you, I never thought it would be you. I'm overwhelmed with happiness and to have that feeling here, in this place. Can you imagine how it must have been for me?"

Tom didn't know what to say. He opened his mouth, but before he could attempt to reply, a sound made him turn his head. It was the sound of a loud whinny, just in the distance. "Eli," Tom shouted in a whispery voice. Amos sat up suddenly, wincing with the pain. "Enoch."

"Will you be okay here on your own for a few minutes?" Tom asked Amos urgently.

Amos nodded, but Tom could see the fear return to his eyes.

Tom ran lightly across the room to the door. He looked back at the young knight. Amos' eyes were on him. Tom opened the door and went through, closing it softly behind him. He ran, swift-footed, down the short passage and opened the door to the outside, taking a breath, almost choking at the rancid smell that filled the air. This side of the corral was empty. Tom went cautiously out and hearing another fierce neigh, he ran around the outside of the castle.

Tom saw a black horse tethered to the dark wooden fence of the corral. It was a beautiful animal except for the ugly wounds on its side. It reared up on two legs and was pulling wildly on the ropes that held it captive. It gave another piercing whinny and redoubled it struggle against the rope. Tom could hear sound of vicious fighting, screaming neighs and thuds followed by gasping breaths, but he couldn't see what was happening. Tom held his breath and walked further out into the corral, past the towering wall of the castle. Then he saw the battle. Tom gasped.

A winged horse, pure white, was fighting against a most terrible beast. "Eli," Tom whispered, pain touching him like he never felt before. "Oh Eli," he said to himself, "please be careful."

The monster, for that is the only way the creature fighting Eli, could be described, was black. Its horse-like shape was much larger than Eli's and muscle bound. The monster's eyes and face made it awful to look at. The eyes were sickly pink, with veins of red streaming through the white. They glinted with malice. The head was that of a dragon, raging and hideous, its long nose was smoking and its wide-spread nostrils flaring.

Tom felt the pain as Eli's screaming neigh echoed across the corral. The dragon-headed beast spat fire again at Eli, burning the side of his lovely white neck. Tom was sick, his stomach churning. Eli leapt away, flying upwards briefly to get away from his horrible enemy. As he winged upwards, Tom drew a sharp breath, for Eli was not a horse. There on the head of his beautiful white Ach, was a silver and grey horn. Eli was a unicorn, a magnificent, winged unicorn.

Tom wanted to run to Eli and help him. He wanted to tell his Ach that he was wonderful. But he could not go to his Ach, because he couldn't deny the cries of the black horse. Tom knew he had to go and release it before he could help Eli. He could hear cries for help in the wild neighs and screams of the tethered animal. The black horse, pulling on the rope and looking round at Tom, kept neighing and whinnying, the urgent and demanding sound of its voice compelling Tom to come to him.

Tom ran across the corral. The horse looked at Tom with such knowing eyes that Tom knew this must be Enoch. Tom pulled his sword from its sheath and slashed the ropes till they gave way. The black horse leapt forward, running towards Eli and the battle with the dragon beast. Tom also ran towards the battle. But he stopped when he heard the neigh of Eli.

"No, Tom, come no further. Not yet."

Tom watched, astonished, as side by side the two Changelings fought with a frightening intensity. Eli charged the beast, head tilted down, his strong pointed horn aimed at the side of the enemy. Enoch rose, towering tall, coming down on the beast just as the horn of Eli pierced its side. The revolting creature roared, but its voice gave way with the pain. It could call no fell help to its side. But it could still fight, and it could still exhale its pain-bringing burst of flame at it opponents and that is what it did. Eli let out another air-shattering scream, piercing Tom with his pain. Enoch yelled too. Then both the black horse and the white unicorn retreated. They galloped to get away from the scorching whips of yellow and orange flames that followed them with searching pain

Tom ran towards the beast, but Eli saw him and turn to canter in front of Tom.

"You can't fight him, Tom." Eli neighed at him. "He is too much. He is the descendant of Arovoit, and I must fight him without you." Tom stepped back, the look in those deep horse's eyes convincing him.

The dragon blew fire again. The flame was white hot this time and blistered poor Eli the moment it touched him. The fur on his flanks burst into flames. Eli rose on his back legs, pawing the air in panic, then ran to find a place big enough to roll on the ground. He galloped to the place where Enoch was already trying to quench the burning on his side from the last wicked attack of the beast.

Tom whirled around, feeling evil coming close to him. It was not a half-dragon, but a person. A person who looked like Eli, with a round Changeling face, tall thin body, straight ear-length hair and almond-shaped eyes. Tom dropped his arm to his side, his sword dangling, its tip touching the ground.

The Changeling drew nearer to Tom. Tom would not be able to fight this Changeling because he was too much like Eli. But as the creature came closer, Tom stared into his eyes and raised his sword again. The almond eyes were little more than slits of hatred and its mouth was a sneer across the marred face. Close-up, this creature was nothing like Eli. It was a descendent of Arovoit, the deformed image of a Changeling.

Tom raised his sword higher, and the sneering ugly face before him laughed. It half-changed into a dragon and from its fearsome head, it issued a low curse and a fire shot towards Tom. Tom jumped, stumbling, and the fire only grazed his cheek. It burnt as nothing ever burned him before.

A thunder of hoofs sounded on the frozen parched dirt of the corral, Tom turned, expecting to see Eli running to his rescue. Instead a galloping Enoch came. For a brief moment, Tom worried for his Ach. It was driven away by wonder. Enoch jumped, it was a leap that went far over Tom's head. To Tom's utter amazement, flames issued from the nostrils of the beautiful horse, taking the enemy with surprise and fire. Then Enoch landed on the beast with powerful hoofs. The dragon beast was wounded, but still lifted its head, breathing fire with even more strength. Enoch cried with pain and rolled off the enemy, whinnying with the agony.

From overhead, Eli's angry neigh echoed. The beast, regaining strength from its latest victory over Enoch, lifted its head to attack Tom with another round of fiery breath. Enoch reared up, kicking at the beast's head with his strong back legs. The dragon-head jerked up when Enoch's powerful kick hit it. The flame shot skywards, missing Tom by inches. Tom thought of his Ach and looked around and up to see if the fire was going to hit poor Eli again. The evil beast laughed as he breathed the fire again, the same thought coming evilly into his mind as well. But Eli was not above them.

The beast moved about, wildly looking for the unicorn. Enoch seized the advantage and kicked it again, hitting the beast soundly in the ribs. Spurts of orange flame flew recklessly about. Then Eli came, charging from the right, diving down on the enemy, his great sliver horn, this time striking hard and fast.

The enemy fell and rose no more.

Chapter Twenty-One

Tom let out one, long, shivering breath, then another. His cheek was burning. The fallen beast lay on the ground beside him. Tom put away thoughts of his own pain, knowing it could be nothing compared to what poor Enoch, lying beside the beast, must feel. Eli must be in horrible pain as well. Where was he now? Tom looked skyward for his Ach. He felt a touch on his shoulder, and turned to find his friend.

Eli's face, neck and clothing were burnt. Across his forehead was a large smear of a nasty black blood that was certainly not his own. Scratches and burns covered his arms and legs.

"Oh, Eli," Tom said, trying to fight the watery sound out of his voice. "Are you okay?'

Eli didn't speak. He stood looking at Tom with liquid eyes, breathing heavily. Eli put his hand on Tom shoulder, and laid his forehead against Tom's forehead. Tom knew his companion, though weary, was okay. After a moment, Eli lifted his head and said, "We need to check on Enoch."

They walked around the dead beast and knelt beside the black horse. Enoch lifted his head as they stroked his sweaty flanks, and then struggled to his feet. Eli stood in front of his brother Changeling and said gently, "Can you transform?"

Enoch whinnied softly. He couldn't.

"Let me help you," Eli said, and he put his hands on the horse's head and closed his eyes. He leaned against the animal, and stood there. Could he give his will to the other Changeling? Tom turned away. When he turned back Enoch was in his Changeling form. "Can you walk? Amos is waiting for us," Tom said.

Eli gave his arm to Enoch saying, "We found Amos already you'll see him soon."

Tom hoped this was true. Now that the fierce battle was finished, he could think again of poor Amos lying there. It was possible that the occupants of this awful place heard the battle. If anyone had come back to the room, they would find Amos much as they left him. Then, they would trap Tom and the Changelings as they walked in the door? Tom spoke none of these thoughts aloud because these two Achs had fought long and courageously. He didn't want to worry them needlessly.

Tom opened the outer door of the castle carefully, every nerve in his body tense as he led the Changelings into the castle. He paused briefly before the door of the room where Amos lay. He opened it. Amos was there. Alone. Tom sighed with relief and felt the hand of his Ach on his shoulder. Eli had known the fear Tom felt.

Amos struggled to sit up as the three entered the door. His face lit up as he said, "Enoch, you're safe." With obvious pain, Enoch bent over and put his arm around Amos' shoulder.

Tom looked up and caught Eli's eye. Prince and Ach were reunited. The pleasure lasted for only a moment. The feeling was quickly ebbed away by the daunting task ahead. "We'd best get on with it," Tom said. He saw Eli move to help Amos up. And Tom steadied the other Changeling.

Enoch was tall and looked to be about the same age as Amos, just as Eli now seemed to be Tom's age. Tom walked to the door, moving as quickly as he could with the weak Changeling beside him. Tom looked out and to his relief the passage way was still clear. Good fortune was with them so far.

He stepped into the corridor and moved to one side to allow Eli and Amos to come out as well. Tom leaned across to close the door and heard voices coming from the outer door.

"Get in here, you fool. Let's see if that nasty changing creature is in here with his weakling prince. He'll pay a high price when the Master finds out what he has done to the royal steed."

The door opposite creaked.

Tom turned to Eli, "Take them and go as fast as you can to the others. I'm going to try and deal with these creatures before they raise the alarm."

Tom heard a gasp come from inside as the creatures found the room empty. This was the end of their luck. Tom silently signalled to Eli. The Changeling grabbed the arms of their charges and ran down the corridor, pushing his weak companions to their limit. Tom drew his sword and he went back into the room.

The creatures looked up as he entered. There were two creatures, mouths hanging open, before him. One was a foot soldier and the other a Grovlin slave, with long dangling arms and a scarred body.

Tom could almost have laughed at the expression on their faces, except he knew this was going to be no laughing matter.

"Wha' the…?" The little slave's squeaky voice started.

"What has happened to make you so chipper and well, young prince?" growled the foot soldier

The little slave squeaked, "It's magic."

The foot solder slapped the Grovlin with the back of his hand, never taking his eye off Tom.

Tom lifted his sword and held it out. "Come find out what magic is here."

The soldier drew his short, curved sword and lunged at Tom. Tom jumped aside laughing. This infuriated the foot-soldier, but his anger didn't help, it only to made him careless. He swung at Tom in anger and missed.

Tom struck the creature, now glad they had done fencing in school. The foot-soldier yelled with pain and then became angry. He came at Tom forcefully, knocking him in the head with the heavy sword. Tom was dizzy and sick, and blood was dripping into his eyes.

The soldier yelled at his slave. "Get in here, you stinking coward. If I have pain, you'll feel it too."

The little slave jumped in. He had no weapon, but Tom soon discovered he had sharp teeth and claws. Now Tom was fighting two. He kicked the slave, feeling a little guilty as it rolled away. All this time he was also slashing with his sword at the foot-soldier. Tom was tiring.

The slave came running back, teeth bared again. Tom kicked, this time feeling no guilt and he kicked hard. The slave flew across the room, smashing its head against the wall, knocking it unconscious. Now Tom could turn his attention fully on the soldier.

He went after it with a ferocity that would have astounded Mrs. Mendor back at school. The soldier was taken aback and he stumbled. Tom was plunging forward as the creature fell. Tom fell too, sending his sword through the creature's chest. Tom stood up, and looked down at the thing he had killed. Now he felt truly ill.

He had to pull hard on his sword to loosen it, and it came out with a sickly squelch. Tom stood frozen, looking down at what he had done. The feelings of regret and sickness passed away. Anger took their place, for this was the work of the Vile One. He was the one who caused Tom to be here to do this terrible deed.

Tom turned and ran out of the door and down the passageway, trying not to think about what had happened. He ran straight through the great hall towards the door before he even wondered whether he would be able to get out or not.

Eli must have found a way to open the door. Desperately hoping to find his friends and only his friends waiting for him, Tom stepped out of the door.

"About time you came back?" said Abigail.

Tom let out a coughing laugh that was almost a cry and Abigail grabbed him in a tight hug. Her body was shaking. She looked at Tom and kissed him. "If my boyfriend knew you'd done that you'd be in big trouble."

"I didn't do…"

Before Tom could finish, Eli stepped forward, and said, "We've been watching every second for your arrival." Tom moved with the others to huddle in the shadow of the doors again.

"Are you two doing all right then?" he asked Amos and Enoch. The Prince and his Ach both nodded, but it was clear they had little strength to do more than that. Tom looked around. Eli understood and answered the question before Tom could ask it, "Eddi has not come back." Tom shuddered then noticed a strange body lying against the far wall. He looked at Abigail and Pan.

"Everything okay?" Tom asked. He looked around for the cat-woman.

Abigail sat down. "We're okay. We've had our bit of trouble, but not as much as you by all accounts." She smiled up at the little faun. "To tell you the truth, Oh Great Leader, Pan here was truly brilliant." Pan smiled and his chest puffed up a bit.

"It was tense, Tom. That ratty creature came in here. At first, it didn't even see me and Pan. We hunched behind the column hoping that it would move on. But it didn't. It saw that cat-woman and stood there. Shivering all over and wiggling its whiskers like it was terrified. Then it seemed to realise the cat wasn't moving. It was almost comical the way it moved up and nudge the cat, started thumping it and then the starts jumping up and down with joy. It kicked the cat, making hissing and spitting noises. When it saw the cat didn't wake up, it giggled with glee. I almost laughed at the sight, but I caught myself. You too, hey, Pan?" The little faun smiled and nodded but didn't say anything.

Abigail continued, "Then the rat jumped and I could have sworn it froze in mid-air when it sees we're over here. It hits the ground and bares it teeth. I'm sure it wanted to eat us. I didn't think there was any way Pan could stand up to something so much bigger than him and I was too weak to get up. Then Pan clouts it on the head with his pot, hard too. And down it goes."

Pan smiled, "Well it had worked for the cat, so…"

"For the cat?" Tom said.

Abigail said, "Yeah, for the cat. She moved see, before the rat came. Pan pulls his little pot out of his pack and hits that witch on her head. She's moved no more since then. And every time ratty moves," Abigail continued, pointing to the rat-creature. "Boom. Ruddy brilliant." Abigail leaned back, still weak. "So we've been doing all that while you've been just lazing about."

Tom heard Amos draw a quick breath. Tom laughed. "You'll get used to the way this girl talks before too long, Amos. She doesn't mean most of what she says."

"You best just be careful, or you'll be laying over there too. That witch thought she could best me in talking and look at her." Tom could hear the sadness in her voice.

"Well, now we have to figure out how to get out of here," Tom said.

"Is Father coming to get us?" Amos asked.

The companions were silent, all eyes looking sympathetically towards the young prince. Finally, Tom answered. "He isn't coming. I don't know your father, Amos, and I'm not judging him. I'm sure he's a good man, but I'm afraid your father isn't coming. It seems Sir Gwain has been put under a spell of some sort. When you were captured he, well, froze up. He isn't able to do anything, nor can his knights."

Amos opened his mouth, a shocked look on his face. But before he could speak, Tom went on. "It's not just your father though, all the knights are cursed. No one is coming. We're on our own."

Amos looked at Tom. "Tom, how can you speak so? Father…"

Before Amos could finish, two tiny creatures rounded the outer wall and came into the castle entryway. Tom shouted, "Eddi."

Eddi bowed. Hanging on his arm was a tiny winged woman.

"Oh Eddi, it was almost more than I could hope," Tom said, bending down.

Eddi looked around at the huddled company and bowed low towards Amos and Enoch. "Prince Amos, it's a joy to see you at last."

The prince smiled and said, "Good Luporchan, thank you."

"So mate you going to introduce that there girl or is she just for show."

Eddi turned, "Abigail, dear dog-girl. It's good to hear your voice. You seem to have a story to tell as well. This is Swen."

The tiny lady curtsied and said in a trembling, elegant voice, "I'm honoured to make your acquaintance." Eddi held her elbow to help her rise from her curtsy. One wing hung low, nearly dragging on the ground.

"I thought I would not live after I ran from you. Indeed, I should not have lived. I ran through the crowds and when those that saw me came after me, I knew I'd done Swen no good by coming into the chase. We ran round the castle. I said good bye to you in my heart feeling I'd never see you again."

Eddi sighed. Then he began again, "A large flying beast came overhead. The creatures that were chasing us stopped running and dropped with fear. I was filled with a cold dread. The black-winged beast landed and I hid my face. The beast was a monster but the rider was beautiful. As he dismounted, he kicked the creatures nearest him shouting, "Show me your allegiance." They kissed his boots, and he kicked them again. I knew this was the son of Evil, the Vile Prince."

Eddi stopped speaking. His listeners were silent, waiting for the little man to regain his composer. With a soft sigh, Eddi said, "I was thankful to be a man of normal size and unnoticed. The coming of this Vile Prince turned became our salvation. I grabbed Swen's hand and ran."

Eddi moved forward and took Swen's hand again. "We ran to a hole under the castle and I heard the Vile Prince say to his steed. 'Go have a bit of sport with that weak creature my enemy calls his friend. I'll have fun with my prisoner.' That is why, Prince Amos, I feel so delighted to find you here. Tom has fulfilled his quest."

"Not yet, Eddi. We have to get out of this here before we can declare victory. I'm afraid we have done the easiest part." Tom's voice broke as he continued, "How do we get out of here when there are such creatures surrounding us?"

Eddi walked right up to Tom. "You will lead and we will follow, even our prince will follow you. There are creatures that are loathsome beyond belief in this place. Even under this castle, creatures dwell. I've seen them. Far below this, we saw sights that would bring fear to the hearts of many larger than us. Down there live snakes, beautiful to look at but mean beyond reason, brown insects with pinchers bigger than their body, and red rats with white eyes. The red rats came down the hole after us, even the snakes slid away for fear of them. I thought they would kill us. But Peregrine Sol, they were good. They came to lead us away. Swen and I live because of the goodness of those creatures that I thought were evil. I'm filled with hope."

"Oh, Eddi, if only that would happen for us. If only some good creature would crawl out of the walls to help us. I would be delighted no matter how awful they looked," Tom said.

Tom put the tiny man back down on the ground beside Swen. "But until that happens, we have to make a plan to try to get out of here on our own."

Amos cleared his throat. The others looked over at the young prince. "Do you really discount the thought that Father will come to get us?" Amos asked, directing his question straight at Tom.

Tom lowered his gaze. He felt for the young prince. Even though he didn't have a father himself, Tom reckoned there couldn't be a worse thing than thinking your father has let you down.

"I don't think we can count on Sir Gwain to come any more than we can count on some good creature coming out of the walls to help us."

The entry way filled with an uneasy silence. Amos' head fell. He looked in as much pain as he had when they found him on the torture table. Enoch's hand lay on the Prince's shoulder.

The heavy silence continued. Tom felt awful, but he had only told the truth. He went to the entryway and looked out. The grounds were still filled with creatures. The scene was actually little different from when they stood at the forest edge. Tom walked back and crouched down by his friends again.

"We need a distraction. Someone, one of us, needs to make a distraction. That's how we managed to get here and that's the only way I can see to get back to the forest's shelter again." All eyes were on Tom's face. He knew what he was asking and he wondered if any one of them had the strength to do this awful deed. He was calling for a task that could be someone's last.

The castle door flew open. A creature ran past so quickly they couldn't even see what sort it was. It ran madly, yelling indistinguishable words as it went. The companions didn't have time to move before they heard more sounds of running and shouting inside the castle. This time the words were understandable.

"A breach? A breach in the hedge, did you say? Where? You stupid fool, where is this breach?"

"On the eastern border, and the western, there are bree-chees ever-where. That's what we was told. And don't you call me names, Maggot. I'm not your slave."

The creatures attacked each other. The fighting lasted only a few moments and the winner growled, "Now, Maggot, you are my slave. Has the alarm been sounded? Does the Master know? You can be the one to tell him and feel his fury, not me. He thought the leader of those stupid people across the hedge was beaten already. Our armies have marched through the land of Adamah with ease. I heard only farmers and little animals defended, but maybe that has changed. Do you think the feared Knight of Adamah has come?"

There was only a whimper in answer.

They heard another thud and then, "Get up you worm, go and tell the Master your news and tell him his faithful servant, Notbug, has gone to blow a horn and rally the defence of his land. Make sure you tell him all I said, or next time you shall lie dead and not just bleeding."

Then a grey man-like creature ran out of the doors into the courtyard. Blood from his victim dripped from his fist onto the floor of the entryway. The companions stayed quiet, waiting for the sound of the other creature's footsteps to echo away into the castle. All was silent in there. Either the creature could not get up and go to its master, or it did not want to. Then a creature came slinking out the doors. Its face was mangled. It stopped and saw that the enemy was at the door. Tom and Eli fell on it quickly, finishing the job its comrade had started.

Tom's chest heaved as he and Eli pulled the body to lay it beside the other two. He went back and closed the doors of the castle quietly.

A trumpet sounded across the grounds and chaos broke out in the courtyard. Tom stepped back against the crevice, hiding behind the column again. No one came into the entryway, but confusion continued to fill the grounds around the castle. The grey-faced riders galloped through, snapping their whips at every creature running on the ground. Chaos reigned.

Two riders came close to the entryway. The first called out, "Is it true?"

"Yes, I have seen it myself," said the second rider. "The hedge is breached. The fools have come into the land. But this taking of their prince, that was a deed…"

"Are you mad, Razeneck? Questioning the Master's son?" the first asked gruffly.

"No, no" Razeneck yelled back. "Of course, I don't question the Prince, Tawz. I only wondered to myself how they did it. That's my question. How did the weak fools break through that magic?"

Taws laughed at his fellow rider. "I think you questioned more than that, Razeneck."

Razeneck's grey face, turned paler. "I'm a loyal servant, you know that Tawz. I have work to do and don't need to stand about here banding words with an idiot. We must away. They have driven our troops back into Sheol. There's a great battle on the plain between the forest and the hedge. I'm off now to drive these monkeys to battle." With that Razeneck dashed angrily into the midst of a group of creatures, whipping them wildly, driving them on towards the outer edges of the grounds.

Tawz sat upon his steed a moment longer. He laughed sourly and then spoke into the air, "Your words will come back to you, Razeneck. You'll feel this questioning of the Master upon your back." Then he whipped his horse and was gone.

As soon as it was safe, Amos lifted his head. A new light was in his eyes. "Father has come."

Tom cut him short. "Whatever has happened, we can't waste time. Our distraction is here and we must make use of it. Eli, help me. All of you, the stronger helping the weaker, let's get out of here. Head for the forest, just as we came."

Tom took Abigail's arm. Pan picked up the two Luporchans and Eli led Enoch and Amos. They stepped into the fray. Creatures were running in all directions. The riders, hundreds of them, dashed through the hordes, rounding up the creatures and driving them to the battlefield. Tom turned back to his companions, whispering, "Keep your heads low and your faces covered. Try not to look around. Being inconspicuous is our best chance."

Tom led them out. They crouched over and ran, staying as far away as they could from the grey riders' whips. They joined groups of creatures chaotic and leaderless. The companions made their way through, avoiding the riders, moving closer to the forest in a wandering fashion. They were so blood-stained and hunched that they looked much like the beaten-down creatures in whose midst they were hiding.

Twice, a wild-eyed creature looked into Tom's face with surprise. Twice, a creature fell to the earth before its mouth could open.

The companions travelled much farther east than the spot where they exited the forest, but Tom didn't mind. All he wanted was to find shelter in that darkness. When at last they were close enough, Tom gave a signal and they lunged almost head-first into the forest.

Still they ran, half-pushing, half-dragging those who were weak. They wanted away from the castle grounds. Tom urged his followers on, to get them to keep going despite their weariness and weakness. A gasp of breath made Tom look at the pale Abigail. He stopped.

Amos and Enoch dropped to the ground.

Eli faced Tom, "It was almost too much for Enoch and Amos. They barely made it here."

Tom felt accused and said, "Well, if we'd been caught, they would be feeling much worse Eli." Tom clinched his mouth and continued, "I'm doing my best." He was sorry for those last words for he knew he sounded like a little boy.

Eli put his hand on Tom's shoulder. "I know you're doing your best. You've done well. But now, they need time to recover." Tom nodded.

He looked back to the edge of the forest. "Do you think those creatures come in here?"

Swen answered him. "They do come, but not often. Picnics, they call it. They tramp and stamp until they root out some creature of our wood, running it down till it has no strength. Then they eat it, while life still moves in its broken body. That's their picnic. That's their fun."

Tom hated the Vile One even more. "I think, they'll take no picnic today as they'll have no time for leisurely acts of violence. We can rest awhile. But only for a short time, I'm afraid."

They answered him only by laying themselves out on the ground. Tom couldn't rest so he decided to have a look around. He walk in what he felt would be the direction of the Enchanted Hedge. All was quiet in the woods. The little creatures must be hiding, and he didn't blame them. It took him some little while, even with running a while, to reach the outer edge of the dark forest. He stepped into an area of thinning trees and looked out warily at the plain before him. Signs of recent battle were apparent everywhere, with dead bodies scattered about. The dead creatures of Sheol were equalled by the number of the dead of Adamah. Tom groaned at the sight.

Taking a deep breath, he stepped out into the open plain and looked around. The battle had moved past this place, apparently moving towards the castle. The army of Adamah must be looking for their prince. They might be sad when they did not find him, but their battle would not be in vain, for it cleared the way for Tom to get Amos out of Sheol. He could now lead his companions across this plain in safety. The dead would not rise up to stop them.

Tom turned and went back into the shelter of the trees. He didn't notice the black speck in the air above him which soared three times in a circle then turned and flew west.

Tom walked back towards his companions but didn't hurry. He would give them only the time it took him to walk back to finish resting. Getting Amos and the others out of Sheol was now Tom's driving ambition. He was so close, but at any minute the tide might turn against him.

As Tom neared the place where he left his companions, he could hear their voices, Abigail's first and then the prince's, answering some question that she asked. What was it about Amos that troubled Tom? This was the young knight that Tom had come for, yet Tom didn't really want to go into that clearing and see him again. What was it? Tom stopped. It came to him. Amos' eyes troubled Tom. They felt so familiar and they looked at him so questioningly. Tom shook his head and walked on. The conversation stopped as Tom came through the trees.

"I've walked all the way to the outer edge of the forest and even stepped into the plain. The way is clear," he said.

"That is great news, Peregrine Sol."

Tom shook his head at Eddi and said, "Only so great Eddi. There's been a terrible battle in the plain, and the dead of the enemy is only part of the story. Many of Adamah have fallen, at least as many as the enemy." Tom looked at Amos. "It's an awful sight. You need to prepare yourself."

The companions were quiet as they dealt with this new information. They were so tired, hurt, and frightened, it felt cruel to push them on, but Tom knew he must. "I'm sorry, but we must go while it's safe to get across the plain. In some ways, it honours those who fell there."

Amos stood first, a determined look on his face. "You're right. A fine knight you are, brother." The others followed Amos and to Tom's surprise, Amos led them out of the clearing. Tom wasn't too sure how he felt about Amos taking the lead. Eli came behind and took Tom's arm. "Come Tom, they're only following your orders." Tom turned and looked at his Ach. Eli smiled at him. Tom shrugged his shoulders and smiled back at Eli. What did it matter who walked in front?

Eli and Tom brought up the rear as they finished their journey through Once Fair Forest. It was a slower journey than Tom would have liked, but he could see from behind that some were barely making it, even at that pace. It was a wonder really that they had been able to keep up the pace he set for them as they crossed the castle grounds.

As the trees thinned, Amos seemed to slow even more. He stopped, lowering his head momentarily, he looked back at Tom. Tom walked forward. "Are you all right, Amos?"

"Yes," Amos replied. Tom was not convinced. He took Amos' arm, "Come on, let's get them out of here," he said. Tom and Amos stepped out onto the plain at the same time. Amos let out a groan.

"It's terrible, isn't it?" Tom said to his fellow knight. Tom looked back at the others. They had been through enough. Pan's face paled and tears poured down. Many of the bodies were animals.

"Try not to look," Tom commanded. He walked on, picking his way around the fallen, trying to keep away from places he thought would be too painful for them to see. Amos fell behind and Enoch slowed down to join him. Meanwhile, Eli had come forward to walk beside Tom.

"Eli," Tom said. "I'm so glad you came with me on this quest. I don't know what I would have done…" He didn't finish, just smiled and said, "You were so little then, but you were right. I'd have failed the quest without my Ach." A look at Eli's face told him he didn't need to say anything else.

Tom stopped to see how his companions were holding up. Something moving in the distance caught his eye. Someone was coming in their direction. Tom turned all the way around, putting his hand to his eyes. His heart began to beat rapidly. It was the enemy, riders with whips galloped at the sides of the troops.

Tom turned to Eli. "I want to say something to you. I want you to know that if anything happens, you must change. You must transform into…." He couldn't finish. He felt embarrassed by the memory of his Ach as a beautiful unicorn. He took a deep breath, "You must take as many as you can carry and fly. No matter what happens to me."

"No," Eli's answered. "I'm your Ach. I could never leave you."

"You're my Ach, and I'm your leader. I tell you now and you must obey. If I tell you to fly, you take Amos and the others and fly."

Then, looking with compassion into his Ach's face, Tom said, "I couldn't live if I failed at this point. It's the best thing you could ever do for me."

The enemy was coming fast. Tom yelled at his companions, "The enemy is coming. Run as fast as you can toward the hedge."

They ran, stumbling, falling, and helping one another, yet they ran. But the enemy ran faster, whipped by the riders.

Tom looked back and gasped. They were close and leading the way on a new and terrible steed, was the Vile Prince.

Amos looked back too. He stumbled and fell, putting his hands over his head. Tom stopped running and called out, "Fly Eli, fly.

Chapter Twenty-Two

The unicorn's nose nuzzled Tom. Tom looked over, as he helped Abigail

climb on to the high white back of his Ach. She clung onto Amos. Enoch was at

the front. Eli's large eyes were frightened.

"I'll be okay, Eli. I have my sword. I'll make for the forest. I'll try to find

the knights of Adamah," Tom said, breathing hard.

Eli whinnied loudly, and then said in his horse-like voice, "I can take you

all Tom. I'm strong enough to carry everyone."

Tom handed Eddi and Swen up to Abigail. "No Eli, you must fly with all

the speed you have and get out of here. You're already overburdened. Pan,

you're not hurt, you stay with me." Pan's face went pale.

Tom patted Eli's strong flanks. "Go now."

Eli neighed furiously. "Tom, let me try to take you all."

The foot soldiers were nearly upon them with their heavy curved swords

drawn. Tom threw Pan up onto Eli's back and jumped on himself. "Hurry Eli,"

he yelled.

Eli ran, raising his white wings at his side as he lifted off the ground. Eli

laboured to go up, but he couldn't move fast, nor could he gain much height.

Tom urged him on, shouting, "Higher Eli, fly higher, we have to get higher."

An arrow whizzed by, just missing Eli's head. Another flew across in front

of Abigail's face. Tom looked back as the Vile Prince, on his steed, lifted off the

ground. The new beast had dragon-wings, and claws of a gigantic hawk. Its tail and face were those of a leopard. It roared loudly, baring enormous fanged teeth. And it flew fast.

Eli was already tiring with the weight of so many on his back. He could not go fast enough, and he was faltering in his direction as he tried to balance his heavy load. They were closer to the forest now, not the hedge. The beast behind was moving high into the air with great speed. Eli was not going to be able to carry them all to safety.

Tom yelled at Pan. "We have to get off so that Eli can get the others out of here." He put his hand on Pan's shoulder and leaned over to drop to the ground, which was now no more than a few feet below them again. He pulled his sword from its hilt and jumped, trying to take Pan with him as he went.

Pan let out a yell of terror and made a grab at Eli's tail. Tom felt a jerk, and the hand that was on Pan's shoulder was empty. Crashing to the ground, Tom scrambled to his feet. Losing Tom's weight was enough to help the unicorn. Eli began climbing again with Pan dangling from the end of his horsetail, swinging to and fro. Eli released a screaming neigh of anguish. But he flew on, this time moving away towards the breach in the Enchanted Hedge.

The beast had gone high thinking he would meet Eli in the air, but Eli had gone down, floundering. The Vile Prince and his steed overshot and were now dots in the air above the white unicorn. Realising their mistake, they turned and made a nosedive towards the unicorn.

Eli was moving faster now, but the enemy was a streak of lightning. Tom watched, willing his Ach speed, as the chase went far away from him.

The Prince turned to see what had fallen from the unicorn's back. One look at Tom, standing on the ground, his face changed, bones appearing and fire issuing. He was once again the frightful, skulled prince of fire and wrath.

The Vile Prince pulled the reins of his beastly steed. Tom saw what he was doing. He turned and began running towards the protective covering of the forest.

Tom looked behind him to see what was happening to his Ach and his friends. Eli was up high now and flying fast. Tom looked back in time to see Eli cross a breach in the Enchanted Hedge. They were in Adamah. Tom turned and ran, hardly seeing where he was going as he ran towards the forest. He ran as fast as he could from the flying beast, the Vile Prince, and soldiers and riders who were still making towards the Enchanted Hedge.

Tom's vision was blurred as he entered the shadows created by leaves and branches. He ran on, stumbling over roots and rocks, thankful the beast had not caught him in the open. It would never be able to fly through these thick branches.

Once he reached the darkness of the forest, Tom stopped, forgetful and tired, and leaned against a tree. It burnt his neck, leaving a stinging welt. Tom jumped back from the black tree and knelt on the ground. He thought hard, but no plan of escape came to his mind. He felt so alone.

Tom's head came up and his breathing became shallow and quick. A lilting voice came through the dark trees. "If you had changed course immediately on my command, we would have caught that stupid Amos. It was your hesitation that let him get away, Guan. My father will hear about this."

The answering voice was harsh, "Your highness must remember the speed at which we were travelling. I could not change any faster without dumping *you* on the ground."

"You say that, Guan, as though you would have liked to dump me," screamed the Vile Prince.

"No master, that's not so. I'm the devoted companion of your father, and I serve you as I serve him."

"How has this happened? That's what I want to know. How has Amos, that pasty-faced son of the knight of Adamah recovered? How has his armour been renewed and his sword returned to him? I will root out the traitor in our midst and make him pay a long sorrowful price for his treason."

Tom didn't stop to hear the steed's answer. He rose and ran on tiptoes to get away from those vulgar voices. A twig snapped under his foot. How could such a small crack echo so loudly? Tom heard the scuffle of feet and then the thud of running footsteps, so he turned and ran, like the hunted creature he was.

Tom felt so exhausted he had no sense of direction or idea of the passing of time. Did they breach the hedge into Sheol, find Amos, rescue Enoch and do battle with so many revolting creatures in just one day? Maybe Tom was locked in some grey cold twilight that would never be the calm of night or the delight of a day. That is what he feared most, that this would never end.

Tom slowed his run so he could listen. There was no longer any pounding of following feet. He slowed to a tiptoe trot again. His side ached with griping pains. If he ever got out of this place and back into the normal world, he would get as fit as possible so that he could run for miles without stopping.

He took the chance of a rest. Bending down in a stoop, unable to trust the trees to lean against, his eyes closed, and waited to hear sounds again.

Then the thought struck him. Why should he wait here like a hunted fox? Why should he not pursue his pursuer? If death was destined to come to him, why not go out and face it and fight it with all the strength he had left in his body. In that resolve, he once again made his way through the forest. He didn't know where he was. So he looked for light. That would tell him when he was close to edge of the forest.

Tom stopped. He could see his enemies outlined in the dim light. They sat close together, crouched down, leaning against a black tree. Was their skin so foul even the trees could not hurt them? The prince seemed tense and anxious, his companion not so. Guan was leaning back, relaxed and uncaring. Tom saw him put a long finger into his nose, swish it around, then pull it back out to stare at it before wiping it on the grass beside him. Then he did the same to other side of his nose. Tom felt sick.

"Guan, are you watching for that maggot?" hissed the Vile Prince.

"Yes master," Guan answered.

Tom thought of his own Ach and wondered where he was. Eli, a companion so different from this one, who cared about nothing, not even his prince.

The noise of a great clash suddenly came echoing across the plain. The battle was moving in this direction. The Vile Prince jumped up, looking out through the trees. Tom craned his neck forward, trying to see out through the distant opening. He could see nothing.

"Look, look at that," commanded the Prince.

Guan pushed himself lazily off the ground and moved to stand beside the prince. He was older and taller than the Vile Prince, and he was much uglier, with a twisted face, sullen and resentful. "What is it, my liege?" he asked, making those words sound almost like an insult.

"Can you see, you idiot? Do you see who is out there? There are knights out there. We were told that no Knights had come, that only weak creatures, children and animals, had come to find their prince. We've been lied to. You must fly to my father. You must tell him that Knights of Adamah from every order are invading. Tell him our servants are falling like flies and running like fools. He must send more or we are doomed."

The companion stood there looking out over the battlefield. The Vile Prince turned and screamed at him. "Can't you hear? Go now, fly to my father." And with that, the prince's eyes flamed, sending shoots of fire out to burn the creature beside him. A sickly smoke billowed around the two and when it cleared, the steed was running through the trees. As he came to the clearing, he lifted into the air on dragon wings.

The Vile Prince was clearly worried about what was happening on the plain. The battle was going against the Vile One's army. Hope returned to Tom that he would be able to find the Knights of Adamah and join them in fighting. He just needed to get past the Vile Prince and onto the plain.

"I know what I'll do," shouted the prince. "I'll curse the entire forest on account of you, Amos. It will burn." Tom realised he had moved and made a sound the Prince had heard. The flesh fell again from the Vile Prince's face, and his eyes burned with rage. Shooting flames of red and orange fire issued from his eyes to the nearest tree. A hot red flame shot up the trunk of the black tree. Then another look from those terrible eyes sent flames up a second tree.

Tom watched, horrified. What about all the little creatures who called this forest their home? What about the faerie people? He would not let the Vile Prince start fires throughout this wood.

Tom knelt on the ground, scrambling around, and finally putting his hand on a stone, he threw it as hard as he could. It hit a tree with a bash. The Vile Prince jumped and ran in that direction, but only for a few yards, quickly realizing that he had fallen for an old trick. Tom ran too, but he ran the opposite direction. The prince once again shot fire from his dreadful eyes. Tom only just made it to the outer edges of the woods before fire flew in at him. He jumped backed and the flames missed him. The feeling of success made Tom brave. He yelled back into the forest, now illuminated by flaming trees. "Come on you coward, come and take on somebody your own size for a change."

Then Tom ran, shouting with the joy of his small victory over his enemy, looking for the battle. The fighting was in full heat on the plains. Tom drew his sword and ran straight into a battle. He heard rather than saw his grim foe exist the forest.

The Vile Prince was attacked the moment he emerged from the trees too. Tom could see as he fought the creatures of Adamah that surrounded him, the Vile Prince was searching for him. Tom moved to help some valiant little antelopes. He looked around and found there were a few small bears, a faun and a woodland nymph there as well. With lashes and strikes of the sword, Tom helped drive back the enemy. Once that was done, Tom ran to help another group of creatures from Adamah. Pleased with his successes, Tom looked around to see if there were any more bands of little warriors who could use his help. Each time he joined a group of fighters, they cheered. Tom was delighted with this response until he heard some shouting victoriously "You're free, you're free, brave Princeling." Tom knew that they, like the Vile Prince, had seen his knight's covering, and assumed that he was Amos. Tom's heart sunk, and though he felt ashamed, he didn't tell them they were wrong. He didn't feel he could bear to see the disappointed look in their eyes.

Tom finished off a tall ugly brute, with long fingers, a short stumpy body, and green fangs, which had been attacking three squirrels and a Rufus. He turned to see where else he might be needed.

As Tom turned from this fight, to find the next, he looked around the battlefield. There were skirmishes taking place as far as his eyes could see. Tom saw a chestnut coloured centaur kneeling beside a fallen comrade, his noble head hanging down with grief. Baring down on the centaur was a Rider with a whip and sword in either hand. Tom ran, yelling with sheer terror in his voice. The Rider was faster, but Tom was closer and they came upon the sad scene at the same time. A clash of metal came over the centaur's head, as Tom's strong sword hit that of the Rider. Tom stumbled backwards and the Rider's horse galloped past. The Rider turned his steed and came back. Tom recovered himself and ran at the Rider again. This time the swords hit with a thunderous crash, but as they did so, the whip of the Rider came round Tom's head. Shredded glass at the end of the whip slashed through the face guard and cut into Tom's cheek. Tom cried out. By this time the centaur was up and he ran at the horse as Tom struck the Rider with his sword. The Rider was knocked to the ground and his whip flung away from him. Tom ran forward as the Rider stood up. Sword upon sword Tom fought the Rider while the centaur fought the evil horse. Tom saw the horse fall, and when the Rider looked towards his fallen steed Tom struck again and Rider fell.

Tom was panting with tiredness at the end of this battle. Blood was oozing down his cheek, falling to the breastplate of his black armour. Tom looked up into the brown eyes above him to see the centaur he had saved. Standing before him was Cimber.

"Well met again, Peregrine Sol Tom, especially for me. You have my gratitude, you saved my life," the noble centaur said, his face solemn and sad.

"I must tell you, Cimber, I didn't know it was you until this very minute. I only saw a Rider bearing down on a centaur. But I'm doubly glad now that I came running when I did."

"I could have wished that you'd come a few minutes sooner, Oh Great Knight of Adamah. For maybe with your help, I would have saved him." A great tear rolled down Cimber's regal face. Never again would Tom see a stranger nor sadder sight than the sight of this majestic creature crying.

Cimber turned back to where Tom first saw him kneeling. Tom's eyes followed him, and then Tom cried too. Walking over to the body lying still and cold, Tom heard Cimber say. "He would follow me to battle, always by my side. I tried to get him to stay behind, using every excuse I could think of. But no, he was sure that I needed him. And so I did. For he stepped in front of me and took the fatal wound that should've been mine."

Tom walked over and stood beside the massive centaur, putting a hand of comfort on his broad back, smooth as silk. And together they mourned, standing over the brown body of Brutus lying dead upon the foul dirt of Sheol.

How long they stood there, Tom never knew. It seemed an eternity of sadness, yet only a moment to mourn. A cry from the field of battle raised their heads and they remembered their fellow creatures, still living, and fighting for their lives.

Tom saw a fray between a small round Gambit and a vulture-warrior. The vulture was overcoming the little fluffy creature. Plucking it off the ground and dropping it. Tom ran in that direction. Cimber ran in another.

The vulture was a cowardly beast, and at the sight of Tom running at him, brandishing his sword, it dropped the Gambit for the last time. He flew away to pick on some other creature that could not fight back. The little Gambit immediately became cheerful. Leaping, bouncing and wobbling all around Tom with happiness, not seeming to remember that battle was still on going all over this wide plain.

Two chipmunks came running. "This way. Follow us," they squeaked and the Gambit followed, forgetting Tom as it forgot all other things. Tom raised his eyes again and he saw the Vile Prince. Their eyes met in hatred.

When Tom's eyes met the fiery eyes of the Vile Prince, his anger returned. The evil prince had been very busy while he looked for Tom in the battle. As Tom looked up, he burned a tiny Luporchan man. When Tom saw that cowardly act, he ran for the Prince, no longer afraid. Tom would not let that brute do any more harm. The Prince's face changed when he saw Tom coming. But this time it was not the icy bones and fires that came, but a look of astonishment.

The Vile Prince, perhaps taken by surprise at Tom's vengeance, turned and ran from the coming onslaught of the young black-suited knight running at him.

Tom saw the retreat of his enemy and he shouted with joy and victory. Running faster, waving his sword and shield before him, Tom looked like a great warrior routing all the enemy as he ran. The troops of Adamah, seeing the bravery of their young knight, shouted in triumph. The fighters rallied at that shout, but the servants of the Vile One trembled. Fear descended on the vile creatures like a tidal wave. As one band of enemy warriors ran, others followed until the battlefield was one long stampede of good creatures pursuing the evil. The riders with their whips lashed out in vain, but they could do nothing to stop the retreat.

Tom did not see the victory happening all around him. All he could see was the retreat of the Vile Prince before him. The Vile Prince didn't enter the smoking forest. He ran towards it and then turned before the trees began. Tom followed, feeling victory before it was won. He followed the prince unthinkingly. The Prince continued to run, leading Tom to a place between the plain and forest where the terrain of the land changed abruptly. Here, the land was pitted deeply in places and in others great boulders stood, as though some long-ago war of giants had taken place, leaving giant cannonballs behind and marking the earth forever.

Tom followed, his bravery growing with each step. He was routing the enemy. Tom continued into this unknown territory, shouting, sure of future conquest.

"Come on you cowardly prince of slime. Come and fight me. Can you only take on those littler than you and weak?"

As Tom came round a huge grey boulder, he froze. Graceful and confident, the tall Prince came from behind the huge rock, his sword in one hand, and a shield in the other. Tom stopped shouting, and skidded to a stop, almost crashing into the strong lean body of his enemy.

A flash, and Tom felt a searing pain down his face and neck. The flame from his enemy's eyes burned the flesh it was true, but as it did so it also froze the soul. Tom fell to his knees, so hurt he could not even cry out. The Prince stepped back and laughed his face now so cheerful and lovely.

Tom staggered to his feet. His enemy allowed him to do so. "I do love to destroy the weak," the Vile Prince answered in a smooth voice. "You are weak, though I have yet to figure out how you have returned to health and youth."

The chilling face was a skull once more and fire issued coldly from his eyes, burning and freezing Tom's legs. He laughed at Tom again. "But this is more fun, now I get to take you down twice, you fool. Even your father wondered if you were worth the effort of saving. He's so strong and brave, so they say in your country. But for you, he couldn't even be bothered to come..." A laugh echoed around the boulders as the prince threw back his head, closed his eyes and howled long and hard. But the words meant to bring so much pain to Amos, didn't hurt Tom at all. Instead of leaping at the ugly prince, as he must have expected, and Amos might have done, Tom leapt behind a boulder.

Tom, panting with fear and pain, stood with his back against the boulder making his sword ready. The Vile Prince laughed more. "There is nowhere you can hide, come out and let me play with you. Remember all the nice little things I did to you in the castle. We can have even more fun than that out here, you little worm of Adamah."

Tom knew the prince was right. There was nowhere to hide. There was also no help coming his way. The sounds of the battle had moved far from this place. There was no one around to hear Tom cry out for help, and no one to hear him cry out in pain. What Tom needed was a way to throw his enemy off guard. A way to make him stumble as Tom had done when he found the Vile Prince standing before him on the other side of this boulder. His enemy was quiet. Tom wondered why. All Tom's senses were alert and his mind was scrambling for a plan of escape.

Tom broke the silence, "You're very quiet now. I thought you like to talk. You seem very able with your tongue, and weak with everything else."

"Keep on, little maggot knight. It will do you no good, soon your whole body will freeze and burn. Excruciating pain and confusion. I'll enjoy watching you."

Tom turned his head. The Vile Prince's voice had come from the other side. So that was his game.

"Oh, you do love hard words. That must be why you kept that black she-cat guarding your front door."

"What do you mean?" The Vile Prince asked, his voice low.

"Oh," said Tom, trying to keep his voice light. "It's just that she too seemed to love to say hard words, poor little pussy cat. Yes, she loved mean words too."

"Where did you see Pardos?"

There was some change in the prince's voice. Tom wrinkled his nose, thinking. This seemed to keep his enemy on edge. He would keep it going and see if it brought his enemy's weakness to light.

"Pardos was that her name? She died well."

There was a most hideous screech that raised goose bumps on Tom's arms and legs. Then the Vile Prince jumped out. In a flash of light he was no longer a man but a full skeleton and his blazing eyes were shooting fire everywhere. Tom was scared as he had never been before. The skull had been enough, but to face a raging, flaming skeleton was too much. He leapt aside and shot his sword forward towards the chest of his enemy. Tom missed the chest, but hit the upper arm of the Vile Prince, who let out another howl of pain and rage. Tom too cried out, for heat and ice came up the sword, shooting through the hilt and into Tom's right hand and up his arm. The pain was excruciating and confusing, feeling both freezing cold and burning hot.

Tom leaned against the rock at his back. He reached over with his left hand and removed his sword from his now lifeless right hand. The touch of his own flesh burned him. Tom's breaths came out quivering, like a baby after a long cry.

The Vile Prince must have been hurt too, for there was no sound coming from behind the boulder. Tom needed the rest, but his courage was leaving him. His arm ached and he was frightened. He could not bear the thought of being burned by those icy eyes again. He fixed the strap of his black shield around his maimed right arm. Wrapping it around and around, cringing at the pressure.

He might as well get it over with. Tom spoke again, raising his voice just a little higher than a whisper. "You love to watch poor wretched creatures suffer and die. Would you like me to tell you how Pardos died? How she writhed on the ground?"

Tom was ready. He held his shield up, sickened by the pain that it caused to move his shoulder, and brandished his sword again. Flames shot everywhere. Then the skeleton disappeared but the skull face remained. The prince shot a fiery dart at Tom. Tom's shield reflected it.

"If you kill me too soon," Tom mocked, "you'll never know what her last words were."

With an electrical blaze, the prince was a skeleton, his sword in the air, shouting, and splashing fire in every direction. Tom sheltered behind his shield, watching in horrified fascination. "He doesn't move." Tom realised. "When he becomes a skeleton, he doesn't move."

The prince was his handsome self again. He rushed at Tom, his eyes fiery and his sword waving. Tom battled him, hit upon hit, he held off his enemy's sword. The crash of metal upon metal, and both fighters' harsh gasping breaths filled the air around them. Tom fought hard against the prince, his sword catching every move the Vile Prince made. But the disadvantage of being left-handed was making Tom tired. The Vile Prince could sense success was almost his and fire came from his eyes again, burning Tom's cheek.

A wretched squeal in the air above caught the attention of both the Prince and Tom. A battle was taking place above them as well. Twenty or so birds of various sizes were circling and attacking one another.

The Vile Prince returned his thoughts to the fight with Tom and swung his sword, catching Tom's mid-driff. His armour tore from his body and he stumbled and fell onto his wounded arm. He let out a scream of pain as the cords binding his shield ripped from his arm. His shield hit a rock and tumbled away. Tom's head smashed against the boulder and his helmet dislodged and fell to the ground beside him.

"And now to finish…" The prince stopped mid-sentence. He stood looking at Tom. His handsome face was marred and twisted with confusion. "Amos? You are not Amos?"

Tom shuffled away, just within fingers reach of his dropped sword.

"Who are you? I demand to know before I kill you."

Tom inched forward a little more as he said, "Can't you guess? Can't you tell?" He wrapped his fingers around his sword hilt. "Who do you think came into your country to rescue Amos? Who found your precious foul-mouthed pet at the door of your father's castle?"

The prince's eyes flashed, and his face was bones for a moment, but no fire issued. Then, as if confused about what to do next, the face was marred, one moment by an ugly scowl and the next by skull bones with no flesh, then back again.

"You play a dangerous game, boy. But you might as well, for no matter what game you play at, today is the day of your death. But who do I think you are?" The Vile Prince once again let loose one of his most ghoulish laughs. "I think that you are one we didn't know about. You are a well-kept secret, our spies have not heard of you. Killing you will be as good as killing Amos. And we will get him soon too." The Vile Prince lifted his sword and his shield and howled his fiendish delight at that thought.

The Vile Prince was gloating, dancing over the body of Tom as if he were already dead. He was now the one counting a victory before it was won. Tom plunged his sword into the foot of his enemy. The Vile Prince screamed in pain and anger. Yet again his anger turned his body to bones. The enemy was once again a maddened, unmoving skeleton with flames shooting from his eyes without control. Tom pulled his sword out of the prince's foot as burning pain ran up his fingers. Then he shoved it into the chest of his enemy, pushing himself up as he did, so that the thrust came with the full force of his young body. Tom pushed long and hard despite the searing pain that flowed down through the sword. Snapping, popping and fizzing, the skeleton disintegrated above Tom, while waves of fire and ice roared through the hilt of Tom's sword, into his hand and arm and down into his body.

The prince fell to the ground, half beautiful and half grotesque, he lay dead at Tom's feet. And Tom fell too, his body burning and freezing.

So Tom lay, and didn't hear or see the Knights of Adamah, led by Sir Gwain, blow the trumpets and declare a victory. He didn't hear the shouts of joy ring out as the troops of the Vile One surrendered in masses. He didn't see the

tears of joy mingle with sorrow as the creatures of Adamah claimed their dead

heroes from the battlefield.

And they did not see him where he laid, hidden in the boulders, the Vile

One's son at his feet.

Chapter Twenty-Three

Tom opened his eyes to find huge sea-blue eyes and a sharp pointed beak looking down at him. Now fully awake, he moved to get away from the attacking bird. But as he jerked his body, searing pain went through every ounce of him. He remembered the horrible burns and freezing wounds made by the Vile Prince.

The sea-blue eyes looked at him again, but this time out of a gentle round face.

"Mim," cried Tom. "Is that really you?"

"Tom," she answered, softly, "Is that really you?"

Tom tried to laugh, but it sent a pain through him that made him cry instead.

"Don't move, Peregrine Sol. Stay still. I'll help you." Mim moved out of Tom's sight. He tried to move to see her but it hurt too much. "Mim, Mim," he called out.

Her face was over his once again. "What is it, Tom?"

"I couldn't see you, Mim. I was afraid you were only a dream."

"I'm here, Tom. I just need to get some medicine for you. I'm going to step away again for just a moment. I'll come back with a dose for you." Mim disappeared from sight again.

"Now Tom, do you hear me? I'll talk with you while I mix this potion. You have been very brave. You've been much braver than I thought you'd be when I first met you. Do you remember how I spoke to you then? The dog-girl was very angry with me."

Mim's face appeared before Tom's eyes again. He was so grateful when Mim smiled at him.

"She's been brave too," Tom said.

"Yes, I know. You've both done wonderfully."

Mim held a strange looking cup to Tom's mouth. The cup was reddish gold in colour and decorated with designs of twisted leaves and vines. Above the vines strange birds flew in two different directions. "You must be brave again. You must drink the potion from this cup." Mim said, 'It might burn your throat, but it's nothing compared to what you've been through. Be brave, dear boy, and drink this down as fast as you can."

Mim helped him to lift his head. He groaned loudly as she held the cold cup to his lips and spilt the liquid into his mouth.

His body began to jerk and his head spun. The face above his contorted into an evil one. He had been tricked; this was not Mim at all. It was some evil creature, come to poison him. The world spun around him and Tom saw large outstretched hands coming down towards his neck. He could do nothing to stop it, because his jerking body was full of pain. Heat burned where once his bones were freezing, cold sheared his burnt flesh. He heard horrendous screams all around him and realised it was his own voice in his ears.

The hands holding him were not around his neck, they were on his shoulders, holding his shaking body down. Tom's vision cleared, and it was

Mim once again, her eyebrows drawn, the sea-blue eyes, stormy. Tom's body went limp and lay still.

"I'm sorry, Tom. I didn't tell you how painful it would be. I thought it might frighten you too much after all you have been through. But it will strengthen you and heal you for a short while till I can get you out of this nasty place."

"I thought, Mim, I thought you turned into another awful creature. I thought…"

"Don't, Tom, don't think about it anymore. I am Mim," she said. "I need you to stand up. You'll feel weak, but for the moment the pain should not be much."

Tom felt weak and stiff but only a little pain. Mim helped him and leaned him against the boulder. She bent down and picked up his helmet and sword and gave them to him. Tom took them in each hand. His arms and hands were charred and felt heavy but no longer ached. Mim then walked over and picked up Tom's shield.

"Mim, have you seen Eli and the others? Are they okay? Do you know if they reached a safe place?"

Mim stood up, holding Tom's shield by her side. "I haven't seen them, but I have heard they reached Hokmah safely. I know some were badly wounded. There is great wonder that they made it out of this awful place when they were so weak and hurt. There is great praise given to you now, Tom.

Tom hung his head. "It wasn't just me. It was all of us. Every one of us played some important part. I think maybe I did the least of anyone."

Mim smiled as she came up to Tom. "That's always the way it is, Peregrine Sol. It's always everyone, never just one person who does great things."

"Mim?" said Tom.

"Yes, what now, dear boy? How many questions are you going to ask me standing here with this awful thing at our feet?"

Tom looked down on the ground. The Vile Prince still lay where he had fallen. His body was half bones. His half-skull face made Tom ill. Yet he still felt ashamed that he had killed. Tom turned his face away and was quiet.

"Come, Tom, the deed you did was awful but good. The two can walk together hand in hand."

"Can you tell me more about Amos and his father?" Tom asked, trying not to think of his slain enemy.

"We need to go, Tom. The medicine I gave you will work only for a little while." Mim stepped up to him. "Can you take your shield? It's cracked in the battle but the Armatura of Hokmah can mend it. I'll transform and carry you, Peregrine Sol. Would you like to ride on my back? Only one other has ever done so and that was long ago."

"Who was it Mim?"

Mim smiled a dreamy smile. "I can't tell you all my stories now. We must fly away. Can you carry your shield as well as your helmet and sword?"

Tom reached for the shield. As Mim held it out for him, she gave out a gasp. "Look Tom. Look at your shield," Mim said, in a stunned voice.

Tom looked at his shield. It was cracked and bits of the black on the front were loosening and falling away from it in small clumps. There, underneath the cracks and crevasses, were symbols. Tom held it up and he and Mim gazed at it. The shield was divided into four by thin gold lines. The black armour covered all but the middle. In the middle, laced through the gold, was a green vine with many leaves. A dove was sitting on the vine, a cluster of grapes in her mouth.

"That symbol in the middle, Mim, is it the same as Amos's shield?"

Mim looked up at Tom, her blue eyes wide. "Yes, Tom. It is. But your shield has more than just the vine. It seems to have something in each corner. I can't tell what symbols are there."

"Can you tell me more about Amos, Mim?"

Mim said with urgency in her voice, "No, Tom, not now. We must leave here. I've lingered too long. Your medicine will soon wear away and your pain will come again." Mim transformed into a huge and beautiful bird with bright coloured feathers mingling with gentle pastels ones. Her voice became high as she spoke again, "Please, can you climb on my back now?"

Tom looked around him. He was tired but felt a strange reluctance to leave.

He looked at Mim, she watched him with her narrow bird eyes. "What kind of bird are you?"

"I told you already, Tom. When you were in Erets, I told you and the dog-girl. I'm a Rara Avis."

"I don't know what that is."

Mim gave a trilling laugh and said in a motherly voice "Did you not look it up when you went home? You should always find out what something means. Meanings are important." Her high-pitched laugh rang out again and she said, "But come now, dear boy. Climb on my back and I'll tell you what it means."

Finally, Tom stepped up to Mim and with great heaviness he climbed on her feathered back

"I'm a Rara Avis, Tom. Have you ever seen another like me?"

"No."

"I'm a Rare Bird." And with that, Mim lifted her wings and flew off the ground.

As they soared upward, Tom looked down. He could see fallen bodies of the good and evil creatures lying across the great expanse of the plain. Captive groups of evil beasts were being guarded by battalions of knights and others. It was busy work down there, and unhappy at times. He could see bodies being moved about for burial, and a hunt for those who lay as though dead but were only wounded.

"Mim?"

"Yes."

"What about the battle?" Tom asked, his voice sounding tired in his own ears.

"The servants of the Vile One surrendered, at least those who haven't run away to hide in holes. The knights and others are hunting down all they can.

Others have come to help carry away our dead and wounded. We had terrible losses, but we claim the victory, so they died for a great cause." Mim's voice was very sad.

"Did the Vile One surrender?" Tom swallowed a lump in his throat. "Does he know I killed his son?"

A shudder went through Mim's body as though she had hit some turbulent air upon her wings. "The Vile One is closed up tightly in his castle. He has not surrendered nor do I think he ever will. But he knows he is defeated, in this battle at least."

Mim stopped speaking, and Tom waited. She spoke again slowly. "That Vile Master knows his servants are weak. He knows we will not hurt or kill where it's not necessary. Nor will we take his land, though by rights we could. But we are not like him. Some cry out to conquer, but we will resist that desire. We will not be like him." Mim's voice rose high and was fierce. Then more softly again she said, "So his creatures will crawl back to him to be whipped and beaten, yet serve him once more. And he will continue to be our enemy and trouble us at every turn." She finished with a sigh. "But one year of peace we will have. One year of pure peace and joy." She seemed then to speed up her flying.

"Is that the agreement with the Vile One, that there will be a truce of one year?" Then more timidly he asked again. "And his son, does he know about his son?"

Mim didn't answer for a moment, and Tom saw they were now flying over a breach in the hedge. "No, this foul enemy of ours would never agree to a truce. He hates us with a passion, as only evil can hate good. The Knights and Wise Ones of our land are at the window of his castle speaking with him now. But no truce will ever come of it. And even if he made such an agreement, we would never trust him to keep his word. No, he only yells out vulgar words and accusations."

"Were you there, did you see him?"

"I was there, but didn't see him."

"Were you there because you are a wizard?"

"Yes. I'm a Wise One of Adamah."

"Do you live in Hokmah?"

"No, you know where I live. You have been to Erets where I care for my little ones. There are Wise Ones living in many places. Maybe even closer to you than you know."

"Was Sanyassi there?"

"Yes, he was there, along with many others. There were many things to deal with, once the battle was fought and won. We needed gifts of many kinds to help us finish the tasks at hand."

"What kind of tasks?"

"Talking with the Vile One, sorting out what to do with his servants we have taken captives…"

Tom laughed, "We left some tied up on his doorway." Thinking about those creatures made him think about his companions.

"Yes, we found one there, tied up tightly, who was very important to his son."

"Pardos?"

"You know her name?

"Yes, I told him, the Vile Prince, that we had killed her. It made him so angry that he turned…" Tom hesitated, not wanting to talk about it anymore. "Well, that is how I overcame him, he couldn't move when he was like that."

Mim seemed to understand without any more explanation. "Yes. His anger was both his greatest weapon and his worst weakness."

"What will you do with Pardos?" Tom asked quietly.

"I'm not sure. She was changed by your encounter, so strangely silent and speechless. More cat-like than I remember her to be."

"Have you seen her before?"

"Yes. She is part of my story. And my story connects closely to yours."

"Have you seen the Vile One?"

"No one has ever seen him. We see only his servants and his son, never him."

"His son was handsome and horrible." Tom shivered with memories.

"You were very brave to fight him, Tom. We were afraid you were taken by him. Some saw you running after him during the fiercest part of the battle. Then no one seemed to know anything about you. Everyone assumed that the

Vile Prince had overcome you and carried you away. We stood in front of the castle window, not wanting the Vile One to know our fear, yet trying to find out if he had you in his castle. We realised, in his accusations towards us, that he did not have you there. That's when I came out with others to look for you on the battle field."

"So the Vile One does know about his son then?" Tom asked again.

"That the Vile Prince is dead? No, he doesn't know. He thinks we have him captive. He accuses us of coming into this land to kidnap his son and hold him ransom. What the foul will do, they accuse others of doing."

A fresh breeze flew into Tom's face as they sailed across the sky. In Adamah the air was clean and Tom felt brave again. "Who will tell him that his son is dead?" he asked.

"Some of our strongest knights will come well-armoured and carry the body to the castle door. They will need to take care, for even touching the dead prince can burn their skin and freeze their bones. Then the father will know his son is dead. And I'm afraid, Tom, he will know who did it. There were birds in the sky today that I didn't know, and they were not driven away in time. And we think we have spies in our midst. That is terrible and sad to us. It's the first time that it has ever been so in Adamah."

Tom sat in silence for a long time, thinking about all that had happened. He still had so many questions, but he was tired. And his pain was returning. "Mim?"

"Oh Tom!"

"Just one more question, Mim."

"Okay, just one more question."

"Did you have a mother, Mim?"

The bird beneath him trilled a happy laugh, long and hard. "Of course I did. We all have mothers."

"Was she a Rara Avis too?"

Mim's voice was thoughtful and maybe a little sad. "No, she was wonderful and a little fierce. I loved her dearly."

"Mim."

"You said just one more, Tom."

"This is part of the other question. Do you know about my mother? Do you know if she's okay?"

Mim was silent, flying strong and hard against the breeze. "Everything will be okay. Now, everything will be okay."

Tom groaned softly as the pain came back upon him.

"Hang on tightly. I'll go faster."

"Tell me about Amos now please, Mim."

"I can't, Tom. I need to concentrate to fly fast and hard. I have already said too much. More than I should. Lie upon my back and rest now, Peregrine Sol. Your quest is finished and you deserve rest."

Tom laid his head on Mim's soft feathers. The icy pain crept back through his body and his flesh wounds burned again. He closed his eyes and thought he heard the sound of his mother's voice calling.

Chapter Twenty-Four

Tom was sitting in a chair looking at a garden full of herbs and flowers. This was the first day that he'd been allowed out of the infirmary. He'd been well cared for, and his favourite healer was Galenic.

Two others also cared for him. They were kind and gentle. Both were green, like Galenic, one was an old man with moss growing in his beard. The other was an older lady. Tom tried to get information from his carers. But the two older ones told him they were obeying the rule, set by the Wizards, which said Tom was to be told nothing until he was well.

Galenic was the only one who talked to him about the things he wanted to know, such as the fact that Eli was fine and was anxious to see Tom. She also told him Abigail was better and staying with some friends in Hokmah. And finally, she surprised him by informing him that he was not in Hokmah's infirmary.

"Where am I?" he demanded.

"You will know soon, Peregrine Sol." Galenic said, smiling at him.

"When?"

"When you are well."

Tom was angry with her for a few minutes. But who could stay angry with a beautiful green girl?

Galenic also told him that Amos and Enoch were recovering and he would be able to see them 'as soon as you are well'.

Tom now felt better and he was getting restless. "I need to go home," he said to Lilium, the older woman who cared for him. "My mother must be frantic with worry."

"Your mother is not my concern, Peregrine Sol. You are. But I do think you are getting well. Perhaps even well enough. We shall see." Lilium turned and with a swish of her green dress, she left the room, leaving behind the dusty sweet smell of herbs.

Tom was allowed to sit in a chair placed in the sunshine. A few bits of gauze were wrapped around his arms and taped to his face. They smelled of herbs. He stretched himself out and closed his eyes.

"Well, Peregrine Sol, do I find you sleeping in the sun?"

Tom opened his eyes and sat up quickly. .

"Sanyassi," Tom said, standing up.

"Sit down, sit down, Tom. Here, I will sit beside you." Sanyassi pulled a chair up beside Tom and sat down. "Oh, this is very nice. Yes, I too could go to sleep in this fine sunshine."

"Have you come to talk to me at last?" Tom said, smiling at the old wizard. "Have you come to tell me how things are in Adamah and send me back home?"

"I've come only to look at you for the moment. To make sure you are well before you have any more thrust upon you."

"Why? What has happened that makes everyone thinks they need to protect me?"

"It's nothing like that. I can see you are well. Well enough that not knowing what is happening is the worst thing for you."

Sanyassi leaned back in his chair and stretched out his legs as Tom had done earlier. "Very well, Tom. Tonight we shall have our celebration."

"What celebration?"

"Dear Tom, the celebration of the fulfilment of your quest. We will celebrate the home-coming of Amos and the victory of the Battle of Sheol, as it will now be called." Sanyassi smiled then raised his eyebrows at the boy in front of him. "Did you think you were the only one who was waiting around here? All of Adamah has been waiting for you to get well so that we could begin our greatest celebration ever." Sanyassi lowered his eyebrows and frowned in a funny way. "We couldn't have the celebration without you, you know."

"Well, I hope all my companions will be there. They were all part of it."

"Yes, of course, they will be there."

"I can't understand why I haven't been allowed to see them."

"You have been very ill, Tom. For a few days we wondered if you would survive. That was some enemy to take on, an amazing victory you accomplished." Sanyassi looked closely at Tom again.

"How long have I been here? Nobody will talk to me about anything. They won't even tell me how long I have been here."

"Six days ago, Mim flew here with you on her back. For three of those, you didn't wake, so no one could talk to you then," laughed the old Wizard. "And for the last three days, at least one person has talked to you." Sanyassi laughed again at Tom's expression. "Galenic is too good a healer to do anything that might bring you harm, of course we knew she was telling you a few things to ease your mind."

"I need to go home, you know. My poor mother must be so worried. I've thought about just saying my words and going. But I can't do that without Abigail."

Sanyassi stood up. "First things first, dear Tom. Tonight, we will celebrate. And tonight will come very soon, and then you can ask questions and be answered till your heart is content as far as I'm concerned." He smiled down at Tom. "You may well learn more than you wish."

"Good-bye till tonight, Peregrine Sol."

"Good-bye, Sanyassi."

Tom leaned back in his chair thinking about Sanyassi's words. Well at least he would get a few answers tonight.

The day was long. Not even Galenic came to see him. She probably knew he would pump her full of questions that she wasn't allowed to answer. But the day finally did pass into evening. Lilium came and mossy Leikhen came with her.

"You need to dress now," Lilium said. "Leikhen will help you. Come, come," she called behind her. Two little creatures came scurrying in to the room carrying Tom's armour. The creatures looked at Tom with wide lion eyes, and snapped their little bird beaks, flapping brown and gold wings. They handed the armour over to the healer then turned tail and ran. The tails they turned were lion's tails and their hind legs were lion's legs.

"What are they?" Tom asked.

"Young Griffins. Cute when they are little, but it's frightening to meet an adult griffin you know."

Lilium left the room after the Griffins and the silent Leikhen helped Tom dress. Leikhen lifted the breastplate of Tom's armour up, and his leaf-green eyes met Tom's. He smiled but spoke no word. Tom held his arms straight out and felt warmth as Leikhen put the armour against his chest. The armour took over, closing in around Tom, fitting against his body like a silk glove does a hand. The leg plates, shoulder plates and the rest of the armour body, all did the same, made themselves at home on Tom's body where they belonged. Tom felt complete.

Finally, Leikhen handed Tom his helmet. Tom put it on his head, feeling a comfortable safety.

"Where is my sword and shield?" he asked the healer.

Leikhen held up Tom's sword. Then Leikhen spoke, his voice a rustle of leaves scratching a tree in the autumn. "The sword I have, but the shield I do not."

Leikhen turned and left the room, not speaking to Tom even to tell him what he should do next. Tom stood there some moments, wondering, but taking the time to enjoy the feel of his armour again.

Sanyassi entered the room. Tom looked up and smiled at him.

"Well, Peregrine Sol, you now look like the knight we sent out on the quest. That's how everyone will wish to see you this evening."

"My shield isn't here. Leikhen didn't seem to know anything about it. Not that he said that, in fact he says very little."

"Then he is probably the wisest among us, dear Tom. Don't worry, Peregrine Sol, your shield will be returned to you in a way befitting the occasion. But come, come, hurry on, there are many waiting to greet you."

Tom walked down a long narrow corridor. Nervousness overcame him. He stopped. Tom called to Sanyassi. The old wizard turned. His white beard swished. He was wearing a long red robe with orbs and crescents that moved about with light. His hat was not as tall as the first one Tom had seen him in, but it was pointed and from it hung long beautiful scarves of many colours. He smiled at Tom. His wrinkled face seemed as dear as a grandfather to Tom just then. "I feel a little uptight, Sanyassi. I mean I don't even know where I am. I thought it might be Hokmah, but Galenic said no."

Sanyassi walked back to Tom and put his hand on Tom's shoulder. "Dear boy, you are in Sir Gwain's home, Avon Castle. It is a special place, in Adamah. Hokmah too is a special place, and there are others. Someday Tom, I think you will know all the special places of Adamah, but first you must know this one."

Sanyassi patted Tom's shoulder and said, "Come, there is nothing for you to be afraid of." But the look in Sanyassi's eyes made Tom's heart beat faster.

Sanyassi turned, walking down the long corridor again. Tom hesitated a moment and then followed the old wizard. At a doorway, Sanyassi turned back

to give Tom a smile. He opened the door. Light came into the corridor.
Then it was darkened by a shadow. Eli stood in the doorway.

Tom fought back embarrassing tears and thumped his Ach on the back. Eli
came round Tom to stand by his side, and said softly, "I am your Ach."
Memories echoed in Tom's head.

Together, Tom and Eli stepped into the bright room. Tom looked up. Pan
was standing beside Abigal. Eddi and Swen were sitting on her shoulders.
Looking down the line of people, Tom saw that next in the line stood Enoch and
beside him Prince Amos. Tom gave them a faltering smile too. Beside Amos
was an older man with dark green eyes. Tom nodded his head, unsure. This must
be Sir Gwain and he was looking at Tom with eyes full of emotion. Tom's gaze
lingered on this man of whom he had heard so much. A helmet partly covered
Sir Gwain's hair which was dark brown streaked with grey. He was not a tall
man, but was strong and held himself straight. His face was kind, etched with
both wrinkles of worry and lines of laughter. Tom glanced back at Amos, giving
him a hesitant smile. Tom envied him.

Tom's eyes travelled to the next person, a woman. The room was silent,
though it was filled with hundreds of creatures watching. A waiting tension
filled every vacant space. Tom's eye filled with those embarrassing tears and he
could look no further. Tom called out in a strangled voice, "Mum, is that you? I
don't understand."

First Tom felt his Ach's hand on his back, and then he was embraced in his
mother's arm. The muffled voice of Sanyassi called out loudly into the silence

of the room. "Here is Peregrine Sol Tom, Knight of Adamah, Fullfiller of a Great Quest, Rescuer of Prince Amos."

An answering cheer came back and Tom heard people yelling his name. There were shouts of hoorays and the sound of trumpets. But it was all far away compared to hearing his mother's voice saying over and over. "Oh Tom, I'm so sorry. I'm so sorry. Please understand that everything I did was because I thought it was best for you." Tom was confused, he didn't know if he should be happy or scared.

Tom's mother stepped away from him. The room was silent once again. He looked up to see Sanyassi standing beside her with his hand on her shoulder. "Miriam, please, go back and stand beside Gwain."

"Sanyassi, I'm not sure this is best."

Sanyassi smiled down on Tom's mum and gently but firmly moved her back to the line of people standing in front of Tom. Then Sanyassi came back to Tom.

"Peregrine Sol, I know this is difficult for you. And you need to be brave as we walk through this night of celebration. You've been brave before. You need to be brave again tonight. Everything you did on your great quest, you did for the good of Adamah. Let tonight be for the good of Adamah as well. There are creatures here representing all the people of this land, they are here to celebrate and to see a time of peace established. This is their time. Your time for answers will follow if you are patient."

Tom whispered, "But my m…mother. I don't understand." A look, a worried look in Sanyassi's eyes shut Tom's mouth. He nodded his head at the old wizard. He could do nothing else.

Sanyassi again turned towards the crowd, speaking to Tom loudly. Tom knew the words were for the listeners rather than for him. "Come, Knight Tom. Come and celebrate a night of peace and joy."

Tom followed Sanyassi as the sound of clapping and cheering filled the room. Eli's hand on Tom's shoulder was comforting. They came to a long white table in front of many other tables. Sanyassi directed Tom to take a seat. The others sat down too, Eli on Tom's right, a knight he did not know on his left. Tom looked around to see where Miriam was. She was sitting at the end of his long table. Beside her on one side sat Mim, and on her other side was Sir Gwain. Close beside them were Abigail, Eddi and Swen. Enoch, and Amos were there too, and some others Tom remembered from Hokmah . Tom's head began to swim. He stopped looking.

Plates of food flew in and all the people rose to say the blessing as they had in Hokmah. Tom looked down at his plate but his mind was busy trying to understand what was happening around him. Serving folk dressed in gold came to fill his goblet. Tom tried to eat, but he could not taste, even though it was the delicious food of Adamah.

Sanyassi rose as the feasting settled into a gentle hum. "Good folk of this great land, we come to celebrate."

The cheering broke out once again. Sanyassi held up his hand trying to settle the people. Finally, a young Niebulung stood and blew a horn. Tom saw a few creatures in the front row duck as the horn went up and under the gnarly nose. Then as the blast rang out they looked at each other embarrassed at their mistaken thoughts that they were going to be hit by a peashooter.

"Good people, we have much to celebrate. No, no, please let me finish. We have our young prince back safely." Sanyassi couldn't stop them so he bowed his head and waited for the cheering to stop.

"And we have quelled our enemy." A small cheer came up this time.

"And the return of those who went out on this great quest." This time the cheer rang out long and loud.

"Good people we have more to celebrate as well. Sir Gwain, your shield," Sanyassi shouted.

Tom, ignoring with great effort the looks his mother was throwing in his direction, watched Sir Gwain rise with a loud ritualistic stamping of his feet. Sir Gwain stood, holding his shield erect, facing towards the watching crowd. He then raised the shield above his head. Following their great leader, all the Knights of Adamah, save Amos, stood, each of them following the same ceremonial stamping as Sir Gwain. A great clash of armoured feet stomping on the floor rumbled through the room, followed by the sound of metal on metal as the knights all over the huge hall lifted their shields above their heads. Tom shuffled, unsure if he too should stand. Eli put a firm hand on Tom's shoulder and shook his head.

Tom looked at the shields of Adamah held proudly in the air, but his eyes lingered on Sir Gwain's beautiful shield. It was divided by gold lines into four corners. In each corner was a different symbol of an order of Adamah gleaming proudly. And looking around, Tom saw those symbols on shields all over the hall.

Sanyassi smiled broadly at the cheering crowd, and then signalled for the Niebulung to blow his horn again. "Amos, show your shield."

Amos stood, stamping his feet on the floor as the other knights had done before him. He held his shield out for those around him to see and then he too lifted his shield above his head. The symbol of the vine and dove shone out.

"Many years ago, the Armatura gave a new symbol to Adamah and we have waited for another to follow suit to create a new order. Now it has come." Sanyassi looked over at Tom with a smile that did not reach his eyes. His eyes were serious and concerned and his voice was solemn as he spoke. "Tom, raise your shield. It's beside your chair."

Tom stood up, trying to do as the others had done, but feeling that he only made a scuffling sound on the floor. He reached down beside his chair and found his shield was there. He held it out before him, facing it towards the watching crowds trying to following the actions of the other knights. Then he held his shield above his head for everyone to see. There was no cheering as Tom's shield was lifted. A great hush fell over the watching crowd.

Sanyassi spoke to the silent crowd. "The vine and the dove have returned, the Armatura has spoken. We now have a new order in Adamah. It shall be called the order of St. Marcus the Healer." Tom looked at Amos, wondering how the young prince felt about this. Then he looked back, the crowd was so quiet and their eyes so wide. They were all looking at him and his shield.

Sanyassi turned towards Tom again and held up his long hand. "The Armatura has spoken. A new heir is established. Tom Wade, Knight of St. Marcus, is declared heir to the throne of leadership. He will be the leader of the Knights of Adamah."

Tom frowned. What was going on? He held his shield a little to the side so he could look up at it. On every corner, surrounding the vine and dove, were the symbols of all the orders, just like on Sir Gwain's shield. Tom shook his head.

"I feel sick, Eli. I need to get out of here."

"Just a little longer, Tom," his Ach said in a gentle voice. "Can you make it just a little longer? Then I will take you out."

"Be seated knights of Adamah," Sanyassi commanded. Tom and all the knights sat down. Sanyassi cleared his throat as though a little choked. "Our greatest celebration comes tonight because a peace has descended upon Adamah. A year-long peace."

The cheering of the crowd could not be quelled even by the Niebulung's horn. Instead more trumpets were blown around the room in response. Sanyassi could do nothing but wait for the excited crowd to settle down in their own time. Finally, it quieted and the old wizard could speak.

"A prophecy has been fulfilled. We didn't know it was happening in our midst, but it did and now we will enjoy the blessing of a year-long peace."

Tom watched, lines forming between his eyes with his intense concentration. Two young women, green and woody in appearance, carried in a large clay pot. The pot had a thorny plant in it, full of buds. Tom looked over at his mother, whose head was lowered, looking down. He then looked back at the pot, now placed by Sanyassi's feet.

Libri walked out from among the crowd, In his hands he held one of the heavy, ancient books that Tom had seen him use in Hokmah. Libri stood on the other side of the pot and opened the book.

Libri's voice echoed across the quiet room, even though he was looking down reading the book. "In the Books of Prophecy, it is found: 'When a brother saves a brother unaware, a year of peace shall descend upon Adamah'." As Libri's voice faded, the buds on the bush burst into bloom. There were hundreds of glorious, multi-coloured roses.

Tom's ashen face turned towards his mother. Sir Gwain's face was full of anguish and Tom saw Miriam mouth the words across to him, "I'm sorry."

Eli was standing beside Tom, his hand on his arm. Tom turned his pale face to his Ach. "Amos…my brother?"

"Half-brother, Peregrine Sol."

"My mother and Sir Gwain are…what Eli? What does this mean?" Eli put his hand on Tom's shoulder. "We can go now, Tom."

Chapter Twenty-Five

Tom sat down on the bench beside Eli. The night was cool and comfortable. Yellow and blue stars twinkled in the black sky. Sounds of talking and laughter filtered from the huge hall. The celebration was still on going inside but outside the mood was somber.

Tom paced and ranted. Eli just listened. Tom wanted Eli to answer back so he could shout at someone. But his faithful friend sat with his head bent down nodding in agreement with everything. Tom finally sat down beside him.

Eli looked up and gave Tom a crooked smile. And Tom grinned back, shaking his head. "How long have you known about all this, Eli?"

"Not long. When we first arrived, I was too weary and sick of heart for anything. We flew into Hokmah. I fell to my knees at the entryway. The doors were shut. I don't know how long I stayed there, kneeling before the doors. We were all weary beyond reason and too frightened to even move."

Eli looked up at the beautiful night sky. "Then the doors of Hokmah opened. They were shocked to find me on their doorstep. Then when they saw Amos, well, I can't even describe the reaction. We seemed buried in people scurrying back and forth to help us."

Tom was looking at the half-hidden face of his Ach. Eli turned around to face him fully, his large brown eyes expressive. "All of us except Pan were taken to the infirmary and didn't see each other. I was only there for a couple of days. Eddi, and Abigail were released a day later. We sat together often. We wondered about Enoch and Amos, who were still in the Hokmah infirmary and allowed no visitors. And we worried about you. We were told that you had come back sorely wounded from the battle and that you had killed the Vile Prince. Your name was whispered all over, a great hero, that's what you are my friend."

Tom looked back down and Eli continued. "Then we were told you were Sir Gwain's son. It seems few people knew of your existence in Adamah. Your mother's marriage to Sir Gwain and your birth had been the private affairs of Avon Castle. Most people were greatly surprised by this turn of events. But it explained a lot to me. All the time, I knew I was your Ach, though I wondered why."

"You mean, you wouldn't want to be my Ach if I weren't Sir Gwain's son?" Tom asked with a smirk.

Eli kicked Tom's foot and they laughed together.

"Where did Pan go, do you know, Eli?"

Eli laughed a little. "I was so angry at him for leaving you. After crossing the Enchanted Hedge, I swerved violently for a while, giving him a most frightful ride. But I think, it was worse for him in Hokmah. Can you imagine having to tell Sanyassi that he deserted you on the field of battle? No, in the end I felt sorry for him, more sorry for him than for any one of us. Though I was very worried about the news you were to receive. But you are okay, aren't you Tom?"

"I think Eli, that I'm more stunned than anything." Tom looked over at his friend, "I've had a father and a half-brother all this time and didn't know. I still don't understand it. They have a good bit of explaining to do, this lot."

A light caught Tom's eye and he looked up. Amos was coming out of the hall, the door letting the bright lights shine on the grass in front. He saw Eli and Tom and walked their way. Eli stood. "I think you need to speak to Amos alone."

Amos came up to the bench and sat down beside Tom, an elbow on each knee and his hands pressed together, his head hanging low.

Amos said, "Are you okay Tom?"

"Barely." Tom said. Amos nodded his head.

"Do you mind that I am here, Amos?"

Amos sat up in surprise, "Mind? You saved my life." Amos pulled out a small bit of square paper from inside his breastplate. "Your mother brought me this last time she came." He handed Tom a photo. Tom stared down at the image of himself.

"It's a lifeless thing, compared to the paintings done by Identity Wizards here. They seem to be able to capture the personality and soul of the person on canvass. This thing Miriam called a photo leaves something lacking around the eyes and expression. But still I liked it. Between the photo and what your mother told me about you, at least I knew you a little. How can I be sorry you are here, my brother?"

"But the shield, the symbols, the business of my being the heir. I mean, all of that should be yours."

Amos laughed loudly, a pleasant friendly laugh that made Tom smile. "I never wanted it. When I was a boy, about your age, I went to the Armatura. I was so afraid. It was assumed that the shield would be the same banner that my father and grandfather had carried. But I live for peace. I think that maybe I am more the healer than the knight. The wizards were in quite a stir when I came out and held up my shield. Quite a stir. But I loved the symbol of the green vine and dove. It suited me perfectly."

"But why me? You're the oldest, and the one who was born here," Tom said.

"You were born here too, Tom."

At Tom's sharp gasp of surprise, Amos said, "I've told them all along that you should know." His voice was tight.

Tom looked at his brother and he could see Amos was angry as well. That thought somehow calmed Tom. "Did my mother come here often? Is she from here? Why don't we live here?"

"I can't tell you her story. Only she should do that. She is not from Adamah, and left when I was a young boy. She only returns during the Season of Peace. That's the only time she can come here. It is all part of the agreement she made when she left."

"What's the Season of Peace? Even after what was said in there, I don't really understand," Tom said.

"When the Soshonanna buds bloom, we have peace in Adamah. The Vile One's creatures cannot come near the hedge, not even to fly over it. The whole plant is enchanted right down to the fragrance. So its flowering is a joyous time in Adamah. Your mother is here and our father is very happy."

Tom nodded his head. His mum and her 'blooming trips'. "So you knew who I was when I found you in that room. You knew I was your brother."

Amos nodded. "Yes, I knew."

Tom shook his head, "That's one of the hardest things. Looking back now, I see how it was. Eli saw it and the Vile Prince and his creatures all thought I was you. I just thought my armour confused them. But they all thought I looked like *you*," Tom said, not able to hide the exasperation in his voice.

Amos moved around to look closely at his brother. Tom found it annoying for a moment. Then Amos shook his head said, "No, I'm far better looking."

Tom's face changed, his mouth opened and his eyes widened. The brothers broke into laughter, Amos punching Tom's shoulder.

Then Tom turned the mood again. "Did you know that I didn't know you were my brother?"

"Oh no, not until I was in Hokmah and healing. It explained a lot that happened in Sheol, of course. Like why you looked at me as if I was mad," Amos said, laughing. "The whole time we were together there I thought, you knew. When you first came into the room, I thought that you and father had come to get me together. I could never imagine the courage of someone your age coming alone into Sheol."

"Well, fortunately, I didn't know what it was. You were hurt when you found Sir Gwain wasn't coming, weren't you?"

Amos looked thoughtfully at his brother at the mention of their father's name. "Yes, you're right. I was upset."

"Imagine what it's like for me, knowing that he has never come for me, not ever," Tom said bitterly.

"You're wrong, Tom. He came for you in Sheol. It was learning that both his sons were in the enemy's lands that broke the spell that held our father and his knights. The wrath that followed when he found that you were there trying to save me, brought the our father's strength in battle upon the Vile One."

Another voice spoke up. "And just think, young Tom, what if life was different than it has been? You two brothers might have known one another, but now be separated forever by the death of one brother. Instead you did not know one another and now have a lifetime to become friends as well as be brothers."

Tom looked up to see Sanyassi walking up from behind them. The old wizard put his hands on the young knights' backs. "It is good to see you sitting here together. I thought it was time you were able to talk. You needed to speak as rescuer and rescued, no less than as brothers. But if I may, Amos, I think it is time I talk to our young hero."

Amos stood. "But we will have time together you and me, Tom. A year of peace is a wonderful thing. Ages have passed since we had such a long peace. Think of it, a year of peace. And we will be together."

Amos turned to walk away and then turned again, walking backwards while talking. "Tomorrow morning we need to meet here on the grass, little brother. Bring your sword. I saw some of your sword play in Sheol, I think you need some pointers." Amos grinned and turned back around.

Tom laughed at his brother's back and called out. "Just don't forget who rescued who." Amos's cheerful laugh rang out into the dark field beyond.

Sanyassi sat on the bench beside Tom, but he threw one leg over and his wide robe skirted the bench. "First I must tell you, Tom, it's my fault you have learned these things this way. We, the other wizards in Hokmah and I, were afraid not to do it this way. The Books of Prophecy were searched and new words found that seemed to tell us that our Year of Peace was dependent upon the surprise of learning that you were Amos' brother. And I think, no, I'm sure, it was correct, the way the blooms burst open when the announcement was made… Yes, we were correct, I think. But prophesies are hard to interpret and mistakes can be made," the old wizard added thoughtfully.

Sanyasis rubbed his bearded chin and said, "Though some mistakes are good, aren't they? We certainly didn't correctly read the Books of Prophecy about you. But if we had, then you would have known that Amos was your brother and there could be no surprise, no rescue unawares so to speak… Oh well, this is too much to think about, it gives even the wisest a headache." Sanyassi rubbed his temples, smiling at Tom.

"As I was saying, it's my fault you found out in such a dramatic way. Your mother wanted to come and tell you gently herself."

"She's had plenty of time in the past to tell me," Tom said, bitterness creeping back into his voice.

"And if she had… what then my boy? She made a decision long ago, painful to herself and all those she loved dearly. Years ago, she left a little boy, Amos, who was younger than you are now, coming only infrequently to see him. Years ago, she left a man she loved dearly, coming only rarely to see him. Years ago, she separated a baby from his kin and I'm sure that decision was hard, and many around her thought she was wrong. She has questioned herself many times over the years, I'm sure. But it's the outcomes of our decisions that are most important. Yet the outcomes are what we cannot see when we are deciding. It's all very difficult, and it certainly makes my head ache thinking about it. But this outcome has been not only good, but also magically wonderful. Don't you agree Tom?"

Tom nodded his head.

Sanyassi laughed, "It's okay if thinking about it gives you a headache, for so the wise suffer too."

"Do you know why she left? Did you know me when I was a baby here?"

"No, I didn't. Much information passes between the special places of Adamah, but not all. What does pass from here to there and elsewhere is for the good of the land and the people. Little of it is personal information. So I didn't know about you and your mother. I guess it is just as well for Amos' sake that the wise are sometimes ignorant."

Tom relaxed a little and laughed.. Then he saw his mother and Sir Gwain coming out of the door and stopped laughing.

"What is this?" he asked the wizard. "A set up? A 'talk to Tom alone' evening, instead of a celebration."

To Tom's surprise, instead of correcting him, Sanyasis tipped back his head and laughed loudly. "Yes, it is a bit of a setup, Tom. But not always to talk alone, these two come together to speak with you. Look up here, boy," the old wizard commanded. Sanyassi stared down into Tom's eyes making it so he couldn't blink. "Ah, my boy. I think you're ready. It will not be easy, but you will be fine." And whether it was what Sanyassi saw in Tom, or what he did to him, Tom did feel ready to meet his mother and father.

As Miriam and Sir Gwain neared the bench, Sanyassi walked away with a wave of his long hand. Tom kept his eyes down as his mother sat beside him. She was wearing the red robe she wore at home. But it shone brighter in its homeland and the colours were true. Others in the hall celebrating had the same kind of robe.

"So now I know the truth about the robe too," he said angrily.

"Tom, I know you are angry with me. But you don't know the reasons for what I did."

Tom lifted up his head. "Maybe your reasons were okay, Mum, I don't know. But to keep a secret for so long… To hide it all from me… To lie to me! To come and see a father I didn't know I had and a brother, telling me you were away at a dig."

"No, I never did that, Tom. I was always careful not to tell you where I was going those times."

"What, you think that makes it all okay?" Tom almost shouted at his mum.

"Not for you maybe, but for me, yes. At least I knew I wasn't lying to you. But remember, Tom, you didn't tell me you were coming here either. And you did lie to me about the Director giving you something."

Tom snorted. "Well, I guess I learned it from the best."

"Tom, that's mean," said Miriam. He looked at his mum. They stared at each other, bristling, for a few minutes. Suddenly he laughed and she smiled.

"I should have told you sooner. I…oh, it was so hard. Once it all started and things were going on, how do you tell a boy his father is a knight in another world?" Miriam reached up and held Sir Gwain's hand. "I couldn't seem to sort it out. Your father was putting pressure on me to get on with it."

She laughed softly, then continued, "We had this agreement that I would tell you soon. Then I was to send you to the wall of King's in Cambridge and the Director would tell you how to come here. When he saw you at the wall that day, he thought you knew about the book. But he had business elsewhere so no one knew he had given it to you."

Sir Gwain bent down on one knee to look into his son's face. "Tom, when I found that you had gone to Sheol, I gathered the armies of Adamah in great haste and we set out to save you. You saved Amos by coming when you did, but you also saved me and all of Adamah as well. Do you understand that?"

Tom looked up. How could he ever see this man as his father? But Sir Gwain's eyes were like Amos' eyes and it was a little like looking into the mirror at his own eyes.

"I think so. But it's hard to understand why I couldn't just be here with you and Amos all along."

Sir Gwain patted Tom's knee. "I think I should leave you with your mother." He put his other hand on Miriam's knee. "But don't be too hard on her. She really tried to do what was best. Now we have a year of peace. It's going to be wonderful for us all. We will be all together for the first time in a very long time." He stood up and touched Miriam's shoulder and then Tom's before walking away.

"My decision was made so long ago when things were not good in Adamah. The Vile One was attacking often and your father was away fighting with his army most of the time. I was frightened. This was not my world. I didn't belong here. I'd come here from Earth. At first I loved it here, but after you were born and the Vile One was being so aggressive, I was frightened. It seemed an evil place for my baby and me. That's the way I felt. The years have shown me that evil is in our world as well and at least in Adamah it is separated by a hedge and they battle against it. We too often embrace the evil in our….. no…. my world."

Miriam shook her head, "When you were a baby, I wanted to run back to the world I knew and understood. So an agreement was struck, a wizard I knew helped me in secret. I'm not sure what all had to be done. It was a dark and difficult thing for him to do and cost him a great deal. But I could return to earth with my baby to live, and only visit Gwain and Amos here during the Season of Peace. I loved them both, that's what made it hard for me, and what made the agreement dangerous for my friend to do for me."

"Were you a Peregrine Sol too, Mum? Is that how you came in the first place?"

"No, my story is different. I was a bit like your friend, Abigail. That's why I can't just come and go as I please. It happens sometimes, for some of us, we come by mistake, as it were."

"So will Abigail be able to come and go now?"

Miriam looked at Tom. "No, Tom. Abigail will go home to her world. It will be fixed for her. They can do it, the wizards. They will fix it with her parents, with her school and her friends. No one will think anything of her absence. In fact, it's probably been magically fixed already, so her parents think or remember sending her away on a school trip. And Abigail will be fixed as well. She will go home and never remember her time in Adamah, though I dare say she will be different because of it."

"Not remember Adamah and the quest, poor Abigail."

Miriam laughed. "Poor Abigail? No, her life is much less complicated. Say poor Miriam and poor Tom instead." But he could never say that. Miriam bowed her head. She could see he now belonged to Adamah.

"Don't worry about your friend. She will probably write a book, a fantasy story. That's happened to some who have come to Adamah and been made to forget. Some memory of the events lives in them forever and comes out of them in some wild fantasy story about talking animals or teachers who turn into cats.”

“And me? What happens with me?” Tom asked anxiously.

“I don’t know, Tom. Many things will have to be sorted out now I guess,” Miriam answered, her voice trembling.

“Couldn’t you and I both come back here to live?”

Miriam shook her head, her eyes filled with tears. “The magic that was used all those years ago is still in place. I…I cannot come back. Sir Gwain, your father, feels there must be something that can be done. But I’m not so hopeful. It was a solemn agreement I made then, very solemn. Oh, how I regret that decision now, Tom. I can’t tell you how much I regret it.”

Tom put his hand on his mother’s arm. “You can’t, that is what Sanyassi has been trying to tell me. It had to be this way or the ending would be different too and awful. Things might be horrible for Amos, for Adamah, and maybe for all of us.” Tom said, forgiving his mother completely.

Miriam patted the hand on her arm. “Yes and we have this year together, you, your father, Amos and I. Oh and we mustn’t forget your Ach.” She laughed, nodding her head for Tom to look. Walking through the distant bushes was Eli, still waiting for Tom.

Miriam rose. “I will leave you to talk some more with Eli and go to sit at the high table with your father.” She turned smiling towards the doors. “It’s wonderful for me to sit there beside him.” Looking back at Tom, she said, “He is such a good, brave man. You’ll like him, Tom.”

"What happened? First he didn't rescue Amos and then he did. Why was that?"

Miriam sat back down. "I think the Vile One has grown stronger. I don't completely understand how it was done, but a curse was put on your father and all the knights. No one knows how yet." Miriam shook her head. "This is frightening, Tom. The Vile One has never been able to do something like this before. It must be strong bad magic to curse your father. All the wizards will be working long and hard to find out how this has happened."

Miriam sighed and then went on, "It was Mim who figured out who you were, but there was a terrible attack on Erets, and a little one gone. She could not leave her home or even send anyone to Hokmah and tell them what she suspected. She had to secure the safety of her own land and her own people first. Then word came that Eli had declared himself your Ach. Mim was of course very happy to know that Eli was safe and this news also confirmed her suspicions, that you were Sir Gwain's son. As soon as she had quelled the attack on her lands, Mim flew to Hokmah, but you were long gone on your way to Sheol." Miriam shuddered and rubbed Tom's arm.

"When Mim told the wizards what she thought, they immediately remembered the prophecy. They debated long and hard about whether Gwain should be told. Mim was furious with them. She was sure that she should fly straight to Gwain, being a mother you know. But most of the wizards were afraid that the prophecy would be made useless if anyone knew that you were

Amos' brother." Miriam smiled at Tom, shaking her head softly. "They say in Adamah that prophecies are fragile things, easily turned aside."

Tom nodded, "Yes, Sanyassi said something like that to me. And that they are hard to figure out too."

Miriam smiled at Tom. "Fortunately, Mim won out. She convinced them that it was right to tell Gwain and that a prophecy should never make a Wise One do the wrong thing. Finally, they let her fly. When she stood before Gwain, telling him that his youngest son had gone to Sheol to rescue his eldest, well no curse or bewitchment could work its power on him then. He says his vision cleared and he plunged into the action he knew all along was the course he should be taking. I guess you know the rest."

Miriam patted her son's arm and stood, saying, "But he feels so awful for his inaction. He keeps saying to me that the pain that Amos suffered and horrors you went through are hard upon him because he didn't move sooner."

Miriam looked towards the hall again. "He's anxious to get to know you again. Very anxious." Miriam turned to walk away again.

"Mum, before you go. Can you tell me how you came here the first time?"

"It's a long story Tom. But something was found on a dig when I was just a young researcher. It started a huge chain of events, Peregrine Sols going from one world to the other, trying to sort it all out. And I came. I was the one who found the thing. So I came here with it. And then I met your father, but I'll tell you all about it another time. When I tell you, I want to do it properly. Around here, the knights and people of the Order tell stories slowly, carefully and beautifully. It takes days. One thing I can tell you, though, although I'm no prince of Adamah like you and Amos, I too had a companion who meant much to me as any Ach could to any prince."

"Who, Mum? Do I know him?"

"Him? It's a her, my boy. And yes, you know her. Mim." Tom's mouth dropped open. "She told me you rode on her back. Did you enjoy that ride? Her feathers are very soft, aren't they Tom? You see now, don't you that I'm the only other to have ever done so? She would never let anyone else."

Miriam turned away and walked towards the doors to the hall. Tom turned to see Eli coming towards him.

Chapter Twenty-Six

Tom was getting ready for school. It was strange to put on his old Colton College uniform in his room at Avon Castle. His mum had insisted that for this year at least, he returned to Earth to attend school. Next year, he hoped to be in Adamah for good. He would have refused to go, but Sanyassi and even Sir Gwain were persuaded by his mum that it was an important transition into his new life.

It wasn't too bad because after school, he was to go 'home' only for show. Then he could walk straight out into the back garden, stand by the odd rosebush and say the words, "Lo bamaqom hazeh. Ba'arets hahi" and fly straight to his father's leather chair by the fireplace in Avon Castle. Sir Gwain promised he would be there waiting to spend the afternoon with him, as they had been doing every day.

Tom and his father had spent every afternoon together since the celebration night. In fact, the afternoons would see him with not only his father, but with his grand-father, his brother, his mother, Enoch and Eli also. Even Mim sometimes flew in to sit on a white cloth spread out in the green grounds of Avon Castle. They had some wonderful picnics. And he knew there would be many more.

One of the biggest surprises so far was watching his mother wield a sword and shield. She and Sir Gwain went out onto the grass to do a demonstration for Tom. He laughed then gasped as his mother held her own for a good long time against the powerful, but gentled, sword of her husband. When they had finished, Miriam's hair hung down in her face, and her eyes were bright and happy. Later, she placed her sword over the fireplace and said to Tom, "I'm terribly rusty. Do you think he went really easy on me, Tom?" Tom nodded and both laughed as Sir Gwain called out from the corridor, "Not at all. I battled you fiercely, dear."

Tom longed to talk to his mother about her journey to Adamah, about meeting his father, and why she had ridden on Mim's back. But he was trying to follow the advice Sanyassi gave him the day after the celebration.

"You must feel, Peregrine Sol Tom, you have many years to catch up on. Remember, the wisest always allow life to unfold slowly. Let the past and the future come together slowly." It isn't always easy to follow a wizard's wise sayings.

Tom had been back to earth for quick visits to sort out little issues. But it was scary to think about going back to school. Tom was just about to utter his incantation to go, when Tegree knocked and enter his room. Tom grinned when he saw the little wizard. "Are you going to school with me?" Tom asked with a laugh.

"Ah, Tom, how I miss our bus rides."

Tegree, a Roweh, worked for Sir Gwain. He, like many of his kind, now shepherded others across Adamah, as they had no land of their own. It was one of the cool things Tom had learned. His father had someone watching over him every day since he'd left the castle as a baby. And Tegree wasn't the only one who'd been Sir Gwain's carer on earth.

"Now, Tom, Ronald is back at school. It would have been easy to fix it so he couldn't come back. It wouldn't even have taken any wizardry at all. That boy deserved to be out. But your father said that we shouldn't even try to get him out. You can handle a boy like that no problem now."

Tom nodded his head. He could imagine his father saying something like that. "Well, I hope he's right."

Mayteria's face popped round the door. "Tegree, I knew I would find you in here. You must get Tom to Earth School."

"Hello, Mayteria."

"Hello, Tom. My man still watching out for you, dear?"

"As always. Are you going to bake chocolate-chip biscuits for when I get home from school today?" Tom asked, grinning cheekily at Mayteria, who had also been taking care of him all of his life.

"Go on with you," Mayteria said, waving her hand at Tom.

"Now, remember young Tom, if you can walk into Sheol and face the down the Vile Prince, you can walk into this earth school and face a silly boy there," Tegree took Tom's arm and they headed through the dark journey to earth. Tom waved at Tegree and turned to go up the path towards Colton College. He walked slowly. It was stranger than he thought it would be. Then he saw James Mason waving at him.

The person Tom most dreaded seeing was Abigail. Everything in her life had been fixed, as his mother put it. Sanyassi said, "She's been adjusted."

They had warned him that Abigail might be cold towards him, like she was

before the quest.

Tom walked through the gates. James ran to him. "Great to see you, Tom.

Glad you're finally back. Your grandfather okay?"

That was part of the adjustment made for Tom. Everyone thought he'd

gone away to see a sick grandfather. It was true, Tom did see his grandfather.

But Sir Thomas, was not sickly. He was a spry old man, still living in Avon

Castle and he could swing a pretty mean sword and wield a shield with powerful

effect.

"Yeah, he's great," Tom said.

"Tom, I have to warn you. Ronald's back. I don't know why they let that

rat back in school after what he did to you, but they did. And he's talking, man.

He's telling everybody that he's going to really bash you this time."

Tom leaned against the wall. "Where is he?"

"He's over there with his gang. Of course they've joined right back up with

him, the weasels."

"Aw, weasels aren't so bad." Tom knew a few very nice weasels in Simkah

Forest who were highly offended when he told them how they were thought of

on earth.

Tom had returned to Simkah Forest, riding on Eli's back. They went to

help Pan, who was frighten to see his fellow Simkah Forest creatures. He was

certainly not coming back as triumphantly as he had hoped. But as the three travellers walked through the dark green trees of the forest towards the clearing, two little baby rabbits ran out.

"Awe you de one dat blew up de 'edge?" they cried.

Pan smiled smugly then began telling the little creatures about his great invention that helped win the Battle of Sheol. Eli and Tom grinned at each other and walked to the clearing to talk to Cimber and remember Brutus.

Tom brought his thoughts back to the present and said to his friend, "Well James, let's go find Ronald."

"No way, Tom. I'm serious. You really need to avoid him. His group have been worse than ever. They even stuck poor Porker in the rubbish bin. Let's just go around to the back and avoid them. It's pretty easy to stay out of their way most of the time."

"James that gives me even more reason to go and find them, Porker obviously couldn't avoid Ronald and his group and I don't plan to. Look, I don't think he'll do anything but run away like the coward he is, but if not, well, I'll just deal with that too. It's about time his dirty business was stopped around here."

A voice from behind the wall spoke, making Tom and James jump. "He's right, you know."

Abigail came around the wall with a friend. She was wearing her green school uniform, and had her backpack flung across her shoulder. A silver-studded dog collar dangled from the backpack. Abigail looked at James, "If you got a problem with someone, well mate, you best jump right in there and take care of it. Go on then, Tom. Go take care of that jerk."

Abigail was holding something in her hand. It was a cut-crystal phial. "That's a nice bottle," he said. "What's in it?'

"Nothing really, just some old liquid that's lost its smell. I just like the bottle." She held the bottle up. "Pretty, isn't it?" She raised her eyebrows and stared at him.

Abigail walked up close to Tom and leaned in close to his ear. "So, are we going to meet at King's wall again?"

"What? I didn't think…."

"Well, we won that debate despite the fact they had the easier bit. It was fun getting ready. But if your mama won't let you," she said, moving back and looking at Tom coldly.

"No, I mean, yeah, sure. After school tomorrow, okay?" He'd have to tell his father he'd be late.

Abigail leaned even closer this time, her lips brushing against his cheek as she spoke. "Okay, and by the way, I broke up with my boyfriend. He really wants to know who you are."

Abigail turned to the girl standing behind her and said, "Come on Jenny, let's go." She smiled saucily at the boys, and led her friend away.

James was staring at Tom. "You and Abigail Meers?"

"Come on, James, let's go and find Ronald"

Tom walked towards the college buildings. James Mason followed behind. They found Ronald with a group of boys at the main school entrance. They were up to their usual trick of intimidating other students.

Tom felt James pull at his backpack, but Tom kept going. He walked right up and stood at the edge of the group. The boys all turned around to look at Tom and James. Tom felt yet another yank on his backpack. It was clear James was terrified of Ronald and his friends. Nathan Shadow tossed his head, sending his fringe flying out. The hair fell back across Nathan's narrow eyes.

Tom stood a little straighter. He clenched and unclenched his hand, missing the feeling of his sword. Tom spoke quietly, "Ronald, I hear you're looking for me."

Ronald turned around. One look at Tom, and his eyebrows lifted just a little. The two boys stood facing each other, Tom standing erect, as if his shield was on his arm. James went quiet behind Tom. Ronald moved threateningly towards Tom, hunching his shoulders and raising his fists.

Tom's right fist shot out and hit Ronald's jaw. Ronald jerked, but didn't fall. Nathan stepped backwards, dropping the fists he had just been raising. "Come on guys." Ronald yelled.

Tom dropped his backpack and stood ready. The other boys didn't move. Neither did Ronald. Moments passed and neither boy moved. Finally, Ronald looked away. He hunched his shoulders and dropped his eyes.

Tom said, "You going to rat on me, you baby?"

"I'm not messing with you, just leave me alone," Ronald said.

Ronald picked up his bag and made for the doors. Nathan gasped, and joined the rest of his friends, who laughed nervously and backed away from the school doors. Ronald kept walking.

Tom walked through the scattering group of boys and into the building. He wasn't too sure about studying Latin, but everything else in life was looking pretty good.

Some of ~~what~~ I saw.

Some of ~~the creatures~~ I met,

Some of the people I met,

Impossible to really get
the transformation of these
creatures.

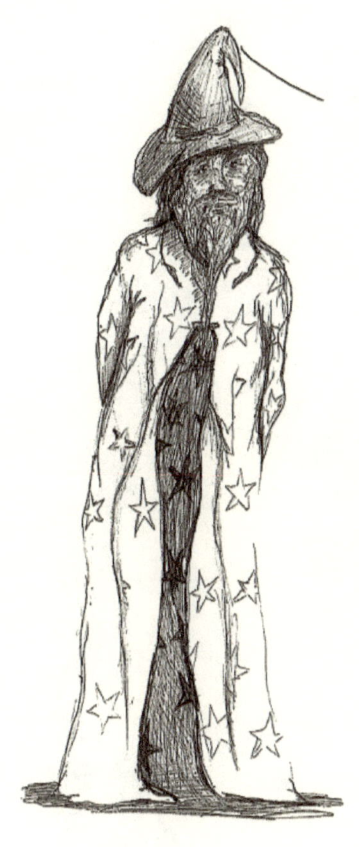

So Majestic

What funny people!

Unbelievable

ABOUT THE AUTHOR

Barbara Mayo-Neville lives in Christchurch, New Zealand with her husband, five children, son-in-law, cat, dog, chickens, goldfish and various other magical creatures. She also writes for adults.